DANTE'S GIRL

KAYLA STEELE IS a sexy young woman trying to hold down her job whilst staying on top of debts. When her boyfriend is murdered, she discovers he has led a secret life, and finds herself suddenly hunted across the dark and glamorous landscape of Los Angeles by a cabal of supernatural beings. Kayla has no other choice but to learn the Dark Arts...

ALSO BY NATASHA RHODES

Blade: Trinity
Final Destination: The Movie 1
Final Destination: The Movie 2
A Nightmare on Elm Street: Perchance to Dream
Final Destination: Dead Reckoning

NATASHA RHODES

DANTE'S GIRL

A KAYLA STEELE NOVEL

SOLARIS

To my wonderful parents Kathy and Frank,
my real-life superheroes.

First published 2007 by Solaris
an imprint of BL Publishing
Games Workshop Ltd, Willow Road
Nottingham, NG7 2WS
UK

www.solarisbooks.com

ISBN-13: 978 1 84416 666 4
ISBN-10: 1 84416 666 X

10 9 8 7 6 5 4 3 2 1

A CIP catalogue record for this book is available from the
British Library.

Designed & typeset by BL Publishing
Printed in the US

PROLOGUE

THERE IS AN old saying in Hollywood that God keeps you alive only as long as you're entertaining; then, when he gets bored of you, he kills you.

Kayla Steele had no intention of ever becoming boring.

For starters, boring people wouldn't own a dress like the one she was slipping her warm, freshly showered body into—wicked black silk that clung to her like a second skin, showing off every inch of her to-die-for figure and stopping just a half inch away from total indecency.

Boring people wouldn't match the dress with six-inch killer heels, outrageously expensive Italian perfume, and a complete absence of underwear. Nor would they put themselves in a position where they would be proposed to in about—Kayla glanced at her watch—thirty minutes and counting, then spend so long getting ready that they were already forty minutes late, without traffic. But to hell with it. He'd been waiting nearly a year for this night. Another half hour wouldn't kill him.

Kayla sighed happily as she flitted around her modest apartment, humming the wedding march under her breath. This was going to be the most wonderful night of her life, and nothing was going to spoil her mood. The dinner reservation was for ten o'clock, so if she skipped the final coat of nail polish, used the quick-dry mascara and picked the heels she could actually walk in, she might, just might, make it in time.

She added the finishing touches to her makeup and studied the result in the mirror, half-watching a CNN news bulletin reflected in the glass.

"In breaking news tonight," the reporter announced cheerfully, "a third badly mutilated body has been discovered in the basement of a nightclub in West Hollywood. Los Angeles Police are refusing to speculate on a motive for the wave of similar killings that have swept the area in the past month, blaming gang warfare, animal attacks, illegal immigration, and the influence of Neptune on Mars. However, an animal specialist has stepped forward to testify that—"

"Yeah, yeah, doom and gloom, whatever," Kayla informed the set amiably, screwing the top back onto her mascara. "How 'bout we get some good news for once?"

She hit the mute button on the set, then turned to a nearby shelf and picked up a framed picture of a smiling, dark-haired young man with unusual sea-green eyes. She studied it for a long moment, then planted a big kiss on the man's forehead and set the picture back down on top of the TV. She gave the frame an affectionate pat, then stepped toward the front door, pausing briefly to give herself the once-over in the full-length mirror.

"Goodbye, Kayla Steele," she whispered. "Hello, Kayla Dante."

She took a deep breath, straightening her little black dress. Then she turned and walked out the front door, slamming it behind her.

A moment later, a picture flashed up on the muted TV screen, a police emergency number scrolling in red above it.

A picture of a smiling, dark-haired young man with unusual sea-green eyes...

CHAPTER ONE

OF ALL THE nights he could've picked to die, Karrel reflected, this was shaping up to be one of the worst.

His dark hair whipped around him as he rose slowly to his feet and gazed down at the body sprawled beneath him, wiping his silver bayonet on his uniform as he did so. He was all alone on the deserted rooftop, save for the rapidly cooling corpse at his feet. For once in his life, he was glad of it.

Karrel shivered, pulling his stolen jacket a little tighter around himself. It was cold. He was cold. The whole fucking city was cold, and he'd bet his last dollar that he was the only one stupid or crazy enough to be out on a night like this. The rest of the world was tucked up in bed, safe and warm. They had no idea that he was up here, freezing his balls off in the name of duty, with only four bullets, a knife, and a Kevlar vest between him and the blackness of eternity.

Still, at least he had a plan. Sort of.

Karrel clenched and unclenched his hands in an effort to get some kind of feeling back into them, and smiled with a bleak humor that rapidly turned into a grimace of pain. It had been nearly twenty-four hours since he had last eaten. It felt like someone had recently and repeatedly punched him in the stomach—which wasn't far from the truth. He knew he was going to get into the worst kind of trouble for what he had just done, but right now, considering what was at stake, he didn't give a damn.

As blood spread around him in a dark pool on the concrete, he removed the laser scope from his modified Remington sniper rifle. He screwed a blocky silencer onto the end, all the while keeping one cautious eye on the body.

Then he stepped back and waited.

A long minute slipped past, during which the lonely wail of a siren sounded in the far distance, floating eerily across the cityscape like the keening of the dead. It was followed by the muted drone of rotors as a far-off LAPD Jet Ranger bird flitted across the urban skyline, flooding the alleyways and rooftops downtown with its cold, clinical light. Karrel paced back and forth restlessly, glancing at his watch and trying to ignore the growling of his stomach. The cops were too far away to cause him any real concern. He knew that by the time they reached him he would be long gone.

That was the problem with the badges in this town. They were always one step behind trouble, which meant that they were always chasing it. The trick was to stand still and let trouble come to you—then cut its nuts off with a blunt knife.

It wasn't much of a philosophy, but it worked for him nine times out of ten.

And on the tenth time...

Karrel stopped his pacing as a strange sound intruded on his consciousness—a wet, crinkly sound, like a child pulling the wrapper off of a piece of Halloween candy. Karrel silently eased back the oiled bolt of his sniper rifle and took a cautious step backward, aiming the muzzle at the body below him as it suddenly moved, twitching and jerking as it flopped over to face him.

As Karrel watched, a wave of spines erupted from the corpse's dead flesh, ripping its expensive clothing to shreds and sending a fine mist of blood up into the night air. The body was a muscular white guy dressed in smart street clothing that probably cost more than Karrel's annual salary. As he slowly backed away, the corpse's exposed muscles bunched and shuddered, straightening out into new and unnatural configurations.

Karrel noted the letter "M" branded into the body's chest, and nodded thoughtfully to himself. One of Magnus's boys. What was he doing so far out from the Strip? Harlequin still controlled most of this part of town, as evidenced by the number of "H" brandings he was still finding on his kills. This guy venturing into Harlequin's territory meant that he was in bigger trouble than he had originally thought.

The corpse groaned as it rolled slowly over, revealing the gaping, bloody hole in its barrel-like chest that was starting to close right before Karrel's eyes. Writhing gray fibers knit themselves at high speed across the white bone of the shattered, exposed ribcage. Karrel's finger tightened on the trigger.

Wait for it.

The corpse's head snapped up and Karrel saw its eyes, burning amber like twin coals beneath the shattered Gucci sunglasses it still wore. Its eyes locked on his with a chilling intensity. Even after all this time, Karrel still felt the old adrenaline burst of shock and revulsion stab through him at the sight. The thing had a hole the size of a bowling ball where its heart should be, and it was still moving.

That wasn't right, not right at all.

As Karrel swung the muzzle of his Remington around, a clawed hand shot up with frightening speed and clamped around the end of his gun. It yanked down hard, nearly ripping the rifle from Karrel's grasp.

With a yelp, Karrel pulled the trigger reflexively, hanging on to the gun with all his might. A vivid picture slammed through his head of the thing wresting the gun from him and blowing his brains out. He pulled the trigger a second time, filling the air with the gritty scent of gunpowder. The corpse jerked, center punched by the twin slugs, but still it held on, muttering an obscene liturgy under its breath. Primal fear battered at Karrel's iron self-control as he viciously twisted the rifle upwards, snapping the thing's head from its body. The head rolled off across the rooftop while the corpse jerked around for a couple more seconds, then rolled over and was still.

Karrel racked a new round into the chamber of his rifle in double-quick time and waited, heart pounding, but there was no need for a follow-up. The corpse lay spread-eagled on the concrete, twitching lightly as its spines retracted with a quiet popping sound and its muscles returned to their normal size and shape. A second later it was nothing more than a hundred and ninety pounds of cold, dead meat, slowly cooling in the chill Los Angeles night air.

Karrel's boots skidded on something slick. He glanced down, then grimaced and took a quick step backward. He always forgot how much blood there was in the human body.

But the thing at his feet wasn't human, not even remotely so.

If he was going to survive the night, he would do well to remember that.

A voice crackled urgently over his radio headset, and Karrel made a face. He listened for a moment, still staring hard at the corpse. Then he ripped off the headset and flung it with considerable relish off the rooftop. Turning his back on the body, he stole over to the low wall that bordered the disused parking lot.

For a few precious moments he stood alone on the empty rooftop, gazing down at the sprawl of glittering lights that blazed a haphazard trail across the darkened plain. Los Angeles could be almost beautiful at night, when the sun went down and the night bathed the concrete ugliness in darkness. From this high up the whole city was visible, from the smog-wreathed high-rises of downtown, to the snaking trails of red and white lights clogging the overworked arteries of Sunset Boulevard, to the pale slice of moonlight just visible on the distant Santa Monica ocean, tinted orange by the ever-present haze of light-pollution. Twin spotlights pierced the smog to his left, wheeling endlessly in the sky as crowds flocked to yet another movie premiere on this busy Friday night. Directly in front of him, a red neon cross blazed on the rooftop of a rundown NoHo church, casting a soothing red glow on the street below and illuminating a hooker and her latest client as they screwed urgently against the back wall of the church.

In LA, life was cheap, death was newsworthy, and the lawyers were never unhappy. Ten million people lived in this crazy, extraordinary city, but tonight, Karrel was interested in just one of them.

Her name was Sarah Preston.

Karrel clicked on his flashlight and carefully studied the blood-flecked snapshot that he'd retrieved from the pocket of the corpse before it had tried to bite his face off. A rush of jubilation sped through him. Sarah was alive—the date printed on the back of the photo proved that—and if his instincts were correct, she should be somewhere nearby.

He glanced quickly at his watch. It was almost seven thirty, which meant that he still had a good half hour left before they killed her. He was cutting things a little close tonight, but if he skipped the final few minutes of training, used the chief's wheels to track down the hostage, and picked the new model Tac rifle that he could actually carry, he might, just might, make it in time.

Easy money.

Even as the thought went through his head, Karrel knew that it wasn't about the money. It was all about a girl, and not the one in the photograph.

It was all about Kayla.

Unconsciously, Karrel reached down to touch the lucky Chinese Dragon coin he wore on a cord around his neck. It was a good luck charm, of sorts, and he hadn't taken it off since she had tied it around his neck last summer.

She had looked so incredible that day...

Karrel blinked and shook his head in a vain attempt to dispel the thought. After tonight, he would have all the time in the world to think about her, preferably when he was in a place where something wasn't trying to eat his brains.

Turning to face the wind, he put away his flashlight and gently buffed his Remington on the grimy leather of his uniform, polishing the barrel to a high shine. He was unsurprised to find that he was shaking. He dutifully tensed and released his muscles, one set at a time, until the sensation passed. But as he stared at his own reflection in the bright metal, a look of worry slid across his face. A long moment passed, long enough and still enough for him to hear the muted sounds of the city drifting up from below.

It was quiet down there. Too quiet.

Karrel's eyes widened and every muscle in his body tensed as he realized what this meant.

"Oh, fuck," he said softly.

Exhaling sharply, he released the pent-up energy in his muscles and exploded into action, taking off across the concrete rooftop in a blur of black leather and flashing steel. Shadows flitted around the sides of the rooftop, but he paid them no heed. He knew what they were, and that they wouldn't harm him. A stairwell beckoned. Karrel flung himself at the door, wrenching it open and barreling into the darkness beyond. The weapons strapped to his lean, muscular frame clattered softly as he descended the steps three at a time, the leather pads on his wrists and elbows cushioning the impact as he caromed off the cinderblock walls, using them as a guide to check his progress. A light in the stairwell would've drawn attention, and if his suspicions were correct, that kind of attention could spell instant death.

A rusted metal door led him out onto a brightly-lit metal gantry on the second floor. Karrel burst through it and ran to the edge of the rail, breathlessly scanning the area below.

They were everywhere. Karrel had never seen so many of them in one place. They were crowded into the alleyway beneath the fire escape, spilling out of the sewers, and pouring off the rooftops in a silent black tide. The sheer size of the creatures gave the impression that there were more of them than there actually were. Karrel made a rough estimate of nine or ten—almost a full pack. His eyes narrowed at the sight; and his hand tensed on the hilt of the street knife he wore in his belt holster.

Werewolves.

KARREL'S PULSE SPED up, pounding strongly in his veins as he stared in horror at the seething mass of werewolves down below. In the semi-darkness he could make out human shapes flitting amongst them, dressed in black clothing similar to his—the rest of his Hunter team. They were fighting what already looked like a losing battle, hopelessly outmatched by the larger and stronger werewolves. Their blades flashed and sparkled in the darkness, cutting the night into ribbons. Other than that the fight was strangely quiet, lacking even the trademark sound of silenced weapons being strategically deployed.

Karrel knew exactly why.

Sweeping the scene with a practiced glance, Karrel locked in on the most viable target—a semi-transformed black werewolf who had one of Karrel's younger recruits pinned in a corner directly beneath him, two blocks away from the main skirmish zone. The recruit's name was Dan, the newest and youngest member of their team. Judging by the look on his face, he was already beginning to regret this particular career choice. Most of the newbies wouldn't know the ass-end of a defensive strategy if it jumped up and bit their heads off, and Dan was no exception.

Even as Karrel watched, the kid brought up his Marines-style Ka-bar fighting knife and waved it at the werewolf uncertainly, the tactical equivalent of threatening a blood-crazed Rottweiler with a rolled up newspaper. The werewolf responded exactly as Karrel knew it would, feinting to one side as if to attack before smacking the weapon from the boy's hand with an easy swipe of its giant paw.

Karrel saw Dan blanch and back away until his back hit brick, mindlessly fumbling at his belt for a weapon Karrel knew wasn't there. At the movement, the creature made a harsh coughing sound that Karrel knew was with laughter. It reared back, ready to pounce.

It let out a shrill scream as one of Karrel's two remaining bullets tore into its left flank, a flower of bright blood blossoming amid its dark, furry hide. Before the werewolf could turn and get a fix on him, Karrel was already airborne, vaulting noiselessly off the metal fire escape and sailing two full stories down toward the clueless creature's head. A moment before impact he smacked the trigger release clipped to the band of his combat belt, popping a four-inch blade out of the heel of his high-laced army boot.

The werewolf yelped in pain and surprise as Karrel landed unceremoniously on top of it, driving his boot-blade deep into the vertebra at the base of its skull. A moment later the creature crumpled beneath him, spilling him onto the foul-smelling sidewalk. There was a brief, queasy moment as Karrel fought to free his blade from the tight gristle of the werewolf's neck, and then he was away, springing to his feet as he simultaneously slapped at his belt to retract the knife.

He spun around fast, glaring at the downed werewolf before redirecting his gaze to the cowering Dan.

"You. Call backup! *NOW!*"

"Yes, sir!"

As the recruit stumbled gratefully away, Karrel raised his Remington and leveled it at the whining lycanthrope. Werewolves were particularly vulnerable when stuck between forms, as this one seemed to be, and Karrel intended to take full advantage of this.

As he sighted the rifle on the unfortunate creature's forehead, he could see it struggling to change, trying to take refuge in the more hardy wolf form to minimize the damage done to it. Karrel had seen a full-form werewolf take a dozen hits from a high-powered AK-47 army assault rifle and keep on coming, whereas in human form similar injuries would have laid it out for at least an hour while its punctured body regenerated itself.

Something caught his attention and he moved closer, lowering his rifle while he peered down at the wounded creature. In the dim light he could just make out the letter "M" branded into its left flank. Karrel felt a surge of elation as another piece of the puzzle dropped into place. This wolf was from the same pack as the one he'd just killed up on the rooftop, which meant it should know where Sarah was being kept.

There was only one way to get the address.

Karrel pulled a green ampoule out of his pocket and shook it up. He advanced on the werewolf, which growled and laid its ears flat against its head as it saw what he was holding. Karrel smiled to himself. You didn't make a living hunting were-wolves and not learn anything about canine psychology, and he knew that this wolf was now very scared indeed. Karrel shook his head in mock sympathy, and then clicked the safety off his rifle as he strode toward it, taking his time.

The creature's face contorted in pain as its muzzle started to flatten, merging back into its face. Karrel knew that younger werewolves were entirely governed by the moon when it came to their transformations, but the older ones were able to control their changes, morphing back and forth at will, although not without the pain this caused them.

After a moment of concentrated effort the were-wolf spoke, its voice little more than a dry hiss. "Wha' you wan'?"

"I want to know where Sarah Preston is. The girl your pack took." Karrel's voice was clipped and cold. "Where is she?"

The black wolf coughed violently, pawing at its face. "Dunno."

Karrel's expression didn't flicker. "Then let me refresh your memory."

Abruptly, he pulled the cap off the green ampoule and flung it at the wolf. The creature yowled as the needle embedded itself with surgical accuracy in the jugular, discharging its chemical contents with a hiss.

The werewolf briefly lifted itself from the ground before crashing unceremoniously to the floor again. It snarled in angry pain as its body began to change, its fur receding as its limbs snapped and buckled, its joints reversing themselves in a series of gristly pops and clunks. It doubled up, growling and clawing at its own body as its internal organs rearranged themselves, its body lengthening and re-forming into a more human shape.

Then the wolf was gone and a naked man was lying on the ground in its place. The man was in his late twenties, thickset and running to fat despite his relatively young age. As his face became fully human his growls became a string of obscenities, which he spat up at Karrel from his prone position in the dirt.

Karrel rolled his eyes. "Yeah, yeah. Death and destruction. Whatever." He jacked a round into the chamber and aimed his rifle at the man's forehead. "Last chance."

The man's fists clenched as he glared up at Karrel, but he knew he was beaten. "Hey, fuck you, buddy. You wanna save the girl? You're already too late. Magnus took her. Said he'd meet us in the Sunset Room. She'll be long dead by now."

"The Sunset Room?" Karrel shook his head, clucking his tongue. "Old boy's showing his age. That place changed hands years ago. It's called, what? The Cabana Club now? Is he even still funding that joint?"

"Look, I dunno anything, I swear!"

Karrel reached into his ammo belt, his fingers brushing the tips of the silver stakes clipped to the back. "We'll see about that."

Then he jumped as a hand suddenly clapped him on the shoulder.

"Pleased you could join us."

The voice behind him was warm and brash, laced through with sarcasm and a healthy dash of irony. It was normally a friendly voice, but on this one occasion it did not sound particularly amused. Karrel paused and pulled a pained face, his finger still on the trigger as he glanced quickly over his shoulder. "Skyler. I was just—"

"You know," Skyler Banks paused as he grabbed a fleeing recruit double-handed, braced himself, and flung the gibbering young man back into the fray, "the common lycanthrope has an excellent sense of smell, full-color eyesight, and, even more startlingly than that, it actually has a strange thing that for want of a better term, I'll call a brain."

"I can see why you're—"

"Unlike you," Skyler went on blithely, "who seems to get by perfectly well without one. Tell me, did you plan on returning to us at any point soon? Or did you intend to invest in property while you were up there?"

"It tricked me." Karrel swung around to face his boss, lowering his rifle in frustration. "I thought it was working alone. I was careless."

"Let me tell you about careless—*McCarthy! On your left!*" Skyler tensed for a second, staring intently at the battle raging just a block away. Then he turned back to Karrel, his ice-blue eyes blazing as he spoke. "Careless is when you burn a cake, *corporal*. Careless is when you forget your wife's anniversary and she gets all huffy and makes you sleep on the sofa for a week. Careless is *not* what you call going bounding off to save the day on your lonesome, leaving eight raw-skinned newbies all alone in the dark with no firepower. We're s'posed to be training these brats to be world-class Hunters, not sending 'em home in body bags."

"I left them with you!"

"You took the damn keys!"

"I—did I?"

"Yes, Karrel, you did. Now we've got forty-six minutes left before they turn our million-dollar hostage into something resembling week-old road-kill, and then come looking for us. I suggest you sort this shit out and then go buy me a beer."

"For what?"

"For saving your life again." Sklyer reached over, unclipped the bayonet from the barrel of Karrel's rifle and flung it with considerable relish over his shoulder.

There was a small, damp sound.

Karrel turned around in time to see a second werewolf—a white female—slump to the ground just three feet behind him, the bayonet buried mathematically dead-center between her eyes. Before he had a chance to react, Skyler had raised his rifle and put a silver bullet through the first werewolf's forehead, as it took advantage of the distraction to try and crawl away. The naked man pitched forward onto the ground and lay still, smoke hissing up from the gaping hole in his head.

Karrel turned back to Skyler in annoyance. "Hey! I wanted to question him!"

"And ask him what? If he would like fries with your ass?"

Skyler looked down at the white wolf with cold loathing as its twitching body returned to semi-human form, finishing up as a young blonde girl no older than her late twenties. She sprawled naked in the gutter beside the dead male, her skull split open by the blade, a shocking redness flooding across her smooth white skin.

Skyler regarded her silently, shaking his head. "Damn. I hate it when they're cute." He sighed, then held out his hand. "Give me your Remmy."

Karrel shook his head. "I've got one shot left."

"Then use it on your damn ego. I'm off to bail out the kiddies."

Skyler snatched the keys from Karrel's belt loop and marched off toward an adjacent alleyway, where the team's black armor-plated SUV was parked. To the naked eye it was indistinguishable from the thousands of beat-up utility vehicles currently cruising LA's highways, but anyone who dared try to break in without first thoroughly grounding themselves would get the shock of their lives. Karrel knew their guns were safe in the booby-trapped trunk, but on this occasion, that was entirely the wrong place for them, or so Skyler would have him believe.

Karrel ruefully shook his head, turning to watch the fight. If he had been in charge, he would never have given the newbies weapons in the first place. Train a man right, his whole body should be a weapon. Relying on something that could be taken away from you was like sending Fate a gilt-edged, hand-engraved invitation to your sudden and very violent demise.

Karrel knew this, which was why he'd taken the keys.

As he watched the short, perfectly dressed figure of Skyler Banks march away, Karrel suddenly grinned. Despite the seriousness of their situation, he was feeling pretty damn fine. He glanced up at the rooftop above him and saw the twin dark shadows waiting there, watching him. An instant later they slipped away, vanishing back into the darkness. The sight of them reassured him, banishing the dark cloud of doubt that had been starting to build in his mind.

He gazed upwards a moment longer and then turned back to Skyler, a smile rising despite his guilt, or maybe even because of it. "Hey!"

Skyler paused only long enough to glare.

"Remember when this used to be fun?"

For a moment, Karrel thought he was actually going to get an answer. Then Skyler turned his back on him and stalked off toward the SUV, muttering under his breath.

Karrel shook his head, wondering if he should tell Skyler he had a lead. Probably best not to. It was his fuck-up, so he would fix it. Besides, by the time his boss had extricated the recruits from the fray and gotten them all organized, onto their motorcycles, and pointing in the same direction, the girl would be dead. She was an innocent in all of this, and he didn't want her death on his conscience, especially not today of all days.

No, he would handle this one himself.

Slinging his rifle over his shoulder, he reached down to retrieve his blade from the body of the wolf-girl at his feet. Pausing only to pull a stray trash bag gently over the dead girl's exposed breasts, he took off up the road at a dead run.

* * *

EIGHT MINUTES LATER, Karrel cut across the familiar parking lot of Amoeba Music, not even out of breath. It was late and a long line stretched behind the red velvet ropes of the Cabana Club, the eager clubbers decked out in Hollywood's latest styles and fashions, keen to see and be seen.

Karrel cursed at the sight of the crowd and ducked behind the squat, neon-emblazoned building, searching for an alternative way to get into the club. Edging his way around a parked delivery truck, he quickly located the service entrance. He forced the door open, slipped inside, and closed it firmly behind him.

Inside, in the thumping, smoky gloom, Karrel tried a number of doors in quick succession before finding the one that led to the basement. Hostages were always kept in the basement, right? It was traditional.

Karrel's hand closed on the reassuring shape of his rifle as he opened the door. He made his way down the stairs as quietly as he could, praying that he wouldn't encounter any employees. In his blood-spattered, exhausted state, the last thing he wanted to do was explain his condition to a skeptical delivery boy, and then have to waste precious seconds hiding the resultant unconscious body.

But tonight, he was in luck. The basement was deserted. He clicked on his mini-flashlight and stepped cautiously into the darkened room, edging his way around broken boxes, moldering pipes and the ancient remains of a seventies disco lighting system.

And in the corner, sitting bound and gagged on a chair...

"Sarah Preston, I presume?"

Karrel crossed the room in three easy strides and a flood of relief. He had made it in time, and what was more, there was no sign of her captors. He was home free, and the million dollar reward from Sarah's fat-cat daddy would do wonders to improve the morale of his team. His last day at work couldn't have gone better.

Karrel heaved a deep sigh. He was really going to miss this gig.

Leaning over Sarah, he pulled out his hunting knife with a macho flourish, ready to cut her free. Her eyes widened at the sight of him and she flinched away, pressing herself back against her chair as she shook her head frantically *no*.

"It's okay. I'm with the good guys," Karrel explained as he squatted down beside her. He pushed the tip of the knife between the tight knots of rope and flexed his biceps, cutting effortlessly through the tough strands. He grabbed Sarah's hand and tugged gently, ready to help her to her feet and flee the building, but the girl didn't want to move. She dug her feet in and pulled away from him, still shaking her head desperately.

Not wanting to further scare the girl by dragging her bodily from the room, Karrel reached out and ripped the silver duct tape off her mouth, hoping to reassure her.

"Come on, girlfriend. Time to go."

"It's a trap!" she burst out, wide-eyed with fear.

"What?" Karrel urgently took her hands in his. "What do you mean?"

Sarah stared at him, wide-eyed. Her body jerked and a burst of dark blood suddenly escaped from her lips, gushing down her chin and pooling in the cleavage revealed by her low-cut, silk halter-top.

Dumbfounded, Karrel glanced down.

A silver blade protruded three inches from Sarah's belly, glinting a shining red in the beam of his flashlight.

Karrel looked back up at Sarah in horror. She coughed, her eyes wide with pain and confusion. Then her body jerked again and a second gush of blood poured from her mouth. Karrel watched the life drain from her eyes and clutched at her hands frantically, as though his touch could somehow keep her on this plane of existence.

But it was no good. Her head lolled back, and she was still.

Sarah was gone.

There was a blur of movement on the periphery of his vision, and then the blade in Sarah's stomach abruptly ripped upwards, cutting through flesh and bone as cleanly as a knife through butter. Karrel convulsively jumped back as the blade exited through her shoulder with a gory *glop*. If it wasn't for her bones her upper body would've fallen away on either side in two halves.

A female figure was revealed, framed by spurting blood and glinting viscera: vampire.

Karrel leapt to his feet as Sarah's lifeless form fell abruptly to the ground, reaching frantically for his rifle. He jacked a round into the chamber and leveled it at the grinning, silver-braceleted siren standing coolly opposite him.

He backed up, breathing hard.

"Tell me," the woman idly raised the tip of her Indian katar sword and watched a drop of blood slide slowly down its length. "What does a girl have to do to get a drink around here?"

KARREL'S FINGER TIGHTENED on the trigger of his Remington, his pulse pounding in his ears as he stared at the beautiful woman standing before him.

"Cyan X," he breathed. "I thought we killed you back in Prague."

Cyan laughed, a dainty sound like the peal of bloodstained silver bells. "You did." She reached up and coyly brushed aside her raven's wing of sleek black hair to reveal a steel plate embedded in her skull. "But they say true love dies hard."

Karrel's trembling fingers found the safety catch on his rifle and clicked it off, but the woman laughed at the tiny sound.

"Easy, lover. Wouldn't want to have ourselves a little accident, now, would we?"

Cyan motioned to the canisters of propane stored on the shelf behind her. She grinned at Karrel, revealing a mouthful of inhumanly sharp, pointed teeth, her violet eyes flashing in amusement. The scent of her Dolce & Gabbana perfume wafted toward Karrel, and he gritted his teeth against the tidal wave of memories it triggered in his head. Cyan was a vampire and, unlike others in her profession, her condition was no accident. He knew her history by heart, although sometimes he wished he didn't.

Sweating, Karrel tilted his head to indicate the flashing CB radio clipped to his belt-band. "You think I came here without backup?"

Cyan shrugged. "Go ahead. Call her. See if I care."

"Fine. I..." Karrel's voice tailed off. Cold dread flooded through him. "How did you know it was a 'her'?"

"Easy, I checked between her legs right after I killed her."

Karrel clenched his jaw tightly. It might not be true. Cyan was an expert at mind games, and for all he knew she was just trying to get him off guard. Concentrating, he got a grip on his emotions, trying not to let her get to him. His eyes flitted treacherously down to the colorful snake tattoo sensuously winding its way up the vampiress's thigh. He shivered despite himself.

"So where's Magnus? Is he in on this little operation too? Or did he dump you again?"

A flicker of anger darted across Cyan's face, then was absorbed quickly into its smooth perfection. She smiled, waving her sword carelessly. "I sent him to the bar to get me and the boys some nibbles." She leaned in closer, her long incisors glinting in mirth. "Between you and me, the service here kinda sucks."

"The boys?"

Even as Karrel said it, he wished that he hadn't. As he raised his rifle to sight on Cyan's forehead, the shadows in the room came to life, peeling themselves from the darkness on all sides and crowding into the tiny, cluttered room. Cyan rested the point of her sword on the ground and watched in girlish glee as six full-form, fully-grown werewolves slunk over to her. They grumbled and raised their heads to her one by one for a caress before falling in behind her, their burning amber eyes fixed unblinkingly on Karrel. Their giant bodies were pitted and scarred from ancient battles, and here and there a tattoo showed through a patch of burnt-off hair. Dark ink snaked across their bulging muscles like tribal brandings. One of them sniffed suspiciously at Sarah's disarticulated remains, nosing her head to one side before taking her skull in its jaws and crushing it like an eggshell. It lapped enthusiastically at the resultant bloody mess, ignoring the sharp glance Cyan gave it.

"Jesus Christ," Karrel muttered.

Cyan gave a small smile. "Bit late for you to discover religion, Karrel, but like you said, there are no atheists in bolt holes. Besides, weren't you were the one who told me that prayers didn't mean shit?" Her smile snapped off. "Right before you shot me."

"Times change," Karrel whispered. His gaze flickered around the room as if he were a trapped animal. If he could just get to the stairs...

"But people don't."

Cyan held his gaze for a moment, and Karrel shivered at the inhuman expression in her eyes. There was no pity there, just dark malice and the faintest flickerings of desire. It had always been that way with Cyan. He had been obsessed with her for so long that he almost felt like she was a part of him, but all obsessions had to end somewhere. He had ended up traveling seven thousand miles and losing a sizable part of his sanity in his quest to kill her.

As he stared at her now, he saw a lifetime of secrets swimming in the eyes of a dead woman, and for the first time in his life he had no idea what to say.

Cyan glanced sharply away and her face darkened. "Harlem! Leave that!" she snapped, as though scolding a dog at the park.

The black-crested werewolf glanced up from its meal of human flesh, strings of bloody drool hanging from either side of its mouth. Karrel could have sworn that the 400-pound killer werewolf actually cringed.

Cyan turned away abruptly, in total disregard of the rifle leveled at her head. "Enough chit-chat. I have work to do. If you have any sense left then I strongly suggest you use that bullet on yourself, Karrel. My boys haven't eaten in days, and I'd hate to think that you suffered."

She paused, flicking the barest glance over her shoulder. "You know I've always had a soft spot for you."

Karrel took a step forward, clinging to one last hope. "Cyan, wait. There's something you need to know—"

"Leave a memo with the devil, darling. I'm taking ten."

Cyan raised a long, lacquered fingernail to her forehead in a mocking salute and repeated the words Karrel had once thrown at her. "Ciao for now, bella."

The vampiress strode from the room in a cloud of exotic perfume, slamming the door behind her.

KARREL STARED AT the closed door, worlds colliding in his mind. His eyes ticked back to the six huge werewolves blocking his escape route, and a chill stabbed through him like an ice pick to the gut. He fumbled for his hunting knife as the enormous creatures rose to their feet, their eyes fixed on his with a terrifying intensity. Their grumbling had turned into a sulky growling now that their mistress was gone, a sound that increased in decibel level with every move Karrel made. The noise was masked by the heavy thump of the club music coming from upstairs, but Karrel knew from long experience that by the time someone came downstairs to see who was screaming, the werewolves would be long gone.

It was just how things worked.

Karrel racked his final round into the chamber and backed away, swinging his rifle from one wolf to the next as his tactical mind ran through a myriad of options, drawing a blank on each one. Even with all his skill and experience as a swordsman there was no way he could take on all six werewolves at once. As they closed in on him he looked from one huge beast to the next, searching their yellow eyes for some vestige of humanity, some shred of personality he could use to his advantage. He found nothing. These wolves were cold-blooded killers. Even if they had been human, he knew that it would be pointless trying to reason with them.

His radio suddenly crackled at his side. A familiar, urgent pattern of Morse code beeps sounded, asking him a question to which he already knew the answer. He knew it was his last chance to live, but he would rather be damned than take it.

Karrel reached down and gently switched the radio off. He fingered his gun, feeling an unearthly calm steal over him. Cyan was right. He only had one bullet left, but there was no way in Hell he was going to take the coward's way out. If he was going to die, then he was going to take one of his killers down with him.

Settling on a target, Karrel carefully leveled his Remington between the eyes of the biggest werewolf. He swallowed hard, steeling himself to face eternity. He had always known that this moment would come, but now that it was here, he was surprised to find that he felt no fear, no panic. All he felt was a quiet sense of resignation, and a profound sorrow that he wouldn't be able to keep a promise he'd made to a girl.

"So, boys, who's it gonna be?" he asked softly.

As one, the pack leapt at Karrel.

A single shot rang out. His flashlight clattered to the ground, plunging the room into darkness.

Two minutes and thirty-seven seconds later, Karrel died.

CHAPTER TWO

KAYLA SUPPRESSED A small sigh of satisfaction as she sat at her table in the candlelit restaurant on the corner of Melrose and La Brea. Everything was perfect, from the soft lighting and the night-blooming jasmine delicately scenting the cool air to the five-piece jazz band playing in the corner of the room. She had chosen a seat out on the terraced patio, after much dithering about the unseasonable cold. The resultant goosebumps were more than worth it for the view of the beautiful nighttime sky, just visible beyond the fog of pollution. An ornamental waterfall splashed and burbled to her right, and a low hum of conversation filled the night air as young Hollywood couples wiled away the evening drinking cheap champagne under the rows of imported Spanish palm trees.

Kayla waved away the waiter as he hovered beside her with a bottle of red wine. She glanced over at the empty place setting opposite her and chuckled to herself, shaking her head ruefully. He was late. Again. That was the trouble with men. They were great at making fire, opening stuck jars and cans, and occasionally dragging home something big and hairy to eat, but there was something about possessing that extra chromosome that seemed to mess with their ability to perform the more simple menial tasks, such as picking up wet towels off the bathroom floor, getting laundry actually into the laundry basket, or, in this case, checking their watches so that they showed up on time. In all of her years of dating, Kayla guessed that she'd spent more time waiting for guys to show up than she'd spent in their presence, but she figured it had been worth it.

After tonight, all that waiting would finally pay off.

A flicker of movement caught her eye and Kayla glanced eagerly toward the door. Her welcoming smile faded as she saw that the newcomer was just a young woman, who took a seat in the alcove across the aisle from her. The woman glanced quickly toward the door before straightening the place-settings and repositioning the candle to create the optimum flattering light, in the well-worn ritual known as Woman Waiting For Man.

Sitting back in her seat, Kayla yawned and rubbed at her eyes. She reached down into her bag and pulled out a small compact mirror to check on her makeup. Tonight was going to be one of the biggest nights in her life, and she wanted to make sure she looked her best.

A loud bang came from the street outside. Kayla jumped, clutching at her purse and looking around in sudden panic. A few nearby patrons looked up too, startled.

A tuxedoed waiter moved in smoothly to reassure them.

"Just a little fender-bender, folks. No need to worry." The waiter tossed his bar towel over his shoulder, smiling jovially. "Anyone want some more wine?"

Kayla nodded unhappily, stealing a glance toward the nearby doorway as the conversation around her resumed. She got the impression that the waiter said that line many times over the course of each week, and her mouth tightened in worry. Living in this city, you soon got used to the sound of gunfire— usually a one-off shot fired late at night, echoing through the back streets and making the neighborhood dogs bark—but it was always far away, disconnected, nothing to do with you. She hoped it was just some kid messing around, taking pot-shots at a street lamp to impress his friends, even though one glance at the local newspapers usually suggested otherwise.

The waiter topped up her glass in silence, his smile as false as his hairpiece. Kayla raised the glass to her lips and took a sip, barely tasting the wine as a torrent of unwelcome thoughts churned in her head. It was her reaction to the sound of the car crash that had annoyed her more than anything. One little bang and her grown-up exterior vanished, making her feel like a child again—small, weak, and helpless.

Kayla hated that feeling.

She always kidded herself, like every other Los Angelino, that she was brave, that if some shady figure ever waved a gun in her face she'd know exactly what to do, but deep down, she knew that she wouldn't. Even the thought of such a confrontation made her feel sick with fear, and she went out of her way to ridiculous extents in her day-to-day life to ensure that it never did. Right now, she wished that Karrel were here to squeeze her hand and crack some joke to make her feel safe again.

She hoped that once they were married, she would never have to feel that way again.

Abruptly cutting off the thought, Kayla picked up her wine glass and raised it in a little toast to the lone woman sitting in the booth opposite her.

"Where're our men folk when we need 'em, eh?"

The woman laughed, looking a little relieved as she raised her own glass in reply. "I hear ya, sister."

Kayla took a calming sip of her drink and reflectively swirled the dregs of the wine around the bottom as she watched the candlelight sparkle and dance on the crimson liquid. She wasn't usually much of a drinker, but the noise of the car crash combined with the long wait for Karrel's arrival was making her nervous, and the fact that she was already onto her second glass betrayed her increasing anxiety.

Where the hell was he?

Stealing a glance back toward the door, Kayla slipped her flip-up cell phone out of her purse and checked the time. She jumped as it rang in her hand.

She flipped it open, her heart fluttering.

If Karrel was calling to cancel on her again...

"Hello?"

The male voice was rich and cultured, with just a hint of a New York accent to it. "So? How many carats, or am I gonna have to break this guy's nose?"

Kayla let out her breath in a sigh of relief. She glanced around furtively, and then ducked her head down in the booth. "I don't know. He's not even here yet."

"What!"

Kayla grimaced and held the phone away from her. Several nearby diners looked up in irritation. She replaced the phone cautiously to her ear. "I'm guessing it's either traffic, or his aunt died again."

"Honey, you forget that dog right away and come home with me. What the hell is he thinking, making the most beautiful woman in the world wait around like that?"

"I dunno about her, but I'm getting kinda bored."

A snort of laughter issued from the phone. "You've got to quit doin' yourself down, girl. I don't know what's wrong with the guy for not snapping you up years ago. Believe you me, girls like you don't just come along every day."

"You're very sweet, Wylie." The reply was automatic.

"And quit sayin' that. You know I'm telling the truth. You know I wouldn't bullshit you, Kayla. Karrel's a very lucky man."

Kayla's cherry-red lips twisted in a wry smile. She waved away the waiter as he approached her with the uncorked bottle of red. "Listen, I gotta go. It's kinda hoity-toity in here, if you know what I mean."

"Sweetie, I always know what you mean." There was a pause. "By the way, you look radiant tonight."

"You can't even see me."

"But I can hear you, and you sound like you look radiant."

"But—"

"Don't argue. You know I'm always right. I'll talk to ya soon."

Kayla grinned and hung up with a beep. She dropped the phone into her purse, then picked up her wine glass and settled back to wait.

FOUR OVERPRICED DRINKS later, Kayla paid the bar tab and quietly left the restaurant, alone. She stood on the street outside for a good twenty minutes, clutching her purse, refusing to put on her sweater despite the cold. She peered down the darkened street, hoping against hope to see the familiar figure of Karrel jogging down the sidewalk toward her, a smile on his face and a rose in his hand to make up for the wait.

There would be a good excuse. There was always a good excuse, but this time, Kayla didn't want to hear it.

She shivered in the rising wind and stepped aside to let a gaggle of drunken teenage girls pass her on the narrow sidewalk. She watched them stagger off down the road, shrieking in merriment. The sound of beer bottles breaking rang out as a bouncer emptied bar trash into a dumpster, and then all was still.

Kayla swallowed. She glanced down the street one last time, fighting a rising lump in her throat. All the bars were kicking out, which meant that it had to be at least eleven o'clock. She only knew two other decent places nearby that were open after eleven, and she would be damned if Karrel was going to propose to her at Chucky's 24-hour Drive-Thru or at Fatburger.

So that was that. The evening was over.

Time to go home.

Kayla took two unwilling steps toward the grimy industrial parking lot opposite the restaurant, and then stopped, staring blindly into the darkness. Tears threatened, and she angrily wiped her eyes with the back of her hand, no longer bothering about messing up her makeup.

How could Karrel do this to her? He'd always been bad at time-keeping, constantly turning up late or breaking dates with her at the last minute, but he had no excuse this time. He'd been building up to tonight for almost a month, dropping subtle hints, giving her all the time in the world to prepare.

"It'll be a night to remember. Trust me."

Karrel's voice echoed in her head. Kayla sniffed, glancing up at the stars overhead. Even his no-good surfing buddies had teased her about it, asking her pointed—if lewd—questions about what she was going to do to him on their honeymoon. They'd been dating for nearly a year; even the postman was asking about when the two of them were going to tie the knot.

All the signs had been there, but as it had turned out, Karrel hadn't been.

A low buzzing drew her attention. Kayla turned to glance up at the sign on the nearby storefront, which announced in bold green neon letters that the World Famous Psychic Palm Reader was having a 20% off sale, ending Tuesday.

The corner of Kayla's mouth twitched up. If Karrel had been with her, she knew that she would've found a great deal of amusement in that.

But he wasn't, so she didn't.

Instead, she stared at herself in the reflective plate glass of the store window. She sniffed. Wylie had been right. She *did* look radiant, although her radiance was starting to look a little tattered around the edges after the night she'd had. Her skin was tanned after a summer spent hanging out at the beach near her apartment every day, and she'd accentuated her high cheekbones and delicate features with just a touch of blusher, plumping up her soft, full lips with sparkly, dewy lip-gloss. There wasn't much she could do about her freckles, but Karrel said he found them endearing, so she left them just the way they were. She'd even put curlers in her long chestnut hair, turning her usually flyaway locks into glossy, bouncing ringlets.

Kayla turned this way and that, sadly admiring the way her dress clung to her sleek curves and how her heels made her gorgeous long legs seem longer still. She'd grown up watching superhero action movies, and Wylie always told her she looked like hot-shot movie star Keira Knightley. She could never see the resemblance herself, beyond a certain jut to her jaw and the proud way she held her head. Her day-to-day looks leaned more in the direction of artistically ripped jeans, beachwear, and cute-but-practical shoes, so if the world ever needed saving, she'd be dressed for the occasion. After all, how could you fight off ravening monsters wearing six-inch heels? The people who wrote those movies were so obviously clueless.

Kayla pulled out a tissue and wiped at her nose. So, here she was, all dressed up with nowhere to go but home.

Screw that.

Kayla abruptly spun on her heel and began walking, not toward the car, but back up the road toward the invitingly bright lights of town, her anger increasing with every step she took.

She should have seen it coming, but her love had made her blind. She'd spent a good portion of her twenty-four years dating a succession of losers, and she'd been so sure that Karrel would turn out to be different. "Never get married until you can't believe your luck," her grandma had once said to her, and she had never really understood those words until the day she had met Karrel. Sure, he had no car or money and worked long hours at that crappy animal charity place. But there was something about his smile, about the way his entire face lit up when he looked at her, as though she were the only thing in the world that had any meaning or worth to him.

Right now, she had never felt more worthless.

Kayla shook herself, angrily tugging her sweater over her bare shoulders. Fine. Karrel could go to hell as far as she was concerned. She was out, she looked great, and she was going to enjoy herself tonight, even if it killed her.

ALMOST AN HOUR later, Kayla was starting to feel a whole lot better. True, this was largely due to the three shots of tequila and the ten-dollar Jack 'n Coke she had just downed, but as far as she was concerned, alcohol was the best invention since sliced bread.

Or was sliced bread invented after alcohol? Kayla's pretty face screwed up as she tried to remember. Whatever. It was all a blur to her.

She was having fun, so it couldn't be all bad, and it was good here, nice and quiet and dark. There was nothing to remind her of Karrel at all.

Kayla reached for her drink and took a sip, getting the straw into her mouth on her third attempt. She tried to empty her mind of Karrel-related thoughts as she gazed around the bar, sucking down the stinging, fiery alcohol to warm her empty stomach.

It wasn't such a bad place, as Tinsel-town's lower-end drinking establishments went. Its main feature was a long steel bar dotted with flickering candles in red glass tumblers, creating a pleasantly warm glow. The insidious smell of marijuana smoke blended with the stench of alcohol and tobacco and traffic fumes drifting lazily in on the night air. Above the retro new-age bar an old-fashioned silver station clock ticked up to a quarter to one in the morning, doling out the seconds to a largely oblivious audience. The bar was ringed by a seedy clientele of Hollywood trash and urban burnouts. Failed middle-aged starlets with Botoxed faces rubbed shoulders with tattooed louts with fake British accents and guitars slung over their shoulders. Furtive-looking men in cheap polyester suits sat in the window and traded tips and smokes with the endless succession of sad-faced bums, who for a shot of Jack would tell you at length the injustices of the Hollywood studio system and which producer had screwed them over back in '55, whether you were interested or not.

Most people were interested, which was why the town survived.

It was The Dream, wasn't it? Come to Hollywood, arrive as a nobody, leave as a somebody. Make a name for yourself and show the world what you were made of.

Yeah, right, thought Kayla, sucking down her drink. Hollywood was a whore who took you in and promised to feed you and love you, before screwing you in the head, taking your money, and throwing you back out onto the street, leaving you with nothing but a worrying rash and a vague sense of unease about where the last fifteen years had gone. It was no wonder that everyone around here was a brighter shade of crazy than the rest of the country.

Kayla shook her head sagely, feeling very wise, then leaned back on her chromed barstool to adjust her dress. She gave a little yip as she started to slide off it backwards. She flung out an arm to regain her balance, then jumped as she felt it being gripped by a warm, strong pair of hands. She blinked muzzily as the hands gently but firmly pushed her back up onto her stool, not even daring to hope.

"Karrel?" she asked, trying to look behind her.

"No. Guess again."

Kayla planted her hands firmly on the stool and twisted her upper body around, wondering why it seemed to take her so long to carry out the maneuver. After what seemed like ages she managed to turn fully around. Her eyes crawled up to take in the good-looking young man standing behind her.

"'Scuse me?" she managed. She clutched at the bar to stop herself from falling sideways. She let out a giggle that seemed strangely loud in the noisy, packed bar.

Man, she was *so* suave tonight.

"My name. See if you can guess it," repeated the man, smiling toothily.

Kayla's brow furrowed. She leaned back and considered the newcomer carefully, taking in every detail from the long black hair flowing over his shoulders to the tight denim of his fashionably-ripped Diesel jeans. His modern biker jacket was open to the waist, revealing a bare, muscular torso, which was coated with a light sheen of sweat from the smoky heat of the bar. A couple of cool tattoos snaked over his hip-line, half-hidden by his unbuttoned shirt.

Kayla realized that her mouth was hanging open. She closed it with a snap. Her eyes began their long trek upwards to the guy's face. When they finally arrived, she found herself looking into the most striking amber eyes she had ever seen in her life. They crinkled in amusement as the man gazed down at her, thoroughly entertained by her intoxicated state.

Kayla bit her lip as she felt a pulse of unmistakable lust go through her, which she quickly put down to the alcohol scorching through her veins. The man was unshaven and kind of rough-looking, but right now he was the most desirable guy she'd laid eyes on in a month. She knew it was wrong of her to feel that way, but considering the way Karrel had just treated her, he was lucky that all she was doing was looking.

Kayla blinked once, twice, frowning as her alcohol-fuelled brain kicked at her. This gorgeous specimen of manhood had just asked her something, but for the life of her she couldn't remember what. She cleared her throat, her own voice seeming to come from a long way away.

"Wha' was the question again?"

The guy laughed, a warm, easy sound, and Kayla found herself relaxing. She was so glad that she had come here tonight instead of going back home to the indignity of the cold, unmade bed in her lonely apartment. The evening had started out badly, but now here she was, looking all cute at an amazingly fun bar, flirting with hot guys, having the time of her life. Karrel could eat his heart out.

Maybe if she drank enough, she'd believe that.

"He sucks!" Kayla announced loudly to the room, lifting her drink in a toast to the ceiling and nearly slipping off her stool again.

"Who sucks?"

"Karrel does! Pay attention!" Kayla lifted her drink to her lips, and was shocked by a sudden burning pain on her tongue. She reeled her hand back in and gazed in befuddlement at the lit cigarette she was holding. Her glass seemed to have disappeared. "Is this mine?" she asked, waving the cigarette vaguely as she hunted around on the bar for her glass. She never knew she smoked.

Another laugh drifted down from above her.

"I think you've had enough to drink, girlie."

"No such thing," Kayla said, the statement coming out harder than she had intended. The cute guy looked at her strangely. Kayla glanced quickly away, stubbing her cigarette out on the edge of the bar.

"Been one of those nights?"

Kayla nodded mutely, staring at the small scorch mark she'd just made on the bar.

She wasn't going to cry.

Strong arms softly encircled her shoulders and squeezed. Kayla leaned back against the new guy as a wave of dizziness passed over her. She rested her cheek lightly on the creaking leather of his jacket, wordlessly accepting the morsel of comfort. She took a deep, aching breath, hating Karrel with everything in her.

"Love sucks," she muttered, wiping at her eyes.

"Love?" the man laughed, mimicking her voice. "No such thing."

Kayla sniffed, dabbing at her nose with a tissue. "You don't believe in love?"

The man shrugged, still holding her close. "Love's a lie. It's just our brain playing tricks on us, pumping chemicals through us to ensure the propagation of the species." He stroked the back of her head softly, letting her silken hair trickle through his fingers like rain. "If you live your life for love, you're a fool."

"Hey, check out Mr. Cynical."

"I'm just being realistic. Way I see it, falling in love's like falling off a building. It doesn't really hurt until the end." The guy shook his head ruefully, clenching his jaw. "Trust me. You're better off on your own."

Kayla sighed, hoping against hope that he was wrong. A moment later she felt warm lips brush her ear as the guy gently pulled her closer.

"So I couldn't tempt you to a dance?"

"If I dance, I'm gonna puke," Kayla said solemnly.

The man gave a short, barking laugh. "No dancing for you, then."

He released her, but one hand lingered on her shoulder for a moment, lightly brushing the soft skin on the inside of her neck with the backs of his fingers. Kayla shivered as he ran his nails teasingly across her shoulders and down her arm before taking her hand in a firm grip. "Want to come to a party instead?"

"We're at a party."

"No, a different one. A better one."

Kayla glanced up at the man, suspicion darkening her eyes. "Is this a private party?"

"Nah," the guy shrugged offhandedly. "Just me and some buddies hitting up some crappy celebrity gig in town. You're more than welcome to tag along."

The man gestured over to the opposite side of the bar. Kayla glanced over to see a second, arrogantly handsome guy in dark glasses, standing by the door with his arm around a pretty young girl. He was wearing a high school letterman's jacket. He nudged the girl and she waved eagerly at Kayla, beckoning her over to join them.

Reassured by this, Kayla turned back to the first guy. "Will there be alcohol at this party?"

The man grinned. "Free drinks, all night."

Kayla reached for her jacket. "Why didn't you say so?"

THE FIRST THING Kayla noticed upon walking into the club was the weird lack of lighting. The place was in almost total darkness. The only light came from the occasional tea light flickering from the depths of the deeply inset booths and a strange red glow that seemed to come from everywhere and nowhere, permeating the air with a sickly luminescence. The club's décor was black-on-black—the walls were black, the carpet was black, even the furniture was black and upholstered with plush red velvet. The sound system was incredible, the deep bass throb of the band coming up from underfoot, making every bone in Kayla's body vibrate like a tuning fork. Electric blue strobes wheeled and skittered over the heaving dance floor, further adding to the feeling of disorientation. The air was heavy with the smell of smoke and hormones, and a damp heat washed through the room as eager clubbers sweated and writhed on the dance floor.

"Nice place, uh…" Kayla turned to the young girl she'd come in with.

"Mia," said the girl helpfully. She gazed around for a moment in fascination, then raised her eyebrows. "Oh my *God!*" She pointed at a nearby seating booth. "Those guys—are they…?"

Kayla glanced into the booth curiously. A young guy in a blue surfer's beanie hat was just visible behind the curtain. He gripped the walnut-finish table in front of him as a pale, willowy girl with bleached white hair buried her face in his lap, not even bothering to hide what she was doing. The guy's other hand was tangled in the hair of a second girl, a punk-rock vixen, who had her skirt hitched around her belly and her legs wrapped around the waist of a severe-looking, tattooed musician-type in black jeans and a ripped Von Dutch T-shirt. As Kayla watched, the musician guy leaned over and pulled the beanie guy closer, licking his way up the guy's throat before gripping his chin and thrusting his tongue into his mouth, drawing delighted giggles from his girlfriend. The four of them seemed completely oblivious to the fact that they were being watched by practically every person who walked by the curtained booth.

Kayla giggled. "Yeah. They are. And don't point."

She took Mia's hand and quickly led her away from the curtained booths as muted moans filled the air, blending with the sultry pounding of the music. Mia was only a few years younger than she was, but Kayla felt suddenly and strangely protective of her. They were both in this together, for better or worse, and it was up to her to make sure they got through the night safely.

Finding a space by the jacket check window, Kayla turned and gazed around at the packed club. Most of the booths seemed to have some kind of noisy debauchery going on in them. Kayla was starting to wonder exactly what they were getting themselves into.

"You been here before?" Kayla waved a hand at the room, taking a furtive sip of the martini the boys had bought for her.

Mia shook her head, fiddling with the gaudy paper umbrella in her own martini. She seemed ill at ease in the dark club, her eyes darting nervously this way and that as her guarded gaze moved around the room, taking everything in. She glanced back at the covered booth behind them, an impish look of curiosity on her young, smooth face. She couldn't have been a day over eighteen. Kayla wondered if she had ever been out clubbing before.

"I don't do the whole 'going out' thing," said Mia, stirring her drink. "At least, not usually, but Jax and Mutt said I'd like this place."

"Who?"

Mia pointed over to the bar where their two escorts were currently deep in conversation with the bartender, who seemed to know them. In fact, everyone in the place seemed to know them, from the valet to the doorman. They obviously came here often.

Kayla snorted with mirth. "Very LA. Their names, I mean."

"But they're cute, right?"

Kayla shrugged offhandedly, taking another sip of her drink. "Known them long?"

Mia shook her head, making her pixie-cut blonde hair slide down over her eyes. She pushed it back and tucked it quickly behind her ears. The noise seemed to be bothering her. "No. Just met them tonight. I thought they were with you?"

Kayla frowned. "And I thought they were with you."

She glanced over at the two guys, suspicion darkening her face. One of them said something to the bartender that made him laugh, and for a moment all three of them turned to stare at the two girls, eyeing them in a way she didn't much like. Kayla felt a chill steal over her despite the stifling heat of the club. She turned back to Mia, warning bells ringing in her head. "What exactly did they say to you?"

"Not much. My guy stood me up and I was so mad, but then Mutt said—" Mia paused at the look on Kayla's face. "What?"

"I got stood up tonight too!"

"No way!"

"Afraid so."

"Jeez! What is it with the guys around here? Bunch of no-good, flakey... Argh. I swear, I'm never dating anyone ever again."

Kayla grinned. "Until next Tuesday, right?"

"Right!" Mia's pout dissolved into a broad smile. "You're cool. I'm glad you're here."

"Likewise, sister." Kayla reached down and took Mia's hand, giving it a brief squeeze. "Don't worry. We'll just chill here for a half hour. Then we can split and... hey!"

Kayla jumped as she felt a hand trail across the back of her hips. She turned around to see Mutt, the older guy, standing behind her. Despite herself, she sucked in a quick breath. *Damn*, the guy was fine. The dim light painted his sculpted bare upper torso in slabs of black and red, his long hair glowing a rich bronze under the strobes. A lit cigarette dangled from his lips as he gazed down at her, the light glinting off his dark glasses.

"You ladies going somewhere?"

Kayla shrugged offhandedly. "Nah. We were just wondering how late this thing's gonna run."

"Late enough." Mutt's face didn't change. He stepped back and lazily draped an arm around Mia's hips, still openly staring at Kayla. His eyes had barely left her all night. Kayla didn't know whether she should be flattered or creeped out by this. She felt a warm presence step up beside her and a muscular arm around her shoulders. She hadn't even heard Jax approach.

"So, you girls been to a lot of these parties?" There was a hint of mockery in Jax's voice that made Kayla bristle.

"I've been to enough." Kayla affected a yawn, then turned away to gaze up at Jax, who she instinctively felt was the weaker target. They both had the brawn, but she got the feeling that Mutt was the brains behind the operation. She felt his gaze burn into the back of her head as she batted her eyelids sleepily at Jax, really working the charm. "But you know what? It's been *such* a long day, and—"

"C'mon, girl." Mutt cut smoothly across her, touching her arm to turn her back around. "You honeys aren't gonna flake on us now, are ya? It's early. I'd hate for you to miss out on all the fun."

Kayla stared up at Mutt's broad, confident smile, and silently cursed. This had seemed like such a good idea back in the safety of the familiar neighborhood bar, tanked up and full of righteous anger at Karrel, but now she hoped that she hadn't gotten herself in over her head. These guys were much older than them, and she had no idea what they expected in return for the ride and the drinks.

Kayla glanced down at her half-finished martini, then came to a decision. She deliberately set her drink down on the table, feeling Mutt's eyes on her all the while. She looked up and met his gaze, then smiled broadly and stepped backward to loop an arm around Jax's waist.

"Wouldn't dream of it," she said.

THE DANCE FLOOR was packed; twisting, gyrating bodies melded together in an orgiastic symphony of movement. The air was stifling, saturated with smoke, sweat and a dozen different brands of industrial-strength aftershave and perfume. Kayla held tightly onto Mutt's strong, cool hand as he led her through the heaving throng, effortlessly side-stepping around writhing leather and latex-clad bodies. She glanced casually around as she walked, trying not to stare.

She'd expected the party to be wild, but the scene on the dance floor was insane, way beyond anything she'd seen before. There was almost too much to see. The girls were all beautiful and dressed in painfully-fashionable clothing. Ultra-hip spider webs of lace and fur spun wickedly across their perfect, tanned bodies, revealing more than they concealed. The women glanced haughtily at Kayla as they ground themselves against their partners, unshaven men with the kind of scruffy, just-got-out-of-bed rock-star looks that took several hours and a membership with a half-dozen major designer clothing stores to achieve. Couples spun past sporting artfully deconstructed bondage gear, the whirling club lights revealing colorful tattoos and glinting off chains and body piercings hidden beneath reflective black vinyl and skin-tight PVC.

The music was savage, hard, primal: white guitar noise over tightly woven bass and drums. Onstage, three androgynous young boys in black eye liner and gaffer-tape costumes fawned to their fans as their squealing guitars drained every last watt of power from the club's struggling generator, throwing their mic stands around as they jumped and spun in choreographed abandon. The crowd roared their appreciation as the music drew to a climax, the lead singer barking lyrics into the mic as the harsh strobe lights illuminated the knife scars and cigarette burns that littered his pale body. A curved tattoo across his lower belly read "Heaven This Way."

Kayla felt Mutt's grip tighten on her hand as he found a relatively clear spot at the back of the dance floor. He swung her around, pulling her in close to dance with him. Kayla gave him a tight smile, keeping her distance, reeling a little from the smoke and the heat. The half-glass of martini she had knocked back was making her head spin. Even though she knew the alcohol would burn off quickly, she was starting to wish that she hadn't had even that much.

The crowd tightened around them as still more partygoers spilled onto the dance floor, fresh from the closing local bars, and Kayla found herself pressed up against Mutt as he moved slowly to the music, one arm locked around her waist. He gave her a saucy wink and she smiled up at him winningly, trying to keep up the fiction that she was cool with this while inside, her head was a mess. She was still seething about being stood up by Karrel, but alone on the dance floor with this almost complete stranger, she was beginning to wish that she'd just gone home.

"Like the music?" Mutt asked, leaning in close.

"Yeah… it's awesome!" Kayla had to shout to be heard above the pounding bass.

Mutt reached out and cupped her chin in one hand, gazing at her thoughtfully while he ran his other hand up the curve of her back, toying with the silken threads that held her dress together. He licked his lips as he leaned in to her again. "As are you, babe," he breathed in her ear. He tightened his grip and pulled her close, grinding himself against her in a way that left Kayla in absolutely no doubt about his intentions.

"Oh, you're just sayin' that," Kayla said with a nervous titter. She playfully pushed Mutt away as she leaned out backward, making the move seem like a part of the dance, scoping around for any sight of Mia and Jax. This act seriously wasn't working, or rather, it was working too well. One more song and she was out of here.

"No, really. You're one *fiiiiine*-lookin' woman." Mutt grinned, revealing teeth that were almost too white. He took his glasses off and stepped toward her, closing the gap between them, his green eyes glinting in the semi-darkness as they ran over Kayla's slender, silk-covered torso. Without warning he gripped her upper arms and spun her around as the wildly gyrating couple next to them swung past in a blur of shiny vinyl, hugging Kayla to him as they pushed by.

Kayla instinctively slid her hands around under his open shirt and grabbed hold of his waist to stop herself from falling backward. She felt Mutt catch his breath at the move. He reached down to cup his hands over hers, leaning into her and burying his face in her neck. He smelled like unfiltered cigarettes and warm male musk. The closeness of him was intoxicating in her inebriated state. Kayla found herself reacting to him despite herself, her fingers moving almost unconsciously over the softness of his skin under his shirt. She pressed harder to feel the firmness of the muscle beneath.

"Why don't we get outta here for a while?" Mutt whispered, his breath hot on her neck.

Kayla glanced up at him in surprise, and then drew in a deep, shaky breath. This guy was seriously gorgeous. For a fraction of a second a treacherous thought went through her mind. Mutt brushed his parted lips softly across her throat as he pressed himself against her again, harder this time, his hands moving tantalizingly down her body.

Reality kicked in with a sobering thump. This wasn't right.

Kayla shook herself. She stepped back from Mutt, disentangling herself from him. "Uh, I gotta go to the restroom," she shouted, with what she hoped was a convincingly apologetic look.

Without waiting for a reply she turned and began shoving her way back through the crowd, swearing under her breath. Who was she kidding? She was mad at Karrel, but she couldn't do this to him no matter how much he deserved it.

She reached the edge of the dance floor and turned around, tensely scanning the crowd for Mia, but the younger girl was nowhere to be seen. Kayla cursed and started moving toward the back of the room, looking for somewhere quiet where she could make a phone call. She had cash on her, not enough for a cab, but if Mia had money too they might just be able to get out of here without further incident.

She started striding decisively toward the back of the club, then paused and backtracked a few steps as something caught her eye. She was sure she recognized those boots sticking out from one of the booths.

Kayla cleared her throat pointedly, then folded her arms and glared down at the smooching couple half-hidden behind the velvet booth curtain. After a moment, the girl disengaged from her guy and pulled backward, gazing up at Kayla with slightly glazed eyes.

"Oh, hey," Mia said with a nervous giggle, wiping at her mouth. Jax leaned out slowly from behind her and eyeballed Kayla, one hand possessively on Mia's slender waist. His expression was anything but friendly.

"Hi. I'm just going to the restroom," Kayla said pleasantly, avoiding eye contact with Jax. "You wanna come keep me company?"

Before Mia could reply, Kayla grabbed her by the hand, hauled her to her feet, and led her across the beer-soaked floor toward the back of the club. As they reached the back door Mia dug in her heels, trying to pull away from Kayla. She pointed to a glowing neon sign beside the bar.

"Restroom's back there, girl."

"I know."

"So where we going?"

"Home."

"But you said—"

"I know what I said, but we're going home," Kayla said firmly.

She pushed her way through the metal back door that led to the exit corridor and held it open for Mia, raising an eyebrow as she took in the younger girl's disheveled appearance. Her lipstick was smeared across her mouth and her black cropped hair was sticking up in random directions

"Yeah, I know," Mia said, catching her look. She wiped at her mouth with the back of her hand in a vain attempt to fix her smudged lipstick. "Shit."

"Here." Kayla fished in her purse and pulled out a tissue.

"Thanks." Mia dabbed at her mouth. She offered Kayla a shy smile. "Talk about in over our heads, eh?"

"Over our heads? More like going down for the third and final time. And not in a good way. Come on. Let's head out."

Kayla stepped out into the cold, fresh air and breathed it in deeply, glad to be out of the hot, smoky club. It was dark outside, the sky tinged with the deep blues of night. The half-hidden moon flooded the scene with a muted silver light.

Kayla yawned, patting her pockets. "Got any cash? I'll get a cab. It's late."

"You don't think the boys will take us home?"

Kayla rolled her eyes, rummaging in her bag. "Not unless you wanna pay the penalty fare. Why don't we just get home under our own steam?"

"Because you girls promised not to flake on us."

Kayla sighed, very deeply. As the door banged behind her she shook her head, gazing up at the night sky, watching as an LAPD helicopter droned past, casting back and forth slowly as though searching for something.

Or someone.

"We never promised you anything, Mutt," she said tiredly, without turning around. "It's late. We just want to go home." She reached back into her bag, rummaging around. Her cell phone had to be in here somewhere.

"Lookin' for this?"

Kayla turned around. Mutt stood behind her, dangling her cell phone between two fingers. The expression on his face made her tense up instantly.

"I'm not even gonna ask how you got that." Kayla's voice was low, measured, her senses prickling with a sudden alertness. "Just give it back."

Mutt ignored Kayla, peering down at her cell phone. He pressed the side button to illuminate the screen. "Cute screenshot. Who's the guy?" He looked up at Kayla, feigning shock. "Is that your boyfriend?"

"So what if it is?"

Mutt held Kayla's gaze for a moment too long, then turned away in disgust to Jax, shaking his head sorrowfully. "Well, I dunno about you, Jax, old buddy, but I feel violated. I mean, how are we s'posed to find a girl these days when we just keep getting lied to all the time?"

Kayla bristled despite herself. "I never lied! I just..." She took a deep breath, feeling her control on the situation rapidly sliding. "I told you. I got stood up."

"Hello? No you didn't, little missy." Jax pushed past Mutt and snaked toward Kayla, his handsome face contorting into a leer. "You never said *nothin'* about that. You just latched onto us, lettin' us drive you places and buy you drinks when you never had any intention of doin' nothin' to pay us back."

"Pay you back? Excuse me?" Kayla swung around to face Jax, the look on her face making him step back fast. "You picked us up! We never asked you for anything!"

"But you let us do it anyway. Same thing," Mutt said quietly. He scratched at his neck, then pulled out a cigarette and placed it between his lips. "You know, there's a name for girls like that, and it ain't pretty."

He lit the cigarette with a click of his lighter and took a puff, gazing at Kayla as smoke twisted slowly between them.

Kayla's temper snapped. "That's it. We're outta here."

She reached out and snatched her phone from Mutt, who held up both his hands, smirking sidelong at Jax as though enjoying the game. Closing it with a snap, Kayla dropped it into her bag and turned her back on the two guys, jerking her head at Mia to follow her. "You boys have a good night now."

"You mean that's it?"

Kayla ignored Mutt, striding determinedly away from the club with Mia trotting obediently at her heels.

"Hey! I'm talkin' to you!"

Kayla increased her pace, ignoring the darting, anxious glance Mia gave her. "Just keep walking," she hissed.

Footsteps clunked along behind them and Kayla scowled. The last thing she wanted to do was to end the night with a slanging match, but if that was what it was going to take to get rid of these two losers, then so be it.

She hadn't walked five more paces before a hand fell on her shoulder. She spun around, anger bubbling up inside her. "Quit pawing me! Whaddaya think I am, a piece of meat?"

Mutt took a step back, once again glancing sidelong at Jax as though sharing a joke. "Hey babe, you said it, not me."

"Get lost, the pair of you." Kayla's voice could have ground down mountains. "You've had your fun. Go pick on someone else."

She glared up at Mutt, rigid with rage.

"Fun? Oh, baby, the party's just getting started." Jax stepped around Mutt and prowled toward Kayla, swinging his hips, giving her the full effect. Kayla glared up at him. He stepped right up to her, refusing to back down. The guy was so full of shit. She would be damned if she was going to let him push her around. She was better than that.

As Jax's lean body brushed hers she raised a hand to push him away, and then yelped as he caught her wrist in a tight grip and yanked her in close to him. Before she could react he grabbed a fistful of her hair in his other hand and crushed his mouth to hers, his tongue seeking to pry apart her lips. He tasted like stale cigarette smoke and cheap rum. Kayla made a furious noise of protest as she drew back her free fist and thumped him hard in the ribs. Jax didn't even seem to notice the blow. He tangled his fingers in her hair as he bent her head back, seeking better access to her mouth.

Acting on pure instinct, Kayla struck him again, then lifted a foot and scraped her sharp stiletto heel down the bone of his shin. Jax pulled away from her with a grunt. Kayla took advantage of the respite to bring up her knee nastily toward his groin. The blow never landed. Before she made contact, Jax twisted away from her and gripped her shoulders. He stepped across her before slamming his hips into hers and rolling her off his body into a nearby doorway in a perfectly executed hip-throw.

Kayla's forehead cracked against the stone doorway. She flung out a hand to catch herself, just managing to regain her balance before she fell. She groggily reached for the door handle to pull herself upright, then swore as she felt a second set of hands grab her from behind.

Before she could move, Mutt had shouldered Jax aside and yanked her to her feet, his hands locking on her biceps in an impossibly strong grip. He smoothed her hair down and glared a warning at Jax, who quickly backed off, staring at Kayla with a deep hunger in his eyes.

Mutt started dragging Kayla off down the alleyway, toward the darkened back lot.

Kayla struggled against him, but he was inhumanly strong, almost pulling her arm out of the socket as he hauled her after him. Kayla redoubled her efforts to break free as she heard a cry come from Mia. She kicked and scratched at Mutt, who swore and grabbed her around the shoulders. Kayla froze as she felt the sharp point of what she presumed was a knife pressing into her throat.

Kayla swallowed carefully, her mind buzzing with fury and fear as Mutt lifted her off the ground and resumed his efforts to drag her back to his car. The eddy of outrage that had been building in her since the beginning of the night flooded through her and she kicked backward as hard as she could, catching Mutt a glancing blow on the kneecap. A sharp pain stung her throat as the knife nicked her, but Kayla paid it no heed, concentrating on twisting her body around as hard as she could in Mutt's grip in an effort to free herself.

As she wrestled with him, a scream tore through the air. For a moment Mutt was distracted. Kayla chose that moment to stamp hard on his toe with her stiletto heel. He grunted in pain and she kicked out hard toward a nearby wall, launching the pair of them backward onto the ground. It wasn't an elegant move, but it did the trick. She landed on top of him in a struggling heap of arms and legs, then swiftly disentangled herself and rolled to her feet, grabbing her purse off the ground and dancing back out of reach.

"You pulled a blade on me? You asshole!" she yelled. She kicked him swiftly in the groin and darted over to help Mia. Mia was struggling with Jax up against a graffiti-covered wall, the pair of them half-hidden in a patch of shadow. Kayla grabbed Jax by the shoulders and tried to pull him off Mia. Jax refused to budge. Kayla pulled harder, slamming him over the head with her purse, shouting at him to let Mia go. She grabbed hold of his hair and yanked him backward. Jax finally let go and swung around to face her.

Kayla screamed.

Jax's face and neck were covered in blood.

He stared at her for a moment, his eyes bright with terror. He slowly reached up to touch his throat, which had been violently torn out. Blood gushed uncontrollably from his ruined flesh. In the wet, purple-black depths of the wound things glistened and clicked as he fought to breathe, his mouth working soundlessly in shock.

His legs gave out and he pitched face-down onto the ground.

Kayla stared down at him for a moment, uncomprehending.

Then she turned to face Mia, and screamed again as her friend stepped out into the light. Mia's features were misshapen and distorted, her sharp elfin cheekbones elongated and ridged and her lower jaw distended as though crushed by a bad car accident. Savagely pointed teeth jutted up from between her blood-smeared lips, and they lengthened even as Kayla watched. As Kayla backed away in blind terror, Mia stretched her muscled limbs, the skin on her face stretching as a set of new facial features rose to the surface. The tendons snapped around the sides of the bones with a series of small, wet noises.

Mia turned her attention back to Jax, a look of feral intensity on her face as she circled him slowly. She pounced on the downed man and locked her mouth on the back of his neck, her razor-sharp teeth sliding deep between muscle and cartilage to clamp around his spine. Before Kayla could draw breath to scream, Mia violently jerked her head up and to the side. Jax's head came clean off his shoulders in a spray of blood and spinal fluid. A dark geyser slowly pulsed out of the massive hole in Jax's twitching, jerking body.

Kayla turned away with a gasp, clapping a hand over her mouth to stop herself from retching.

"Jesus fucking *Christ!*"

Mia's head snapped around at the sound. She fixed Mutt with a baleful, hate-filled glare, her face a shining mask of blood that glinted and dripped in the moonlight. She stared at him blankly for a moment, and then released Jax's head, which fell to the ground beside his desecrated body. Her long, flat tongue came out and swiped once, twice, at each side of her face, neatly cleaning off the blood like a dog smacking its lips after a meal.

The spell shattered. Mutt took off like a rocket, his boots pounding the hard concrete as he sprinted off up the alleyway. Kayla registered a blur of motion as the Mia-thing instinctively whirled and gave chase, snapping her jaws and baying in a sudden and shockingly loud explosion of sound.

Then Kayla was running too, not caring where she was going or how she got there. She was driven only by the powerful urge to get the hell away from whatever it was that Mia had become. Screaming erupted from the alleyway behind her. Kayla kicked off her heels and ran, and ran, and ran.

CHAPTER THREE

DETECTIVE JAKE Collins scratched irritably at his four-day stubble as he pondered the report file before him, reading it a third time in as many minutes to make sure he had understood it correctly. In his late forties, with almost half those years on the force, he was no stranger to late nights, but this night was becoming later than most of them. It was coming up to four in the morning, although he hardly noticed the time.

This report was far more important.

Without thinking he reached out and pulled open his desk drawer, then blinked, sighed, and closed it again, tightening his jaw as he gazed around his new office. Everything in him was aching for a cigarette, but he'd given them up three days and nine hours ago and he wasn't about to cave now. His wife had told him to quit smoking because it was bad for his health, which was crazy considering the nature of his work and the fact that he lived in LA.

Still, sometimes you had to make sacrifices for the ones you loved, even if they were nagging old trouts.

As Jake pondered the file, the door creaked open and a handsome female cop with gray eyes and no makeup leaned into the room and deposited a cup of coffee on his desk. Her face was puffed with sleep deprivation but her eyes were kind. She scanned the cluttered room, and the corner of her mouth lifted in a half-smile. "Glad you're making yourself at home, Jake. You've had this office ten days and already it looks like the back of your car."

"How would you know what the back of my car looks like, Gracie?"

"I read the graffiti in the women's restrooms." She was smiling as she said it. "How's your wife doing?"

"Still not dead."

"Just checking. Hey, you've got a visitor. Want me to send him in?"

"Give me five."

"You're the boss." Gracie winked at Jake and blew him a kiss before disappearing back through the door. The shadow of the word *HOMICIDE* stenciled on the glass fell across Jake's desk, backlit by the lights still glaring next door. Nobody in this place slept much, but this month Jake was going for a record.

He picked up the cup of coffee and sipped at it thoughtfully, then settled back into his padded leather chair. He flipped through the pages of the report for the fourth time. He'd been working as a detective for almost ten years now, but this case blew all the crazy shit he'd seen so far out of the water. He knew with a terrible certainty that this report would mean that his lunch breaks would be shot to hell for the next month, if not longer. As though on cue, his stomach rumbled. Jake made a face, glancing toward the door. If there was one thing he hated, it was working on an empty stomach. But if his suspicions were confirmed, then every single minute of overtime he'd put in during the last few years would be worth it.

Jake pulled out a thick manila forensics file and thumbed through it. The top picture showed a nightmare Technicolor image of a young guy in a high school letterman's jacket sprawled dead in a back alleyway, his throat ripped open, surrounded by a wide crimson pool of his own blood. The guy couldn't have been any older than twenty-two.

Screw it, he was having a cigarette.

He pulled out the pack of unfiltered Camels and lit up with a sigh, feeling the subtle nicotine rush course through his system. He dropped the photograph back into the file and flicked through the rest of the images, blowing a plume of warm smoke toward the ceiling.

It was always the same damned thing: throats torn out, heads ripped off, limbs severed, and always the same kind of teeth marks on whatever remained of the victims' chewed bodies. The way this town was run it was rare for the boys in forensics to bat an eyelid at yet another decapitated stiff, but the increasing brutality of these cases was causing a stir, even in this jaded force. During the three years he'd been on this case he'd had several leads, but each one had gone cold before he had even gotten close. It was something of a personal mission to find the evil sonofabitch who did all this and put him behind bars for life.

The door flew open and a young, fresh-faced officer burst into the room, his eyes alight with
excitement. "We got another one!"

"Two hits in eight hours? You gotta be shitting
me."

"No shitting involved, sir." The young man held
up a pink file. He was practically dancing with
excitement. His name was Ned, and he'd been on
the force just long enough for Jake to decide he
didn't like him. There was nothing particularly dis-
agreeable about the man, which in Jake's book was
grounds for instant suspicion.

Jake flicked a gaze up through bushy eyebrows,
but he took the file anyway and opened it. He gazed
down at the grainy black-and-white forensics pho-
tos, and then pressed a hand to his mouth. He felt
something in his stomach start to burn.

He swallowed, breathing carefully. "Do we have
a name for the... casualty?"

"Karrel Dante," said Ned, tapping a pen on the
photo. "Worked for the American Humane Society.
We found his wallet amongst the remains. Looks
like some kind of animal attack... if you get my
drift."

Jake lit a second cigarette, sighing. "Got it. Has
his family been notified?"

Ned shook his head, glancing down at a printout.
"No living family members on record. Parents died
in an auto accident twelve years ago, or so it says
here. However, we found this in his wallet."

He held out a bloodstained photo-booth strip.
Jake took it and gazed down at it. "Good-looking
guy. Shame. Who's the girlfriend?"

"Kayla Steele, twenty-four. Some kind of beauty
sales rep. Her business card was with the photo,

and it all checks out on the digi-photofit. The cell phone number listed was switched off though, so she hasn't been notified of his death yet."

"Interesting. Any dirt on her record?"

"None. Clean background. Moved here from New York a year ago. I'm heading out to break the news. Wanna come with?"

"Only if we stop at Bravos after. I need some serious pizza after this shit."

Jake Collins got to his feet, steeling himself. He hated deaths where youngsters were involved. Usually it was gang-related shootings, but this was something else altogether.

As the pair moved toward the door, Jake raised an eyebrow and touched Ned's arm. "By the way, what's with that tattoo of yours? I saw it on one of the paperwork guys in my old division." Jake gave a little sleep-deprived laugh. "The chief make you office boys get it when you sign up?"

Ned's hand moved instinctively to tug down his cropped shirt sleeve, beneath which a branded letter "H" was just visible.

He looked up at Jake, a strange smile on his face. "Something like that, sir," he said.

ON THE OTHER side of the city, four hulking shapes sat around a table, wreathed in cigarette smoke and barely visible in the gloom. The table was covered in broken glass, empty liquor bottles, and a ripped-open grocery store bag containing a stash of drug paraphernalia rested on the one vacant chair. The overhead light had been smashed and hung sparking from its socket. At the head of the table sat a woman in her mid-thirties, terrified. A foul wind blew through the broken window behind them as a nighttime bus sped past, kicking up trash and making the bells strung above the door chime.

The woman's name was Lucy Luck. Not her real name, of course, but she'd been in this city so long she couldn't remember ever being called anything else.

Tonight was not her lucky night.

She felt the business end of a semi-automatic pistol prod her knee under the table. She willed her hands to stop shaking as she reached out to draw another card from the pack on the table. She laid it facedown on the table and stared at it.

"It ain't gonna flip itself, sister."

Lucy clenched her fist under the table. She slowly reached up and took hold of the corner of the card.

She took a deep breath, then turned it over.

The skinhead werewolf thug named Skeet sitting next to her leaned forward in a creak of leather. He snorted. "What the fuck's that? A hamster?"

The other three werewolves sniggered. Lucy shook her head too quickly, setting her horseshoe earrings jingling. "It's the Fool."

Skeet's pierced lip curled in distain. "I don't like that card. Pick another."

"Don't you want to know what it means?"

"Fuck, no. I want a better card."

Harlem rose from his seat, the chains draped over his torn jacket jangling, and snatched the deck. Ignoring Lucy's protests, he pulled off his studded gloves and thumbed through once, twice, the colorful devil tattoos wrapped around either arm bulging and flexing in the half-light. He peered up at the others suspiciously.

"I think the lady's dicking us around. They're all different."

"They're supposed to be different." Lucy stretched up a timorous hand toward the deck. "If you'd just let me—"

"Did he ask you to speak?" Jackdoor snarled across the table, flaring his ragged, deformed wings.

"Shut yer hole, or I'll rip ya a new one." Harlem glowered at the younger man, then turned to Lucy. "Did I ask you to speak?"

Lucy shrank down in her chair obediently.

"Good girl." Harlem peeled one card off the pack, nearly tearing it in half. He held it up, a wash of acidic green from the broken neon sign flickering across his mean, feral face. "I want this one."

"That's the Moon."

"We can see it's the moon, lady," said Flame in a guttural whisper. He reached up and scratched at the burned, scarred side of his face. The other half was smooth, pristine, the face of an angel gone to Hell. His lungs wheezed as he spoke. "Wassit mean?"

Lucy cleared her throat, trying not to stare. She read from the script inside her head in a vain attempt to calm herself. She had given this reading a hundred times before, but now, as she felt what she instinctively knew to be the last few minutes of her life ticking past, she struggled to remember the words.

"The... traditional meaning is one of a journey to be made, through good and evil, of passing behind the veil of perception. Here are the mysteries you seek, in this land beset by dark forces linked to the most primal and ancient powers: powers of nature, not of civilization. It is a land beloved of artists and madmen, a terrifying, seductive place, with very different rules. Wolves run wild across this land, hunting alongside maidens with bows and arrows; a land where creatures from childhood nightmares peer from the shadows, ready to pounce on the weak or unwary—" Lucy jumped as a loud crash came from the back of the shop, followed by the sounds of a scuffle.

"Mitzi! Shut the fuck up back there!" bawled Harlem. He turned his palm up to Lucy with mock courtesy. "Go on."

"Please don't hurt him," Lucy burst out. "We told you where the cashbox—"

"We don't want yer stinkin' money. We want our fortunes told," Harlem growled. He cocked his head at her, his spiked neo-punk hairdo blotting out the light on Lucy's face as she shrank from him. "We just had a death in the family. Knocked us for six." He sniffed irritably, rubbing at the faded tattoos on his knuckles. "Really makes you wanna think, death, dunnit? Re-evaluate. Put your pri-orities back in order."

A muffled cry came from the back of the shop. Lucy squeezed her eyes shut, a tear slipping down her cheek.

Harlem tossed the remainder of the deck against the display counter in a fantail of fluttering paper. He banged the moon card down in front of Lucy, shoving his face into hers. His breath was a stale gust of rotten meat and tobacco.

"So what's my fate, fortune-lady?"

Lucy slowly leaned away from Harlem and took a couple of careful breaths, glancing helplessly toward the back of the shop. Her voice wavered as she continued. "The path... through the land of chaos you've been walking... it's become a raging river, and you are standing waist-deep in its powerful, moonlit waters. In the middle you see a small boat tethered to a post, but it has no rudder, no oar—"

A bottle sailed past her ear and smashed on the wall behind her. Lucy went on desperately. "You have two choices. You can give up and turn back, lose yourself in the desolate, primal land of madness and illusion, howl with the wolves, be hunted down… or you can risk everything to get to that boat." She took a deep breath, her voice steadying. "But if you do, you need to trust yourself to the river. The moon controls the river, the tides of fate, but with the choice to go on, you at least have a chance for freedom… the freedom to continue your journey, wherever that may lead you."

Harlem gnawed on a nail, his eyes flicking suspiciously to the side. "So does that mean I'm gonna get laid tonight or not?"

The other three men exploded into laughter. The sound shattered Lucy's last vestiges of self-control. She lunged to her feet, making a frantic break for the back of the shop. Harlem caught her on one arm and effortlessly hurled her back across the table. Lucy sailed across it and slid to the ground in a storm of broken glass and bottles. Even before she hit the floor Skeet and Jackdoor were upon her, tearing at her clothes and cackling at her shrieks.

Harlem cracked his knuckles. "I'll take that as a no."

As he started to move around the table, a slender African-American man emerged from the back of the shop, a rapier sword resting casually on one shoulder. His black hair flowed like spun silk across his back, rippling in the moonlight as he shrugged his head from side to side, popping the muscles in his neck.

"Dinner's up," he said, his voice as expressionless as his face. There was a *thunk* as he dropped the severed head of a middle-aged Latino man down onto the table.

Under the table, Lucy started wailing.

Harlem snorted. "Everyone in this stinkin' place is out to lunch." He cast a bleak look around the palm reader's shop, then made a face. "But I ain't hungry."

With a swift, savage movement he reached into Mitzi's belt, pulled out a pair of throwing knives, and hurled one at the struggling woman under the table.

Lucy's cries stopped.

Skeet's head popped up, his pierced lips stained with blood. "Hey! No fair!"

"Blow me. I've got a headache."

A shrill sound pierced the silence of the decimated shop. Harlem spun around, his second knife at the ready. Then he relaxed and fixed Flame with a disgusted look. "Your ass is ringing, bro."

"It is? Sorry." Flame reached into the back pocket of his ripped black jeans and pulled out a cell phone. He clicked it on. "Hello?"

He turned away, one finger in his ear.

"Jeez. There's no fucking escape around here, is there?" Harlem turned back to Mitzi, massaging his temples, then dropped the knife into the top pocket of Mitzi's Chinese gangster-style trench coat. He patted it. "Nice action. Bit heavy on the back end."

"I'll fix it." Mitzi regarded Harlem with his soulless, black eyes as wet, hungry sounds came from beneath the table. "You're not eating?"

"Lost my appetite." Harlem gestured back toward the table, disgusted. "It's like hanging out with a pack of animals."

Mitzi's eyes continued to bore through Harlem, who found his own eyes beginning to water involuntarily at his buddy's unblinking stare.

He turned away, pretending to check the street outside. "Those black contacts of yours are fuckin' creepy, man. Can't you just wear shades or somethin'?"

"Shades come off. That would be bad. These don't."

"Point taken. Hey, next time that casting kiln of yours explodes, remember to look away. Boom, chhhhh."

Mitzi continued to stare.

Harlem rolled his eyes as Flame walked up to him, phone in hand. "Kid's got no sense of humor. What?"

"Shore leave got cancelled, boys. We're going back in."

"Says who?"

"Guess."

"Crap."

"Right."

"Who's the hit?"

"Some broad. Girl our guy from earlier was banging."

Harlem swung around to face Flame, his fists clenching. "The shit-for-brains who killed Rocco?"

"One and the same."

Harlem turned to face the broken window, the harsh moonlight turning his face into a deranged jigsaw puzzle of highlight and shade. His burnt amber eyes flashed as he reached into his pocket for his leather gloves. He pulled them back on with slow, deliberate menace. "Well. I think it's time we paid the little bitch a visit, don't you?"

CHAPTER FOUR

"BEWARE THE MOON. And keep off the moors."

The werewolf opened its jaws and let loose a long, drawn-out howl before leaping at the unwary backpacker. Its amber eyes blazed as it mauled him, blood and torn flesh flying as his companion screamed in terror.

Kayla clicked the button on her remote control, freezing the DVD on the last frame. She stared at the onscreen image of the snarling werewolf and felt a shiver run down her spine.

Okay, that was that. She was officially, undeniably losing it. Here she was, a grown woman, slacking off work and risking what little credibility she had left in order to watch monster movies.

She snuck a furtive glance back toward her counter, relieved to see that it was still quiet. It was nearly closing time, and around her the department store buzzed with its usual late-night crowd, a hectic mix of badly-dressed tourists and tanked-up locals swarming around and making the place look untidy. In the end-of-day lull she had strayed from her post, drawn as though magnetized to the new plasma screen array at the far end of the store. A traded pack of smokes with the bored punk kid behind the counter had given her access to a remote control and the master video that supplied the feed to the TV, usually devoted to screening glossy MTV music videos, but now showing *An American Werewolf in London*.

Kayla adjusted her skimpy perfume girl uniform. Shivering, she looked again at the frozen image on the screen. It was beyond ridiculous, but she knew what she'd seen. Again and again in her mind she saw Jax fall to the ground, blood pumping from his throat while Mutt fled down the alley. She'd called the police from her cell phone on the way home, then hung up, sick and trembling, when they asked for her name and contact details. She'd turned the phone off so they couldn't call her back and had spent the night lying awake, clutching her pillow and staring at the ceiling, trying to come to terms with what she'd seen and drawing a blank on every theory she'd come up with to explain it.

Twelve hours later her phone was still off—she didn't dare turn it back on in case the cops tried to call her—but as soon as she got up the nerve she'd turn it on for a quick call to Karrel. Right now she desperately needed to talk to someone about this, and soon, or she was going to go nuts. Karrel might be officially the world's biggest jerk, but he would know what to do, whom to contact, how to deal with the police in a way that wouldn't land her in even bigger trouble than she was in right now.

Kayla blinked and rubbed her eyes, making purple lights dance across the insides of her eyelids. What on earth was she going to tell Karrel? *Something* had attacked Jax, something that looked like Mia but wasn't, something that had big teeth, amber eyes, and had looked for all the world like...

Kayla shook herself, a part of her mind shutting down in an attempt to preserve what little was left of her rationality. She looked around the room, blinking rapidly, seeking comfort in the familiar tedium of the store and the things in it. It didn't work.

Just say it.

Kayla took a deep breath.

Jax had been attacked by something that looked like a werewolf.

There. She'd said it. She was officially crazy. Not just regular crazy, either, but full on, screaming, underpants-on-the-head crazy.

There had to be some other explanation.

A shadow fell across her and she looked up, vaguely aware that she had been asked a question.

"Can I help you?" she asked indistinctly, frowning at the screen.

"You tell me," said a smooth voice. Kayla winced in recognition. Her body straightened automatically and she swept a hand through her hair, cranking up something that resembled a smile as she fought a long-buried primal instinct to flee.

She turned around, discretely slipping the remote control into her back pocket as she did so. "Mr. Holt. I was just—"

"Oh, I can see *exactly* what you're doing," sniffed Mr. Holt. His watery blue eyes glinted as he looked her over and adjusted his cheap polyester suit. He was pushing fifty and his skin was lined and weathered from years chasing ass in the Californian sun, but in his mind, he was the most desirable man who had ever walked the planet.

Moving still closer to Kayla, invading her personal space, he dropped his voice to what he obviously thought was a seductive murmur. It came out more as a condescending whine. "As your boss, right now I should be giving you a hard time for slacking off... but if you're *exceptionally* nice to me, there's a possibility I may overlook it. Just this once."

"How nice?" The question was out of her mouth before Kayla could stop herself. She backed off slightly, keeping her distance.

"Say... dinner at my place? Eight o'clock?"

Kayla sighed, inwardly marveling at the eternal optimism of the male mind. The guy had asked her out practically every day since she'd first started working here, and showed no sign of giving up any time soon. It seemed like the more she turned him down the more eager he became. Typical guy.

She forced a smile. "I already told you—*sir*—you're my boss, and besides, I'm seeing someone."

Mr. Holt's broad grin didn't waver.

"A man. Who I love," Kayla added, somewhat defensively.

"Splendid. I'll pick you up around seven-thirty?"

"No, because I'll be with my boyfriend."

"So who is he?" Mr. Holt folded his arms and tapped his foot impatiently.

"His name's Karrel. I already told you like a hundred times—"

"No—I mean, *who* is he?" Mr. Holt ran a hand through his slick hair. "Is he an actor, a director, a model, maybe? Does he run stocks and shares when he's not jetting to Tahiti on business?"

"No, he works for an animal charity. But he's—"

"So... he's not *really* anybody, you're telling me?"

"Hey! He's somebody to me!" Kayla opened her mouth to go on, but she blinked and shook herself before refusing to get drawn into the argument. "Besides, that's none of your business, *sir*."

"My business is this store, *Miss* Steele, and you're in this store, so that makes you my business." Mr. Holt reached out and pushed a stray lock of hair off Kayla's shoulders, ignoring her instinctive cringe. His hand lingered longer than was strictly appropriate. Kayla fought the urge to slap it away as if it was a poisonous insect. "To be totally honest with you, if I were in your position, I'd make more of myself. You're a beautiful girl. You ought to be with a beautiful guy."

"Like you, perhaps?"

Mr. Holt beamed. "You read my mind."

Giving up on sarcasm, Kayla tried tact. "No disrespect, sir, but I've already made my choice, to be with the man I love."

"This is LA, sugar pie. Love won't get you anywhere. You need ambition, looks, drive, passion, me."

"So you're saying I need you so that I can make it in LA?"

"Precisely." A sneaky look came into Mr. Holt's eyes. "If you want to keep working in this store, you do."

Kayla gave Mr. Holt her second best glare, and was rewarded with a wink and a saucy smile. She shook her head, shuddering inwardly. The guy really had no clue. Kayla knew deep down that if she had any self respect at all she'd tell the lecherous son of a bitch exactly where he could shove his cruddy minimum-wage job, but she needed the cash to pay her rent. Otherwise she'd have to go back to New York, face her past—

She cut the thought off and abruptly turned to go, but was restrained by a hand on her shoulder. Kayla froze, fighting down the terrible sense of deja vu.

"By the way," Mr. Holt drawled, "there's some loser friend of yours here to see you." He put a clammy, too-warm hand on her shoulder and pointed. "He's currently destroying the display on the cosmetics counter. If you value your job I suggest you get rid of him before security does."

Kayla glanced guiltily across the room, where a tall, spiky-haired goth boy looked up from the eyeliner he was applying in copious amounts to his face and lips. He gave her a happy little wave of recognition. Kayla winced inwardly. Wylie Thompson had been her best friend since she'd moved here a year ago, but today, the timing of his daily visit was not the best. As she watched, he put down the liner, then jumped back as the display pyramid collapsed, sending tubes of makeup tumbling and bouncing across the counter. He glanced up guiltily, and blew Kayla a kiss.

Kayla pretended not to see him.

Mr. Holt paused for effect, a look of grim glee on his face as he delivered his punch line, trying to make it sound offhand. "Oh, and while I remember, there are also two police officers here to see you. They say it's urgent. Come to my office once you've closed up your counter."

Then he was gone, striding triumphantly back toward the store office.

Kayla's stomach lurched, and she felt the color drain from her face. The cops were here. How had they found her? Now she would have to face them alone, without Karrel's support. She knew she was innocent, that she had nothing to do with Jax's death, but would they believe her? And what in the hell was she going to tell them?

Above her, David Naughton's head popped up onto the screen, his eyes blazing, a torn-off deer's head in his mouth.

Kayla shivered.

Werewolves, indeed.

"THE PACK WAS last seen heading down Highland. Five werewolves, full-form; to be considered top priority and extremely dangerous. I suggest we mobilize Special Unit C and smoke them out before they rendezvous with whoever sent them and get a fix on our position."

"Yes sir."

Skyler Banks strode through the underground mess rooms of the Hunter's HQ, an empty ammo case slung over his shoulder, two Tac-team reps with clipboards scurrying at his side. It was early in the morning and the grimy, low-ceilinged room was filled with the muted sounds of hungry Hunters refueling, pouring drinks, and swapping gossip over a beer and a burger. A respectful stillness spread out in Skyler's wake as hard-bitten troopers and new recruits alike watched him pass. Some offered a nod of condolence and sympathy, others briskly saluted in a gesture of solidarity. Skyler could feel the tension in the air, as though a cold mist of worry and anger hung in the atmosphere, corroding everything it touched.

He paused by the battered drinks machine to pour himself a Pepsi. Knocking it back, he pushed his way through the swing doors at the far end, where the reps peeled off with a salute, heading back to organize the day's new mission. He continued on down the corridor outside, moving deeper into the base until he reached an imposing set of cast-iron doors emblazoned with yellow warning signs.

As he reached out for the door, a hand touched his elbow. Skyler turned to find himself looking into the earnest, scrubbed face of a new recruit sporting a white bandage across one shoulder.

He cleared his throat. "What is it, um…?"

"It's Dan, sir. Just wanted to thank you."

"For what?"

"That speech you gave. In the Ops room earlier?" Dan swallowed, fiddling with a strap on his unlaced body armor. "We're all going to miss him… you know, Karrel, but the stuff you said about him?" He shook his head, looking wistful. "If I ever go out, I want someone to say stuff like that about me."

Sklyer nodded kindly. "He was a good man. I'll miss him too."

Dan sniffed, pushing his mop of curly brown hair out of his eyes. "I know you will, sir, but you really helped. We were all freaked out about what happened, Karrel just running off like that and getting himself killed. But the way you put things… it made us all want to do better, to really nail these sons of bitches. And then you taking the rap for him like that, in front of everybody… that was just…"

Dan looked away, blinking hard.

"Don't you worry, kid," Skyler said quietly. "We'll get the bastards who did this."

Dan nodded, straightening up. "We all knew what Karrel was like, sir. We know it wasn't your fault." He looked up at Skyler, his eyes bright. "I've only been with you guys a couple months, but I hope that one day I'll be good enough to fight under a team leader like you. You make us all proud, sir."

Skyler gave a half smile, fingering the ammo case. "Don't mention it, kid. It was the very least I could do."

He touched his finger to his cap. Dan stepped back and saluted him fiercely as Skyler pushed his way through the door, closing it quietly behind him. On the other side, the lights were out. He strode on down a short, modern hallway lined with carpet and entered a second key code into the door at the far end.

The door hissed open, and Skyler stepped through.

Depositing the ammo case inside the door, he kicked off his shoes and stretched hugely. He crossed his opulent quarters, his feet leaving deep impressions in the thick carpet. Loosening his tie, he picked a control unit off the top of the big plasma screen TV facing the bed, examined it, then hit a button. An oak-paneled hatch swung open on the wall beside him. Skyler reached inside to retrieve a bottle of black Russian vodka and a clean crystal glass. He knocked back a shot and was about to pour himself another when a tiny noise intruded on his hearing.

Skyler froze. He turned his head to the side, listening carefully. He quietly placed the glass down on the sideboard and moved soundlessly toward the bathroom, stealthy as a cat. He paused outside the door, every muscle tense, then grasped the doorknob and turned it, taking great care not to make any sound.

Inside, steam hissed and water splashed. A slender, fine-boned woman stood beside the curtained bathtub, gloriously and unashamedly naked save for a pair of intricate leather armguards. She hummed softly to herself as she tended to the running water. Her waist-length black hair hung in ringlets from the steam, tumbling over her smooth, pale shoulders and coyly resting on her perfect breasts as she reached inside the curtain to add more hot water. She seemed completely unaware of his presence, pouring foamy pink bubble bath in lazy sweeps under the running water.

Skyler swallowed. As though in a trance he started moving across the bathroom toward her, his eyes fixed on the curve of the woman's back.

He was almost upon her when she sighed deeply and said, "You know I could smell you from three rooms away."

Skyler stopped dead. "But I just showered this morning."

Cyan X turned around to face him, her violet eyes glinting wickedly in the subdued light. "As I recall, you didn't get much washing done."

Skyler smiled, stepping forward to slide his hands around the vampiress's waist, brushing his closed lips against hers as he nosed for a kiss. "Care to finish the job?"

Cyan ran her tongue along his lower lip, then pulled back and regarded him shrewdly. "What's in it for me?"

"About nine inches."

"Liar."

Cyan took a step back from Skyler, easily breaking his hold on her waist. She reached out to lift her newly cleaned Katar sword off the stand beside the bath. Swinging it slowly upright, she touched the razor-sharp tip to Skyler's throat, just beneath the knot of his half-undone tie. Before Skyler could react she gave a quick downward flick of her wrist, slicing his shirt open down the front. Skyler caught his breath and moved toward her. She took a step backward into a smooth en garde position, cocking her head at him in warning and resting her sword point above his heart.

"Just the truth from now on."

"No such thing." Skyler pushed her sword aside with care and reached out to take Cyan's delicate wrists in a firm grip, although he knew his control over her was an illusion. He closed his eyes and inhaled, breathing in the scent of her. He knew that she could tear his head off without breaking a sweat, and the thought made him almost dizzy with desire. He could feel the power in her, thrumming just below the surface of her deceptively slender, lightweight frame, and a shiver of unreality ran through him. He'd never been with a vampire before, but right now he couldn't think of anything in the whole world he wanted more.

"Hope you weren't bored today," he said, when his vocal cords started working again.

Cyan shrugged. "I managed to entertain myself."

"I bet you did."

Cyan laughed and stepped in closer, her voice hypnotic. "So. Tell me. They don't suspect...?"

"Not a thing," Skyler said smugly. He opened his eyes and a smile slipped across his face as his eyes roved hungrily over Cyan's toned body. "Bunch of half-wits, the lot of 'em. We got them right where we want them. One more day and everything will be ready. Once the werewolves put their master plan into play, they won't know what hit them."

"So no more screw-ups?" Cyan smiled coquettishly. Her voice was light, but there was an undertone of menace that made Skyler's pulse skip a beat.

"No more screw-ups," he confirmed, resting a possessive hand on her bare hip and using the pad of his thumb to trace the cryptic tattoo scrawled there.

"You promise?"

Cyan considered Skyler for a moment and then gave him a small shove, sending him reeling backward into the china-tiled wall. He pulled her after him, stopping with his lips just a fraction of an inch away from hers. Skyler's heart sped up. He opened his mouth to kiss her, then changed his mind and grinned instead, playing along.

"Cross my heart."

"Cause you know I'd have to kill you if anyone else found out."

Skyler laughed right along with her, licking his suddenly dry lips. "Can't we just skip the foreplay, babe? You know I'm onto it."

He moved toward her, biting his lip, but Cyan put a hand on his chest.

"I'm three wolves down because you were 'onto it,' Mr. Banks," she murmured, almost brushing her lips across his, then reached down to cup a hand over Skyler's groin. She squeezed hard and Skyler groaned.

"And the other... little thing?" he managed, breathing raggedly.

"I'll take care of it. Tonight." Cyan smiled impishly. "So, what if it had been Phil who had found out, hmm? Would you have had my boys kill him, too?"

"If need be, I'd have killed him myself," Skyler breathed.

"Do you mean that, or is that just the hormones talking?" Cyan asked. She ran her tongue across his throat, pressing a gentle line of kisses along his jugular, then bit him on the back of the neck, hard and sexy, before starting to snake her way down his body. Mischief danced in her violet eyes.

"Both." Skyler swallowed as Cyan fumbled with his zipper and slowly pulled down his cotton boxers. He gasped as she took him inside her mouth. Her cherry red lips moved slowly but surely, giving him a spectacular visual.

"Oh, *shit*, girl."

Skyler watched with bated breath as Cyan leaned forward, gripping his hips as she moved teasingly. When she flicked her catlike tongue around the tip, he gasped, clutching the towel rail as he stared down in awe. He panted as he leaned his head back on the wall, losing himself in the sensations.

He didn't notice the rap at his door, not even when it sounded for a second time. The door burst open, and rebounded off the wall with a crash loud enough to wake the dead.

Skyler's eyes flew open and he jumped, instinctively yanking his pants back up as he spun around.

A tall, swarthy man dressed in combat fatigues and a military issue cap was standing in the doorway to the bathroom, his arms loosely folded and a look of ironic amusement on his hard-bitten, scarred face. Beside him, a petite vixen-faced blonde woman in a white fur coat lounged against him, her arms wrapped possessively around the man's waist.

"Are we having a Kodak moment here?"

Cyan giggled as she climbed to her feet, wiping her mouth on the back of her hand. Skyler hurriedly zipped up his fly and pulled his ripped shirt back around him, pointlessly attempting to button it.

There was only one button left. He let it drop.

"Magnus," he said, as casually as he could, "I didn't hear you come in."

"And you're still alive, so that means I like you," Magnus rumbled. The mob boss werewolf transferred his burning gaze to Cyan and his silver eyes lit up with mirth. "Cyan X. Well, I never. To what do we owe the pleasure?"

"The pleasure's all yours, I can assure you." Cyan sounded bored already. She put her sword down on the marble top and turned around to pick up the bottle of bubble bath, taking her time, completely unashamed of her nakedness. "But seriously? My whereabouts should be the least of your concerns right now, *baby*. Did you know you have a werewolf stuck to your side?" Cyan dropped her voice to a stage whisper. "You know you can get ointment for that."

"Her name is Dana. She's none of your business." Magnus put his arm around the blonde woman and gave her a squeeze. She glared up at Cyan with suspicious honey colored eyes, baring her teeth churlishly.

"Quite the little hellion, isn't she? Does she do tricks?" Cyan asked brightly. She popped the cap on the bubble bath and waved it back and forth in front of Dana. "Here girl! Fetch!"

Magnus sighed. "When you're done peeing on my new girl, I suggest you put some clothes on and leave us. We have business to discuss."

Magnus held the bathroom door open, the movement casually exposing the large gold-plated Desert Eagle pistol stashed in his waistband. A faint blue glow emitted from the barrel.

UV rounds, Cyan guessed. How passé.

She stared at Dana just long enough to cause discomfort, then smiled warmly. "But of course. Must let you boys have a little guy time together. All three of you."

"That's enough, Cyan."

"It's never enough. Not with you."

"Out."

Cyan gave a girlish giggle, then contained her mirth with visible effort and made her way toward the door. As she passed Dana she reached up to touch her jaw, casually pulling down her lower lip with her thumb, exposing her glinting canines, and ignoring her warning growl. "That all you got? Sorry to disappoint you, doll, but he likes at least an inch of fang. Better tell him now before things get heavy between you guys. Just a word to the wise."

Dana's teeth snapped, but Cyan's hand was no longer there.

"Back in ten, darlings. Dinner's gone cold. I'm getting take-out."

With a wave of her ringed hand, Cyan was gone.

Magnus cocked a scarred eyebrow. "Dinner?"

Skyler shrugged. He let out the breath that he didn't know he'd been holding and gave Magnus a curt nod of his head, hiding his disappointment as the bathroom door swung closed. He swept a hand through his mussed hair, trying to sound professional. "So. How's tricks?"

"I won't keep you. I can see you have other business to attend to." Magnus glanced over his shoulder and gave Skyler a knowing look. "How much did she charge you, by the way?"

Skyler stroked his jaw, stalling for time. "Ten K, but it was well worth it. No one else is going to find out, I promise, and with Karrel out of the way—"

"No. I meant to sleep with her." Magnus's gaze was piercing.

"Oh." Skyler glanced around, flustered. "We haven't..."

"I'm joking, Mr. Banks," rumbled Magnus. "She would never sleep with a human, at least, not one she wanted to let live." Magnus broke into a throaty chuckle that abruptly ended as soon as Skyler joined in. In the uncomfortable silence that followed he inclined his head, considering the figure. "Ten K, eh? I'll beat that for the next job. This is a dog-eat-dog world, after all. So to speak." Magnus smiled broadly, revealing enormously sharp yellowed teeth.

"Gotcha." Skyler distractedly moved over to the bathtub to let the water out, buying himself some thinking time.

He started to pull back the curtain, then froze.

"So tell me, is everything in place for tomorrow night?" Magnus asked.

"Hmm?" Skyler stared down at the pale, mutilated corpse of one of his recruits spread-eagled in the bathtub, then quickly twitched the curtain back into place. He cleared his throat and swung around to face Magnus, his face glassy. "You were saying...?"

"Saturday night. The grand unveiling party. Much progress has been made, and we're eager to test the results. Word from the lab is that we've finally nailed it, or so they say."

"Have you? That's nice," Skyler burbled, the face of the dead recruit hanging before his eyes. His guys up in Reports were going to have one hell of a time writing up this one, but hell, that was what he paid them for.

He only hoped it would be worth it.

"Yes. Cracking the secret of the vampire's immortality is... *nice*, considering we've been working on it for the last decade." Magnus gave a strange smile, then stepped forward and picked up Cyan's Katar sword, weighing it in his hand experimentally. A touch of reproach entered his voice. "I'm not getting any younger, you know. We werewolves age, unlike *them*."

"Indeed." Skyler shook himself. His eyes refocused on Magnus, a sick sheen of sweat suffusing his face. The man actually had a mane, Skyler noticed with a touch of hysteria, his thick, shoulder-length hair sweeping back almost to a point behind his powerful shoulder blades. The guy looked like an ex-wrestler stuffed into a business suit. Skyler knew without a shadow of a doubt that all those muscles didn't come from working out at Bally's gym.

He inched away as Magnus spun the sword in his hand with easy skill, watching the way the light played along the razor-fine blade as he waited for him to speak.

"Hey, it's not my fault it's taken so much time," he burst out, his voice rising in frustration. "You know that shit's not my department. I kept my end of the bargain. You got the technological stuff you wanted from us—"

"And you got the protection you wanted from us." There was a measured, dangerous pause. "Even at the expense of our own."

Skyler held up his hands. "Hey, you know I do all I can to keep our guys away from your guys. It was just a matter of time before somebody went against orders and screwed things up. I can't go on every mission and play chaperone, you know."

"I don't want excuses. I want results." Magnus slammed his fist down on the luxurious countertop, cracking the heavy marble. He watched Skyler's eyes widen at the sight of his filed-down claws, and curled his lip in contempt. "Any more leaks, you're off the project, and when I say 'off the project,' I mean..."

"You have my word," said Skyler fiercely, sweating.

Magnus nodded, gazing at the spinning blade as though hypnotized. "Soon, our wait will finally be over. We've had ninety-three percent of our test subjects survive the process in the last month."

"And the other seven percent?"

Magnus stopped his sword-spinning and gave a broad smile.

Skyler swallowed. "Right."

A small, excited sound came from behind him. Skyler turned around, gazing anxiously at Dana, who had been pottering around the bathroom as they spoke. She was sniffing the air around the bathtub, drooling at the smell of fresh blood. As she reached out for the curtain Skyler stepped quickly in front of her and blocked her way. He glanced at Magnus and started fiddling with his shredded shirt, his mind racing.

Oh, this wasn't going to be fun.

"Hey," he started, his pulse starting to pound in his throat. "While I remember, there *was* this one other thing."

"Yes?"

"Karrel. The guy who found out. He..." Skyler paused while he tried to think of how to put this. The wrong words could be disastrous, particularly while Magnus was still holding that sword. He licked his lips, his gaze flickering toward the door. "He didn't have any family left, but our sources indicate that he might've been involved with a girl."

"A girl?"

"A girl," Skyler confirmed, willing his voice not to shake. "Just a little girl though, nobody important, hardly worth mentioning, in fact. I just thought that, well... maybe we should, you know, kill her. Just in case Karrel said anything. Not that he would say anything, mind you, because of the Hunter secrecy oath, but still. You never know. You know?" Skyler lapsed into a sweating silence.

Magnus considered this. At length he said, "Does Cyan know this?"

"Yeah, I already paid her," said Skyler, trying to keep his tone light, flippant. "But the girl she sent last night goofed. She already called her boys in to try again tonight, but I was thinking, if you could give me a deal, maybe send someone a bit more professional...?"

Magnus's brutal, weathered face settled into a frown. "Cyan will do the job, and you'll pay me double for her services. That's cheap, for you."

"Cheap?" Skyler's jaw dropped. "Compared to what?"

"You have health insurance?"

"Of course."

"Then you'd better check your policy. Read the fine print." Magnus loomed over Skyler, flexing his claws as the man shrank back, a sick look on his pale, sweating face. "You stiff us on this payment, you'll be needing it."

WYLIE TOOK KAYLA'S hands in his as he leaned back against the counter, regarding his pale-faced friend with concern. His usually jovial expression was somber, although the upturned corners of his mouth and the laugh lines around his warm brown eyes hinted that this was not a natural state for him.

"I came as soon as I heard. Tell me all."

"There's not much 'all' to tell." Kayla pushed her hair back and shrugged, trying to put on a brave face. "He just didn't show, but there's something else I need to tell you."

Wylie's breath hissed through his teeth. "Son of a bitch. I knew he'd do this to you. Remind me why I didn't hook you up with that other friend of mine instead?"

Kayla paused despite herself. "Who, that Norman guy? The one with the bad breath and the evil teeth?"

"You can fix bad teeth, sweetie. You can't fix a bad personality."

"Karrel doesn't have a bad personality! And by the way, actually you can. With drugs, and lots of vitamin C, and, er, electroshock therapy." Kayla paused as she looked up into Wylie's knowing, kohl-rimmed eyes. "But you know Karrel, he's not a bad guy, really, deep-down. He just..." she paused while she ran a couple of sentences past in her mind and discarded them all. "He just..."

"He just proved himself to be the big lame ass coward he is and upset my favorite-ever girl. C'mere, give me a hug."

Wylie swept Kayla into his strong, greasepaint-scented embrace, squeezing her tight. Kayla relaxed against him, but only slightly, resting her head on his shoulder and snuggling into his neck.

"You know what I keep tellin' you," he said quietly. "You should *never* have to make excuses for a guy. Any man who genuinely gives a damn about you will move heaven and hell to be by your side, and he'll do it right away, not three days later when he remembers to return your phone call. Trust me on that one."

"He was probably just kept late at work," Kayla sniffed, not sounding at all convinced.

"So, the California Humane Society had some big animal emergency that needed him there on his one night off?" Wylie snorted. "Sounds likely to me."

"Maybe," Kayla pouted, fiddling with a thread on Wylie's T-shirt.

"Bullshit. I know that guy, sweet as anything, but monumentally dumb when it comes to commitment or making any kind of decision. Guy can't even pick a fight in a bar without phoning a friend." Wylie leaned forward to plant a kiss on Kayla's forehead, leaving a sticky print of lip-gloss behind. "Enough is enough. The guy's gotta go. We can't be having you upset like this, not on my watch."

"And who would I date if I wasn't dating Karrel?" Kayla asked, her voice light, teasing.

"Hmm. Well. Let me think now." Wylie blushed slightly and blew out his cheeks, before fixing Kayla with a frank grin. "I can think of at least one guy."

"Really? And who would that be?"

"Hello? Pest control?" said a voice from behind them. "Yes, I need a van sent out right away. I seem to have a swarm of losers infesting my counter. Please hurry, I think they're about to start breeding. Thanks. Bye."

Kayla peered around Wylie. "Nice to see you too, Julissa. How's life treating you?"

The tall, leggy, cosmetics counter girl tossed back her ebony locks and considered the question. "Much worse now that you're here."

"Pleased to hear it," said Kayla pleasantly. "Oh look, there's Paris Hilton."

"Where?" Julissa spun around, sweeping her hair back and reaching into her pocket for her lipstick. Her perfect, mixed-Mexican features crumpled as she surveyed the empty bar. "That was so lame."

"But still funny."

"In a 'not' kind of way."

"Ladies! Enough with all the estrogen! How 'bout a little love?"

"Love is on the third floor, Aisle C, in the 'fiction' department," Julissa snapped. "I suggest you go look for it and stop cluttering up my bar with your 'Hi, I'm a goth, so I have to wear black with everything' lack of trendiness. Have you ever even heard of individuality?"

"Hello, issues," muttered Kayla.

"At least I know what my issues are. I suggest you take a look in a mirror sometime." Julissa peered at Kayla with disdain over the top of her Police brand half-frame glasses. "At least fix your skin. How can you even stand to go out in public looking like that?"

"Hey! Late night, okay?" said Kayla. She remembered why she had called Wylie here in the first place. She turned urgently back to him, but Julissa cut her off.

"Get with it, perfume girl. If you give me that 'beauty is only skin deep; it's what's inside that counts' crap again I'm gonna shoot myself." Julissa picked up a brush and dabbed it into a jar of loose rouge powder that she had magically produced from somewhere about her person. "It's what's *outside* that shows. Honestly, I don't even know how you survive without basecoat. If God had meant us to look like you, he would never have given us the Mac range."

She swept the brush across her cheeks and beamed. "See?"

Kayla glanced sidelong at Wylie. "Don't worry. She'll turn back into a human being after her daily fifteen-hour sleep quota. Now, about this thing I wanted to tell you—"

"Hey, if you're happy to go around looking like Miss FreeRadicals 'R' Us then that's your business. My business is all about looking good. I look good, therefore I am." Julissa blew Wylie a kiss. "Get it?"

"Got it. Just not sure that I want it."

"All the more for me, then." Julissa grabbed Kayla by the wrist as she started to walk away. "Let's face it, girlfriend, you'll still be here, working this counter when I'm sipping lattes with the rich and famous." Julissa let go of Kayla's wrist and tossed her hair demurely, lowering her voice. "I mean, look around you. This place is a hotspot for directors and producers, and all those delicious movie people who do the hiring. It's your problem if you don't take advantage of that." She reached for a nearby display, tilting it to face Kayla. "Talking of taking advantage… are you gonna enter this competition?"

"What competition?" asked Kayla.

"With Genetica. That new hot-shot beauty company? They're looking for a new cover girl. Look, you get a free beauty treatment if you enter."

"I'll pass, thanks all the same."

"So I can have your coupon?"

"Knock yourself out." Kayla half-heartedly saluted Julissa. "Now, if you don't mind, us 'losers' have important business to discuss. The fate of the world hangs in the balance."

"Yeah. You wish," sniffed Julissa. Grabbing two Genetica coupons and a makeup mirror, she vanished into the stock room with a whirl of perfumed hair, closing the door behind her.

Wylie looked at Kayla quizzically as she peered after Julissa, checking that she had gone before he continued. "Something's up. Am I right?"

"You could say that." Kayla paused, trying to work out how she was going to say this. She knew she could trust Wylie with anything, and right now she desperately needed someone to run this by before she talked to the cops. If they thought she was messing with them with her "werewolf" story, she knew that things could go real bad, real fast.

She took a deep breath, working up her nerves. "Wylie... you've known me a long time, right?"

"Twelve whole entire months. Ever since you moved here," said Wylie proudly.

"So you know I'd never bullshit you."

"Right. Or if you did, you'd send me a three-page message on MySpace explaining your somewhat shoddy and to-do-with-a-guy reasons, and I'd ignore you for two days before I forgave you."

"That's our song. Listen." Kayla pressed her palms together, glancing quickly over at the office door. "There's a cop here to see me. I need to tell you some stuff."

"What!" Wylie stared. "Kayla, you ain't in some kind of trouble, are you?"

"No! I mean, I don't know. Maybe. Perhaps yes."

"I like a woman who knows her own mind." Wylie paused and his eyes flicked sideways. "On second thought, I'd just like a woman, any woman. But enough about me." Wylie leaned back against the counter and eyed Kayla with great concern. "Tell me all."

"I'm not quite sure how to."

"Why? Is it illegal, gross, scandalous, or a combination of the above?" Wylie parked himself eagerly on the edge of a display block, nearly dislodging a pyramid of herbal moisturizers. "C'mon, girl. Don't cheap out on me. Spill."

Kayla breathed in deeply through her nose and let the breath out through her mouth, her mind whirring. "Okay. The Yahoo News version. I saw a guy get killed last night."

"You what?" Wylie stared at her.

"Or maybe he wasn't killed. Maybe he survived." Kayla glanced up at Wylie, picking fitfully at her sleeve.

"Whoa, whoa, whoa! Hold your horses, sailor! Start from the beginning."

"I can't. It'd take too long. I really should be going."

"No way! You tell me you saw someone get..." Wylie glanced around furtively and lowered his voice. "You saw someone get killed, and you don't have time to tell me about it properly? This is like the biggest news ever in the history of us! What are you, crazy?"

Kayla gave Wylie a pained look.

"Just tell me one thing. You didn't do it, did you?"

Kayla shook her head.

"Did you see who did it?"

A pause, then a nod.

"So…?"

"You'll think I'm nuts."

"I already think you're nuts. That's why I hang out with you, to take all the attention away from me."

"Fine, then. It was a werewolf."

Wylie stared at her. Then his cheerful face split into a smile and he thumped her on the shoulder. "That wasn't funny! You had me scared to death for a minute there!" He reached out and mussed her hair. "You're weird, but still cute."

"But it's the truth!" Kayla burst out, dropping her voice. "I saw a werewolf kill this guy! It had claws and teeth and everything, and it ripped this guy's throat out, right in front of me!"

"Yeah, right." Wylie shook his head good-naturedly. "Just stick me on the short bus and call me George. You nearly had me that time."

"But it's true! And now there's a cop here to question me about it, and I don't know what I'm going to tell him!" Kayla's lower lip started to quiver.

"You're not messing with me? You really saw a guy die?"

Kayla nodded, not trusting herself to speak.

"And this werewolf… It couldn't have just been some big guy with a beard and bad teeth?"

"It was a girl, not a guy. One minute she was normal, the next she—" Kayla broke off and shook her head. She swallowed hard, feeling tears threaten.

"Wylie, what am I gonna do? What am I gonna tell the police when they—"

"Miss Steele! *Today*, please!"

"Shit. I gotta go." Kayla reached down and gripped Wylie's hand, pressing it to her heart. "If I go to jail, you can have my Batman comics."

"You're really serious, aren't you?"

"Just pray for me." Kayla threw a hunted look toward the office. She gave Wylie a quick peck on the cheek and quickly turned away from him, swearing to herself. Just five more minutes, and maybe they could've worked out a story together, something about a mad dog, maybe? She had always been a shitty liar, so the cops probably wouldn't have believed her, anyway. Now she was going to have to tell them the truth, and she knew for a fact that they weren't going to like it.

She strode quickly across the store, her heart thumping in her chest.

Kayla knocked confidently on the office door and waited. There was a murmur of conversation and the door opened a crack. Mr. Holt peered out, an odd look on his face. Behind him were two cops. One was a nerdy-looking uniformed cop clutching a cup of Starbucks coffee. The other was a tall, well-built man of mixed race, wearing a rumpled shirt and tie and a look of kindly concern. He stood up straight as he saw her, holding his cap in his hands. He looked ill at ease and Kayla felt her heart sinking.

She cleared her throat. "So, what's all this about?" she asked, trying to sound cheerful.

Mr. Holt opened the door wider.

"Miss Steele... um..." He flicked her eyes down to Kayla's name badge and her heart sank further. "Kayla. You'd better come in." He paused for a second. "It's about your boyfriend, Karrel."

Kayla stared at him as the bottom fell out of her world.

DOWN BY THE ocean, a chill wind rose off the dark sea by the rocky breakwater, a thousand glimmering lights of the city reflected in its murky, disease-ridden depths. The local surfers would joke that they could tell who surfed which beach by the exact type of bacterial poisoning their friends had, and very frequently, they were right. It rarely rained in LA. When it did, every bit of crap coating the streets and buildings washed down the storm drains, eventually finding its way to the oceans of Santa Monica, Venice, Marina Del Ray, and even the less built-up areas of Hermosa, Redondo, and Manhattan Beach.

Despite the state of the waters, the tourists still flocked to them, crowding the beaches with their white, pudgy bodies and making entertaining targets for locals' surfboards. This evening, though, the water was almost empty. It hadn't rained in a while, and the gray, sludgy foam on the oceans was at its thinnest in months, which was what passed for beauty around here. Venice truly lived up to its reputation as being the place where the debris met the sea, in more ways than one.

Two young surfers paddled the calm, tepid waters, enjoying the stillness and peace after the noise and bustle of the day. Their names were Gridz and Bradley. They'd been in the ocean since noon, carving through the water on their fish shortboards, enduring the heat of the day to catch waves long past the routinely beautiful sunset, with the light refracting through the hazy yellow pollution. Now they were drinking in the beauty of the falling evening.

They paddled surely, confidently, leaving the beach far behind as they ventured out into the deep dark waters a short distance from the pier. The stars were coming out and the water beneath them was smooth and glassy. Big ripples moved through the water like muscles moving beneath the velvet skin of a giant panther. The waves were small and mushy, not even reaching four feet, but they'd heard rumors of a storm swell coming in. Even after the slow day they'd had, they still held out hope for some action.

They were in the middle of discussing Gridz's latest audition, lazily dangling their limbs into the cool water, when a light flickered beneath them through the glassy depths of the ocean, moving slowly but surely toward the shore.

Gridz sat up on his board, warily watching the light as it passed beneath him. It was blue and pulsed regularly like a fucked-up jellyfish, lighting up the water and revealing all kinds of things floating in the ocean that he would rather not know were there.

He stared at it for a long moment, his handsome, tanned face creasing into a frown.

"Brad, bro, you getting this?" he asked quietly.

Brad wiped a hand over his face, sending a powder-like residue of crusted salt drifting down onto his board. "Yeah. What the fuck?"

They watched in bemusement as the strange, disembodied light flooded toward the shore, then left the water and flowed up onto the sand, drifting lazily over a set of old, rusted beach swings. There it seemed to hesitate, drifting aimlessly back and forth and casting weird jumping shadows off the underside of the pier. Then, just as suddenly, it seemed to decide on a direction, zipping up the steps toward the road and shooting off inland in the direction of Hollywood.

"They shooting some kinda ghost flick 'round here?"

Gridz ran a hand through his drenched, sun-bleached hair, feeling suddenly cold despite the snug warmth of his wetsuit. "Beats me."

"Wanna paddle in and find out?"

The two surfers looked at each other, sharing a thought. Then they dropped back down on their boards and resumed their expectant positions, gazing out at the horizon as the moon came up.

Life, they knew, was all about priorities.

They already had theirs.

A few minutes later, the moving light reached the noisy bustle of Sunset Strip, barely visible amid the ultra-bright lights and glaring neon of the street. Reaching its destination, it flew in through a top window, danced down some steps, then coalesced into a spinning vortex of light in a dark, cluttered basement filled with yellow police caution tape and a number of small, sad chalk outlines. A cloud of spinning paper was whipped up as ticket stubs and abandoned band fliers formed a merry vortex with a glowing blue light at its center. It stretched upwards until it was roughly man-shaped. A desolate keening sound filled the air, blending with the strident sound of badly played electric guitars echoing down the steps from upstairs.

Then, just as suddenly, the light winked out.

"NOOOOO!"

The sound came from deep inside him, from the black abyss that until just a moment ago had swallowed his soul. Karrel screamed as every muscle in his body tightened, his heart pounding painfully in his chest like a bloody, broken fist driving through concrete.

Gasping, he opened his eyes, his body arching off the floor as a hideous spasm of pain wracked him. The world loomed around him and he screamed again soundlessly. His fingers scrabbled the dirty floor, clutching at nothing as his consciousness hit him full force, boring hideous, unwanted, bloody images into his brain.

A second later his training kicked in and he was on his feet, sprinting for the door. Then he was spinning backward and downward as vertigo body-slammed him, snatching him up like a giant hand and hurling him to the floor in slow motion. As he fell, he instinctively snatched at a nearby chair to catch himself.

His hand passed right through it.

Karrel hit the ground with a bruising thump and lay there, his bloodshot eyes wide with confusion. A moment later he blinked and his gaze flickered around to take in the room. The chalk outlines. The bloodstains on the walls. Police wasp-tape strung around the door.

Karrel's terrified, half-crazed gaze came to rest on the shattered remains of his Remington rifle lying on the ground next to him. He stretched out a trembling hand toward it.

His fingers went right through it.
He squeezed his eyes tight shut.
"Ah, crap."

CHAPTER FIVE

JULISSA SIGHED AS she swiped her card through the machine lock on the staff exit. She pushed her way through the heavy gray door, leaving the late evening bustle of the mall behind her. She was not having a good day. It was only eight o'clock, and already three bad things had happened to her. Firstly, her brand new suede jacket had been ruined by a piece of gum she was sure one of the other counter girls had stuck onto her chair. Secondly, that perfume girl's boyfriend had gotten himself killed, and their supervisor had sent her home, meaning that she and the other girls had to cover her slot tonight. A double shift was the last thing she needed, but for the sake of keeping her lousy job she had to put up with it.

Life, in Julissa's book, sucked.

And thirdly—

"Hey there Miss Julissa, any word back yet 'bout that audition?"

Julissa winced. She turned and flashed a thin smile at the hulking security guard holding the outer door open for her. "Still haven't heard back," she lied.

"They turned you down?" the guard boomed, oblivious to her discomfort, his weathered face settling into an expression of bemusement. "Man, those guys have gotta be insane to toss out a beautiful woman like you. I mean, look at you." He moistened his lips, looking her up and down appreciatively. "If you were *my* woman, I—"

"Well I'm not, so you don't have to worry about it, do you? Ta-ta."

Julissa pushed her way past the guard and marched toward the parking lot as fast as her legs would carry her. She waited until she was out of sight of the guard before cupping her hands to her face and groaning loudly.

Great. Now the whole world knew she was a failure. She'd been so sure she was going to get the part that she'd just gone around, willy-nilly, telling everyone she met how she was soon going to be a big star, only to have yet another agent crap out on her. Just another indignity to join the long line of embarrassments she'd suffered so far since arriving in LA, three years ago.

It was her age, or so they told her. The girls starting out in the film industry these days were anorexic girls of sixteen, so of course they had flawless hair, perfect complexions and legs to die for. Even getting an audition was a battle for her, as form after form was returned to her citing her age as the reason for her rejection.

At twenty-six, Julissa was "officially" too old for the film industry.

Still, at least her parents were proud of her, or rather, they were proud of the girl who had gotten three starring roles on soon to be major movies. Julissa was sure that they'd share her disappointment when the movies all had the plug pulled on them by their backers at the last minute. She didn't like having to lie to them, but then neither did she like being seen as a failure, even by her own parents.

Well, she'd show them.

She'd show them all.

Julissa tugged down her absurdly short counter-girl skirt and strode across the crumbling employee parking lot, holding her breath and muttering to herself as she strode past rows of dumpsters overflowing with food from the café and sticky bottles from the bar. The whole place was a dump. The sooner she got herself out of here, the better.

She climbed in her car and sat for a moment with her head resting on the steering wheel. She tried to focus on her breathing, as her yoga teacher had taught her.

In... and out.

In... and out.

In, and... Oh, who the hell was she kidding? She was going to die poor and friendless, rejected by society, snubbed by those who mattered the most.

Still, she had one last hope.

Carefully, she slid a hand into her pocket and pulled out the two tiny silver Genetica coupons. They were a simple design printed on quality stock paper with a silvered, mirror-like surface.

She checked the address on the back, and a slow smile spread across her face.

Two free beauty treatments. Cool.

Maybe there was hope for her yet.

She put the car into gear and pulled out of the mall parking lot, heading for the open road.

TWENTY MINUTES LATER she pulled into the wide, impressive parking lot of Genetica, Inc., located deep in the heart of the more fashionable end of Beverly Hills. She carefully guided her vintage VW Beetle down the sweeping white gravel driveway, beneath the lush, overhanging canopies of palm trees planted around the perimeter. She drove past floodlit granite sculptures of beautiful, athletic men and women, and cheerfully splashing fountains, before pulling into a wide, easy space between two sleek white Mercedes.

Julissa switched off the engine and gaped.

Genetica was a tall, architecturally daring building dominated by a sleek, multi-layered mirrored spire, which made the place look a little like a chromed wedding cake. The building was brightly lit and shone like a white beacon of hope in the darkness, surrounded by grass hills, through which clients and employees strode back and forth, most of them dressed in suits and carrying briefcases.

Julissa locked her car and hurried toward the main entrance, coupons in hand.

Despite the lateness of the hour, the path was swarming with clients. Julissa had barely taken more than a couple of steps before a tall man on a cell phone bumped rudely into her. He pushed past her and carried on walking without so much as acknowledging her presence.

Julissa bristled. "Hey, jackass! Watch where you're going!"

The man spun around to face her, his eyes flaring. His retort died on his lips at the sight of her, and a look of faintly horrified surprise spread across his face.

"Julissa?"

"Tyler?" Julissa stared. She hadn't seen her ex-boyfriend once in the six months since they'd split up, and seeing him again now was something of a shock. Tyler was loud, brash, annoyingly confident, insanely handsome, and—judging by the sweep of his bulging biceps under his expensive suit—he'd recently been cast in something big that featured at least partial nudity. They had met at an audition and dated for a whole three weeks, which by LA standards made them practically married. Then he'd ditched her when he'd found out that she worked in a downtown mall rather than, as she had claimed, in a Beverly Hills boutique.

Julissa turned to face him, brushing back her hair and wishing she was wearing anything other than her scruffy counter-girl uniform. She peered at her reflection in his silvered shades, hoping she didn't have lipstick on her teeth. "Wow. You look... great."

The words were out of her mouth before she could stop herself, but it was true. Tyler *did* look great. The sparkling white of his suit really brought out the mahogany hue of his skin, and his ripped, muscled physique was to die for.

Maybe, just maybe he would give her another chance.

Tyler smiled, sweeping her with an ironic look. "At least one of us does."

And there it was, the reason she wasn't so cut up when they split up. He may be good looking, but the guy was an asshole. He didn't need to be nice to get women. He didn't need to chase them, either;

they chased him, and if they were really, really unlucky, they caught him.

Julissa bit back her instinctive recrimination and forced herself to smile, her eyes covertly sweeping his jacket until they found the designer's tag. Her eyebrows went up. Tyler was wearing a jacket that cost more than her annual rent.

She licked her suddenly dry lips and her gaze darted over his shoulder to the parking lot, wondering what car he was driving these days. Something big and shiny, she guessed. The kind of car that would look great with her in the back of it.

"Come, now," she wheedled, half distracted by her fiendish internal calculations. "You think it's easy looking this good on a budget?"

"If you're on a budget, you shouldn't be in this place."

Tyler turned to go, dismissing her with a sneer, but Julissa quickly caught him by the sleeve. She swallowed her pride. There was rent to pay. It was now or never. "Wait. I've been doing some thinking about you and me. See, when we met, my life was—"

"I'm not interested in your life, princess. I'm interested in my life, and right now, I have much better things in it than you."

Tyler glanced pointedly over her shoulder. Julissa turned to see a long-legged, young blonde girl waiting beside the open door of a mint autumn-black Jaguar, her luscious red lips set in a sly smile. She couldn't have been any older than nineteen.

Julissa's heart sank. She turned back to Tyler, rolling her eyes. "Do the words 'cradle-snatcher' mean anything to you?"

"Very little." Tyler grinned, giving a sickening little wave at the girl. "Now move. We have a plane to catch."

Pushing her aside, he strode on up the path to his car.

Julissa stood for a moment staring after him, watching as he joined the blonde girl and swept her up in a tight embrace. He kissed her in an obvious, drawn-out way that left her no doubt that the little spectacle was entirely for her benefit.

Julissa shook herself. Whatever.

Turning her back on him, she angrily adjusted her short black skirt and began marching up the path to Genetica, the comforting shape of her Free Trial coupons clutched tightly in her hand. There were plenty more fish in the sea, whatever the hell that meant, and once she was rich and famous, he'd be begging her to take him back.

She'd show him.

"TYLER, BABY, WHO was that?"

"Her? Nobody." Tyler settled back into the leather-padded interior of the Jag, dropping his Genetica treatment pack onto the floor. He flicked the car's mirror up and peered into it, running a hand approvingly over his face. His skin definitely seemed much smoother and tighter after that last session, and he was sure that his agent would be thrilled with the results. This place really was everything it claimed to be and more, and he made a mental note to get some new headshots done immediately to make the most of the big bucks his top-of-the-line treatment had cost him.

Removing his sunglasses, he gave a sigh of satisfaction and swept his new girl with a long, lingering look. "But you... you're really somebody." He clasped his hands together, gazing into her deep blue eyes. "Remind me of your name again?"

The girl chuckled, then stopped as she saw the look on Tyler's face.

"No, really," he said. "I'm serious. I've got a lot on my mind, what with that big shoot coming up tomorrow and everything."

"Of course. You poor thing." The girl reached out and stroked his forehead lightly, then ran her cheek across his freshly-shaven jaw before whispering in his ear, "It's Ocean."

"Ocean? That's a pretty name. A pretty name for a pretty lady."

The girl giggled, and Tyler smiled a wide, generous smile. This was going to be too easy.

He leaned over with a creak of leather to run his fingers over the girl's fine-boned jaw, basking in her beauty for a moment before cupping her head and leaning in for a kiss. Their tongues met in a sugary tangle of breath mints and spearmint gum. Tyler made a small noise of contentment as he reeled her in closer, breathing in the warm honeydew scent of her perfume. Ocean was five foot eight of pert perfection in a figure-hugging white cotton dress. She'd been hanging around him since she'd met him at that last Pepsi commercial audition, obviously convinced he was "the one" who was going to get her started in the movie industry. Tyler wasn't about to start complaining. Money had a way of attracting beauty, provided that beauty was young and penniless and desperate for its big break.

Tyler loved it.

He rolled his eyes as he felt Ocean's slim, warm fingers slide beneath his shirt, tugging softly but insistently at the buttons. Cute girl, this one, but not very bright. Most of the "movies" he'd done were in fact indie shorts that hadn't even found buyers yet, but it was amazing what you could do with a rented suit and a buddy who worked at a classic car showroom. That Julissa girl had fallen for it too, as had all the others. If she hadn't stopped getting the check for him after all those big expensive dinners, he might still be dating her.

In less than a minute he was tugging off his shirt, his face buried in the soft warmth of Ocean's full, curvaceous breasts, breathing in the heavenly scent of her. The tinted windows hid them from the prying eyes of the outside world, but as he reached down to unbuckle his pants Ocean pushed him back gently. "Not here," she whispered.

Tyler made a disappointed noise. He had to be back at his mother's house for dinner at nine, and he needed to get some action before then so he could put up with yet another night of her whining to him about him getting a job and getting the hell out of her basement.

"Then where?" he asked her, getting impatient.

Ocean pointed to a nearby side street, around the back of Genetica. "Move the car, at least."

"Gotcha."

Tyler eagerly scooted back over onto his seat and started the engine, pulling his rumpled clothes back around him. Two minutes later he'd found a secluded spot near the back loading bay of Genetica, away from the bright lights of the parking lot and hidden from prying eyes by a lushly overgrown bank of foliage.

Putting the car into park, he rolled up the windows and turned back to Ocean.

This was more like it.

Reaching out, he slid the slender straps of Ocean's cotton dress off her shoulders one by one. She was gloriously, spectacularly naked beneath the sheer dress, her coppery skin making a startling contrast with the cream-colored leather of the car's luxurious upholstery. Tyler took a deep breath, his eyes roving hungrily over the supple perfection of her young, slender body, lingering on the full swell of her breasts—a C-cup, he guessed. If they went out much longer he'd suggest that going to a D-cup would increase her chances of success, if not in the movies, then at least in his bedroom.

His eyes moved down her flat, brown belly with its jutting hipbones to where her dress lay in rumpled folds around her waist. The muted dusk cast a blue glow over the gentle sweep of her body. She was watching him eagerly, her eyes alight with a hunger that was part lust, part financial desperation.

Tyler smiled to himself. He had seen that look a hundred times, and it never failed to get his motor running. That look meant he could do anything he wanted, anything at all, and get away with it. After all, it wasn't as though he promised these girls anything. They just assumed that he could help them, because he had—or appeared to have—what they wanted. All he did was smile and look the part, and they flocked to him.

Tyler sighed happily, trailing his fingers across Ocean's stomach, taking his time. It was all part of the illusion, wasn't it? Real power didn't look like him, or drive show-off vintage cars like him, or have big muscles like him. Real power drove discreet, company-leased, tax-deductible cars, dressed casually to avoid drawing attention, and rarely had time to shave, let alone put in the long hours required to build and maintain a strapping physique like his. Real power was in bed by nine to be up at six for board meetings, followed by a doctor's appointment to deal with hypertension and peptic ulcers. The closest they got to a perfect body was a trip to the edit suite to watch the golden angels their people had hired to put their dreams onto the screen, and even then they kept their distance.

Still, there was always some new girl in town willing to believe the illusion.

As long as they kept on coming, so could Tyler.

With a chuckle, Tyler turned his attention back to Ocean, drinking in her youthful beauty. He slid her dress further down, just far enough to prove his theory that she didn't wear underwear. He confirmed that fully with his fingers as he ran them up the inside of her thigh to feel how wet she was.

He kissed her greedily, pulling her over the gearshift to his side of the car while pushing the seat-recline button with practiced ease. Ocean giggled as she straddled him, her hair falling around her bare shoulders in a shining curtain of gold. Her fingers wandered across his well-defined pectoral muscles and down the ridged symmetry of his stomach, then moved lower. Tyler groaned, lifting her slightly on firm biceps to take some of her weight. Long days of unemployment wiled away at Gold's Gym were certainly paying off, but Tyler didn't have the patience to savor the moment.

His mouth curved into a self-satisfied smirk as he felt her pull him free of the confines of his boxers. With a quick, easy thrust he was inside her. He gasped at her tightness as he began to move, measured out his pleasure in short, shallow strokes. He closed his eyes and gave himself over to the simple pleasure of fucking. His hands climbed blindly up Ocean's body as she moved over him, sliding over the baby-soft silk of her skin, roving over her firm breasts, enjoying every inch of her, as she moved over him, panting softly and moaning in his ear as he neared climax.

God, she felt so...

Ocean was slowing, stopping. It took Tyler a moment to register that something was amiss. He wriggled down further in his seat, angling his body to thrust deeper, entirely caught up in the moment. An instant later he heard Ocean gasp, then let out a muffled scream.

Tyler smiled to himself.

Damn, he was good.

But Ocean went on screaming. Tyler's eyes flew open to see the girl staring down at him, a look of disbelieving horror on her face. She pulled away from him and yanked her dress back up. She made a mad grab for her purse and fumbled blindly for the door handle.

Tyler sat up. "Babe. What's up?"

Ocean didn't reply. Instead she wrenched the door open, and threw herself out. She stumbled to her feet and started running, casting horrified glances back over her shoulder. Her feet were bare but she didn't seem to notice. She picked up speed as she sprinted away from the car.

A slow, stupefied look spread over Tyler's face. He pulled himself back upright in his seat, buckled his pants with difficulty, and leaned out of the car, watching in bemusement as Ocean ran smack into a bull-sized security guard. The guard took the girl by the shoulders to calm her, frowning as she turned and thrust a trembling finger back toward him, then looked up at the car, suspicion written all over his swarthy, bearded face.

"What the *hell*?"

Tyler smoothed his hair down, quickly checked his fly was closed, and then climbed out of the Jag as the security guard marched sternly toward him. Crazy chick. Whatever he had done to the girl, she was obviously overreacting. Some messed-up psycho-drama trigger from the past, in all likelihood. A few quiet, mano a mano words with the guard should straighten this one out, and if not, he had a hundred dollar bill in his wallet especially for the occasion.

His mother need never know about this.

As the guard neared him he saw the man hesitate, then speak urgently into his radio. A few moments later the side door to Genetica flew open and three other guards stepped out, wearing sunshades and identical expressions of menace. The first one moved to intercept the distressed girl, putting an arm around her shoulder as he led her quickly back to the main Genetica building, while the other two fell in behind the first guard as he resumed his ominous march for the Jaguar.

Tyler slammed the car door and started walking, working up his best movie-star smile and mentally checking that he had no drugs about his person. He froze as the first guard drew a weird, blocky-looking gun and aimed it at his chest.

"Stay where you are, sir."

"Sure, no problem." Tyler raised his hands and smiled ingratiatingly. "But there's been a misunderstanding. That girl, see, she's—"

"I said freeze, asshole!"

"Fine. Jeez!" Tyler backed up a little and scratched his head, hoping this could be taken care of quickly. His hair felt weird, as though it wasn't quite attached to his head right. He smoothed it down, hoping he didn't look too messed up. The last thing he needed now was to get a ticket for public indecency.

Trying to make the move look casual, he turned to check his reflection in the tinted car window. He let out a yell of fright, staring in horror at his reflection. His features looked like they were melting, misshapen and oddly flattened. Bony ridges jutted out of his cheekbones, and swollen lumps framed his jaw line and brow. Even as he watched, more ridges sprouted on his forehead and chin, as his hair continued to grow. When he'd gotten into the car it had been freshly cut and ear-length. Now, the back of it was touching his shoulders.

"Jesus!"

Tyler leapt away from the car as if stung. Gingerly, disbelievingly, he ran his fingers over the lumps and bumps that had sprouted on his face. They didn't hurt, although his skin was starting to tingle as if it were sunburned.

He spun to face the security guard. "Help me!" he cried.

The security guard didn't have time for this shit. He raised his Taser gun and gave the freaky guy 50,000 volts of juice, holding down the trigger long after he'd dropped him. Just to be sure.

As the other two guards moved around him to haul Tyler's unconscious, limp body away, he raised his radio to his lips, a look of grim glee on his face. "Get a containment unit down here. We got another one."

Then he turned and walked back up the steps to Genetica.

CHAPTER SIX

As NIGHT FELL Kayla sat alone on the edge of her bed, staring at the wall.

Karrel was dead.

It couldn't be real.

Yet, somehow, it was.

She shifted her weight on the creaking mattress and glanced helplessly around her, at her things, at the bed, at the four walls of her ramshackle studio apartment.

Everything seemed so real, so solid, so... normal.

That couldn't be right, could it? Karrel was dead, and her entire life had suddenly, horrifically changed, but nothing had changed here. There should be bloodstains on the carpet, flames licking up the walls, smoke obscuring the cheery arrangement of photographs lining the shelves.

Then maybe she'd believe this was real, that this was her life.

Thunder grumbled outside. A storm was coming. A rush of cold air blew in through the barred window, setting her makeshift gauze curtains fluttering, but Kayla had no energy left to get up and close it. Instead, her eyes traveled over the accumulated possessions of her small, unremarkable life, and she fought a strange urge to flee the place.

Everything reminded her of Karrel. The apartment was barely more than an industrial steel shell with a bed and a few belongings on a stripped wooden dresser, but it was hers, and she was proud of it. What with all the break-ins around here nothing of value lasted long, but she'd made the living unit as comfortable as she could. There were a few red throw pillows, and she had even hung some warmly-hued strips of red and orange gauze from the ceiling in a mad fit of alcohol-inspired creativity to curtain off her sleeping area from the small, tattered kitchen-slash-dining area.

She remembered the day when they'd tried to hang those curtains. Karrel had come around after work clutching a stolen power drill, a roll of duct tape, and a big bottle of her favorite Caribbean white rum. How pleased with himself he'd looked when he'd finally got the damn things both straight and the right way around. Then they'd found some much more interesting things to do with the duct tape, and promptly lost all interest in decorating the apartment.

Kayla cut the thought off abruptly and waited for the tears to come, but they didn't. She reached up to touch her dry cheeks, uncomprehending. Her chest was painfully tight, as though a steel band was constricting around her heart. She didn't understand why she wasn't crying; it added to the feeling of unreality that had been building in her ever since her meeting with the office cop and the detective.

A dog had killed him, they'd said, possibly a neglected club guard-dog he'd been called out about. They'd found a business card in his wallet and tried to call his employers—the American Humane Society—to inform them of his death, but the organisation had told them they had no record of him, information the police were treating as highly suspicious. They'd asked Kayla pointedly if she knew anything further that might be of help to them. Without thinking, she'd told them about last night, about the club, about Mutt, Jax, and Mia. It wasn't a dog that had killed him, she'd assured them fervently. She knew exactly who Karrel's killer had been, because she'd met her.

They'd calmly asked her to explain, so she told them as much as she'd dared about the attack. They were cops, she'd reasoned. They'd listen and understand. They would thank her for giving them some vital information, and tell her that they'd heard of the killer before. They would reassure her that she wasn't going crazy. But by the time she'd registered their frozen expressions and their hands tightening on their radios, it had been too late.

They'd clapped handcuffs on her and taken her down to the station, where they'd spent hours grilling her. They had shown her photographs she hadn't wanted to see, blurred crime scene images of Jax lying dead in an alleyway with his throat torn out. They'd spared her the ones of Karrel, thank God. They carefully wrote down everything she'd said, took her fingerprints, and photographed her before finally discharging her hours later. She'd felt like a criminal. They told her they couldn't hold her for longer without an arrest warrant, but that she might eventually have to go to court and testify against Jax's killer—if indeed she was telling the truth. They had time-logged CCTV footage of her in the club that effectively exonerated her from a murder charge in Karrel's case, but they warned her that if their investigation revealed the slightest question about the possibility of her being an accessory to Jax's murder, she could be brought back in for questioning at any time.

And that had been that.

Kayla shivered, feeling fear and worry seep into her mouth and fill it with the acrid taste of tin.

She bit her lip, her red-rimmed eyes tracking slowly around her room. Karrel had been here just twenty-four hours ago, sitting on her bed right where she was now, and everything had been normal. She had been getting ready to be proposed to, with no idea that just a day later the engagement would be off permanently, and she would be "an accessory to murder." There was a half-empty coffee cup on the dresser that he'd put there, rushing off to answer a cruelty case call. The folded jacket on the dresser, that was his, waiting to be returned to him after he'd lent it to her to keep her warm after a night at the pier. That crumpled ball of paper on the floor beside the trashcan was a list they'd made together of things they wanted to achieve in the next year, a list that seemed almost comically, tragically point-less. All she wanted was Karrel, and no matter how many lists she made, she could never, ever have him back.

Kayla looked down at her hands, lying balled and white-knuckled on her lap. A thin black cord trailed out of her fist. She stared at it for a moment, then slowly opened her hand. A Chinese coin with a square hole in it lay in her palm, the black cord running through the center making it into a necklace.

There was dried blood on the cord.

Kayla stared down at the coin listlessly. He'd won the necklace for her on their very first date at the pier. Karrel had tried to win her a fluffy pink teddy bear on the shooting stand, but he had proved to be such a comically poor shot that he ended up with the booby prize, a cheap brass dragon coin necklace. He'd handed the rifle to Kayla and she'd fared equally badly, ending up with the exact same necklace, which they both thought was hysterical. The wizened Irishman who ran the stall had told them that far from being the booby prize, the dragon-coins would bring them luck, and so neither of them had taken them off since. Until now.

Kayla squeezed her eyes shut, completely and utterly numb, feeling the pressure of grief grow inside her until she thought it would suffocate her.

It was no good. She had to get out of here.

Jumping up, she grabbed her sweater and keys from the nightstand and ran out of the room, slamming the door behind her.

She didn't stop running until she hit the main road and slowed a little, clutching at her side as a stitch cramped it. Months working at the mall had left her badly out of shape, and the discovery of this pissed her off. Yet another reason for her to quit that damn job, as if she needed one. She bent over to relieve the stitch before setting off again at a fast, furious walk, not really caring where she was going. Karrel was dead and was never coming back. All she wanted to do was be as far away from her house and her memories of him as possible.

Kayla focused hard on her anger as she walked, almost grateful to finally feel something besides numbness. She had spent the day in a daze accepting everyone's condolences: her supervisor's awkward apologies, her co-workers' platitudes, Wylie's sympathetic ministrations with hot tea and wise words that seemed to be more about making him feel he'd done his "job" by consoling her than they were about making her feel better.

None of it had helped. If anything, it had only made her feel more alone.

She carried on down the hill toward the ocean, the sound of booming surf audible as the storm picked up. She tried not to look around her as she walked, but couldn't help herself. Everything she passed reminded her of Karrel, every graffiti-tagged tree, every bench, every grungy café, every bar. They all held memories for her, trivial at the time, now given desperate importance by the inescapable fact of his death.

The grief inside her grew until it was almost unbearable. Karrel's face began to form in her memory, but she slammed the door shut in her mind, unable to cope with even the thought of him as her mind raced, turning the situation over and over. The whole thing was just so unreal. It *had* to have been Mia who killed Karrel, no matter what the police said. How could a dog kill a full-grown man, especially a strong, fit man like Karrel? She hadn't even seen the body, for crying out loud. All she had was some cop's word. What if he had been wrong? There was always a chance, wasn't there?

Kayla turned a corner and stopped dead. She felt something clench nastily in her chest as she recognized her surroundings.

This was where she'd had her first date with Karrel.

The street opened out into a concrete plaza area, ringed with little merchandise booths selling seaside souvenirs and cotton candy and churros and soft rolled pretzels. The distinctive smell of the ocean flooded her senses, a pungent mixture of salt spray and gas fumes and dead things floating in the water, not all of them fish. The plaza joined onto the funfair pier, with wooden steps down each side that led down to the beach. Fog from the rumbling ocean below drifted up the eroded steps and flooded across the pier, curling in ankle-high drifts like dry ice on a movie set, giving the scene a feeling of unreality.

As though in a dream Kayla began walking, moving haltingly through the darkened relics of the funfair, drawn as if drawn by a magnet. She bypassed the sprawling clutter of the fast food stands until she reached the boarded-up shooting stall. Kayla stopped walking and stared at it, her gaze far away. It was closed up with a graffiti covered wooden shutter, the plastic guns chained down to the counter. She reached out with trembling hands to tenderly touch the barrel of the rifle Karrel had used, all those months ago, to win her the dragon coin necklace.

She crossed the splintery boards in a daze and stepped quietly down the worn, weather-beaten steps at the side. A short walk across the sand and she was at the swings, where they had ended up at sunset at the end of their first date. Kayla reached out to trail her fingers across the railings bordering the swings. As her fingers touched the blackened, salt-corroded metal, a tidal wave of memories rolled over her, making her gasp, painting the night as bright as day.

She remembered the gleeful look on Karrel's face as he had spied the swings from the pier and dragged her down to them. She'd followed him down the steps half-heartedly, protesting all the while that swings were for kids. She burst out laughing as Karrel eagerly crammed his six-foot-two frame into a kiddie swing and nearly tipped the frame over backward. He called her over to join in the fun, fun that was cut short a few minutes later as the spoilsport lifeguard radioed the beach patrol to chase them off. They'd gone back and broken into the lifeguard hut that very night and, giggling and shushing each other, had stolen the guy's radio. That radio sat proudly on Kayla's dresser, a small badge of honor to commemorate their small victory over authority. It made her smile every time she looked at it.

But now Karrel was dead, and he would never break into the lifeguard's hut with her again.

The tears came, as unstoppable as the night. Kayla slumped down in the worn plastic seat of the shooting stall as her legs gave out.

She had no idea how long she sat there, head in her hands, tears flowing down her cheeks and dripping off the end of her nose. After a while she felt a cold sea breeze blowing across her, ruffling her hair and raising the golden hairs on her forearms. Kayla sniffed, rubbing her eyes blearily. She sniffed again, more deeply, feeling a shiver pass through her that had nothing to do with the cold. Godammit, she missed Karrel so badly she could almost smell his aftershave.

A moment later, her forehead crinkled in a frown.

Wait a minute, she *could* smell his aftershave!

Kayla looked up and saw Karrel.

It had to be Karrel, because it was the same shape and height as him, and nobody else wore those god-awful Seventies style surfer hats any more. Something instinctively told her it was him. The figure was standing silhouetted at the top of the pier steps, just fifty yards away, watching her. The second Kayla's eyes lit upon him, he turned and started walking unhurriedly away across the pier. A moment later he disappeared into the rolling sea fog, just visible as a faint gray shape within, backlit by the orange sodium lights of town.

"Karrel?"

Kayla stood up abruptly, her heart in her mouth, squinting into the light. She could just make out the figure walking up the gentle slope of the pier, heading toward the backstreets. Within moments it disappeared around the corner and vanished from sight.

Kayla took a few faltering steps forward, disbelieving, then broke into a run.

Behind her, five dark shapes emerged from the darkness beneath the pier and started moving swiftly after her.

CHAPTER SEVEN

"KARREL!"

Kayla's lungs heaved as she ran across the sand, her mind racing. Sprinting up the steps to the pier, she paused, looking around her wildly before taking off in hot pursuit of the figure. Her footsteps rang out in the silence of the night as she ran back the way she had come, her gaze fixed firmly on the end of the street.

She arrived at the end and turned the corner.

There was nobody there.

Kayla spun around with a cry of frustration, her eyes seeking to pierce the gloom around her. She was at a crossroads, common in the honeycomb backstreets of her neighborhood. In all directions the roads were empty, stretching away to a vanishing point of blackness.

Karrel—if that's who it had been—was gone.

Kayla sagged, leaning back against the rough stone wall and bowing her head as she pressed her clenched fist to her forehead. This was ridiculous. She was seeing things. Karrel was dead. It couldn't possibly have been him, could it?

A faint noise came from behind her, a whisper of skin on concrete.

Hardly daring to hope, Kayla turned around and saw the dog.

It had to be a dog. Kayla had no other frame of reference for what else the creature could be. As far as she knew, there were no wolves living wild in the city, and she had heard no reports of escaped bears in the area. The creature was huge, well above waist height, its flanks paved with slabs of overlapping lean muscle and covered in speckled silver fur. The hair on its back was ridged and ran up to a peak on its shoulders, where the fur was so thick it almost looked like a mane. Its head was blunt and wedge-shaped, and beneath a pair of pale, strong eyebrows, its eyes were the brightest gold she had ever seen. It was looking at her in an oddly human way—head lowered and cocked to one side, eyebrows drawn together in a look of wary feral intelligence.

A crazy thought struck Kayla.

She cleared her throat. "Mia?"

The dog's muscles tensed, the fur on its shoulders rising up, its black lips drawing back into a sound-less grimace. Kayla took an instinctive step backward at the gleam of its huge teeth, terror flooding her like molten lead.

It had been a dog that had killed him, they'd said.

Kayla backed off two steps as the creature growled at her, her eyes wide with terror, the clunk of her heels overwhelmingly loud in the narrow alleyway. If she kicked off her heels, perhaps she could outrun it.

A second, answering growl came from behind her.

Kayla turned slowly around, her blood turning to ice at the sight of five more of the enormous dogs padding up the alleyway toward her. Lightning flashed above her, illuminating the pack in a nightmarish freeze-frame. They were big and ugly, and their eyes gleamed as they closed in on her. They spread out in a horseshoe shape to block the alley, silent and terrifying, cutting off her escape route.

Kayla spun back to the first monster-dog. Its growling increased in volume tenfold to become a rattling snarl, every hair on its body bristling. She knew instinctively that the pack was about to attack her, and that she wouldn't be able to stop them.

If only Karrel were here, he'd know what to do.

Kayla clenched her fists, an electric buzz of white-hot adrenaline flooding through her as she readied herself to fight, desperately wishing she had some kind of weapon on her. She saw the first dog's muscles tense as it prepared to launch itself at her. Kayla cried out in fright, closing her eyes and shielding her head as the dog flew at her, teeth bared.

Then there was a loud yelp, and the sounds of a scuffle.

Kayla's eyes flew open and she glanced left, right, and then turned around, disbelief welling up inside her as she watched the silver dog fly past her and viciously attack the nearest pack member, seizing its throat and biting down deeply. Blood spurted and the creature howled in pain, then retaliated by rearing up backwards and flipping the first dog over, teeth still embedded in the dense fur of its throat.

Kayla stared. It was almost as if the first dog was trying to protect her.

The other four members of the pack took off like a set of snarling guided rockets toward Kayla, who turned to run.

Too late.

The lead dog slammed into her with the force of a pile driver, sending her flying through the air. She hit the ground a half-dozen feet away and rolled painfully across the concrete, finishing up in a crumpled heap by the chain-link fence. She cried out as a huge black dog the size of a small lion stampeded toward her, its eyes alive with malevolent glee, its claws extended and ready to slash her to shreds.

A blinding white light suddenly exploded on the periphery of her vision, followed by a loud *CRUMP*. Kayla screamed, curling up into a fetal ball as the aftershock of the explosion echoed through the nighttime streets, setting off several car alarms. The wailing electronic shrieks blended with the roars of the dog pack as they howled in pain. As the afterglow of the flash faded from her overloaded optic nerve, Kayla saw the creatures running blindly about, shaking their heads and snarling in rage.

"Hey, you! Get the hell outta there!" cried a female voice.

An engine roared loudly in the night, followed by the slamming of doors. Confused and disoriented, Kayla shrieked as the silver dog blundered into her, knocking her back against the fence and almost trampling her in the process. She felt its teeth graze her forearm as it seized her sleeve. She yelled as the creature tried to drag her bodily along the road away from the pack, stumbling blindly back and forth. Karrel's lucky dragon coin necklace caught around her throat, almost choking her. Kayla twisted wildly in its grip, reaching up to try and pull herself free.

A moment later a silver-heeled stiletto boot flashed down into her field of vision and connected hard with the dog's skull. The animal let out a muffled cry of pain, but didn't let go. There was a muffled curse from above her, then the sound of the slider on a rifle being racked back.

K-CHAK!

BOOM!

Kayla yelled out in fright and rolled away from the dog as it finally released her with a yelp, blood flowing from an ugly gunshot wound in its shoulder. Recovering, it wheeled in a tight, dazed circle and went for Kayla again, its golden gaze fixed determinedly on her arm.

A weird sense of strength filled Kayla. Without thinking, she caught the creature by the scruff of its neck as it trampled over her prone body, then snapped her knees to her chest. She jammed her feet into the soft flesh of its abdomen and heaved with all her might, using the dog's momentum to send it flying through the air end-over-end, pitching it an astonishingly long distance down the road. It landed with a crash on the hood of a parked derelict car, smashing the windshield and denting the hood.

Kayla watched in disbelief as the dog tumbled off the side of the car in a rain of shining glass, flopped to the ground, and rolled over. The whites of its eyes showed as it fought to get up again. It collapsed with a howl of what sounded very much like frustration, its foreleg buckling beneath it.

Kayla heard the sound of a high-powered weapon reloading and flung up her arms to shield her face.

Nothing happened.

Cautiously, she lowered her arms to fix the newcomer above her with a wary look. Her gaze traveled up the vinyl boots and a long, tan legs to see a lithe, intelligent-looking woman peering down at her, an expression of curiosity on her high-cheekboned face. She clutched a silver pistol in one long-fingernailed hand. In the other she held what looked like an old-fashioned blooper gun that almost dwarfed her voluptuous upper body, her arm crooked back to balance its weight.

Tucking the pistol back in her leather hip holster, the woman pulled down her mirrored sunshades and gave Kayla the once-over.

"Well, shit-a-dog," she said. "Are you human?"

KAYLA ROLLED ONTO her side and regarded the newcomer with a look of bewildered suspicion. "Excuse me?"

"You heard me. Human or not? It's not a complicated question." Thunder rolled overhead. The woman stepped up to Kayla's cowering form and nudged her gingerly in the ribs with the tip of her boot, as though she thought Kayla might explode.

"Well, I *think* I—"

"Phil! Get the hell over here!"

Kayla removed her hands from her ears and cringed away as the gun-toting woman bent over and calmly extended a hand.

"I'm Ninette. Come with me if you want to live."

"What?"

Ninette snorted back a laugh. "Sorry, big Arnie fan. I love that shit." Her glitter-red lips spread in a smile. She slammed the butt of the blooper into the dirt by Kayla's ear, almost making her jump out of her skin, and used the fearsome weapon as a prop to push herself back to her feet. She regarded Kayla from her full height as the sounds of shouting and snarling came from behind her, straightening the olive-green skintight uniform that did nothing to hide the curves of her perfect, athletic figure. She pulled out a miniature radio and pressed a button on the side. "Tony! Get a containment unit down here, stat!"

Slipping the radio back into her pocket, she stifled a yawn and waved her rife half-heartedly at Kayla. "C'mon, kid. Get the fuck up and let's go for a drink. Phil will take care of the werewolves. Is there anywhere decent around here that serves martinis after midnight? I'm parched."

"Martinis?" Kayla felt her grip on reality threatening to tear. Here she was, lying in the dirt after being attacked by a pack of what she'd just been told were werewolves, and now some strange, crazy woman was threatening her with what she was sure was an illegal weapon, and asking her at gunpoint if she'd like to go out for a drink.

She started to laugh, the convulsions racking her and making her bruised ribs ache. She coughed her way into silence as she felt Ninette's bemused gaze on her. "Sorry," she said, "I'm not having an entirely sane day."

She glanced away, feeling oddly embarrassed. "And who's Phil?"

A trio of dark shapes flew over Kayla's head, landing with a thud and a noisy clash of metal against the chain-link fence. Kayla got a quick, confused impression of a pair of chunky boots sticking out from beneath two of the monster dogs, which scrabbled and snarled at the man beneath them before suddenly being launched through the air as though flung outwards from an explosion. A scruffy, handsome young man dressed in a similar olive-green uniform was revealed. His face was warm and friendly, and he wore a futuristic-looking jointed brace on his left knee, the hydraulic actuators on either side whirring and clicking as he rolled over.

Without even bracing himself he vaulted smoothly back to his feet, simultaneously drawing a souped-up Tac rifle fitted with a bulky homemade silencer. Rising to his full height, he spun around and fired a controlled burst of rounds at the approaching dog pack, sending them running for cover.

As the last dog disappeared around the corner he turned and glanced down at Kayla, then broke into a broad grin. "Neat trick, huh?" he said with a wink. "I also do birthday parties."

Kayla shook her head in bewilderment. "Who are you people?" she asked.

"Us? Oh, we're—"

"Phil!"

The man immediately looked abashed, but his eyes flickered with guarded amusement nonetheless. He grabbed Kayla's hand and hauled her to her feet, then turned to Ninette and grinned at her disarmingly. She arched an eyebrow at him and the man beamed back, affectionately rubbing a smudge of dried blood off the woman's nose before planting a quick kiss on her forehead.

Then the two of them turned back to Kayla, leveling their guns at her chest.

"We're the people that just saved your life," said Ninette. "Who the hell are you?"

* * *

ACROSS TOWN, KARREL crouched in the corner of the darkened club basement, his head pressed against the wall. His whole body was shaking. Hot tears of pain and confusion streamed down his cheeks. He cupped his face in his hand, his forehead pressed against the cold, damp wall, his brain refusing to grasp what had just happened.

And behind him... He didn't want to look behind him. Hell, no.

An ungodly sound looped around and around in his head, the noise of snarling and tearing flesh interspersed with his own agonized breathing and the echo of a single gunshot, ringing on and on and on.

Karrel grabbed fistfuls of his hair and rocked, his eyes shut, fighting off the insanity that threatened to steal what was left of his mind. Whirlwinds of purple spun through his head as he pressed his balled-up fists against his eyes, trying unsuccessfully to erase the hideous images that swamped him.

He had known for as long as he could remember that he would die, someday, but the possibility had seemed so remote that he had never truly had to face it. Until now.

But death hadn't been the worst of it. In those last bright, blinding few seconds of his life, all he had been able to think about was Kayla. All his imaginings, all his training, all his fears hadn't prepared him for this, for his love—the brightest spark in his life—to be so cruelly snuffed out. When he ceased to be, he had realized, his love for her would be gone, and the thought had hit him in the stomach like a full swing from a baseball bat. He hadn't thought about his family, his friends, or even the loss of his own life. All that had mattered to him was Kayla, and the danger she would be in without him there to protect her.

That thought had kept him moving, kept him fighting, trying to raise his useless rifle again and again until the werewolves' jaws had finally deprived him of a means to lift it. The pain of death and loss had swirled together in a burning red tide of eternal despair inside him, his heart breaking even as his body was torn apart.

As he lay dying on the floor of the club, he had seen Kayla's smiling face right in front of him, bright as the sun and as clear as day. He had reached out to stroke her cheek even as the vision began to fade before him. He knew that this wasn't right, that people shouldn't leave each other this way, that there should be some kind of power in the world to prevent such things from happening.

He had fought the darkness that had reached up to swallow him until the very last, his eyes fixed on the dimming vision of Kayla even as the dark shapes of his killers closed in on him. One thought repeated over and over in his mind, so loudly that he thought it might be the voice of God. *I'm not leaving you.*

The words had seemed to echo off the ceiling, filling the room, crashing through the walls and windows like the sonic boom of his soul. His spirit had gone with them, fleeing his mangled, useless body, and soaring up into the sky. It busted through the poisoned atmosphere to look down on the City of Angels in all its necrotic glory, on the hunters and the hunted, the scavengers and the prey, seeing for the first time the dizzying interconnectedness of it all and not giving a flying fuck. He wasn't meant to go out this way, to leave the one he loved at the mercy of the universe.

It wasn't fair, it wasn't right, and he sure as hell wasn't going to stand for it.

As he hung there, suspended above the clouds, there had been a sensation of movement, infinitely slow while at the same time stunningly fast. It was as though he were moving at light speed through clinging tar and the world had slowly faded away from him, to be replaced by...

This bit he struggled to recall a little. They weren't people, or beings, or any of the wise and knowing creatures with long flowing beards usually portrayed in these circumstances. They simply *were*, and for the first time in his life Karrel had felt completely known. A great warmth had surrounded him, infusing his being with a sense of infinite completeness, of belonging to the universe.

As his physical body finally died back on Earth, he watched in wonder as a ghostly vision suffused his disembodied senses, of all the energy of the universe pouring past in a great white tide like a raging river, timeless, ageless, never changing. Time had no meaning here, nor did space. Here was the final resting place of the precious spark that caused the freak chemical reaction known as life. And that eternal fountain had its own guardians, the last gasp of the conscious mind trying to make sense of what it saw before it was consigned to blissful oblivion.

And on that river of light had been a boat, manned by a pink, fetal thing, something so terrifying that he had barely dared to look at it, although he had known instinctively that it meant him no harm. It held out a clawed hand to him, softly cooing with its raw hole of a mouth, a vision of the wonders that awaited him on the other side, of peace and acceptance and forgiveness and beauty and love and...

Karrel had told it to fuck off.

He wanted to go home, back to Kayla.

If it wanted him, it was going to have to come get him.

That hadn't pleased it.

Next thing he knew it had him by the throat, and Karrel had felt the terrifying sensation of his being seeping into the thing, drawn upwards against his will to The Other Side.

And that was when he'd made it a bargain.

CHAPTER EIGHT

THE JET BLACK SUV slowly rumbled its way through the backstreets of downtown LA, neon lights flowing across the glossy paintwork like streaks of nighttime gunfire. It bumped and rocked its way through urban desolation, rolling past tall brick buildings emblazoned with angry curls of gang graffiti, ram-raided studio lockups with burned-out vehicles embedded in their buckled rollup grills, and pawn shops protected by dented metal cladding and razor wire. Although the place was deserted at this time of night, an almost palpable menace hung in the air. It was as though the streets were alive and watching, just waiting to inflict ugly and inventive death on unwary travelers who strayed too far from the flock.

Kayla shifted uncomfortably in her leather seat in the rear of the SUV, gazing out of the tinted windows. Her whole body ached and her arm throbbed from where the dog... werewolf... whatever... had grazed her with its teeth. Her two new friends sat in the front, Ninette driving, Phil flicking restlessly between radio stations, keyed up and practically vibrating with an adrenaline wash of energy. They hadn't spoken much during the long drive, their frequent worried glances at one another and at Kayla in the rearview mirror indicating that she was in some kind of trouble that they clearly did not want to tell her about.

Kayla leaned forward, clearing her throat. "So," she said, "I need to be tied up... why, exactly?"

Phil shrugged, fiddling with the rifle on his lap. "Standard procedure."

"And the bag over the head?"

"So you can't find your way back here."

"To this place?" Kayla curled her lip, glancing out of the car as they passed the hollow shell of a rusted-out RV vehicle. "Anyway, there's a hole in the bag. I can see fine."

Phil glanced sheepishly at Ninette, who merely shook her head and continued driving. A moment later she cut the wheel hard to the right, causing Kayla to lose her balance. Hauling herself back upright, she stared through the hole in the bag to see their SUV pull up outside a giant, boarded-up warehouse, its front a mish-mash of chipboard and corrugated iron paneling.

As they drew level with the building, a pair of guards who looked like they could be the doormen to Hell detached themselves from the shadows and lumbered over to the car, shining their flashlights into the windows. They wore long trench-coats and expressions of deep suspicion. One of them held a large black dog of indeterminate breed on a thick chain. It popped its head up at the window and shoved its snout into the cracks in the frame, snuffling loudly and leaving a trail of white foam on the glass. Kayla spotted a large semi-automatic weapon stashed in the first man's belt. She shrank back down in her seat.

What kind of a place were these people taking her to?

Phil rolled down the window and handed over an ID pass, nodding amiably at the guard, who pulled a hand scanner from beneath his ratty clothing and swept a spinning green array of lights over the pass. The lights instantly turned red and a warning tone sounded.

The doorman frowned, peered more closely at the card, then handed it back. "This is a Blockbuster Video card."

"Is it? Sorry, buddy." Phil rooted around in the glove compartment before producing the correct pass. The doorman scanned it, flashed a gold-toothed grin, and traded a complicated handshake with him.

"Be safe, sir."

"You too, Doug."

With a *clunk* and a *boom*, the front door swung open. Ninette hit the gas and turned the wheel, nosing the SUV inside the building.

The car drove through a series of giant metal shutters, which rose sequentially in front of them, green lights sweeping the SUV and its occupants at every stage before disengaging the locks with an automated beep. Muted blue light flooded the car as the final shutter rose, revealing a scene that looked more like the interior of a spaceship than the inside of a derelict downtown warehouse.

Kayla stared. The ceiling overhead was high and domed, dotted with chromed UV lights strung from painted black metal support struts. The room was divided lengthways into a number of bays, each of which contained a small army of vehicles sitting silent and gleaming under the overhead lights. Kayla counted at least twenty more black SUVs, each identical to the one she was now sitting in, as well as several dozen racks of customized motor-bikes. The further up the room she looked the weirder the customizations became, culminating in a row of hulking hybrid vehicles against the far wall that were like nothing she'd ever seen before. They had sleek, pointed noses, jointed segments, and wheels absurdly sticking out of their roofs. Each vehicle had a pair of ominous-looking grappling guns affixed to their hoods, aimed up at the sky. It gave the vehicles the look of having giant, tufted ears.

Kayla pointed, unable to help herself. "What're those?"

Phil looked where she was pointing. "Things I'm not allowed to drive."

THE CORRIDOR WAS brightly lit in contrast to the dim blue light of the loading bay. The walls were painted charcoal black. There were thick steel doors with Plexiglas portholes set into the brick-work every ten feet or so, although the windows were too high up to see through. An intermittently pulsing blue strobe flickered down the length of the corridor every few seconds, making it annoyingly hard to concentrate.

Ninette led the way, her steel-tipped boots click-ing on the white tile floor.

Kayla followed her, feeling dazed, unreal, as though this wasn't really happening to her. As she walked, she glanced at the brass signs affixed to the doors they passed. They were labeled things like "TRAINING ROOM 7," "HOLDING PEN 3," and more ominously, "DISSECTION LAB 12/ FORENSICS."

Unnerved, she hurried to catch up with Phil. He was lagging a few paces behind, laden down with the weight of several silver weapon cases.

"So," she said in a coversational tone, "am I crazy, or are you crazy?"

"Possibly both." Phil shrugged his rifle strap back up onto his shoulder, catching it just before it fell. It immediately slipped down again. "Here, could you hold this?"

Kayla took the rifle from him awkwardly, looping the strap over her neck. "And you're really…?"

"Werewolf hunters? Sure."

"Was there, like, an ad in the paper for that or something? Or did you just wake up one day and think, 'Yes, this is what I want to be?'"

"Hey, that's sarcasm, right?" asked Phil.

"How could you tell?"

"Because the tone of your voice goes up at the end of the sentence. Listen," Phil stopped and put a hand on her shoulder, "I know you're probably all like 'What the fuck?' right now, but don't you worry." He winked at her, light glinting off the silver ring that pierced his right eyebrow. "All will be explained."

"Looking forward to it," Kayla muttered.

THE NEXT SET OF doors led them out into a small steel debriefing room, which Kayla thought was almost anticlimactic after the huge vehicle bay. She didn't know what she had expected, but it wasn't this. The room looked very definitely lived in, and smelled as though a large number of people had recently been breathing the air for a long period of time. It was the kind of room found in large businesses everywhere, a place where the real work went on. The room was a study in barely controlled efficiency, mountains of papers neatly stacked in, on top of, and beside a set of large gray filing cabinets. Weapons racks hung on every wall, loaded with an assortment of pistols and machine guns. Beside the shiny new coffee machine was an old-fashioned TV, bracketed to the wall, currently tuned to the Cartoon Channel.

Ninette shed her jacket and dumped a pile of weapons on the table before striding over to the coffee machine. "Espresso or decaf?"

"Decaf," Kayla said automatically, then frowned. "With two milks, a sugar, and a side order of telling me what the *hell* just happened tonight, please."

"I already told you. We're—"

"I know what you *think* you are," said Kayla, with what she thought was a great deal of patience, "but really, what's the deal? You come storming down here, save me from those—"

"Werewolves," said Ninette, calmly pouring a coffee.

"Whatever, which was very nice of you, but then you tell me that you can't let me go home because you think I might be in mortal danger?" Kayla glanced helplessly around the room. "Call me Miss Delusional, but I think the only danger I'm in right now is from you people. You believe in monsters, fine. But what I saw, it could've been some kind of… I mean… what you're expecting me to believe is just…"

Kayla's voice tailed off as a picture of Mia's face, dripping with blood, swam guiltily before her eyes. She floundered for a moment. "What exactly *are* you expecting me to believe?"

"That your life is in danger and that we can help you." Ninette turned around with a cup of steaming espresso. "Phil, honey, why does our hostage have a gun?"

"Sorry. I'll take that." Phil took the gun from Kayla, pulling the strap over her head.

"As I was saying," Ninette went on, shooting Phil a pointed look and wrinkling her nose at him as he beamed at her. "You can't go home until we've taken care of a few things. Namely, why that were-pack was after you. We intercepted radio communications from some seriously big players in town saying they wanted you dead. They gave your name, address, physical description, everything. Must've hacked your file from Social Security. You're lucky we got to you in time."

Kayla clenched her fists. "I already told you. I was—"

"…out walking and the pack just attacked you, yes. Tra la la, skipping in the woods, then boom, werewolf. We've been through all of this." Ninette plunked Kayla's coffee on the table, spilling most of it. She unzipped her tunic and started unlacing what looked like a metal-plated corset that she wore beneath her uniform. "Just tell us the truth, 'kay? We'll get out of here much quicker and I'll get to watch my yummy TV show which starts in eighteen minutes and counting. No pressure or anything."

"Why don't you believe me?" Kayla shouted in frustration.

Ninette wheeled to face her, all trace of humor gone from her face. "Because half an hour ago I saw you throw a werewolf fifteen feet down an alleyway. No one your size should be that strong, not without training, not without drugs, and not without muscles the size of his."

"Thanks," said Phil dryly.

"It was just a small werewolf," said Kayla, then added dutifully, "if that's what it was."

"Bullshit, girlfriend," snapped Ninette. "That thing was nearly full-grown. Do you know how much those guys weigh? And you just..." Ninette whistled and made a flipping motion in the air. "Tell us who trained you, and we'll go from there. Was it Karrel?"

"No! I told you! I have no idea what you're..." Kayla stared hard at Ninette as her brain kicked at her. "What did you just say?"

"Who trained you?"

"No, the other thing, about Karrel."

"Karrel? Of course. Poor guy. You must be devastated." Ninette didn't sound sorry at all. "I told him not to tell you what his deal was, but you know what he was like with keeping secrets. So much for the oath of secrecy." She took a sip of her coffee and looked at Kayla with interest. "So where did he start you? He was our best field operative, so he must've at least taught you the basics."

Kayla's mouth opened and closed a couple of times, then she shook herself and tried again with the only thing that had registered. "You knew Karrel?"

"No need to get jealous, honey. He was a cutie, but not my type. Besides, I already have my hands full." Ninette glanced meaningfully over at Phil as he tried to switch channels on the TV, found the remote didn't work, and started pulling the AA batteries out of the laser scope of a sniper gun.

"I didn't mean... Never mind." Kayla sat down heavily on a nearby chair, her mind on overload. "How did you meet him?"

"Basic training, twelve years ago. Same year as I met Phil. Crazy times, right?"

"Best years of my life," smiled Phil. "Travelin' around, seeing the wonders of the world, learning to say 'Oh shit, we're gonna die!' in eighteen different languages... Those were the days."

Dropping the remote, he picked up Ninette's hand and pressed it to his lips, his eyes twinkling.

Kayla was still floundering. "Basic training for what?"

"Oh, c'mon on, girl. Drop the act. I know you want to protect Karrel, but he's not gonna get into any trouble now, 'cos he's..."

Ninette tailed off, then she smiled brightly.

"Welcome to the Hunters. Do you want to choose your own code name, or shall we get the computer to pick one?"

KAYLA STARED HARD at Ninette, then relaxed, a flood of relief surging through her. "No, it's okay. We're talking about different people. Karrel wasn't a field operative... or whatever it was you just said. He worked for the California Humane Society."

"Big dark-haired guy? Weird tattoo? Annoyingly cheerful? Always had to be right about everything?"

"Yes, that's him," Kayla said with feeling, then stopped as her lower lip started to tremble. Karrel *did* have to be right all the time. God, she missed that.

She fought to regain her composure, trying to act tough in front of these crazy people. "He worked with you guys? Doing what?"

"Uh, hello? Killing werewolves?" said Ninette. "Drink your coffee, there's a good girl. That was quite a clunk you got on your head back there." Reaching into her bag, she pulled something out and fiddled with it. "Gimme your arm."

"Why?"

With a put-upon sigh Ninette grabbed Kayla's wrist and briskly pulled up her sleeve. Before Kayla could move she jammed a syringe full of red liquid into the top of her shoulder and depressed the plunger. Kayla yelped and tried to pull away, but it was like trying to pull her arm out of a rock.

"Fuckin'... *ow*! What the hell was that?"

"ADHT. Or as we call it, anti-werewolf goop." Ninette pulled the empty syringe out and tossed it into a trashcan. She touched the long red welt in the top of Kayla's arm where the werewolf's teeth had grazed her, ignoring her wince of pain. "Skin's not broken. You might be lucky. It's their saliva that transmits the virus, but it needs to get into your bloodstream first."

Kayla pulled her arm back, staring at Ninette warily. "You're saying I've been bitten by a werewolf? So what? Now I'm gonna turn into one?"

"Unlikely," said Phil, looking up from the television. "It takes a very deep bite to get enough of the virus into your system to bring about a full change, but a nasty scratch can have weird effects. You're too much of a babe to start growing a beard."

"Gee, thanks." Kayla rubbed her arm and glanced warily at Phil. He pulled a big, ugly gun out of an oilskin bag and started field stripping it methodically, his movements easy and practiced, his eyes glued to the onscreen antics of the X-Men. Ammo cases spilled to the ground as he emptied the bag out and started on another one. Kayla stared at them, her eyes huge. She pointed to something silver lying amid the debris.

"Are those guitar strings?"

"No," said Phil, as he quickly shoveled the tangled mess back into his bag. "They're, uh, bow strings. From the archery department."

"They look like guitar strings to me," said Kayla, folding her arms suspiciously.

Ninette ignored the pair of them, opening a silver weapons box and stashing several of her bags inside. "Look, I'll cut to the chase. You're in deep shit, girlfriend. I've seen that pack before, and they work for someone you don't even wanna know about. I'm guessing it's Karrel's mess you've gotten yourself into. Just tell us what you know, so we can work out what to do with you."

"How 'bout letting me go?"

"No can do, kid. You already know too much, and the whole innocent act ain't fooling anyone. The wolves are up to something, and we need to get to the bottom of this quick. If you do know anything, now would be the time to fill us in on it. We need all the help we can get."

"Help? For what?"

Ninette glanced up at the flickering TV set, the blue light playing across her face. "We're not sure. Something's going on with the wolf community right now. It's big, so big that nobody's telling us shit. We caught three wolves last month and they all chose to die rather than spill. One guy mentioned building an army, about two seconds before his head came off. Talk about bad timing." She glanced over at Phil meaningfully. "The boss thinks we're chasing shadows, but me and Phil have a hunch. We've gotten close to it a couple times, but each time we always just seem to miss it. It's like they knew exactly what we were planning. It's bugging the shit outta me."

"And this is my problem... why, exactly?"

Ninette sat down on the table next to Kayla. "Karrel kept dropping hints that he had some new info for us about the werewolves' master plan, and then he got whacked before he could tell us. But you're his girlfriend, right?" Ninette went on, ignoring Kayla's pained look. "I'm guessing he told you what he was thinking. If the werewolves really are building some kind of army, we want to be there before they can finish it. In return, we'll stop anything nasty from biting your head off before we figure this one out. You help us, we'll help you. Deal?"

Kayla backed away, her grief and confusion resolving into a cold fist of anger. "You want help? Then go get help of the professional kind. Seriously, I don't know what kind of drug you're all on, but either give me some of it or let me go. My boyfriend just died, for chrissakes. What is this, some kind of sick joke?" She got up in disgust and backed toward the door. "Karrel's dead and he's not coming back, and all you can do is stick me with needles and talk garbage about werewolf communities and master plans—please! Exactly how stupid do I look?"

Phil held up a finger and opened his mouth to speak, but Kayla cut him off. "Don't answer that. Just let me out of here. There's no such thing as werewolves. And if you wanna believe that—"

She jumped as the door suddenly slammed open. Ninette and Phil both rose to their feet expectantly as a muscular, tattooed guy with a shaved head burst into the room, dragging a black bag and wielding a steel grabber pole like a magician's staff. He was dressed in a crazy-looking outfit that looked something like a cast-off from an S&M party: an overlapping swathe of cut-to-fit chain-mail interspersed with thicker, molded armor protecting the vulnerable areas of his body at groin, stomach and neck. Kayla switched her attention to the bag. Judging by the various snarling and growling sounds coming from inside, the newcomer had brought a crocodile to their little tea-party.

"Whatcha got, Tony?" Phil asked, apparently relieved at the distraction.

"A new volunteer for the lab boys," replied Tony.

He pulled an enormous knife out of his boot and cut the thick rope tying the top of the bag, the tattoos on his strong arms rippling with the movement of the muscles beneath. He tightened the buckled straps affixing the thick, sculpted armbraces to his forearms, then took the jointed steel pole and slid his fingers into the mechanical grip at one end.

Cautiously, he pushed the steel noose at the other end into the bag.

All was still for a moment. There was a resounding snap, and a scream of outrage. Tony's muscles tensed with wiry strength as he lifted and pulled out...

"Oh my God! How cute is that?"

Everyone turned to look weirdly at Kayla as she got up from her chair and walked over to Tony, entranced.

A gangling, half-grown puppy hung from the end of his noose, the flexible steel bands circling its ribcage and pinning its furiously kicking legs to its body, which was wrapped in a torn blanket. It was of no breed Kayla had ever seen before, its long, dainty snout and feathery ears curiously juxtaposed with a solid, almost hyena-like build. It whined pathetically as Tony lifted it up onto the table and dumped it down on its side, its tail thrashing, and wrathful bubbles forcing their way out of the duct tape gag that bound its muzzle.

Ninette stepped up to the table and gave Tony a look. "You know you're gonna get into shit for this. We're not s'posed to take the pups. Remember what happened in Encino?"

Tony waved a hand dismissively. "Ah, phooey. They were sloppy in Encino. Don't worry, I covered my tracks."

He reached into his bag, winking at Kayla. "And now, for my next trick…"

Kayla watched in bemusement as Tony pulled out a shrink-wrapped plastic syringe full of green liquid. Ripping it open, he jammed the syringe into the puppy's hindquarters. The pup began thrashing around in its bonds, foaming at the mouth.

"What the hell?" Kayla stepped up beside Ninette and stared down at the writhing creature on the table.

A moment later her mouth fell open. "I think I'm gonna throw up."

"Basin's to your right," said Phil automatically.

"Thanks," Kayla said faintly. She stared down at the bloodstained two year-old girl lying on the table growling at her. She swayed slightly on her feet. She felt hands guiding her to a chair and was glad of them, because her legs suddenly didn't want to support her any more.

After a while she stirred. "Tell me again how you met Karrel?"

CHAPTER NINE

ACROSS TOWN AT Genetica, Julissa pulled out her silver Free Trial coupons and flashed them hopefully at the receptionist. It was late, past nine-o'clock, and she was getting tired. She had an hour of freedom left before she had to be back in to cover Kayla's night shift, and once again she cursed the girl for messing up her evening.

She tried to smile as the immaculately dressed receptionist looked up at her expectantly. "I'm here for the free trial thing?"

The receptionist glanced at her coupons and pointed a manicured finger. Her name-tag read "Cindy" and she looked like she had just stepped off the cover of Vogue. Julissa hated her immediately.

"Take a seat in the waiting room, darling. We'll be with you shortly." Cindy smiled an annoying little receptionist smile.

"Thanks, doll," gushed Julissa, not to be out-smarmed.

Smoothing her work clothes down as best she could, she stepped back from the silver desk and made her way across the wide, impressive reception area. This place obviously had class. Who knew what cosmetic wonders lurked behind each of the silver doored treatment rooms? Judging by the expensive outfits worn by almost every person here, the full treatments would be too expensive for her. But she had savings, or rather, she had her father's savings.

Julissa was so involved in her own thoughts that she didn't notice the Italian man in the blue suit until she bumped into him, knocking the cup of freshly squeezed orange juice from his hand and sending his balanced stack of notes tumbling. Juice spattered all down the man's suit and his papers went flying, fanning to the floor like a flock of birds.

"Oh, shoot. I'm sorry."

Julissa immediately bent over and reached out for the papers, helping to gather them up. After a couple of seconds she realized that she was picking up the papers alone while the guy just stood there, checking her out.

Julissa's hand flew to her barely-there skirt, checking to make sure it was still covering her. She quickly straightened up and thrust the handful of notes at the man. "Here, why don't you get an eyeful of these instead?"

The Italian man gave a laugh, warm and heartfelt, then stepped back and folded his arms. "Turn around for me." He raised a finger and made a little spinning motion.

"Excuse me?" Julissa could barely believe her ears. Not only was this guy leching on her, now he was giving her orders!

That was it. She was *so* outta here.

"Forgive me. My name is Jagos," said the man. He stepped forward and held out his hand. His voice was as thick and rich as molten chocolate. Julissa's eyes narrowed shrewdly as she swiftly checked him out, from the tips of his Kenneth Cole shoes to his crisply cut Spencer Hart cotton suit, to his four-thousand dollar Gucci wristwatch and heavy Prada designer sunglasses. By the time her eyes had reached his handsome features and softly upturned lips her annoyance had abated somewhat. Still she hung back, looking down at his outthrust hand like he'd just asked her to shake a dead fish.

"Jagos Kensington?" he prompted.

Julissa indicated with a curl of her lip and a shrug of one shoulder that not only was his name not ringing any bells, but that she didn't want it to ring any bells. She hiked her purse higher up on her shoulder, eyeing the door.

"I run the place?"

Immediately, Julissa's whole demeanor changed. She broke into a warm smile, smoothing back her hair. "Of course!" she gushed, reaching out to touch his arm. "Silly me. I was just on my way back to the movie set. You know how crazy you get when you're filming a big feature."

"Naturally." The man's smile grew wider. He flicked his eyes down to Julissa's hand, which was still caressing the fabric of his suit. "Nice material, isn't it? I mean, the bits without the orange juice."

"What? Oh, yes, amazing." Julissa withdrew her hand with reluctance. "Soft as baby skin. If they made suits out of baby skin, which of course they don't, and in fact that's quite a revolting image. So sorry about the orange juice. I'm going to stop talking now." She beamed brightly at Jagos.

"Indeed." Jagos raised a finger to his lips and considered her. "What are you, five-eight, one-ten, thirty-two C?"

"That's my code name," lilted Julissa. "Wow. You're good. Wanna try guessing my phone number?"

Jagos suddenly clapped his hands together, making her jump. "You're perfect."

"I know." The response was instinctive. Then Julissa frowned. "For what?"

"The commercial."

"You're shooting a commercial?"

"Of course. We have to promote somehow, expand our client base." The man waved a testy hand around him, as though the lines of well-dressed people thronging the plush reception area weren't enough for him. "There was a competition, but I'll cancel it. You win, hands-down. We shoot in two hours. You come with me now." He reached down to take Julissa's hand.

Julissa hung back, a flare of doubt sparking inside her. The man was almost too smooth. There was something odd about him that she just couldn't put her finger on.

"Is this 'commercial' in a private little room somewhere with a big couch?"

The man broke into a hearty laugh. "My dear. How long have you lived in LA?"

"Long enough."

"Then you know at least one martial art and have pepper spray in your bag, right?"

"Got my black belt in June," Julissa confirmed.

"Then you have nothing to worry about. Come, we must hurry. There is much to arrange."

Jagos walked over to the huge oak door of the main office and held it open for her. Seeing Julissa's hesitance, he gave an elegant shrug and pointed to the beautiful receptionist. "Of course if you don't want to be our new cover girl, I can always give the part to her."

"I'm there," said Julissa with feeling.

"Good girl," smiled Jagos. He gave her shoulder a little squeeze as she walked past him through the door.

Julissa glanced up at him as she slipped past. "Wow. You've got long nails for a guy. Not that that's bad or anything."

"It's a new fashion," said Jagos, with a wide smile. "Now come. We have work to do."

He followed Julissa though the door, pulling it closed behind him.

NINETTE OPENED THE door to the main Rec area of the base, ushering Kayla through. Kayla trailed behind the two Hunters as they took her on a guided tour of the building, gawping around, her bullshit detector primed and ready to roll.

"The Hunters have existed, in one form or another, for the best part of two thousand years," Ninette was saying. "We follow the werewolves' migrations around the world and set up camp whenever they start to get a foothold in the community, like they've done here in LA. We keep their numbers down, and stop the media and the cops from getting hold of any bodies. So far, we've been successful."

She paused at a door, and slid a keycard through. They walked into a room that looked like a cross between an off-road racing lab and a scientist's techno-haven.

"This is our main lab," Ninette continued. "All kinds of shit goes down in here that you don't even wanna know about. Don't touch anything that looks like it might bite, break, or explode. That goes for both of you."

"Wouldn't dream of it," said Phil, surreptitiously sliding a shiny metal gauging device back onto the work surface. He caught Kayla's eye and winked at her, then followed Ninette down the central aisle.

After a moment's pause, Kayla trailed after them.

"Basically," Ninette went on, "we got a thirty-room top secret nuclear bunker located beneath some of LA's worst neighborhoods, deep in the heart of downtown. Nobody comes pokin' around down this way. The cops, the military, the street grease—they all leave us alone. Occasionally some homeless guy takes a wrong turn down a bad alley and winds up with eighty thousand volts up his ass after trying to cop a snooze in a vent tunnel, but aside from that, the compound's pretty secure. It needs to be, considering what's after us."

A door hissed open, and they all stepped through it. Ninette strode on ahead down the long, clinically bright corridor as the door *za-zinged* shut behind them. "We got guards on twenty-four-seven detail at every entrance, triple-reinforced compound walls, hydraulic bank vault doors, motion-activated UV floods, a heat-seeking containment system in case of breakouts, a ten minute auto-destruct system in case of break-ins, atomized colloidal silver mixed in with the water in the fire sprinklers, and a really shitty voice recognition system on all the computers that keeps locking me out of my email account. Why we need all this crap in a nuclear bunker is beyond me, but the rules are the rules."

"A nuclear bunker? Underground?" Kayla frowned. "What about earthquakes?"

"And, in two seconds, our new girl clocks what three hundred illegal Mexican workers were trying to tell the government officials for the whole four years it took to dig this place." Ninette waved to Phil to hurry up. "It cost close to a billion dollars to construct the bunker, then they boarded it up and abandoned it the second their big cheese managed to wrap his head around the whole 'earthquake' concept. That's upper-level management for you."

Kayla glanced around her. "So what happens if there really *is* an earthquake?"

"We die," replied Ninette calmly, "but until then, we get free rent. Moving swiftly on..."

She started to enter her pass code on the second door keypad, her movements brisk and businesslike. "We got three hundred folks down here, working in army-style units. Unit A contains the big boys of the fighting core, the most experienced and highly trained of our Tac teams. In Unit Z are the newbies, most of whom are lucky if they get through the first year without shooting themselves in the ass. We've got technical and medical support, on-site kitchens, vehicle bays, training rooms, soundproofed firing ranges, the works. Everything is run by the cadets, who each train in a trade while learning to hunt beasties, like in the Army. So we're entirely self-contained."

"That's gotta cost a few bucks."

Ninette nodded uneasily. "Funding comes twice a year from an anonymous source. Rumor has it that it's someone in the US government, but we've been told not to ask who, so we don't. Skyler and his team of accountants handle the money side of things, so I'm guessing that someone pretty high up got wind of the wolf sitch and decided to do something charitable with our tax dollars. The money keeps on coming, so we don't complain."

"I still say the cash could be coming from the vampires, funding us to wipe out the werewolves," said Phil, with a little laugh. Ninette playfully swatted at him.

"Yeah, right. As if Skyler would take money from vampires. A guy with his background… You checked out his file, didn't you?"

"I was with you when you hacked it off the mainframe," Phil reminded her.

"Oh yeah. Right." Ninette looked faintly guilty. "Squeaky clean. Scarily so."

"Our funding's more than tripled since he joined us."

"Which is a *good* thing, Phil." Ninette turned back to the keypad and finished punching her pass code. "I know you don't like him, but he's part of the team now. How 'bout you get off his case for ten minutes?"

"Oh, but I was having so much fun jumping up and down on it."

"So how do you recruit people?" Kayla asked, changing the subject to Ninette's obvious relief. "Don't tell me that somehow you've managed to track down and bring in three hundred people who all had their families or loved ones eaten by werewolves and have now sworn to wreack bloody revenge on them and all their kind?"

Ninette paused, her head down, her finger still on the keypad.

Kayla blinked. "Oh."

"As I said," said Ninette quietly, "moving swiftly on."

The door hissed aside, revealing a second lab. It was smaller than the first and packed full of sophisticated equipment. At the far end, a group of people stood locked in what sounded like a heated debate.

They fell silent as Kayla approached. There were three guys and a girl, dressed casually in civilian clothing. Kayla eyed them apprehensively as she felt their curious stares burning into her. She immediately recognized Tony and gave him a little wave, relieved to see a familiar face. Ninette quietly greeted the girl, while Phil gave the three men a high-five each. One of the men stepped forward, a heavyset, proud-looking white guy with a blue bandana wrapped around his wrist. He put down his wrench and jerked his head derisively at Kayla.

"This her?"

Ninette nodded.

"Sheeit, woman. You know Skyler's gonna flip his wig when he hears about this."

"I told you, Motor. We couldn't just leave her."

"But you know the rules!"

"The rules can go hang," said Ninette calmly. "This is Karrel's girl. We don't just abandon our own. You think we'd bring her back here if she were just some ordinary civilian?"

"She's just a girl," said Motor, curling his lip. He adjusted the bandana on his wrist, looking Kayla up and down in disgust. "There's nothin' to her. Get her outta here before she hurts herself, or us."

"You hear what she did? With the werewolf?"

"Oh, I heard," snapped Motor, "and I ain't impressed. With either of you." Folding his heavily muscled arms, he leaned back on a pitted and scarred bench, glaring at Kayla. "What if she's a spy, sent to take us down? Huh? Look at her, dressed like that. Who the hell goes out fightin' werewolves in a skirt that short?"

"These are my work clothes!" protested Kayla. That morning suddenly seemed like a very long time ago.

"Where do you work, Hooters?"

Ninette crossed the room and leaned on the bench next to Motor, bumping him gently with her hip.

"Remember what you were wearing when we found you?"

Motor gave Ninette a long hard look, unconsciously reaching up to touch the scars that looped twice around his neck.

He scowled, letting out his breath through diamond-studded teeth. "You'd better know what you're doing, Ni. This comes back down on us, in *any* way—"

"I know. It's my neck on the line, not yours."

Motor narrowed his eyes at Ninette dangerously, cracking his knuckles. "Anyone else but you..."

Ninette grinned and blew him a kiss, then gave Kayla a faintly apologetic look. She pointed around the room as she made her introductions.

"Kayla, meet our team—otherwise known as Unit D." She nudged the scowling man beside her. "This is Motor. Used to be in the Crips until his kid shot him in the kneecap and tried to hang him from a tree."

"The little fucker," rumbled Motor, still glaring at Kayla.

"Now he fixes tanks and gives me shit for a living."

Ninette saw Kayla's questioning look and touched her arm reassuringly. "I know what you're thinking, but it's all totally legit. Most of our new recruits come from local gangs. Werewolf activity is heaviest on the South Side, so we send a team out once a month to recruit. Most of the kids out there ain't got a thing going for them besides the will to fight, and they don't need no home address to get a pay check. Once they get a load of the fact that they'll get paid for shooting guns and blowing shit up, they're all over us."

"Isn't that dangerous?"

Ninette shrugged. "So long as we don't mix rival factions, we're cool. Had a lot of trouble with that at the start, before we did our research. Now we got it down pat."

"So you used to be in a gang too?"

Ninette shook her head, suppressing a smile. "Our Unit is mainly ex-military. There's a story behind that, for another time." She turned back to the room, seeming eager to drop the subject. "You already met Tony. That's Allan, our bike guy. The guy beside him's J-Bo."

Allan was a cheerful guy in his early thirties. He had longish blond hair and an earnest, eager expression. He was wearing a faded AC/DC T-shirt stained with engine oil, and his lace-up black pants were ripped in so many places they were more hole than denim. He put down a tiny screwdriver that he was using to adjust the scope on a large, unwieldy rocket launcher and reached out a hand to Kayla, his bright blue eyes crinkling with good humor.

"Welcome to organized insanity. You'll fit right in."

Kayla returned his firm handshake and turned to the girl next to him, who looked less than thrilled to meet her. The girl had sky-blue hair which contrasted almost painfully with her pure white skin. A richly detailed tattoo of a red snake wound its way up her leg, vanishing under her severe military-gray skirt.

"So we're hiring kooks now, that it?" asked the girl, watching Kayla warily.

"Giselle, play nice. You know we're short-staffed."

Giselle tossed her head, folding her arms. "She sure don't look like she could fight no werewolf."

"Neither did you when you first joined. Tell her, J-Bo."

"Yeah, you sucked."

"Hey, bite me, bitch."

"With pleasure."

J-Bo was a lean, tattooed guy in his mid-twenties with shaggy red-streaked hair that threw his face into shadow so all that was visible was his perpetually broad grin. He hung back and stuck his hand into the pocket of his camo pants, looking Kayla over with shrewd interest before reaching out to touch her head.

"Cool hair," he said. "Did you grow it yourself?"

"All my own work," Kayla confirmed, throwing Ninette a helpless glance.

"Groovy. I have hair too." He leaned forward, grinning. "Wanna touch it?"

"I'll pass... thanks."

"Suit yourself." The guy leaned back on the bench next to Phil contentedly, his work apparently done.

"J-Bo heads up our technical department," said Ninette, with affection. "He can calculate the reduced tensile strength of a damaged Glock bow to three decimal places, but we don't allow him near any sharp pointy objects. J-Bo, show her what happens to people who touch shit they're not meant to."

J-Bo silently lifted his ribbed gypsy vest to reveal a nasty-looking scar tearing across his muscular upper chest. He beamed happily at the attention.

Ninette turned back to Kayla. "J-Bo has something of an... interesting history. I'm sure he'll fill you in on it if you don't run away fast enough. Let's just say that the werewolves won't be messing with him again. He's been with us about five years, ever since the LA branch opened up. He taught us a lot about werewolves, and his expertise in biochemistry helped us perfect our most ingenious weapon."

Ninette picked up a rack of colored syringes from a nearby bench and held them out to Kayla to examine. "Biophetamines, or BPMs. You've already seen them in action with that wolf kid. It's a chemical cocktail of agents that bind with the virus in the host's body, the main ingredient being tiny shavings of magnetized iron."

"How does it work?"

J-Bo stepped forward, taking the rack from her. "Very cleverly. When catalyzed by adrenaline, it bonds to the ultra iron-rich blood of the full-form werewolf and creates a counter-magnetic field that freaks out the virus, tricking it into thinking that conditions are no longer optimum for it to manifest itself. Put simply, the virus thinks that the moon's gone down. So one shot of this, and the wolf becomes human again. In older werewolves, the virus eventually bonds with its brain and becomes part of its DNA, so they can actually learn how to control their transformations. Newly turned werewolves are pretty much bound to the moon—or whatever we inject into them."

Ninette picked out two glass vials and waved them at Kayla. "The effects of the drug can be reversed by an antidote. Green for go; red for stop. Even a child can remember that. Handy in the heat of battle when one of our lads has their back to the wall and a wolf in their face."

"BPM also stands for Beats Per Minute," added Phil, fiddling with a centrifuge device, "an important musical term, without which there would be no music, only chaos, or classical music, which is infinitely more terrifying."

"Anyway," Ninette went on, ignoring Phil. "We've been testing the stuff for about four years. It's been a massive success in field trials, and has let us catch werewolves for study for the first time ever. A full-form wolf is practically impossible to bring in, but now we can just shoot them with a dart of this stuff, make them human, and then change them back again once we've got them locked up. So rather than just killing them wholesale, we can keep them alive in captivity definitely, in whatever form we choose." She glanced toward the door. "Which leads me onto our next lab…"

"Boy." Kayla attempted a smile as she felt her sanity starting to tear. "And I thought the scariest thing I'd have to deal with today was Julissa."

"Who?"

"Never mind." Kayla cleared her throat as the room started to sway gently around her. "Just one question. Can I go home now?"

"No. You'll have to stay here tonight. Whoever sent those werewolves won't give up after just one go. We've gotta figure out why they attacked you and what they want before we can even think about releasing you."

"So what now?"

"We call Skyler."

"Who?"

"The boss. Nothing around here goes down without his say-so. He'll know what to do with you. Don't worry though, this place is unbreachable. You'll be safe here with us."

Kayla nodded unhappily and relaxed slightly, chewing on her fingernails.

As Ninette pulled out her two-way radio, a siren suddenly sounded, ear-splittingly loud in the close confines of the room. The team jumped to their feet, staring at each other in confusion. Then as one, they put down their drinks and raced for the door, leaving Kayla alone with Ninette and Phil in the empty lab.

"What's happening?" asked Kayla in panic.

Ninette reached for her gun, a look of astonishment on her face.

"We've got a break-in," she said.

CHAPTER TEN

KAYLA HAD TO sprint to keep up with Ninette as she raced back down the corridors and burst out into the main weapons room. Tony was already in there ahead of her, securing the werewolf child in a cage. The toddler was wrapped in a blanket, yelling her lungs out as the sirens wailed, creating an ear-splitting din.

Two side-doors thumped open and a dark stream of what looked like army cadets flooded into the room. They formed a tense crowd in front of the weapons cabinet. Phil bounded over to join them, disengaging the lock, pulling out dozens of guns, and handing them out to the troops like candy.

Kayla grabbed Ninette's elbow. "What's going on?"

Ninette pressed her finger to the miniature radio in her ear. "We got a breach in Quadrant C. I got Sklyer on the line saying something about a very pissed wolf trying to get in." She turned to

Tony, eyeing him accusingly. "Gee, I wonder why?"

"That's nothing to do with me!"

BOOM!

Everyone jumped as a heavy impact rocked the main door, a thick indention appearing in the center. There was a loud scrabbling noise, like claws on metal, then the sounds of snuffling and snorting from beneath the door. In the cage, the little girl awkwardly pushed herself up on her forearms and began to cry loudly, her bawling partially muffled by the blanket.

There was an answering howl from the other side of the door, followed by a ringing flurry of impacts as whatever was outside renewed its efforts to get in.

Ninette strode over to join Phil, her gazed fixed on the door. "I think Mama's mad."

"You don't say." Phil reached into his big oil-skin bag and pulled out a pair of pistols, weighing them in his hands. "Beretta or Glock, honey?"

"Pass me the Glock. The Beretta sticks."

"I love you too, honey." Phil passed Ninette the pistol, then tossed the Glock aside and rummaged around inside the bag until he found what he was looking for. With an effort, he pulled out an enormous AK-74M assault rifle and slammed in a new banana clip. He racked back the bolt, chambering a round, then struck a heroic pose, grinning.

Ninette glanced at him sidelong. "Just be sure to clean it when you're done."

Hopping down off the bench, Ninette took up position beside Tony and the other Hunters. She pointed her pistol at the door, now almost off its hinges from the furious onslaught.

A moment later it gave way with a splintering crash. Something big and brown and angry barreled into the room, knocking aside tables and chairs in its haste to get in. Ignoring the combined fire of the Hunters, it stalked over to the bench and sniffed at the air, then spun around and howled at its attackers in a terrifying blast of noise. Rounds tore into its flank as it jumped up onto the main conference table, clattering across the polished mahogany surface toward the bawling, caged wolf child. Reaching the cage, it sniffed at it briefly before drawing back a paw and sending it flying across the room in a fit of rage.

Ninette glanced over at Phil, sharing a thought.

Whatever the werewolf was after, it wasn't the child.

A young recruit bravely approached the beast, holding down his trigger. Bad move. The big wolf instantly crashed down off the table and lunged at him in fury, snatching him off the ground by the shoulder and pitching him bodily through the air as though he were nothing more than a toy. The recruit struck the crumpled door with a sickening thud before dropping to the ground in a lifeless heap, blood pouring from his mouth.

Kayla gave a little scream of horror at the sight of the dead man, then clapped a hand over her mouth as the werewolf's huge head whipped around. It froze, one paw off the ground, its entire body pointed at her. Its dirty orange eyes locked on hers and narrowed dangerously. Kayla's breathing stopped. She had no difficulty recognizing it as one of the pack "dogs" from the alley.

With a snarl, the creature sent tables and chairs flying as it plowed through the room. Ninette stepped into its path, laying down a barrage of covering fire.

"Get her outta here!"

Phil seized Kayla's arm and took off toward the back door, slamming through it and dragging her with him. Then Kayla was running, barely able to keep up with Phil as he sprinted down a series of long, carpeted corridors, the shouts and screams echoing in the hallways behind them. Her muscles burned as she strove to keep up with Phil, but despite her best efforts she quickly found herself falling behind.

She rounded a corner, lungs heaving, and nearly ran into Phil, who was standing stock still in the middle of the hallway at a T-junction. The corridor was blocked by an advancing group of strangely-dressed men and women armed with an assortment of crude weapons: table-legs, broken bottles, and what looked like stolen lab tools.

Judging by their expressions, they were not friends.

A stocky man with biker-length gray hair advanced on them, wielding a thick steel radiator pipe. He bared his oddly sharp teeth at Phil, who hefted his AK-74M, aimed it at the man, and pulled out his radio with his free hand.

He hit the talk button, his jaw tight.

"Drew, we got a breakout in the vamp sector."

"In the *what* sector?"

Phil ignored Kayla, backing up two steps before dropping to one knee and firing a shockingly loud round at the advancing figures.

Kayla screamed again and ducked, clapping her hands over her ears. The glowing tracer rounds tore down the corridor and struck Biker Guy, spinning him half around and slamming him back into the wall in a spray of blood.

To Kayla's horror, Biker Guy simply peeled himself off the wall and continued rushing up the corridor, smoke belching out of the bullet holes in his chest. Phil backed off, holding the trigger of his AK down, blowing chunks of flesh from the man's chest and face and spraying the walls with blood. As the smoldering man reached him he used the butt of the rifle to deflect a wild blow from the guy's steel pipe. He dealt a swift volley of blows to the man's head and midsection, knocking him off balance. Catching the man by the lapels with one hand and reloading with the other, he jammed his AK into the man's chest and let a single bullet fly.

An intense blue-white fire poured out of the bullet hole above the man's heart and rushed upwards to engulf him, lighting up the hallway in a blaze of incandescent light. He gave one last scream of rage and then suddenly and shockingly exploded, sending a grisly rain of burning flesh and carbonized blood down onto the carpeted floor.

Kayla stared, cowering back against the wall. "Oh, you have *got* to be kidding me!"

CHAPTER ELEVEN

PHIL BACKED AWAY, the muscles in his arms bunching as he held his huge AK-74M aloft, eyeing up the approaching vampires. The shattered overhead lights flickered on and off spastically, illuminating the oncoming monsters in nightmare snapshots. Noticing Kayla as though for the first time, he stabbed a finger back along the corridor.

"Get out of here!" he cried.

"By myself? No way!"

"Fine." Phil swiftly reached into his belt clip and handed Kayla a blackened handgun. "Sig 226 army pistol. Safety's off. Use it."

Kayla took the gun gingerly. "But I don't know how to kill a vampire!"

Phil stole a glance at the mass of vampires striding down the corridor, then swung back to her. "Okay. Vampire physiology 101. To kill a vamp, you gotta destroy its heart. That's the one part of it that can't regenerate. Either shoot it through the heart, or use this." Phil pulled out a silver stiletto and handed it to Kayla, one eye on the approaching vampires. "So... take one sharp, pointy object. Figure out what side the vampire's heart's at. If it's coming at you, it's on your right. If it's dangling you upside down and trying to eat your spleen, it's on your left. Insert pointy object into vampire heart, then stand at a safe distance until vampire has detonated. If bits come off and stick to you, you go 'urgh' and wipe your sleeve on the nearest convenient recruit. You got that?"

Kayla grabbed his arm. "Wait! How do I kill a werewolf?"

"You don't. The werewolf kills you." Phil paused, thinking. "Unless you're me, in which case the werewolf asks you out to dinner, tries to eat the maître d', and gets you in shit with the manager, but more on that later."

Abruptly turning away from her, Phil sprinted down the corridor to engage a group of eight vampires as they swamped him, canines flashing.

As the sounds of snarling and rapid-fire gunshots echoed back at her, Kayla raised her own pistol, trembling, lining up the sights on a scrawny vampire with matted dreadlocks at the back of the pack. Feeling her gaze, the creature hissed and shoved its way past Phil, wielding a foot-long dissection knife. Kayla felt herself go pale as it stalked toward her, its sulphur-yellow gaze fixed unerringly on her throat.

Here goes nothing.

Her hands shook as she lined up her sights on the vampire's heart and pulled the trigger. To her surprise the shot went wide, taking a chunk of plaster out of the wall behind it. The vampire grinned as Kayla raised her gun and fired at it again and again, but once more the vast majority of her shots missed completely, blasting through the wall and shattering the overhead lights. The noise was deafening. She felt blood start to trickle from her ear as the close-range gunfire battered her eardrums.

BLAM-BLAM-BLAM-BLAM-click.

Click. Click-click-click.

Shit! Her pistol was empty!

Kayla shook the gun, as though that would somehow magically make more bullets appear in it. Phil's little lesson hadn't stretched to reloading. Her mind went blank as she gaped up at the knife-wielding vampire pounding toward her. Of all the ways to die, this wasn't one she had imagined. She heard Phil yell something and turned just in time to see him fling a small Colt pistol end-over-end at her. She snatched it out of the air gratefully and unloaded the fresh clip into the creature's chest, knocking it backward, wincing as it splattered her with gore.

But still the vampire kept on coming.

The next thing she knew it was upon her, opening its mouth wide to bite.

Reflexively, Kayla drew back her elbow and slammed it with all her might into the creature's throat, then ducked and kicked backward, driving her heel into its kneecap while smoothly ducking out from under its reach. A strange rush of knowledge, of *power* suddenly swam through her as she touched the creature. The vampire gagged and reached for her. She spun around and body-slammed it against the wall with her shoulder, her heart hammering. She trapped its knife-hand under her arm and brought her pistol up to fire a round through the bone of its wrist.

It was as if she had done this before.

The vampire's hand exploded in a fine spray of blood and its knife went clattering to the floor. Operating on pure adrenaline, Kayla swept the blade off the ground and buried it up to the hilt in the vampire's heart with a shout of defiance, driving the knife through its body with such force that it punched through its back and *thunked* into the wall behind it. The creature gave a ghastly scream before the all-consuming white fire flashed through it, spreading out from its heart and turning its flesh to cinders. Then its skeletal structure collapsed inwards, raining to the floor in a pile of bone fragments and ashes.

Kayla backed away, trembling, the pistol falling from her suddenly-nerveless grip. She turned to see Phil staring at her, covered in blood and cinders and surrounded by a wide circle of heaped ash.

The inside of her head pounded with blood and violence. There was a haze of red over everything. She had no idea how she'd done what she'd just done.

"Beginner's luck?" she hazarded.

Phil opened his mouth to reply, then froze as a low howl rang out, reverberating down the corridor, sounding oddly muted. There was a moment of ominous silence before galloping footsteps sounded on the other side of the wall, followed by an ear-splitting crash.

The wall at the end of the hallway erupted inwards in a smoky shower of cinder bricks and plaster. The huge furry shape of the brown werewolf barreled through, kicking and bucking free of the debris. It gave a growl of triumph at the sight of them, silhouetted against the light blasting through the hole in the wall.

Phil pulled a fresh banana clip out of his belt and slammed it into the AK. "At this point I'd advise you to run."

"Where to?"

Phil gestured to the T-junction in the corridor, two ends of which were blocked by oncoming monsters. "Pick a direction," he said, his voice heavy with sarcasm.

Kayla didn't have to be told twice. As Phil stepped in to cover her back, she spun and hared off down the clear branch of the T-junction, light-headed with fear.

KAYLA HAD NO idea how far she ran, careening through an endless maze of corridors as footsteps and snarls echoed behind her. Eventually she saw a sliver of light up ahead of her—an open door— and focused everything she had on getting to it before whatever was chasing her got to her. She wrenched the door open, hurled herself through, and then slammed it shut and twisted the lock. It was a restroom. Wooden cubicles lined the wall to her left, and a row of stainless steel sinks sat underneath a large mirror.

She clapped a hand over her mouth to muffle a scream as something large and heavy struck the other side of the door with such force that it tore the hinges half out of the frame. The last shred of doubt vanished in her mind. It was *her* that the werewolf was after. The people in the room out-side meant nothing to it. It wasn't hungry. It wasn't chasing her out of blind instinct, it wanted her dead. It wasn't going to stop until it had accomplished that mission, and she had no idea why.

Kayla backed away, numb with terror, then jumped as the lights around her suddenly exploded. The werewolf struck the door again, shaking more bolts free. The sound of gunfire snickering back and forth down the corridor filled the air as Phil tried to reach her. Kayla heard doors slam down the length of the corridor and booted footsteps pound past, followed by a series of heavy impacts and the sound of agonized screaming.

She ran to the far end of the long restroom, hunting for a way out. There was a small window about twelve feet up the wall, but it was too high for her to reach. Kayla looked around for something she could use to stand on to reach the window, but the restroom was totally empty save the toilet pedestals and cubicle walls.

She was trapped.

The gunfire from outside stopped.

Silence.

Unnerved, Kayla's gaze slipped sideways and she regarded herself in the big bathroom mirror. She hardly recognized the person she saw, pale and haggard, a livid bruise marring one cheek, her hair tangled and wild. Blood stained her rumpled work uniform, and the flickering fluorescent light overhead revealed that her mascara was badly smudged.

Great. Not only was she about to die, but she was going to do so looking like a crazy homeless bag lady.

Acting on twenty-four years of pure ingrained instinct, Kayla reached into her pocket for a tissue and fixed the smudge. She glanced down at the tissue and took a big, shaky breath. Things couldn't possibly get worse than this.

"Come on, Kayla," she whispered. "You can do this. Even if you do look like crap."

"I think you look incredible," said a familiar voice from behind her.

Kayla's heart stopped. Her eyes flew back to the mirror and the tissue dropped from her suddenly nerveless hands and fluttered to the floor.

"Karrel?" she gasped.

CHAPTER TWELVE

KAYLA STARED INTO the mirror. Behind her, Karrel took two steps toward her, his movements unsure, hesitant.

Kayla stopped breathing.

Her mouth worked frantically as she locked eyes with Karrel, afraid that if she looked away he would vanish again like pixie dust in the night. He was dressed in a way she'd never seen him dress before, a sleeker version of the Hunters' uniform she'd seen on the recruits. It looked great on him, fitting his hard-cut, lean body like a robotic second skin. His eyes were soft, dark, adoring; his face was strained and somber.

He was the most wonderful sight she had ever seen in her life.

She whirled around, holding her breath, half expecting him to be gone, but he was still there, still gazing at her with a strange, terrible expression on his face.

"They told me you were dead!" Kayla whispered. Her entire body vibrated with shock and relief.

Karrel didn't reply. Instead, his eyes ticked sideways to the door.

Kayla's gaze followed Karrel's as a faint clicking sound reached her ears.

The door handle was slowly turning.

Kayla's eyes flew back to Karrel's, her soul on overload.

Karrel drew a deep breath. "Kayla. I need you to listen to me. We don't have much time."

Something inside Kayla burst, as if a great dam in her heart had been released. "Oh my God, you're alive!" she cried.

With a sob she rushed at Karrel, her arms outstretched, ready to give him the biggest hug she'd ever given anyone in her life.

Five seconds later, she got up off the floor, her brown eyes saucer-wide.

"Karrel?" she said carefully. "What just happened?"

Karrel's gaze didn't waver. A look of profound sorrow entered his eyes as he gazed longingly at her.

"Karrel?"

The door handle rattled loudly as whoever was turning it discovered it was locked.

"Karrel, don't do this." Kayla's voice was shaking. "You're scaring me." She backed up two steps, staring at him.

"I'm sorry, Kayla," said Karrel softly. "I'm so sorry."

"For what?"

Karrel silently bowed his head.

Kayla's heart started thumping. Hot tears welled painfully in her eyes. She took a step toward him, hesitated, then backed off again. "Karrel, what's going on? Please talk to me. What is this, some kind of test?"

Karrel looked up at Kayla, an oddly harsh expression on his face. "It's not a test, Kayla." Karrel reached out a hand to stroke her jaw, wavered, and then dropped it again.

When he next spoke, his voice was cold, drained of emotion. "I can't see you again because I'm dead." He glanced fitfully toward the door. "I was murdered, Kayla. I don't have much time."

"What?" Kayla's throat closed up and she started trembling. "But you're here."

"Not for long. I made a bargain to come back… it'd take too long to explain. I have to find the guys who killed me, and fast."

"But who would want to kill you? And why?"

Karrel's jaw tightened. "I was in the wrong place at the wrong time and overheard some things I shouldn't have. I'll tell you about it some other time, but somebody here at the Hunters' base was responsible. Someone I worked with. Someone I trusted." Karrel swallowed and turned away, a haunted look on his face.

"Karrel." Kayla wiped away hot tears as the vision of him started to waver. "Tell me this isn't happening."

"If I had the power in me, I'd make it so," Karrel said fiercely, "but I've been given something else, something that not many people get: a second chance. I came back for you, Kayla. I love you, and I need you to help me. I need you to avenge my death. You have to find the people responsible for murdering me, and kill them."

"What! Me? Kill people? Are you out of your mind?" Kayla's jaw dropped. "Karrel, I couldn't even kill that wasp that got into our apartment. You remember?"

"And I loved you for it," Karrel said gently, "but anyone can kill, given the right circumstances, and these aren't people. They're werewolves. Whoever ordered my death sent a pack after me. There were five of them, and a vampire. That makes six—"

"But Karrel—"

"*Listen to me!*" Karrel shouted. "I don't have much time. The werewolves' names are Harlem, Flame, Mitzi, Jackdoor and Skeet. Remember those names! They're old-timers, real low-down nasty street scum. They were led by a vampire called Cyan X—she's a traitor too, a real head-case. She needs to die, along with whoever issued the order to have me killed, and anyone else who was involved. Only then will I be free. I wish I could help you more, but that's all I know right now."

"How exactly am I supposed to kill them?" Kayla's voice was a teary whisper.

"I'll help you," said Karrel gently, "but first, you need to get out of here. As long as you're here, you're in danger. I don't know who ordered my death—it could've been anyone here—but if they find out you're here, they'll try to kill you too."

At that moment, a loud crash reverberated through the restroom. The door jumped in its frame and a large part of the steel lock hit the ground with a clatter.

The spell shattered. "Kayla. You have to go, *now!* That's Skeet outside, one of Cyan's little errand boys. He's one of the wolves that killed me, and he'll kill you, too, just on the off-chance I told you anything. You have to get out of here!"

"But there's no way out!" Kayla was practically in tears.

"There's a window back there. Use it."

"I can't reach it!"

"Try," Karrel said savagely.

Fear hot-wired Kayla's muscles. She looked up, her nerves doing a tap dance in the pit of her stomach. The window was half ajar, but it was still a good four or five feet above the top of her outstretched finger-tips. It was too high! There was no way she could reach it without standing on something.

"Help me!" she cried.

"I already have," replied Karrel. "I've given you my strength, but I don't know how long it's going to last."

"What?"

Gunshots sounded outside the door, blowing the remainder of the lock out. Light stabbed through the holes, crosshatching the restroom.

"Just jump! I'll explain later."

Shaking her head with the futility of it, Kayla jumped as hard as she could, her fingers reaching for the sill. To her utter amazement, she reached the window easily, catching onto the sill by pure reflex. She felt herself slipping almost immediately and hauled with all her might, her legs flailing for a grip on the wall. In one smooth, athletic movement she pulled herself onto the narrow ledge. She peered through the window. There was nothing but an unnerving blackness on the other side.

The door gave way with a resounding crash.

Kayla took a deep breath and jumped through the window.

CHAPTER THIRTEEN

"OKAY, PEOPLE. I'VE been sitting in this makeup chair for five hours. Please tell me I'm not going to die here."

Julissa tapped her fingers on the leather arm of the chair, waiting for her freshly-painted nails to dry. She watched dozens of black-clad people scurry around her, doing obscure technical things to cameras and setting up lights in the brightly lit studio. There was an inordinate number of people who seemed to have no particular job other than standing around peering down at clipboards and looking worried. Julissa reached out in a vain attempt to capture the attention of one of them as he scurried by.

"Really, I'm ready to go whenever you guys are."

The makeup artist who'd spent the last half hour ignoring her turned away—ignoring her even more, if such a thing was possible—and Julissa rolled her eyes. She felt a movement behind her and turned, looking into the charismatic blue eyes of Jagos. "Please tell me we're ready to roll."

Jagos put a comforting hand on her shoulder comfortingly. "All in good time. We just have to wait for the injection to take effect."

Julissa reached up and rubbed the side of her face. An hour ago they'd given her the first of her two free treatments, an injection that was meant to knock at least five years off her appearance. She had been suspicious at first, but then when they told her that people normally paid over a thousand dollars for the treatment, she had jumped at the opportunity. The injection had stung a bit, but now she felt great, warm and glowy with a surplus of energy she put down to the excitement of it all.

"Tell me again what was in that thing?"

Jagos smiled, revealing unnervingly white teeth. "It's a new formula. We've been testing it for many years now. When we finally get it right, it will change the world."

"Whaddaya mean, 'when you get it right?'"

Jagos gave a little laugh. "It's still in the experimental stage, but don't worry, it won't harm you."

"Then why won't you let me look in the mirror?"

Jagos looked at her sideways, then smiled and reached down to take her hand.

Julissa beamed and followed Jagos as he led her into the darkness the back room. He pulled a dusty cloth off an old-fashioned vanity mirror and clicked on the set of bulbs that ringed it.

Julissa gasped at herself in the mirror.

The skin on her face was smooth and plump and baby soft. The fine lines around her eyes and mouth had practically disappeared, as had most of the faint freckles on her nose. Her chocolate eyes were brighter than ever and even her hair was shinier and fuller.

She really did look five years younger.

Jagos clapped his hands together in delight at her reaction. "Not bad, no?"

Julissa reached up a hand to touch her face, still hypnotized. "Where can I buy this stuff?" she murmured.

"You can't. We produce and administer the formula here. We can't risk our... competitors... getting hold of some and analyzing it."

"Incredible." Julissa tore her eyes away from her reflection and looked up at Jagos. "You use it yourself?"

"Of course. You wouldn't believe that I'm a hundred and thirty, would you?"

Julissa shook her head. "You don't look a day over a hundred and twenty-nine."

Jagos smiled, although not for the reason Julissa thought. "Come now. We should be ready for you short—"

A gunshot rang out, blasting through the muted hubbub on the set. When Julissa's ears recovered from the shock, she heard a female voice screaming.

"Jagos!" cried the voice. "I know you're in there! Come out, you son of a bitch!"

Jagos blanched. Julissa tried to peer around the curtain, but Jagos stopped her.

"Who's that?" Julissa mouthed.

"That's Loki. She's an, er, an ex-patient." Jagos glanced toward the door, his normally calm face displaying a tic of anxiety. "She has a few... issues."

"You're telling me."

From next door came the sounds of shouting and banging, followed by a zap of electricity and a shriek of outrage, abruptly cut off.

As the main door opened, Julissa leaned around Jagos and peered out onto the set, even as he tried to block her way. She caught a glimpse of an older woman, maybe in her early thirties, struggling violently as a pair of gruff security guards carried her off the set. As she passed through the door her head lolled backward, into full view. Julissa gave a little gasp of shock.

"Her face..." she started, then stopped as she saw Jagos's expression.

"A sad case," he said after a moment. "She had a nasty skin disease, wouldn't respond to conventional medicine. She thought I could cure her, but I couldn't. So she broke in here one night, stole some of our newest trial medications, and, well..." He waved a hand ineffectually.

"She had... it looked like she had..."

"Scales?" finished Jagos, with as much bluster as he could manage. "Yes, an unfortunate side effect. The medication reacted badly with her own topical creams. Shocking, really. We've refined the treatment a lot since then."

He flashed Julissa a tight smile. "Excuse me. I have to go... make some arrangements."

He crossed the room and drew one of the med assistants aside, pointing to Loki.

"Bring her up to the main lab, Rob."

Rob, a doughy 200-pounder in a worryingly white uniform, saluted sharply. Apparently, he had wanted to be in the Marines when he was younger, and took his current job just a little too seriously. He was exactly the kind of man a company like Genetica tended to employ, the LAPD having already rejected him when he'd failed the IQ test.

"Yes, sir!" he barked.

Jagos flinched away from the man, wiping the spittle out of his eyes with a touch of reproach. "Oh, and Rob?"

"Yes, sir?"

"Try not to use the whole bottle of chloroform this time. I want this one alive."

JAGOS STRODE RAPIDLY through the crowded back corridors of Genetica, muttering under his breath. He burst into the main control room, letting the door rebound off its hinges. Three uniformed guards looked up from their half-eaten tacos, startled, rising guiltily to their feet under the heat of Jagos's glare. One of them swiftly stuffed a small radio into his pocket. It continued to blare the local baseball game from his camo-pants, much to the guard's embarrassment.

"Where is he?" Jagos snapped.

The second guard nodded toward the back room. "I wouldn't go in there. He's not happy today."

"*He's* not happy?" Jagos glared at the bear-sized man, who cowered.

Jagos stormed past the guards and stood in front of the small metal door, hesitating only briefly before knocking.

There was no answer. Jagos felt his anger rise. He put his hand on the handle, let go again, and stepped back, looking up at the door with distrust. Then he clenched his jaw and pushed his way into the room, slamming the door behind him.

The long room on the other side of the door was cold. Refrigerated air swirled in icy clouds down from big air vents near the ceiling. Hidden machinery flashed and beeped, and there was a strong smell of antiseptic and disinfectant.

All around him…

Jagos tried not to look at the various human and non-human test subjects strapped into the complex biofeed tanks that lined the walls. The hiss and hum of life-support machinery echoed eerily back from the stainless steel walls. As he passed by one subject, a creature that looked something like a man with grotesquely overgrown furred forelimbs, he could've sworn that its cold, sightless pupils widened at the sight of him. Some kind of primitive reflex, Jagos hoped. He had been reassured time and again that the test subjects were all put into chemically-induced comas before the start of each trial, but walking through this particular room still gave him a serious case of the heebie-jeebies.

As his eyes adjusted to the gloom he saw a gurney pushed against the wall about halfway down the room. The woman with the scaled face lay upon it, motionless. A blackened patch of skin on her left shoulder bore testament to the high-voltage Taser charge that had been pumped through her.

Jagos approached her cautiously, running one hand down the cold metal rail that bordered the gurney. He gazed down at Loki sadly, noting how the pearly iridescent scales that covered her cheeks and jaw line had spread since he'd last seen her. Two weeks ago the scales had been the size of pinheads, like new feathers pushing their way through the skin of her cheeks. He'd reassured the terrified woman that the effects were temporary and sent her on her way with a pat on the hand and a case of "antidote" pills that were nothing more than vitamins, making sure to send an e-memo to the guards on this level not to admit her again.

Now, several weeks on, the scales were fully grown, meshing together to form an overlapping metallic weave that covered almost her entire face, spreading down the side of her neck and starting to erupt on her shoulders.

Jagos peered down at the clipboard lying next to her, but couldn't make sense of what was written there. There was a nice gold pen lying on top of it though, which he examined for a moment before pocketing it. He reached out to lift the neckline of Loki's cashmere sweater and grunted softly to himself, peering down in fascination. The scales were spreading all over her body, already forming a ruff around her shoulders and breasts, just visible under the skin of her ribs. He idly stroked the scales with the back of a knuckle. They were soft to the touch, like warm goose feathers, and really weren't that unattractive.

Except, he thought, women weren't supposed to have scales, were they?

Still, if this new trial succeeded, it would all be worth it.

The door banged open and he jumped, hiding Loki with his body almost guiltily. He relaxed only slightly when he saw who it was.

The man—if he could be called that—standing in front of him was scrawny and haggard, with a pinched, wizened face and wild black eyes shot through with a heavy dose of contempt. His skin was so white it was almost luminous, the bones visible as duller white shapes beneath, and his hair was a dull, lifeless black. Cerik was a vampire currently working as their head lab tech guy, although not of his own free will—the slender UV collar around his neck bore silent testament to that fact. Jagos knew that without it, he would've been dead about eight seconds ago.

Cerik blinked at the sight of Jagos, his pupils briefly contracting sideways, like those of a goat, before returning to a more human, round shape. He shot Jagos a cold look. "You're here. Why?"

Jagos crossed his arms across his chest defensively, trying to keep eye contact with the man while simultaneously fighting the urge to turn and run for dear life. There was something about the way the guy moved—like a snake moving through long grass—that made the hair stand up on the back of his neck. Jagos knew this was a perfectly normal reaction of a human being in the presence of a vampire, but he prided himself on being above such things.

Steeling himself, he made a slight motion of his head to indicate Loki. "She wasn't supposed to be able to get in here."

"She's here now."

"That's unacceptable." Jagos pushed past Cerik, flinching noticeably when his arm touched the vampire's shoulder in passing. The guy's skin was freezing cold, like a walking corpse's. Jagos shuddered in revulsion. He knew that they needed Cerik, that it was his genius at biochemical and genetic engineering that kept the whole project moving forward. But as soon as the project was completed he'd take great pleasure in personally activating that collar and blowing the guy's head off.

Cerik looked at him sharply, as though reading his thoughts. Jagos swallowed, feeling the parched tissues of his throat creak together with the effort. Despite popular myth, vampires were not psychic, but that knowledge didn't reassure him very much.

His fingers crept up to touch the small steel cross he wore around his throat.

"Because...?" Cerik prompted.

"Because the new girl saw her, that's why." Jagos spun around to glare at Cerik. "This new formula's dead-on, I can feel it. If she gets freaked and doesn't come back, we'll be royally screwed. She needs that second stabilizing injection in twenty-four hours, or we're going to have another circus freak to add to your little menagerie." He waved a hand to indicate the rows of sedated subjects lying on the gurneys around them. "I'm running out of lawyers to bribe in LA, for fuck's sake. How is that even possible?"

Cerik sighed. "How is this my problem?"

"Because, if your damned formulas had been right from the start I wouldn't have to be dealing with this bullshit!"

Cerik stared at Jagos blankly. His hand blurred and suddenly he was holding a gold pen, just like the one Jagos had just picked up. Jagos flinched slightly, his hand dropping surreptitiously to his jacket pocket.

The pen wasn't there.

He felt beads of sweat break out on his brow.

The vampire turned away from Jagos and picked up the clipboard from Loki's gurney. He *tsked* softly to himself, tapping the paper with the gold pen.

"She got batch three. Unfortunate."

"Meaning...?"

"An early run that should've been destroyed."

"Destroyed?" Jagos rubbed a hand over his eyes, mentally counting to ten. "Great. We just gave the new girl batch three. What was wrong with it?"

"Nothing was wrong. It worked fine, but there were... side effects, as you have seen." Cerik gestured toward Loki's body. "We tried splicing in a salamander gene to assist with cell regeneration problems, an action that was perhaps unwise."

"You put fish genes into a human?"

"Precisely."

"Any reason, or were you feeling a really special brand of crazy that day?"

Cerik's goat eyes contracted sharply and Jagos tensed, but the vampire merely dropped the clipboard back on top of Loki and turned to a nearby basin to wash his hands. "We needed something to bridge the divide between human and vampire. Early trials revealed that vampire and human genes were non-compatible. So we attempted to create a pathway between the two with animal DNA."

"How?"

Cerik set the hot water running, then rolled up his sleeves and started scrubbing his hands. "The human body is quite fascinating, a biological triumph, some might say, but certainly not a masterpiece, as many of your species would claim. The design is inherently flawed. A human being is a limited-run organism with a built-in self-destruct date. It is not designed to regenerate above a certain level. Your low-level cells—blood, bones, hair, skin—constantly die and are replaced, but the program has its limits. You only get one set of teeth, for instance, and severed limbs will not grow back."

"Some animals can do that, yes?"

"Correct. Shark's teeth are constantly replaced, and many creatures—salamanders, Zebra fish, certain types of lizards—can re-grow missing limbs, their spinal cords, even parts of their hearts."

"Like vampires?"

"Like vampires. Some might even say that the vampire is the logical fix to the human condition, the next step in the evolutionary tree. Vampires do not age, and they have almost unlimited regenerational abilities."

"So what's the difference?"

Cerik tapped the side of his nose. "That's what we're trying to find out. In humans, as your body ages, the program responsible for continually renewing your cells gradually becomes corrupted. The instructions contained in your DNA get scrambled over the years, destroyed by free radicals, chemicals, and your body's own cellular junk. DNA is like a set of written instructions on how to make a human, chemically encoded into every cell of your body. The older you get, the more illegible your DNA gets. Your body eventually gives up trying to read it and ceases functioning altogether."

Cerik shook his hands off and reached for a paper towel. "Vampire DNA is a hundred times more hardy than human DNA. Our powers of regeneration are enormously accelerated, but we too have our limits. We can close any wound, mend any broken bone, re-grow any body part except for our heads and hearts. Cut off a vampire's head or destroy his heart, and he is as dead as a human."

Jagos gave a snort of mirth. "Speaking of destroying hearts... you seen Cyan today?"

Cerik grew very still. He reached down to turn off the taps, studiously avoiding looking at Jagos. "She is no concern of mine."

"That's not what I heard."

Cerik didn't reply. Jagos grinned widely. The vampire scientist's weakness for Cyan was what had got him caught in the first place. Word around the lab was that he was deeply ashamed of it. He moved closer to Cerik and clapped him on the shoulder, ignoring the vampire's look of disgust at his touch.

"When you see her, do me a favor. Tell her that I just talked to the chief, and everything's ready for tonight. The big plan's going ahead at midnight."

"The Genetica opening night party?" Cerik gave him a look of calculated disdain. "But of course. The wolves must have their publicity, and Magnus must expand his client base."

"No. I mean the other plan, and the other chief."

Cerik's face froze. Jagos was pleased to see that the vampire was genuinely surprised. He wheeled around to stare hard at Jagos, and once again Jagos flinched at the deeply unsettling sensation of an alien mind touching his brain, searching...

He shook himself, fighting off the sensation.

"Come now," he said quickly, to distract Cerik. "You don't think I was taken in by all this?" He reached out to touch the vampire's UV collar. "I know the deal, what you vampires are really planning. Hell, I'm impressed."

"Cyan told you?"

Jagos nodded. "But there's a stinger in the tail that could really mess things up for you guys." He pulled a sheaf of papers out of his bag—a large purchase order—and dropped them in front of Cerik. He watched the vampire's eyes scan over the papers and widen in alarm.

"That's right," said Jagos, trying not to sound too pleased. "Top dog ain't so dumb as you guys got him pegged. Looks like he got your number."

"So what do you want me to do about this?"

Jagos hesitated. His macho bluster dropped for a moment, and he looked up at Cerik with worried eyes. "Warn her."

Cerik sniffed and turned away. "You warn her. You're the one who wants to fuck her."

Jagos's normally calm expression flickered, just for a second. Then his face closed up abruptly, and he lunged forward and grabbed Cerik by his lab jacket. He slammed him back against the wall, flushing with rage. "You think you know everything, you little creep? Huh? Then how 'bout you get your low-down vampire ass back to work and fix that damn drug before I blow your worthless head off?"

Cerik smiled, revealing a hint of fang. "Cool it, boss. I'm on my lunch break."

Jagos glared in disbelief at the vampire. Then his eyes focused on the vampire's fangs. He released him, hurriedly backing up two paces. Overconfidence was a killer in any workplace, but in this job, that was quite often literally the case. True, the vamp was wearing a UV collar, but the activation unit was with the guards outside. By the time they heard his screaming, it would be too late.

He backed up, breathing hard, trying to hide his sudden fear. "They give you scumbags lunch breaks?"

"Correct."

"But the cafeteria closed at two."

"Also correct."

Cerik moved aside casually, revealing a sight that Jagos really, really didn't want to see lying on one of the covered gurneys.

Jagos got up and walked toward the door, trying to make the move seem casual, then he cursed inwardly as he bumped into a tray of instruments, which clattered noisily to the floor. "Well then, don't let me keep you. I'm glad we had this little chat."

Cerik eyed him, the faintest glow of triumph in his eyes. "And the girl?" he asked.

"Right, the girl." Jagos felt a twinge of guilt, but swiftly banished it, crushing it behind the iron wall of his ego. There were more important things at stake here. "She is of no consequence. Get rid of her."

"She's human, like you. You do not wish to save her?"

Jagos shook his head. "If these experiments succeed, we will be gods. Since the dawn of time, men have been trying to crack the secrets of aging, to become immortal. Finally, we have the technological power to alter our destiny. With one little injection, we could fix our human defects forever, become immortal in the space of a lunch break, and you expect me to care about the life of one girl?" He made a dismissive gesture. "Don't waste my time."

Cerik looked at him for just a moment too long. "As you wish."

CHAPTER FOURTEEN

KAYLA WALKED BLINDLY through the darkness on the other side of the restroom wall, limping slightly but moving as fast as she could. She had twisted her ankle after jumping from the window, and every step sent a throbbing jolt of pain up her leg. She tried to ignore the pain as best she could, glancing fearfully over her shoulder every few steps and concentrating on getting the hell away from the restroom window. She'd pulled it shut behind her as she jumped, but even through the thick glass she could hear growls of frustration and crashes coming from the other side of the wall as the werewolf—she presumed—trashed the place looking for her. She knew it would only be a matter of time before the creature noticed the window and came looking for her.

A winking red light caught her attention about a hundred yards ahead, along the darkened hallway. Straining her eyes in the darkness, she could just make out the rough outline of a door. She quickly made her way toward it, flinching as a fresh volley of gunfire rang out from one of the rooms on the other side of the wall.

The opposite room was equally dark. Kayla groped for a light switch, and was surprised to actually find one.

She was in an enormous, black room, easily several football fields long and equally wide. The room resembled an aircraft hangar. It had the same oil-stained concrete floor and domed, intricately-strutted ceiling she'd seen in the vehicle bay when she'd first arrived, an hour and several lifetimes ago.

However, there were no vehicles. Instead, the room was lined with over a hundred enormous steel cages, some of them with bars so thick there were barely any spaces left between them. The larger cages seemed to have their bars electrified, a low crackle of energy filling the room. As the light came on, a flurry of movement rippled around the room as the cages' inhabitants awoke, stretching hairy limbs and pressing their faces against the bars of their cages.

Kayla gasped. The cages were full of werewolves. Either that, or she'd inadvertently stumbled into the world's scariest petting zoo.

One by one they got to their feet and stared at her intently, in unnerving silence. There had to be about thirty werewolves in total, ranging from half-grown pups to one massive, red old-timer in the end cage, big as a mountain lion and twice as muscular. Every one of them wore heavy iron collars fitted with red blinking LED lights—tracking devices, Kayla guessed—linked to steel posts embedded in the corners of each cage by four heavy-duty chains.

Inch-long hooked claws clicked on metal tile floors as the creatures paced back and forth, snorting at the air and swiping at the bars of their cages as though in contempt of their confinement.

But it was their eyes that really freaked her out. As she looked from cage to cage, every pair of eyes was riveted on her, checking her out, forming opinions, making direct and unflinching eye contact in a way that made her shiver. It was as if she were a single woman who had just wandered into a downtown bar at the end of the night, and all the single men were looking her over with pathetic hope, praying that there was still time for them to get laid.

Kayla looked around the room, searching for a way out. In the far corner she could just make out a pair of steel doors, partially hidden behind a big stack of what looked like big-game hunting gear. She pried herself away from the door and walked as quickly as she could through the room, feeling the back of her neck prickle as she passed within mere feet of the cages. She reached the exit door and had her hand on the handle when she heard an oddly familiar voice call out to her.

"Hey!"

Kayla paused, curiosity warring with her urgent need to get out. The room was empty apart from the cages. Could werewolves speak? She guessed not, but with the night she was having, anything was possible.

Her gaze came to settle on a big male werewolf in the cage nearest to her. Its jut-jawed mouth was open fractionally, strands of drool hanging between its teeth.

"What?" she asked it, feeling slightly silly.

Laughter came from behind her. "Oh my God, Jax was right, you *are* as stupid as you look."

"Mutt?"

Kayla spun around and stared in shock as Mutt lifted a bloodied hand and gave her a little half-wave, lounging back against the bars of his cage. Judging by his casual body language he could have been waiting for a date, rather than trapped inside a ten-foot steel pen. The fact that he was completely naked destroyed the illusion somewhat. Shadows from the cage bars fell like tiger stripes across his lean, sinuous body. The darkness in the room did nothing to hide the sculpted perfection of his form, nor the blood that seeped from an ugly, partially-healed gunshot wound in his shoulder. It trickled down his bare torso to mingle with the dark line of hair running down his muscled stomach. His hair fell in a ragged curtain over his face, the tips dyed red with his own blood, and a bruise flared angrily across his cheekbone.

But despite his sorry state, or maybe because of it, his eyes were amused, relaxed. If he'd had a cigarette, he would have been smoking it.

As she stared at Mutt she found her eyes slipping down his body. She quickly glanced away, embarrassed.

Mutt chuckled, low and dirty. "What's the matter, babe? You never seen a naked guy in a cage before?"

"I don't get invited to those kinds of parties," Kayla replied, flushing. She forced herself to look Mutt in the face, her mahogany eyes sparking a warning. "Until last night."

"Yeah, well, shit happens," said Mutt. He leaned back into the corner of the cage and touched his thumbnail to his lips. "Looks like you got your full share tonight."

"It's been a night for it," Kayla admitted. Despite her dire predicament she found to her surprise that she was almost glad to see Mutt. Last time she'd seen him, things had been normal, albeit briefly.

She moved closer to the cage and studied him, the door temporarily forgotten. Mutt was the kind of guy who dressed to leave nothing to the imagination, so seeing him without clothes actually wasn't too much of a shock. He wasn't particularly tall, but his body was well proportioned and well muscled, without an ounce of fat. Intricate black tattoos wove their way around much of his upper body, a mixture of tribal markings and what looked like Latin inscriptions. The ends tapered off down his powerful, lean legs. He had a large, ragged scar on the left side of his chest, positioned right above his heart.

Kayla purposefully avoided looking anywhere else; the shadows in the room helped him protect a little of his modesty, although from what she knew of him, she doubted he'd care.

Kayla realized she was staring, and her gaze flew back up to Mutt's face.

"Seen enough?" he asked.

A flash of anger went through Kayla as she remembered the circumstances of their last meeting. Just thinking about the way Mutt and his friend had treated her was enough to make her blood boil, but the recrimination died on her lips as she recalled how the evening had ended. "Jax. Is he...?" she asked.

"Dead? Yeah," replied Mutt brusquely.

"Why are you in a cage?"

Mutt shrugged, eyeing her darkly. "Maybe I feel like being in a cage."

"So you're one of them?" Kayla flicked her eyes toward the next cage where a young werewolf studied her with bright, hard eyes.

"A werewolf?" Mutt laughed dismissively. "What do you think?"

Kayla shrugged, running the tip of her tongue over her back teeth. Even in her crazed, worn out state, the sight of Mutt naked was doing inexplicably wrong things to her head. She quickly clamped down on the thought before it could spread further. "You're in a cage in a room full of werewolves, so I'd hazard a 'yes' to that."

"Think what you want. I'd advise you to hitch up your skirts and get out of here before somethin' graphic happens to you."

"You always this charming, or are you making a special effort for me?"

"Both," Mutt drawled. "And I've a favor to ask."

"Is this the bit where you tell me you're innocent, they got the wrong guy, then ask me to bust you out of there using a big jangly set of guards' keys conveniently hanging nearby?"

"No, this is the bit where I ask you to kindly turn out the light and fuck off."

Kayla stared at Mutt.

"You want to stay here, in that cage?"

"Yup."

"All night?"

"Yup."

"Any special reason?"

Mutt stepped out of the shadow, gripping the bars with slow, unmistakable menace. "Because your *jackass* of a boyfriend got my girl killed last night, then I got shot and nearly had my head torn off trying to protect you."

"What?"

"Yeah, and now I'm stuck here in a cage like some whipped little playboy up at Club Rage, and in the morning Karrel's little Tonka toys are gonna come in here, very probably whip my bits off, then put a collar on me and make me look like *that* for the next thirty days while they decide what to do with me." He stabbed a finger at the snaggletoothed werewolf in the next cage. It stared unblinkingly at him, threads of slimy drool cobwebbing its long black whiskers.

"You were trying to protect me?" Kayla's exhaustion vanished, and she was suddenly angry. "Like hell you were! You pulled a knife on me!"

"So? I got carried away. Don't we all?" Mutt coughed loudly, clutching his chest. "It was for your own good. If it wasn't for me, you'd be dead."

"My own good!" Kayla exclaimed. "Just how was groping me and trying to drag me off down an alley for my own good?"

Mutt rounded on her, his eyes flaring. "Because, you silly bitch, I was trying to get you away from them!"

"Away from whom?"

"The dude and the girl."

"Jax and Mia?"

"Whatever. They were both following you. Karrel said to keep an eye on you until he arrived. So I did. Figured the best way to do that was to pick you up." Mutt inspected his fingernails, looking faintly smug. "I gotta say, it was easier than I thought it'd be."

Kayla bristled. "Karrel stood me up! And I was drunk!"

"That's what they all say," smirked Mutt. His smile vanished as though it had been switched off. "But that doesn't matter now. He's dead, my girl's dead, and you're dead. So go on. Fuck off, and do that thing with the light on your way out. I just want to sleep."

Mutt turned his back on Kayla, who once again found her gaze sliding downwards, drawn against her will.

Nice ass, she thought, then shook herself, ashamed.

"And quit lookin' at my ass," snapped Mutt.

"Wouldn't dream of it," said Kayla weakly.

She turned to go, anger still boiling within her, then she stepped back up to the cage, unable to let go of one thought. "Does everyone around here know Karrel?"

"What's it to me?" growled Mutt. "He was a stinkin' Hunter, bad as the rest of 'em. I shoulda killed him way back, but I figured I owed him one for what he did when…" Mutt's voice tailed off and his mouth snapped shut. He eyed Kayla suspiciously, as though trying to work out how much she knew. "Anyway. I did the kid one lousy favor, and now I'm paying for it, me and my girl both." A muscle twitched in Mutt's jaw as he tipped his head into a shaft of light. Kayla was amazed to see a tear roll down his cheek, although he didn't appear to notice it.

"You did him a favor?" she asked, trying to keep her voice hard. "You're a werewolf. He's a werewolf hunter. What's up with that?"

Mutt looked right at her, naked hostility in his dark eyes. "Let's just say there was a girl involved."

"A girl?" Kayla felt her heart flutter.

"Ancient history, girlie. No sense in diggin' it up now. She's dead, Karrel's dead, you're soon-to-be-dead, and I'm stuck in here trading breath mints with Scooby Doo over there."

"Look, about that soon-to-be-dead thing," Kayla said desperately. "Is there any way you could, you know, help me with that?"

Mutt waved a hand dismissively. "Go talk to Karrel's little Hunter buddies. You're human. If you're lucky, they won't get all slap-happy and kill you for just existing, unlike yours truly here." He turned his back on her. "Now go on and get the fuck outta here before someone catches you."

"But Karrel told me a Hunter was to blame for his death!"

Mutt paused and glanced over his shoulder, his brows drawn together in pitying bemusement. "Karrel's dead, girl, d-e-d. He didn't tell you nuthin'."

"But I saw him!" Kayla ran to Mutt's cage bars, buzzing with sudden excitement. "He talked to me! He told me he was murdered and that someone here was to blame!"

As Mutt opened his mouth to continue, a roar sounded in the next room followed by the tinkle of broken glass.

Kayla blanched.

"Never mind. Good luck."

With a movement too quick for Kayla to follow, Mutt grabbed her arm through the bars of the cage, quick as a striking cobra. He held onto her tightly, staring off toward the door.

"What was that?" he asked in a dangerously calm tone of voice.

"That? Oh, only some big ugly werewolf that followed me here and is trying to kill me," said Kayla gaily. She tried to pull away. Mutt held on, tightening his grip.

"And *now* you tell me about this?"

"I didn't think it was… you were all naked, and… I should really be going."

Mutt closed his eyes and banged his head against the bars of his cage. Then he looked up and heaved a very deep, put-upon sigh. "I can't believe I'm doing this."

"Doing what?"

"Giving a shit." Mutt rolled his eyes at Kayla. "God help me. You know that big, jangly set of keys you mentioned? It's actually a control board. It's over there. I've seen the guards work it. You just hit the button by the cage you want opened, and hey presto." He licked his lips, glancing toward the door. "Trouble is, there are no numbers, and I don't know what button opens which cage. Things could get messy 'less you know what you're doing."

He gave the door another wary look, then reeled Kayla in with a quick flex of his biceps. "I'm going to let you go now. You have two choices after that. One, you can go on your merry way, flounder around for a bit, then probably get eaten by something nasty and hairy. Or two, you can let me out of here, go find me some pants, and live for a while longer. Your call."

"Um…" Kayla licked her lips and looked desperately at the other werewolves and the door behind her. She hadn't locked it, and it suddenly seemed a very long way away.

"If I let you out," she said slowly, "what's to say you won't kill me too?"

Mutt shrugged, his eyes still fixed on the door. "You're just gonna have to trust me."

Kayla shook her head firmly. "Nu-uh. Call me Miss Suspicious, but if you knew Karrel you also know that I have trust issues the size of Outer Mongolia, and that's just for starters."

"Suit yourself, but guess what? You have a new choice to make."

"Which is...?"

"Whether you're going to trust me... or him." Mutt jerked his head toward the door.

Unwillingly, Kayla turned around.

A squat, ugly man who looked like a pit bull in human form stood at the door, casually buttoning up a pair of bloodstained Hunter's slacks. Kayla froze, staring at the man in horror. No way was this guy a Hunter. She knew that with everything in her. The guy's body bulged with over-pumped muscles. Everything on him that could be pierced had been pierced, and his exposed arms were almost hidden beneath a multitude of overlapping pornographic tattoos. His acne-scarred face lit up with feral glee as his black eyes locked in on Kayla's face.

He grinned, exposing blunt, rotting teeth.

"Hey there, pretty lady," said Skeet.

CHAPTER FIFTEEN

PHIL SKIDDED AROUND the corner, his rifle raised. His face and hands were covered in blood, but not his own. A few vampires were going to wake up back in containment minus a number of their favorite extremities.

He smiled grimly to himself. Since the new rules had come in about not killing what you caught, he and his team had to vent most of their wrath at the creatures in the field before dragging what was left of their sorry carcasses back to Skyler and his team of mad scientists. Every Hunter had some kind of dark history involving one of the creatures they were now hunting. Some of them had lost parents or siblings to the undead, bitten by vampires or demons or chewed on by zombies. Others had had friends or loved ones torn apart by werewolves. It was a fairly universal reason for joining the Hunters—the only way you learned of their existence was if you were rescued by them. You couldn't take a vampire to court, or lock up a werewolf in a human jail, so the only form of revenge was to bite the dog that bit you, so to speak, and to hope that you survived long enough to spare others a similar fate.

Phil yawned. That was one of the two reasons why he was here, and right now, the other one was late.

Reloading his AK-74M with practiced ease, Phil shrugged off a shattered armor plate and placed it soundlessly on the ground before hefting his gun and creeping forward, every sense alert for the slightest—

CRAAAASHH!

The large tinted window above him exploded as the blazing remains of a two-hundred pound vampire sailed through it. It struck the wall opposite and burst into a cloud of black dust. Rapid-fire pistol shots rang out and the rest of the glass gave way, shards of spinning glass embedding themselves in the wall amid the ashen remains.

Ninette vaulted through the empty frame, drawing her silver pistol as she did so.

Landing with feline grace, she turned to face Phil in a low crouch, her hair swirling around her. She looked right, then left, then straightened up and lowered her pistol with a sigh, tapping it impatiently against her vinyl-covered thigh.

"Where's the girl? Please tell me you guys are playing hide and seek."

"Hey, there were vampires, okay?"

"Yeah, I know. There were vampires, there was traffic, it was raining meatballs down on Sepulveda. I don't care!" Ninette swept a slender hand through her glossy blonde and black hair, struggling to remain calm. "Okay, I'll bite. Where did she go?"

"Dunno. She ran off after dusting two vampires."

"By herself? You're kidding." Ninette stepped closer, her hazel eyes sparking with sudden interest. "Fine. I won't be annoyed yet. I don't care what she says, Karrel must've trained her. There's no other explanation."

She checked the chamber in her silver pistol, then slid in two more bullets and racked the cylinder shut. "There's gotta be a reason the werewolves want this girl, and I'll bet it's the same reason they killed Karrel. Let's just hope we find her before they do."

At that moment, Phil's radio buzzed. He held it to his ear and listened intently for a moment, then turned to Ninette in excitement. "Tony's got her on the Infra-Scope. She's down by the holding pens."

Ninette swore.

"What?"

"That's where they put the new guy we picked up tonight."

"So?"

"So, he was spinning our boys some line about him being Karrel's best friend."

Ninette gave a snort of laughter. "Nice one. I like to make friends with the monsters that killed my family, too, just for shits and giggles."

"You think *she* knows that?"

The two Hunters looked at one another, sharing a thought. Then as one, they drew their weapons and sprinted off down the corridor.

KAYLA STOOD HER ground as Skeet sauntered across the room toward her, still grinning that awful grin of his. His features were unshaven and cruel, and there was something not quite right about his face, as though he was at a slightly lower stage of evolution than the rest of humanity. His low brow and flattened, pug nose framed eyes that shone with greasy malice. Kayla wrinkled her nose at the smell of unwashed skin and rotting meat that emanated from the man. The guy was like a garbage heap on legs. She could almost see the flies circling around him, in a cartoon visage of decay and death.

She shivered involuntarily, casting her eyes desperately around for an escape route.

There was none.

Skeet cranked his grin up a notch as he neared the girl. The only thing she smelled like was fear. He liked that. His drug-addled brain ramped up a gear in anticipation of the fun to come. He cracked his knuckles, reaching down to brush his fingers over the assortment of Hunter weapons that hung on the belt of his stolen uniform. He knew he didn't need them, and he suppressed a chuckle of glee at the thought. Then he realized he had no reason to suppress it, and laughed out loud.

He looked the girl over, his eyes creasing in lewd pleasure at the sight of her. Pretty, pretty lady. She had it all: great tits, legs to die for, and that wonderful, almost orgasmic look of fear on her face as she looked at him. Oh yeah, she knew what was coming, and he'd make sure she was conscious long enough to enjoy every single blood-sodden minute of it.

He watched as the chick made eye contact with the puny, naked whelp in the cage, then glanced over to the big control board at the side of the room that was covered in a checkerboard of numbers.

They were meaningless to him, but judging by the look on her face they were somehow important. Skeet watched the girl's eyes track back to the whelp's cage, staring at him almost pleadingly.

Skeet gave a laugh that was as short and ugly as he was. "Don't worry 'bout him, precious, I'll show you a far better time than he ever could."

Mutt gripped the bars, every muscle in his body tense. "Touch her and you're dead."

Skeet drew a pistol from his belt and aimed it at Kayla, stopping her in her tracks as she started creeping toward the control board. "How about if I shoot her? That don't count as touching, does it?" He laughed uproariously, making a sound like a cat coughing up a pound of sand.

A strange prickling feeling traveled up the back of Kayla's neck, as though she were being watched from behind. Unable to resist the compulsion, she tore her eyes off the grinning madman in front of her and cast a quick glance over her shoulder.

A sea of eyes met hers. Each werewolf was standing stock still in its cage, staring past her at Skeet. A low rumbling sound filled the air as the wolf in the cage nearest her began to growl, a low, D-minor tone of warning. The creature in the next cage picked up the note and took it down a few keys, to a major sound of threat. The noise traveled around the room as one by one the werewolves got to their feet and snarled at Skeet, their fur bristling. In one of the end cages, the biggest werewolf started pawing the ground, barking harshly as it jerked on its chains, its gaze locked on Skeet's face in fury.

Mutt stepped back from his bars, glancing around him with raised eyebrows. "Looks like you make friends everywhere you go, Skeet. I gotta say, I'm jealous."

Skeet cracked his knuckles. "It's a talent." He swung around suddenly, his face darkening into a scowl. "Hey, shuddup, alla you!"

The growling only increased in volume.

"Ah screw this shit." Skeet twisted his pistol sideways, sighting it on Kayla's head. "Any last requests?"

"How 'bout you don't shoot me?"

Skeet gave a slow, stupid smile. "Ha! Good answer. I like that one. I'll put it in my screenplay." He guffawed loudly, then racked back the hammer on his pistol, tensing the muscles in his arm to take up the recoil as he prepared to fire.

Kayla swallowed, staring into the blackness at the end of the gun's barrel. She had never felt so desolate in her life. There was nothing she could do, nowhere she could run. At the movies, she'd always been the one yelling at the screen "run, you fool!" when someone was threatened with a gun and just stood there like an idiot.

Kayla stood there like an idiot. She knew with an overwhelming sense of futility that whatever she did, Skeet was going to shoot her.

So she did the only thing she had left to do.

With a cry of defiance, she lunged for the control board.

She managed to hit the first three buttons before the gun went off. Kayla's heart nearly imploded in fright as Skeet's bullet whizzed over her head and struck the board, which exploded in a geyser of sparks. All the colored lights on the board immediately started flashing, and a shockingly loud klaxon sounded in the room.

A rumbling sound filled the air. Kayla turned around fearfully.

"Oh, my God," she whispered.

Almost every cage in the room was open. The werewolves inside strained against their bonds, desperate to free themselves and get to Skeet. There was an explosion of metal links as the big red werewolf snapped three of the four chains binding him. Skeet spun around wildly and fired his gun at the big creature, putting six rounds into its flank. The werewolf didn't so much as flinch. Foam dripped from its mouth and its eyes blazed in fury, jaws agape as it fought to get Skeet.

Kayla spun back to Mutt to find that his cage was still locked. She ran across to him, tugging on the bars in case the lock had by some chance disengaged.

Mutt slapped on the bars. "Forget me. Get out of here!" he yelled.

At that moment, the red werewolf's final chain snapped.

The giant creature burst out of its cage like a derailed train and barreled across the room, smacking into Skeet headfirst and sending him flying across the room. Skeet struck a bank of lockers, smashing them to a crumpled mess of sheet metal before falling to the ground in a flailing heap.

Kayla's eyes widened as the creature flew toward her at full tilt, a crazed look in its eyes, foam flying from its gaping nostrils. Some long-buried instinct made her stand her ground, waiting until the werewolf was nearly upon her before throwing herself to the side.

With a loud *CLANG!* the big werewolf ran straight into Mutt's cage, its momentum buckling the bars and driving its head and shoulders through. Mutt leapt back as the big creature flailed helplessly, half in and half out of the cage, digging its huge claws into the ground as it snapped and howled in frustrated rage.

Mutt looked up at Kayla through the three-foot hole in the bars, ran forward, and jumped onto the werewolf's back, using it as a springboard to vault through the gap. He landed on the ground outside the cage and straightened up, grinning at Kayla.

"Now... about those pants..." he started.

He spun around as a loud *crrr-aaa-ccc-kkk* rang out. The big werewolf planted its feet squarely on the ground and started backing toward him, dragging the half-ton cage with it, step by step. Mutt clapped his hands over his ears, wincing in pain as steel shrieked and concrete scraped beneath the cage, sparks flying. The creature's muscles bulged like sacks of watermelons as it braced itself and heaved a second time. The bars trapping it started to bend outwards, buckling under the strain.

Mutt darted over to the groaning figure of Skeet and snatched a rolled up pair of jeans from the wreckage of the troops' lockers. Pausing only to kick Skeet nastily in the ribs, he hurriedly slipped the jeans on, ran back to Kayla, and grabbed her by the hand. "Let's fly, girlie."

TOGETHER THEY RAN through the empty rooms and corridors of the base. Kayla saw more cages in a blur as they passed through the darkened labs. She saw things with claws, things with fur, things with horns. She passed by a big tank full of things that looked disturbingly like scaled babies with forked tails and enormous eyes. She almost ran into a post when one of them popped its head out of the water and started crying, reaching out toward her beseechingly with tiny, wrinkled white fingers.

"Jesus! What is this place?" she gasped, appalled.

"A bad place," replied Mutt grimly. "Keep moving."

Kayla redoubled her pace, darting around cages and jumping over stacks of equipment. Loud crashes and snarls came from behind them. Kayla knew it was only a matter of time before Skeet and the red werewolf finished duking it out and the winner came after them.

She felt cold air on her face as they neared a set of large, steel-shuttered doors. Moments later, they burst out into the main vehicle bay, back where she'd first come in.

With a gasp of relief, she ran toward the nearest parked SUV, trying the handle.

It was locked.

The next car was locked too. Kayla made her way swiftly down the line, trying the door handles of each vehicle with no luck.

As she neared the end of the line, a loud growling sound came from behind her. Kayla tensed, spinning around in panic as headlights flashed on in the darkness. She shaded her eyes and squinted painfully into the light as one of the black hybrid vehicles she'd seen earlier rolled forward out of its bay, its engine growling, and drew to a halt alongside her. Kayla saw the letters "SBV" stenciled on the side, and in smaller letters beneath the hand-written acronym, "Stupidly Big Vehicle."

A window rolled down with the hum of an electric motor to reveal Mutt, shirtless in the driver's seat. He waved to her cheerily, looking extremely proud of himself. "Get in!" he shouted.

Kayla wasted no time in complying.

As she slammed the door the bay lights suddenly blazed on, flooding the place with blue UV light. A series of panels slid up in the walls, revealing dozens of black-outfitted troopers. They were all armed, and did not look friendly.

She glanced over at Mutt, raising an eyebrow as she watched his bloodied hands surf over the panels of technological equipment, an intense look of concentration on his face. To Kayla the controls had no meaning. Nevertheless, Mutt took hold of several levers and pulled back on them confidently, revving the motor as he gazed through the windshield at the troopers, a look of glee on his face. With a whoop he hit the gas, laying down a thick track of smoking rubber as he headed straight for the closed door ahead of them.

The troops opened fire, spraying the vehicle with bullets.

"What the hell are you doing?" Kayla yelped as Mutt floored the gas, aiming right for the center of the door.

"Having some fun."

Mutt flicked up a recessed panel hidden beneath the steering wheel as though he had done it a hundred times, and stabbed his finger down on the green button inside. A flash of brilliant white light filled the car. Kayla threw up her arms to shield her face. Through the blinding brilliance she saw what looked like an anti-tank missile streak out of the cannons on the side of the vehicle, punching a smoking, six-foot hole clean through the thick metal shutters before them.

"Man! I have got to get me one of these!" Mutt said.

"I think you just did," replied Kayla, clinging grimly onto her seat.

A second later the car struck the shutters with a jarring crash. For a moment it stuck in the hole, wheels spinning. Then the sheer power of its engine peeled the hole wide open and the car jolted through. Mutt blasted through the second shutter with a whoop, heading for the next door.

Kayla yipped as the back window erupted in a shower of glass. Bullets tore into the upholstery behind her. She threw herself down in her seat, shielding her head as the main door came toward them at breakneck speed. Mutt hit the rocket-launcher button again and again, each missile blasting a bigger hole in the door, but nothing like the size they'd need to get through it. The door was reinforced somehow, Kayla guessed.

Not good.

A second later the vehicle struck the main door with a deafening *clang* and stuck fast in the hole melted by the rocket launcher. Kayla plunged forward, hitting her head on the control panel. As she hauled herself groggily back upright she heard the sounds of yelling and the rattle of gunfire from behind them as the Hunter troops caught up with them. One of the side windows went out with a bang, spilling nuggets of safety glass onto Kayla's lap. She gave a little yip of panic and ducked down in her seat as a second volley of gunfire sparked off the semi-destroyed door in front of them, bullets ricocheting in all directions. Then the gunfire stopped and Kayla lifted her head cautiously, peering back at the troops through the glassless back window.

"Christ! That was close!" she gasped.

There was no reply.

Kayla glanced back at Mutt, and her blood froze. He was lying half-slumped in his seat, clutching the steering wheel, a glistening red crater in his stomach oozing blood all over the seat. He looked up at her in disbelief and slowly brought up his hand to touch the hole. Then he slumped, his eyes rolling back in his head.

A club of cold fear slammed down on Kayla.

"No!" she cried.

Footsteps pounded behind them.

Frantically, Kayla leaned across the unconscious form of Mutt and slammed her foot down over his, hitting the gas again and again. It was no good. The car was well and truly stuck.

A scream cut through the gunfire, followed by a loud roar. Kayla glanced into the rearview mirror to see a werewolf crash through the hole in the first door and pounce on the nearest trooper. His gun immediately went off, taking down one of his buddies. She immediately recognized the werewolf.

It was Skeet.

Kayla started pushing buttons and pulling levers at random, making the car shake and vibrate as smoke poured up from the tires. She had to get out of here. If what Karrel had told her was true, going back to the Hunters could mean the end for her. It certainly would be for both of them if Skeet caught up with them. Hits pinged and plinked across the chassis of the car as the Hunters opened fire on her once again. Kayla slammed her fist down on the dashboard in frustration.

"Quit shooting at me!" she yelled. "I'm on your side!"

She saw the reflections of troopers running toward the car and she stabbed impotently at more buttons, sweat running down her forehead. She hit a green button at random and yelled in surprise at a sudden whir of motors. The cab started shrinking as the rocket launcher retracted and the roof lowered itself with a busy hum of machinery.

A moment later the vehicle popped out of the hole in the doors like a cork shot from a bottle. Kayla hit the gas with a gasp of relief and the engine sucked fuel, sending the SBV blasting up the dirt track away from the base, heading for freedom in a swirl of discarded newspapers.

The vehicle vanished into the night, a howl of frustration ringing out behind it.

CHAPTER SIXTEEN

MAGNUS STALKED THROUGH the heated crush jamming his opulent penthouse party suite on the top deck of one of LA's most notorious new downtown clubs, Wolfbayne. He owned most of the clubs in the city, in one way or another, and this place was just the latest in a series of new openings set to usurp the old music-biz-dominated ownership of the town's most popular watering holes.

A hush fell over the crowd as Magnus reached the inner room of the club. He was looking mighty fine tonight, and he knew it. He was dressed fashionably in supple black leather jeans and a velvet shirt, the top few buttons open to expose his impressively cut upper body, his enormous muscles covered in reams of scar tissue from ancient duels. Magnus stared straight ahead as he walked. His dark sunshades hid the movement of his burnt umber eyes as he casually scanned the crowd, taking in and memorizing the faces of the partygoers for future reference as he searched for the one who had displeased him.

The long, dark room was packed almost to overflowing. The worn leather couches and scattered throw cushions were occupied by an energetic mix of vampires and werewolves, talking, laughing, drinking, and kicking back at the end of the week to discuss business deals, mergers, and pack negotiations. Topless male and female human waiters moved through the room, drink trays held aloft, plying members of rival packs with high-grade alcohol and cocaine to keep them, however briefly, from each other's throats. Magnus didn't tolerate rowdiness at his nightly parties. The fully armed guards standing at each exit were a good visual reminder, should anybody forget it.

Magnus nodded faintly with approval at the sight of the turnout. It was better than he had hoped, for tonight was a special night. All the main local drug mob bosses were there, grouped in close circles around the chromed bar, perusing the entertainment and sipping hundred dollar cocktails alongside representatives from the European, Asian, Mexican, and Japanese drug trade. Word of Magnus's latest deal had gone around quickly, and tonight he had enough buying power under this one velvet-lined roof to outsource anyone in town.

Tonight however, it wasn't drugs they were going to be dealing in.

Proto-rock music pumped from oversized speakers as Magnus moved silently toward the group of five rough-looking figures lounging around a cushioned cabana booth beside the indoor waterfall, lit only by the red glow of the inset flame pits.

Just the sight of them sitting there, smoking his weed and enjoying his booze, burned him inside.

Magnus ground his teeth as he stepped around a pair of long-legged vixens reclining on an over-sized stuffed pillow. They broke into fawning, coy grins at the sight of him and reached up to stroke suggestively at his leg. Magnus wasn't in the mood. He brushed the two ladies off, ignoring their disappointed pouts as he strode onwards.

Reaching the cabana booth, he drew his trade-mark Desert Eagle pistol and calmly leveled it at the nearest man's head.

"So tell me," he said in a conversational tone of voice, "which one of you little fuckers do I have to kill first?"

Harlem spoke up, fisting the coke residue from his nose. "I dunno what you're talking about, buddy."

"Oh, really? Word on the street is that someone just went crash and boom over at Skyler's place. So now you got five seconds to tell me what the fuck you were thinking, before I blow each and every one of your stinkin' worthless cur heads off."

Harlem giggled and then quickly sobered up, focusing on Magnus with an effort. "What makes you think we dunnit?"

"I'm psychic," said Magnus, eyeing the bloodied, bullet-riddled form of Skeet half-slumped in the end seat, a bottle of Jack clutched in one white-knuckled fist. Mitzi was bending over him, an impassive look on his face as he pulled flattened slugs from his friend's body with a pair of needle-nosed pliers. Across the table, Jackdoor and Flame looked on in amusement, sipping cold beers.

Harlem's gaze didn't flicker. "Take a chill pill, old man. We was just followin' orders. The hit got away, see? Skeety-boy here was just takin' care of her."

Magnus stared at him blankly. "That's four seconds. Three. Two…"

A red-haired woman lifted her head from Harlem's lap, her lipstick smeared and her gaze unfocused. "Boys! I already told you once. No guns at the table!"

"Don't you worry, darlin'." Harlem pushed the woman's head back down between his legs and settled back with a sigh of contentment. "Everything's under control."

"No, Harlem, everything is *not* under control," Magnus snapped, his meager supply of patience fast running out. "Everything is royally fucked."

"How's that, then?"

Magnus whipped off his sunshades and fixed Harlem with a chilling stare. "Number one, we're not supposed to know where Nancy Boy's little hidey-hole is, and number two, that joint is supposed to be unbreachable. Now we've got every little soldier boy in the place running around like decapitated poultry looking for where the big bad werewolf got in, and I got Mr. Fancy Pants himself on the phone having kittens, because now he has to send out a team to track your mangy ass down and bring back your head on a platter."

"What does he care?" sniffed Flame, rubbing at his gums. "He knows it was us."

"Because, you moron, the other Hunters don't. Way they see it, now that the evil werewolves know where their little top-secret base is, what's to stop them from going back there next week with a bunch of their buddies and killing everyone in the place?"

"That's exactly what we're gonna do, right?" asked Flame, his voice rough with alcohol.

"Oh, very good. A round of applause to Freddy Kruger's stunt double," snapped Magnus. With a swipe of his gloved fist he cleared the table, sending empty bottles flying in all directions. Nearby party-goers ducked as they smashed against the wall. "Idiots! You think Skyler would be so cooperative if he knew we were planning to kill him and all his little Buffy wannabe's once we were done with him?"

Magnus swept the gang with a fierce glare. "The European deal goes down tomorrow night, gentle-men. Once Genetica launches, we won't need the financing from the Hunters. When the media gets a load of what we're developing, we'll be set for life. We've got thirty of the most brilliant minds in the world working on a cure for aging, racing against the clock to crack that stinking vampire DNA before someone twigs what we're doing and shuts us down for good... And you're willing to risk all that, everything we've worked for, for a single hit?"

The hum of conversation died down as the party-goers around them turned to stare accusingly. Harlem ignored them all and yawned loudly, lazily stroking the silky head of the woman in his lap. "Skeet dunnit, not us. You wanna waste his scrawny ass? Go for it. An' pass me his beer when you're done."

Magnus casually raised his Desert Eagle and pulled the trigger.

When the smoke cleared and the screaming had stopped, Harlem gave a put-upon sigh and reached down to push the lifeless red-haired woman off his lap. As she slid to the floor, blood gushing from the fist-sized hole in her head, he sighed and flicked Magnus a disgusted look.

"You owe me three hundred bucks for a new pair of pants, man."

"I don't owe you anything, you bottom-feeding *freak*."

"Is that so?"

The other four werewolves instantly tensed up at Harlem's tone of voice. They scraped their chairs back as Harlem rose slowly to his feet and stepped around the table, deliberately walking right into the werewolf leader's gun. He stopped barely an inch away from it and eyeballed Magnus, his golden eyes glinting in the low light. The music had stopped, and in the ensuing silence the tinny metallic *tk...tk...tk* of the strobe lights flashing was audible.

Harlem smiled cruelly as he stared into Magnus's rheumy yellow eyes, noting the fury and defiance there. He knew it was all show. That wasn't what he was looking for.

Concentrating, he gathered his mental strength and looked deeper. He couldn't read minds in the traditional sense, like some vampires could. He couldn't hear the words that beat like burning butterflies in his victim's heads, but he could feel their thoughts, see images, almost taste their emotions as though they were living entities. He'd been able to read minds since they'd done those experiments on him, pumping him full of vampire genes, unlocking a part of him that should never normally be activated.

Now that Pandora's Box was opened, there was no going back.

Harlem's eyes gleamed as he pushed past the pride and the bloodlust and the petty jealousy in Magnus's mind. Finally he came to the part of the older werewolf's brain that was filled with fear.

Now, this was interesting.

It wasn't just normal, healthy fear, the kind that kept you alive on the streets of gangland LA. This was a dark, screaming wasteland of mortal fear, barely under control, and getting worse by the second.

Harlem locked his mental hooks into the void, seeking to pry it open and take a closer look. Harlem saw Magnus flinch as he tapped further into his memory. He gave an ugly chuckle, his hand flashing out to grab Magnus's lapels to keep him from turning away.

"Whatcha afraid of, old man?" he asked, his voice a dry whisper.

As he had hoped, his words sent a fresh stream of images racing through the man's mind like cool, clear water, playing out on the internal cinema screen of Magnus's subconscious.

Needles plunging through sun-splotched flesh... A cold draft through the indignity of a backless surgical gown... A nurse dressed in white, carrying a clipboard... Naked fear rising, the burnt aluminum taste of adrenaline... A heart-rate monitor, going into the red... A cry of disbelief ringing long and loud... Hospital corridors flashing past through blurred, tear-blinded eyes... Driving wind and rain and a scream from the depths of hell, then a parking valet hitting the ground, blood gushing from the ruin of his throat... A cemetery flashing past a leather steering wheel as claws erupted from flesh in a burst of defiance...

Magnus jerked himself free from Harlem's grasp, his face suddenly ashen. His gun clattered to the floor and he took two shocked steps backward.

"How *dare* you?" he gasped.

Harlem grinned, exposing pointed, gleaming teeth.

Magnus swallowed and swept a hand through his mane, attempting to recompose himself and drive the unwanted images from his head. His throat tightened at the memories and he cursed as the stress made his lungs start to convulse. He began coughing, hacking, his hand over his mouth as he fought for air.

When he took his hand away, there was blood on his lips.

Harlem raised an eyebrow as Magnus shrank from him, his pupils dilating in fear. "Well, looks like the big bad wolf ain't so big and bad anymore."

Magnus glowered at him for a long moment, his hand straying inside his jacket to touch the warm, smooth shape of his other gun. A warning series of clicks came from the cabana booth beside him. Magnus turned his back on Harlem and swung around to face the other four werewolves, raising his voice to divert attention from the shaking of his hands.

"You've got twenty-four hours to find that sniveling little bitch of Karrel's and kill her," he snapped. "If she's spoken to anyone, I'll kill you. You get seen in that base again, I'll kill you. You put one foot out of line without my express written permission, and guess what?"

"You'll kill us?" hazarded Skeet.

Magnus smiled icily, the strobe lights flashing off his jagged, yellowed canines. "And to think Cyan told me you were all half-breed fuckwits." A group of female werewolves sniggered, and Magnus flicked his gaze back to Harlem in triumph. "Apparently, she was misinformed."

Then he was gone, storming off through the swiftly parting crowds.

The stony silence that followed was broken by Skeet's nervous giggle. "Cyan would never say that about us, would she?"

Harlem rolled his fire-colored eyes as he reached for a fresh beer. "You do know she's met us, right?"

CHAPTER SEVENTEEN

THE ENGINE OF the SBV growled as Kayla wrestled with the unfamiliar steering stick, turning the car out onto the 10 freeway. She shot a fearful glance at Mutt. He was out cold in the passenger seat beside her, a thin sheen of perspiration covering his face. He was still breathing, but only just. Blood pooled on the seat around him, dripping stickily down onto the floor.

Kayla swallowed hard as she accelerated up the darkened highway, the car barely under control. She didn't dare stop the car to check on Mutt for fear of not being able to start it again. A glance in the cracked rearview mirror showed no sign of pursuit. That was one good thing, at least.

She crested the top of the hill, heading toward West Hollywood. The familiar sprawl of the Hollywood Hills rose up before her like a beacon of light. The sight of it reassured her, the lights dotted on the dark hills gleaming like an oasis of sanity and normalcy after a night of anything but.

Kayla took a few steadying breaths to calm herself as she edged the stolen vehicle into the sparse night traffic, ignoring the curious looks of other drivers and praying she could get to safety before someone called the police. She had retracted the SBV's cannons after a few heart-stopping moments of trial-and-error, but the cops out here would stop you for as little as a busted tail-light. She guessed that the bullet holes peppering the back end of the car would get her more than a road ticket.

Beside her on the seat Mutt stirred, groaning weakly.

"Don't freak. I'm taking you to hospital," Kayla said in what she hoped was a soothing tone of voice.

Mutt's eyes half-opened and he gazed up at her, his eyes unfocused. "Screw that. They own the hospitals."

"Who do?"

Mutt just shook his head. "Take me home."

"My home or your home?"

"We can't go back to yours. They'll be waiting for you." Mutt squeezed his eyes shut as a wave of pain hit him. "Fuck, that hurts. Just get this thing off the road before we hit a cop. I don't want to be on the news. My hair looks like shit and these pants make me look gay."

"But you're bleeding—"

"Werewolf, remember? I'll be fine." Mutt's eyes slid closed again and he sagged down in the seat, breathing shallowly.

Steeling herself, Kayla put her foot on the gas and drove on, heading deeper inland.

Twenty minutes later, the black Hunter SBV turned into a garbage-cluttered side street and coasted to a halt outside a dark, foreboding tenement building. Kayla switched off the engine and peered out the window.

"Please tell me you're kidding."

Mutt opened his eyes and coughed into his fist, then wiped blood from his lips with a shudder. "Do I even remotely look like I'm kidding?"

Kayla shrugged. This wasn't the kind of place she'd want to drive past at night, let alone think about getting out of the car and going inside. She shivered as she took in the rusted strands of razor wire climbing like deadly steel roses up the thick black fences that flanked the dilapidated eight-story building. Snowdrifts of trash were pushed up against every vertical surface and hanging from every fire escape like stinking decorations. Threatening, angular gang graffiti decorated the lower portion of the building, and an intermittently blinking street lamp shed light on the surrounding area. Kayla counted at least nine homeless people curled up on cardboard around the outskirts of the building, huddled in shadowy corners.

"People really live here?" she asked fearfully, peering up at the tenement.

"We try."

Suddenly, Kayla's own life didn't look so bad. She looked sidelong at Mutt. His face was ashen from blood loss and she wondered exactly what she was getting herself into.

Kayla drew a shuddering breath, trying to stay focused, rubbing her grimy face with her equally grimy hands. She felt sick and tired and cold, and had never wanted to sleep more in her entire life. "So what about my workmates? And Wylie? Will the werewolves go after them too?"

"You already called them from the gas station, remember? They'll be fine."

"Yeah, but what if—"

"Don't worry about them. It's you they're after. The wolves won't want to draw attention to themselves by racking up a body count near a hit's home. Last thing they need is the cops crawling all over your place when they're trying to stalk you. They figure you'll come home eventually. Then they'll get you."

"Glad to hear it," Kayla muttered. "So when can I go home?"

"I just told you," said Mutt, irritation creeping into his voice, "you can't. You wanna risk your life, feel free, but they could be anywhere, and they could be anyone. You can't tell a werewolf by sight without training. They may wait a week, a month, a year before they come after you, but they will come after you. It's your job not to be there when they do."

A moment's banging and fiddling around disengaged the multi-jointed driver's door, which rolled upwards into the roof with a whisper of oiled bearings. Kayla made her way around to Mutt's side of the car, keeping one eye open for danger as she scanned the building. Graffiti on the front of the building read: "I Know Why Jesus Wept—Rent Control."

Kayla shivered.

For a moment she contemplated dumping Mutt before jumping back into the car, slamming the door, and roaring off home, but she knew that if she did, she would be on her own, and that thought terrified her more than anything else she'd seen that night.

Rolling up Mutt's door, she hesitated before extending her hand. To her surprise, Mutt hauled himself upright and jumped down by himself. He turned to face her tiredly, looking a lot younger than she remembered him being. She wondered how much of his personality was for show, whether the bravado and swagger he'd shown when she'd first met him was real or if it was just an act, a role he'd been playing to throw her off-guard.

No matter. Right now, she had more important things to worry about.

She cleared her throat, hardly daring to hope. "You wouldn't by any chance have a shower in your place, would you?"

THE SHOWER WAS warm. That was the most important thing. Kayla could barely stand as the water sluiced over her, washing the grime and sweat and blood from her tired body. Her legs shook with exhaustion and adrenaline burnout. It was all she could do to keep them under her as she methodically scrubbed at her skin with the razor-thin fragment of soap she'd found beside the sink. She guided the sliver across the smooth expanse of her skin, running it up and down her long, lean calves, around the her flat stomach and across her slick breasts. She leaned full into the blast of the water, the stinging droplets bouncing off her skin and forming a mist that surrounded her in an ephemeral, soothing cocoon.

Heaven.

As she washed she tried not to look around at the grime and the mold and the black mildew that reached head height on all four walls. She prayed to God that there weren't any spiders.

When she was clean she got out and dried herself as best she could on a towel that was only slightly less damp than she was. She hesitated as she passed the cracked mirror. She backtracked, stared at herself in it, and then gazed with forlorn hope over her shoulder.

Of course, there was nobody there.

Heaving a deep sigh, Kayla roughly toweled her hair off. She gazed with something less than enthusiasm at the clothes Mutt had found for her to change into.

Gingerly, she sorted through the pile. "Hmm. One halter top, bloodstained... one pair of Lucky Brand jeans, boys cut... three T-shirts touting bands that ought to be shot... and possibly the world's ugliest Hawaiian shirt." She sat back, perplexed. "Great, I've been kidnapped by Bon Jovi's kid brother."

Pulling the least offensive of the three long white T-shirts over her head, Kayla unlocked the bathroom door, pushing it open a crack to peer into Mutt's room.

The main light was out. The only illumination came from a small, ineffectual bulb dangling from a bare wire at the end of the bed, which mingled with the stray beams of moonlight flooding in from the low bay window. There was only one piece of furniture in the room, a rickety double bed shored up on cinder blocks, adorned with a single sheet and a lumpy pillow. Kayla had seen worse guy's rooms, but not many. Mutt was sitting on the bed, his back to Kayla, the moonlight painting his exposed upper body with a dozen curved brushstrokes of white light. A half-empty whisky bottle lay on the bed beside him.

If he'd heard her come in, he didn't acknowledge it.

Kayla hesitated, then stepped into the room and closed the bathroom door quietly behind her. She cleared her throat, feeling awkward. "Are you showering tonight, or should I just hose you down?"

Mutt looked up at her, his face expressionless. "Hoobastank. Good choice."

"Hmm?"

"The shirt." Mutt reached for the whisky bottle. Uncapping it, he took a hefty swig before pouring the rest of it down his front, wincing as the alcohol washed over the wound in his stomach. He clenched his teeth and hissed, then turned back to Kayla, gesturing at her T-shirt with the bottle. "Not mine, just so you know."

"Heaven forbid." Kayla gave Mutt a doubtful look as scotch trickled down his torso, soaking his stolen jeans. "I guess that answers the shower question."

"I guess it does."

Mutt's dark eyes glittered in the lamplight. A mournful look briefly crossed his face, and he quickly upended the empty whisky bottle over his mouth, tipping the last few drops down his throat. He tossed the bottle with a clink into a trashcan already full of empties. He weakly got up off the bed, swaying slightly on his feet. Stopping barely inches away from Kayla, he reached out toward her throat.

Kayla instantly tensed up, but Mutt merely touched her dragon coin necklace gently, turning it into the light.

"What's this?" he asked.

Kayla reached up and took it from him, turning it around to gaze down at the design. She'd forgotten she was still wearing it.

"A good luck charm, of sorts," she said quietly. "It was Karrel's."

"Oh." Mutt stared at it for a moment, and then blinked. "Luck. Ha."

He reached out again and gently stroked Kayla's damp ringlets away from her face. There was a far-away look in his eyes.

Kayla's breathing quickened, uncomfortably aware that she was naked beneath the T-shirt. She hadn't even thought about putting her underwear back on beneath it, and was starting to doubt the wisdom of her decision. Being clean was once thing, but not at the expense of putting herself in a compromising position.

Kayla glanced down at the wound in Mutt's torso, hoping to distract herself with a jolt of reality. The hole was only about the size of a quarter, but it looked pretty nasty. Kayla had never seen a bullet wound up close before. The sight of it made her empty stomach churn.

She tried to be encouraging. "Doesn't look too bad."

"No? Check out the back." Mutt gave a little spin as though he were in a dressing room trying on clothes. Kayla gasped as she saw the large, ragged exit wound just to the left of his spine, above the small of his back. Blood slowly seeped out, staining the back of his jeans a dull red.

"Sexy, huh?"

Mutt gave a little laugh as he turned back around with a visible wobble, perspiration running down his brow despite the chill in the room. He was white as a sheet and trembling with shock. He ran a hand through his sweat-drenched hair, trying to tidy it, then gave up with a wince.

"Shouldn't we be taking you to the doctors'?" Kayla asked, worried.

"I'll live. It'll be healed by the morning."

Mutt's eyes lost their focus for a moment and he swayed slightly, throwing out a hand to catch his balance. Kayla caught his arm without thinking and steadied him.

"You sure?"

Mutt's eyes refocused and he gazed at Kayla's face, his hand still on her arm. His hands were very warm. Regaining his balance, he slid his mournful gaze down to her lips, and then looked back up to her eyes.

He started to move forward, closing the gap between them.

Uh-oh, thought Kayla. She knew how this one went.

Before Mutt could move any further she cleared her throat, diffusing the situation the only way she knew how. "So what was she like?"

"Who?" Mutt drew up short, his face flickering from sadness to anger and distrust in a second. His gaze became guarded. It seemed suddenly important for him to look at the walls, the floor, the clutter on his unmade bed. He smelled very strongly of alcohol, and Kayla started to regret spending so long in the shower. She wondered how much of that whisky he'd drunk while she was in there.

"You know who. Your girlfriend."

Kayla backed off slightly, studying Mutt's face as she watched him wrestle with himself. It was a nice face, really: unruly black hair, swept back at the temples; overgrown forelocks falling in random curls over strong, sculpted cheekbones; a patchwork of bruises on one cheek, already fading to dull charcoal smudges like the daubings of a mad artist; strong white teeth, the canines pointed and just a little too long for comfort; faint laughlines around his eyes, betraying his age while somehow adding to his surly good looks; dark, curving eyebrows, a good balance for his powerful jaw. His intense green eyes were now watching her steadily.

All in all, he wasn't bad looking. Not bad looking at all.

Kayla shook herself, trying to remain focused as the silence between them deepened. "Did she have a name?" she prompted.

Mutt shrugged, his expression unreadable. "Her name was Bea. Doesn't matter now. I told you, she's dead."

He started to move toward her again, all lean muscle and animal grace, gazing down at her through heavily-lidded eyes. Kayla took a step back, putting some distance between them. She shook her head fractionally, an unspoken "no." Mutt's eyes flashed with hurt. Kayla cleared her throat, hearing her own voice banter on cheerfully as though from a distance.

"That's a crazy attitude to have. What if they ran the world like that?" She put on a somber newscaster's voice. "'Two hundred people were killed last night in this big crazy-assed explosion, but it doesn't matter now because they're dead. And now back to our main story about a cute little kitten stuck up a tree.'" Kayla shook her head, backing away from the bed, trying to put some distance between them. "Doesn't really work, does it?"

"Works for me," Mutt said softly. He reached out and determinedly ran his hand down Kayla's forearm, watching his fingers move over her bare skin as if hypnotized. "No sense in wallowing in the past."

"But she only died last night!"

"Right. That's the past."

Before Kayla could protest Mutt slid his arms around her. He pulled her in close to him, holding her tight.

Kayla flinched and went to pull away, but after a couple of tense seconds she realized that all Mutt was doing was holding her. She cautiously relaxed into his embrace, resting her wrists on the back of his neck and breathing carefully. Mutt squeezed her more tightly, crushing her breasts against the firm muscle of his chest, pushing his nose into the damp mass of her hair and inhaling. He felt so warm and real and solid, and an uncontrollabe sigh came from within Kayla, like a cool wind blasting away the shadows of the night. It felt so good to be held, to be touched. The warmth of Mutt's embrace started to thaw the bleak emptiness that had been growing inside her since she'd heard the news of Karrel's death.

She felt hot blood start to seep through her already damp T-shirt, mingling with the moisture from the shower. A faint echo of worry sounded in her mind. She was making a big leap of faith by doing this, by being here at all. Mutt was practically a stranger, yet here she was, alone and semi-naked with him in a small room in a strange part of town, literally trusting him with her life because he said he'd been friends with Karrel.

What if he'd been lying?

Kayla felt a small chill of fear go through her. She was painfully aware that her T-shirt was riding up, that her heart was beating far too hard against her breastbone, that it was late and she was going to have to stay here tonight, and most of all, that there was only one bed in the place.

Enough. This was stopping right here.

Kayla pulled back and put a hand on Mutt's shoulder, searching his eyes for something that said she could trust him. Mutt blinked and glanced away almost immediately, his gaze sliding off hers like water off a hotplate. That fact alone should've been enough to set all her warning bells ringing at once, but right now she was pathetically willing to disregard them. She wanted Mutt to be a good guy so badly, to be someone she could trust, someone who would get her through this despite his behavior toward her so far.

After all, if Karrel really had sent him to protect her, he couldn't be all that bad, could he?

Kayla clung desperately to that thought as Mutt's fingers ghosted over the loose folds of the T-shirt covering her, tracing the lines of her slender hip-bones, still not quite meeting her eye. Kayla felt her legs start to tremble again, but this time it wasn't from tiredness.

"Did you love her?" she asked quickly, to keep their safe little conversation going.

A pause, the slightest hesitation. "None of your business."

"That's a 'yes,' then?" Kayla said.

Mutt's grip tightened on her hips and his eyes finally met hers with a flash of black fire, as though he was pissed at her for not dropping the subject. In the semi-darkness his eyes were the only things that held any kind of color, twin pools of amber light that seemed to glow from within. In the stark moonlight his face looked harsh, almost feral, with a pained kind of intensity.

"So what if I did?" he said in a low voice that barely left his throat. "She's gone now. You can't change the past. You can't bring back the dead, so why worry?"

Mutt licked his lips as he moved in closer to Kayla, noting the faint glow of desire mixed with the exhaustion and defiance in her eyes. He knew that she wanted him on some level, but he wondered whether she'd let herself give in to the compulsion.

They'd both lost someone. What else did they have to lose?

He felt her cool, soft hands touch his chest, not holding him back, just showing him where the limits were. He knew that if he really wanted to he could make those limits go away. But when he moved in closer he saw her fists clench at her side and a pang of guilt went through him. Bea's face swam before his eyes, and he quickly shook his head to dispel the image.

He almost succeeded.

Time ramped back to full speed and heat blossomed within him, partially inspired by the alcohol, and partially inspired by the half-naked human girl standing in front of him. He hadn't meant for the night to play out like this, but he wasn't about to start complaining.

He looked Kayla over with approval, taking in her fine-boned, heart-shaped face with its frame of damp, bouncy ringlets, her delicate features, her golden skin. Her ridiculously cute nose was smattered with freckles, just visible in the moonlight, and her shining brown eyes were narrowed at him in a look that was half fear and half arousal.

The tip of her pointed little tongue darted out to moisten her full lips and her breathing quickened, teetering between fight and flight. Unable to help himself, his eyes flicked downwards. Her T-shirt clung in strategic places to her lithe, athletic frame, and the legs that emerged from beneath it were long and deliciously tanned. Mutt imagined them locked around his neck and shivered, trying to suppress the thought.

Okay, so she was Karrel's girl, but so what? The guy was dead, right? What did he care?

Fuck. He really shouldn't have had that whisky.

Mutt leaned forwards again, holding his breath to try to quell the raging need, the mental and physical pain that filled him. He could hear the girl's heart beating loudly beneath her soft, sweetly scented skin and smell the blood pumping through her veins.

As his lips made soft contact with Kayla's he heard her small, urgent intake of breath.

"Don't," she said, the word sounding like a painful confession.

"Why not?" Mutt whispered, his lips not leaving hers.

Kayla swallowed, although she didn't move back. The smell of warm male animal coming from the guy was intoxicating, and her head swam as she gathered all her mental resources. "You know why."

Mutt took a couple of deep breaths, breathing in her scent, then traced his lips over her cheekbone, down the side of her neck and along her jugular.

"Tell me you don't want this," he said quietly, "and I'll go."

His touch sent a bolt of electricity through Kayla and she closed her eyes, reeling with a shockingly sudden burst of need. Maybe it was the lateness of the hour, or a sickly cocktail of emotional overload and stress, but the thought of being with Mutt wasn't all that terrible. She knew in her gut that it was a really, really bad idea, but, like most bad ideas, it was almost impossible to resist.

She felt Mutt's breath on her neck, and she reflexively turned her head to allow him better access. When his tongue flicked out and lapped against the hollow of her throat she gasped. He chuckled low in his throat as his hands moved up to gently cup her breasts, his thumbnails scratching lightly over her nipples, his touch awakening a burning urgency that she didn't know she still had in her. When Karrel had died a part of her had been wrenched away. Now, she desperately wanted it back.

Kayla's lips parted and her gaze grew unfocused. She held herself almost unnaturally still as she silently submitted to his touch, as though moving or speaking would make the situation real. Her eyelids grew heavier with each passing moment. A tingle raced up the back of her neck and spread out over her chest as Mutt kissed her there. When he moved around behind her and lightly nipped at her neck Kayla let out her breath in a quick pant, pressing herself back instinctively against him. Her body was rooted to the spot as all her attention focused in on the hot, wet touch of Mutt's tongue and lips and teeth as they roved unhurriedly over her cool, damp skin.

Any minute now, she told herself, I'll tell him to stop.

Any minute now...

Her eyelids slid closed as he nuzzled the sensitive skin on the back of her neck, and she reached up behind her and ran her fingers through his tangled locks, gripping the back of his head to draw him closer. She leaned back against him, rubbing her check against his, luxuriating in his touch and the sandpaper feel of his stubble against her own smooth skin.

Impatiently, he tangled his fingers in her hair, pulled her head further back on to his shoulder, and nosed his way back up her neck. Then he sealed his lips over hers and pushed his tongue deep inside her mouth. Kayla gave a small sigh. She felt as if she was falling forward into the sweetness of Mutt's mouth. He made an urgent noise of need and enjoyment. She turned while keeping her lips locked with his, sliding her hands around his waist. She pressed herself against him as he pushed her back step by step toward the bathroom door, his tongue exploring her mouth, his erection showing through his denim.

Kayla's head bumped against the door and she gave a faint giggle that turned into a groan as Mutt slipped a denim-clad thigh between her bare legs. He tried to ease her thighs apart.

Kayla reached down to grab his hips, pulling him against her even as a red warning light flashed madly in her brain. What the hell was she doing? Her boyfriend had been dead twenty-four hours and already she was fooling around with one of his best friends. That was so, *so* wrong she couldn't even begin to process it. They probably had a special level of hell reserved for people like her.

Kayla tried to concentrate on the glowing picture of Karrel in her mind, clamping down on her emotions as they boiled over, flooding through the breach in her defenses. She tried to block them, but it was late, and she was tired, and Mutt's touch felt soft and good.

When she finally found the strength to pull away, she did so with regret. She turned her head away from Mutt, licking her lips as he continued hungrily kissing her, slipping down her body. She shook her head and blinked in a vain attempt to focus.

"Hey," she said quietly.

Mutt grunted and nipped her on the muscle of her back while he shouldered her a little too hard against the door, his hands running swiftly to the bottom of her treacherously short T-shirt. Kayla caught his wrists and held them tight, moving them firmly back up to her waist. After a moment Mutt's head came up and she saw that his eyes were on fire, burning with desire and something that it took her a moment to identify as a sullen kind of despair.

The look stilled something in her. She cupped his face in her hands, her thumbs stroking his jawline in concern. He tried to pull away, to hide his face in the darkness of the room. When she said his name he snapped at her, his eyes meeting hers in defiance and anger. With a sudden lunge he tried to kiss her again, but she braced her elbows against the door and flattened her palms against his chest, holding him back.

"We can't," she said simply.

"You mean *you* can't," said Mutt, his voice roughened with arousal. He pulled away from her slightly and looked her right in the eye. Kayla shook her head and gave him a look of such pity that Mutt drew back.

He stared at her intently, his face a broken jig-saw puzzle of highlight and shadow in the moonlight. "What?" he asked, the sound more like a growl than a word.

Kayla turned her head away to hide the desire in her eyes. "This can't happen. I'm sorry."

"What, you think I need your permission?" Mutt asked, in a low, cold voice.

Kayla stood up straight, moving away from the bathroom door. She reached out to lightly touch Mutt's face. "You tell me."

Mutt's body tensed and Kayla braced herself, but he merely nodded slightly to himself. He cleared his throat and looked her over with something very much like regret. "You know, Karrel always told me such great things about you. I was beginning to wonder if any of them were true."

"What?" Kayla stared. She felt like she'd just been slapped. "Hey, I didn't *mean* for this to—"

"Yeah, sure. You didn't *mean* for it to happen." Mutt lowered his gaze, but he didn't move away. "I didn't mean to get mixed up with your crazy boyfriend. I didn't mean to let my girl get herself killed. My whole stinkin' life is made up of things I didn't mean to do, same as everybody else, but shit happens, girlie. You just gotta pick yourself up and get over it, because this is your life, right here, right now. It doesn't always get any better. Things fall apart and people you love die on you and it hurts like fuck, so why even bother about what's right and what's wrong? And so here we are." He tossed his head slightly, his jaw tighten-ing. "Or rather, there we were."

"Look, I said I'm sor—"

"Forget it. My bad." Mutt laughed suddenly, although there was no humor whatsoever in his face. He eyed her ruefully, shaking his head. "I guess I just mistook you for someone who cared."

"What? I don't even know you!" Kayla cried, exasperated.

"Exactly," Mutt said, as though that explained everything. He gave her a black look and drew a deep breath, folding his arms. "There's a spare blanket next door on the back of the chair. I suggest you use it. It gets real cold on the sofa at night."

He met Kayla's gaze steadily, a steely glint in his eye.

Kayla stared back at him, shocked at his sudden rejection. She felt her eyes flooding with hot tears and turned away, trembling, confused, sick with guilt. She'd screwed up, somehow. She'd hurt him, and she'd lost something. She wasn't quite sure what, but its loss made her feel colder and emptier inside than ever before.

She stepped quickly around him, refusing to meet his eyes, and walked unwillingly to the door. She put her hand on the handle and paused, her mind racing, wishing that she could say something, do something to make things all right again...

Mutt lunged forward, grabbed her, and slammed her back against the door. Kayla drew a breath to cry out and Mutt kissed her, hard, brutally, desperately. He pressed himself against her, crushing her, the heat of his body almost suffocating. She tried to pull free but he held her tight, the look on his face making a mockery of his words as he gasped into her mouth, his hands sliding roughly down her body.

With a cry, Kayla wrenched free and shoved him away from her. To her immense surprise Mutt flew backward as though hit by a pile driver, smashing into the rickety bed, knocking it off the concrete breeze blocks that propped it up, and sending it tumbling to the floor. Mutt hit the ground and rolled over, groaning softly and clutching his ribs. He turned his head to stare up at Kayla, his dazed expression registering shock and bewilderment.

Kayla gaped at him, then looked down at her hands as if she had never seen them before, her whole body shaking. She looked at the floored Mutt, the smashed bed. Her mouth fell open, but no words came out.

In a daze, she whirled and ran out of the room, down the stairs and on through the living room. She slammed her way out into the crisp, cold air outside the tenement building, then wrenched open the door of the Hunters' SBV. She jumped inside, starting the engine on her third attempt. The lights flashed on and the powerful engine growled as she hit the gas and peeled out of the driveway in a cloud of blue smoke, leaving Mutt's place far behind her.

THIRTY MINUTES LATER she pulled up outside her house. She backed the huge Hunter vehicle into an empty space in her apartment block's underground garage. Another five minutes and she was back in her bedroom, curled up in bed, her door locked and a chair shoved underneath the handle, overwhelmingly glad to be home.

She had never been so relieved to lie down in her life.

Kayla drew a deep breath as she lay trembling in bed, her mind flitting back and forth like a trapped insect as she calmed down. Karrel's face loomed in her dimming vision, and Kayla's throat tightened as she realized how close she had come to betraying him. Grief made people do crazy things, but thinking about what she had done, or rather nearly done, made her sick and cold with disgust.

Reaching beneath her pillow, her hand closed on the cold steel shape of the Smith & Wesson handgun that lay beneath it. It had been Karrel's; he'd insisted she keep it for home defense. Right now, she was just glad to have it near her.

Gradually, her hammering heart slowed down. The pull of sleep grew stronger, until it was impossible to resist. Kayla's eyes slid closed, blinked open, and then finally shut as she fell into a deep, black sleep.

CHAPTER EIGHTEEN

"SO... WHAT WOULD you do if you knew you'd never get caught?"

Skyler pressed himself against the wall of the plush shower room of Cyan's luxurious hotel suite, his teeth chattering, the cool spray drenching his Armani silk shirt and running out over the over-flowing sill of the stall. He'd only been under the shower for two minutes and already he was shaking, and not only from the cold. How many pints of blood could you lose before you actually passed out? Skyler blinked hard, trying to focus. His grasp of human biology was fuzzy at the best of times, but right now, with a purring female vamp nuzzling against his throat, he quite frankly didn't give a rat's ass.

"Christ, I dunno," he muttered. "This, probably."

"Only probably?"

Skyler gave a shaky laugh and ran a trembling hand through his soaked hair, tightening his grip on

Cyan as she slid her slick, naked body against his in a maddening rhythm. His shirt was open, shredded. A dozen nicks and cuts marred the pale skin of his muscled torso, tiny dribbles of blood washing out and turning pink under the spray. His thousand-dollar outfit had been ruined the moment Cyan had dragged him into the shower, but at the moment he didn't give a damn. All of his attention was focused in on the beautiful vampire moving against him. The cuts stung, sensitizing the skin all over his body with a pins-and-needles wash of sensation, but that wasn't all bad.

Nothing was bad, where Cyan was concerned.

He gasped as a sudden warmth enveloped his nipple. Cyan's delicate sharp teeth pulled on his sensitive flesh, and caused a wave of goosebumps to flash across the surface of his wet skin. A groan escaped his throat and he closed his eyes and tipped his head back, resting it against the cold white tile of the wall. Cyan chuckled low in her throat as her mouth plundered his body, moving across his chest, lapping at the wounds she'd created just long enough to make him squirm before moving on. He turned to face the wall and shivered under the pressure of a line of kisses and small, shallow bites that raced up his spine. His knees buckled slightly and he braced his hands against the wet tiles to stop himself from falling.

Cyan lifted her head, blood glistening on her pale lips as she turned him back with a deft movement. She gazed thoughtfully at him, notic-ing the faraway look on his face.

"You're not still freaking about Magnus, are you?"

Skyler shook his head absently, too breathless to speak.

"He's out of my life," Cyan reassured him. "Done and dusted."

"That's what you said last time," said Skyler. As he opened his mouth to continue Cyan pressed a cool finger against his lips.

"So now you've got me... tell me what you want from me."

A rush of dark, treacherous thoughts danced through Skyler's mind, swamping all thoughts of Magnus. Black lust swept through his veins. Could vampires really read minds? Christ, he hoped not. He would rather die then tell Cyan what he really wanted from her, even though part of him was sure that she already knew. There was something about the way she looked at him, the way she held his gaze just a split second too long, the twitch of her lips as she coolly looked him up and down before turning away, utterly dismissing him in a way that was as maddening as it was erotic.

Oh yeah. She knew all right.

Fuck.

Skyler's heart gave a quick thump as a freezing spike of fear and lust ran through him, blending with the ice in his veins to create a sickly cocktail of biochemical guilt. What the hell was he doing? Here he was, the supposedly great leader of the Hunters, doing incredibly wrong things with one of their most dangerous enemies. What he was doing was so wrong, so risky, and above all so unbe-fucking-lievably stupid, that he may as well just kill himself right now and be done with it. The penalty for fraternizing with the enemy was secret court martial followed by instant dismissal, but for fraternizing with an enemy like Cyan? Skyler shivered. He already knew what the official records would say, although anyone wanting to verify his post mortem report would spend a long time looking for his body.

"Well?"

It took Skyler several attempts to speak, and when he did, his voice came out as a dry whisper.

"You. I just want you."

"Coward. That's the easy answer, and quit thinking. I can hear the cogs grinding from a mile away."

That made Skyler smile. He gazed down at Cyan, watching the fine spray of water bead on the smooth curve of her softly muscled back, fighting a growing feeling of unreality that he knew was only partially to do with the blood loss. He'd needed her so badly, for so long, that to finally have her was so surreal that he could barely believe it was happening. A hundred nights spent lying alone in bed in his Hunter's quarters, gasping her name at the ceiling, had only given him fuel for an increasingly destructive fire that threatened not only him, but everybody around him.

Trying to shut off his endlessly whirring mind, Skyler reached out and ran his shaking hands over Cyan's small, firm breasts, cupping them and squeezing gently before moving on to reverently stroke her wickedly flat belly. He trailed his fingernails over the bone china perfection of her lightly muscled ribs, marveling at how something so delicate could be so deadly. She was too damn perfect, every inch of her an outright denial of the existence of God. After all, what creator would make something so beautiful, so exquisite, and then let his masterpiece be perverted in such a terrible way?

No, Cyan was proof of the existence of something else, something Skyler didn't want to think about.

"So what about you?" he asked, trying to distract himself from his guilt, catching his breath as Cyan slipped a hand down his body and started unbuttoning his jeans. "What would you... do if you knew there'd be no comeback?"

"Now, *that* would be telling," Cyan murmured, slipping down his body with a wink. She licked her lips and stared up hungrily at him, her violet eyes betraying what her mouth was about to do. Skyler gulped. Common wisdom said that being on your knees was supposed to be a submissive position. With Cyan, it was anything but.

Damn, but he loved that.

He watched with bated breath as the vampiress tilted her head and nosed inside his open fly, running her closed lips down his hard length still encased in the black silk of his boxers. She pulled back with a grin as Skyler tried to press himself against her. The small noise of disappointment died in his throat as Cyan opened her mouth and gently gripped him through his boxers with her teeth, her lips wrapped around them to shield him from their sharp points. She squeezed so delicately that all he felt was a sensation of pressure, moving upwards in frustratingly brief pulses of warmth.

Skyler gripped the back of her head, desperate for more sensation. He froze as Cyan growled softly in warning under her breath, squeezing down with just enough pressure to make him gasp. The message was quite plain—if he wanted her, he'd have to wait.

He buzzed with frustration, every muscle in his body tensing as she ran her fingers briefly down his length.

She released him and eased his jeans down his muscular legs, trailing a line of cool kisses behind them. His belt buckle hit the floor with a clink, and he kicked his clothing away. Skyler moved toward her, but Cyan once again held him back. She rose to her feet and shoved him back against the shower wall. She seized his mouth in a punishing kiss.

Her mouth was warm, filled with the rich flavors of red wine and the faint, sharp taste of blood. Skyler deepened the kiss with a groan, and wound his arms tighter around her neck as he pulled her ever closer, his patience running out as he ground his hips against her aggressively. Cyan gave a purr of contentment and rocked her pelvis against his, matching his pace. She raked her nails through his hair before breaking their kiss to trail her tongue down his jugular, kissing and licking the soft spot just beneath the angle of his jaw. Skyler gasped, his spine trying to crawl out of his shirt. A familiar ache spread suddenly, and he bit down hard on his lower lip to keep himself from crying out.

"Cyan... Please..."

"Shhh, baby."

Cyan held him still by both hips, grinding herself against him playfully until his grip on her shoulders drew blood and his knees started to buckle. With an impish grin, she reached down and squeezed him, laughing as he bucked against her, sucking in a harsh breath through his teeth. The sensation almost made him lose it. Skyler swallowed hard, starting to move with increased urgently against her. Cold water from the shower beat down around them, providing an icy contrast to the molten heat in his groin. He was surprised he couldn't hear steam sizzle.

He stopped breathing when Cyan finally tired of her game and ripped his boxers down. She guided him inside her in a sudden lunge that made him cry out.

Hot and cold waves flooded through him as she circled her hips slowly, sending a pulse of sensation through him so strong that he almost blacked out.

Gasping, he grabbed her slender waist, spun them around and shoved her up against the wall, thrusting himself so deeply inside her that her growl of protest turned to one of pleasure. He felt her fingernails rake his back as she kissed him furiously, her tongue a ruthless lash inside his mouth. He braced himself on the faucet and pounded into her, feeling hands strong enough to tear him apart grabbing desperately at his hair, his skin. Her body arched against his as she locked a leg around his waist, tightening her slick grip on him, making him shudder and bow his head against her body. He bit down on her shoulder as he fought for control.

Cyan chuckled against his throat, her teeth scraping over his skin before a well-placed nip on the side of his neck made him jerk against her and raise his head, gazing pleadingly into her eyes. She shook her head with a grin and grabbed his hair, enjoying the game. She continued to jerk her hips against his and he moaned in frustration, gripping the thigh clamped around his waist and roughly yanking her leg higher.

It was too much, and still not enough.

Skyler gritted his teeth. Cyan was so damned hot, wet and ready, and the adrenaline pounding in his veins told him that he had about ten seconds before he lost it completely.

In a panic he grabbed her and tried to pull out, but with a quick, balletic movement Cyan ducked around him and gave a quick heave. She caught him in her strong, lithe arms as he fell.

The next thing he knew he was lying sprawled on the shower room floor with Cyan straddling him, somehow still inside her, the impish look on her face as she pinned him to the floor almost undoing him.

The pleasure swelled to almost unbearable levels as she expertly thrust her hips over him, squeezing her slick internal muscles on the down stroke and forcing a groan up from deep inside him.

Skyler gasped and moaned and writhed under her. He fought against his looming orgasm, but was powerless to stop its approach. Fuck, it was too soon! She increased the pace and the friction, deepening her thrusts until he couldn't stand it anymore.

Skyler swore as he felt his muscles tense, preparing for the inevitable.

It was no good. He couldn't hold out any longer.

He was going to—

In the split second before his body erupted, Cyan's head flashed down with the speed of a striking cobra and she slid her razor-sharp fangs deep into his throat, sending a shocking bolt of white-hot pleasure shooting through him. As she deepened the bite he cried out soundlessly, his body jerking convulsively as wave after wave of ecstasy ripped through him, washing through his veins in a flash-flood of searing liquid heat that shot from the wound in his jugular to his groin.

He was barely aware of Cyan's lips working against his throat, draining the blood from him in long, languid pulls that dragged further convulsions from his aching body, the pleasure lasting longer than he'd ever thought was possible. His vision went gray, then black as fireworks went off in his head and buzzed across the surface of his skin. He gasped at the incredible sensation of a thousand mouths moving relentlessly against every nerve ending in his body. Then he felt Cyan tear her mouth from his throat as her own body seized him. He reached blindly for her even as she bucked and gasped, before finally falling limp and panting on top of him.

Skyler drew her shakily to his chest, his eyes staring sightlessly at nothing.

An eon passed, maybe two.

He felt Cyan stir, lifting her head from his chest. Too spent to move, Skyler rolled his head over to face her and gazed up at her numbly, his eyelids heavy with exhaustion.

"I hate you," he whispered.

Cyan smiled faintly as she took his hand and pressed it against her bloodied lips.

"That's what you said last time," she said.

CHAPTER NINETEEN

As THE MOON rose, Magnus brooded alone out on the patio deck on the rooftop of the club. The air was chill but he liked it that way. His thick leather and fur jacket kept him more than warm enough. Nobody dared disturb him when he came out here. They were fearful of his wrath. Even the burly guard who protected the door to the rooftop had slunk away upon sensing his master's mood.

The deck was bordered by a low wall draped with imported honeysuckle, its heady perfume hanging heavily on the night air. Magnus wandered across to it and sat down heavily, placing his shot glass of absinthe down on the wall beside him. He clasped his hands and gazed down ruminatively at the bright lights of the city below him, spread out from plain to plain and interspersed with the liquid channels of moving red and white lights of the city's freeways. Down below him he could hear a thousand voices beneath the ever-present rumble of traffic, as late night clubbers and shoppers and tourists went about their petty, small-minded business, but they were unimportant to him. They all were.

Magnus took a sip of his absinthe, rolling the flavor around his tongue. It burned with a rich, dark piquancy but it was a poor substitute for blood and flesh, the flavor that had come to haunt his dreams with ever-increasing frequency in the past few months. In another life he knew he would have been a great ruler, a king of kings. In this one he seemed to be stuck lording over a rapidly dwindling race of brutes and idiots who needed water wings to compete in the gene pool. They spent their time fighting and whoring with never a thought as to where their once-great race was heading.

All that was about to change.

Magnus shifted on the wall, reaching up to rub at the ugly lateral scar that ran the length of his throat. The scar represented the werewolf medic's best attempts to clear the thick deposits of tar that had built up on the inside of his trachea after a lifetime of smoking fifty cigarettes a day. When he'd first been turned he'd thought he was immortal. Despite assurances to the contrary, he'd gone on a self-destructive binge that lasted for the next two decades, buoyed up by the feeling of power and invulnerability the werewolf gene had given him.

Finding out that he had cancer had brought him back down to earth with a nasty bump. Unlike vampires, werewolves were not immortal and, despite their superior powers of healing, they could still fall prey to most common human diseases. After being told that his cancer was incurable, Magnus had turned his attentions to the next best thing—cracking the complex vampire gene. He had picked up the gauntlet that every generation of werewolves since time began had at the very least had a shot at. Thousands of years ago werewolves would eat still-beating vampire hearts and bathe in their blood in the hope that they too would become immortal. Now, in the age of gene therapy and DNA sequencing, the werewolves finally stood a chance of taking what they felt was theirs by right. The vampires' immortality.

Magnus picked up his glass and knocked back the rest of the shot, wincing as the absinthe burned his throat on the way down, but the physical pain helped drive the mental pain out, and for a moment he felt soothed.

He set the shot glass down beside him on the wall, hoping that the pain in his lungs would be masked by the alcohol. Last week he'd been told he had maybe three months to live, if that. Overnight his world had come crashing apart, giving his mission to crack the vampire gene a new and very personal urgency. Magnus gritted his teeth, gazing down at his clasped, trembling hands. He'd worked so damned hard to get where he was, wrestling control from the accursed vampires street by street over the course of the last couple of decades. He owned this damned town. Or rather, he owned the bits of it that mattered—the underground drug factories and club networks that had between them supplied him with enough cash and contacts to start up Genetica. The vamps might still own the cops, paying their office guys to doctor paperwork and cover up vampire-related murders, but that wouldn't be the case for very much longer. Harlequin was out of the picture now. If his plan succeeded, they would have enough money to buy the cops back from the vampires. It would be plain sailing from then on.

If Cyan's little team of meat head freaks screwed things up **for** him before the lab came through with its results, he'd personally devote the rest of his life—short though it may be—to inventing five new and entirely insidious ways to die.

Speaking of which...

Taking a deep, painful breath, Magnus counted to ten.

"Are you going to stand there all night, or are you going to come out here and fuck me?"

A small noise sounded in the cool of the night, a muted sound of female amusement. Then a slender figure stepped silently from the shadows and stood before him, wiping her hands on her black velvet dress. Immaculately dressed and groomed as she was, she could have been on her way back from an Oscar party.

The broken body of the guard on the ground behind her suggested otherwise.

"And they say romance is dead," Cyan said, delicately licking the last of the blood from her fingertips.

Magnus gave the vampiress a long, appraising look, and then deliberately turned his back on her. A great weight of tiredness pressed upon him. "Romance never came into it," he said, gazing down at the lights of Hollywood beneath them. "As you've always said, we're just animals. Don't try to pretend there's any more to it than that." He waved a hand half-heartedly. "Strip. Let's get this over with."

Cyan stepped up behind him, her heady perfume washing over him like a warm caress. "*You* might be an animal, Magnus old boy, but I'm something more than that, something better." She paused, cocking her head in mischief. "You of all people should know that."

Magnus nodded faintly, his face expressionless. Beneath his hand, the plaster of the ledge crumbled as he tightened his grip on it. "You're right. You *are* something more. An animal could never be truly monstrous."

"It takes one to know one," murmured Cyan.

Magnus's meager temper gave out. He spun around, his words cracking across her like an angry whip. "What do you want from me?"

Cyan stepped back, a flash of amusement momentarily sparking across her face before being absorbed into its smooth china perfection. Werewolves never were much good at controlling their emotions, and it never ceased to entertain her how easily she could rile them, Magnus in particular. She had only slept with him a couple times in their brief courtship—if you could call it that—but she knew that she had awakened in him a craving that he could never satisfy with a werewolf or human lover.

She had him right where she wanted him, and she knew that he hated her for it.

She ran her finger teasingly across the pommel of her sword, her voice light. "You know what I want."

"I'm not asking you what," Magnus spat. "I'm asking you why."

"Why do I want you?" Cyan tipped her head forward so that her ebony hair spilled over one eye. She gazed up coquettishly through the living curtain. "Why do you think?"

Magnus got up slowly and stalked toward her, desire and anger mingling inside him in a deadly cocktail. "You tell me. Why sleep with a mere animal like me when you could have any man you desired?" He stopped in front of her and traced her jaw lightly with the crooked knuckle of a gloved forefinger. "Or any vampire?"

Cyan froze for the briefest of instants, and Magnus was gratified to see the look of hurt that flashed deep in her beautiful eyes. With an effort she managed to contain it, locking down on it with an iron control born of years of practice. Magnus could never tell how much of Cyan's personality was an act, the camouflage of a predator, but he knew that for once what he'd seen in her eyes was real, much as she despised him for knowing it.

She tilted her head and looked up at him, her tone light but her voice as steely as the Katar sword in her hand. "That was uncalled for."

"No." Magnus dropped his hand from her face and stepped back, looking her up and down with undisguised contempt. "It was perfectly called for."

He felt a secret sense of triumph as she instinctively backed off. He knew how much vampires hated werewolves, and he could only guess at what Cyan had gone through in order to be in any way intimate with him.

He cleared his throat, reaching out to brush her long hair back off her face. "I'll cut to the chase, kitten. If you think you can get back at Harlequin by fooling around with me, you're as crazy as he is. He doesn't care that you exist. Why should he give a damn about who you're screwing?" Magnus's eyes lit up with unholy mirth, and he smiled for the first time that evening. "You're a joke, Cyan, a living freakshow. Your own kind won't accept you, and we sure as hell don't want you."

"My boys love me," said Cyan quietly.

"Hello, newsflash? They just wanna bang you, darlin'. That guy Harlem? He'll do anything that don't get up a tree fast enough." Magnus gave a snort of contempt. "Go back to Prague and join the circus, Cyan. At least then you'll get paid when people laugh at you."

He reached out to grab her arm, but Cyan was already moving, unsheathing her fangs in a flash and reaching for her sword quicker than he could follow. She managed to half-draw it before he blocked her move and slammed his gauntleted fist across her elbow, instantly deadening her arm and making her drop her sword. He caught her wrist on the rebound, twisting her arm around until her elbow locked, and then used all his strength to shove her down to her knees. Her stilettoed foot flew out as she hit the ground and caught him a painful blow on the ankle. He ignored the pain and grabbed her other hand as she went for her sword again, bringing both her wrists together in a cross and holding her pinned as he reached down to fumble with his fly.

CHINK!

Magnus gasped in pain as a foot-long serrated bone spur shot out of Cyan's wrist and impaled him through the arm. He felt it grate between the two bones of his forearm and fought the urge to jerk himself free. Instead, he clenched his fist and turned his wrist ninety degrees to lock the bones of his arm down on the spur, trapping her. His free hand flashed out and plucked the sword from her belt, flinging it across the rooftop and out of reach. He bent over and crushed his lips to Cyan's, kissing her deeply and ignoring the pain as her half-inch incisors nicked his tongue. He ripped his arm free and shoved her as hard as he could toward the edge of the rooftop.

Cyan hit the patio deck heavily, crashing through the low wall that rimmed the deck and throwing her arms out to stop herself from tumbling off the edge. Her head snapped up and she watched Magnus prowl warily toward her, blood running freely down his arm. She enjoyed the spectacle. She shook her head dizzily and hissed at him, hanging partially from the roof. He smirked before lifting his foot to kick her in the face and send her plummeting to the streets below.

His foot never made contact. As his leg descended, a dozen other spikes and spurs—some bone, others titanium-plated metal—erupted from Cyan's shoulders and the joints of her ribcage. Deadly arcs of electricity snapped between them like electrified wings. With a flick of her shoulders she instinctively crossed the spurs over her face, interlocking them like an organic shield. Magnus's foot touched the uppermost spur and he yelled as a jolt of electricity went through him, throwing him backward through the air. He smashed through an elaborately painted Chinese screen, vanishing in a storm of flying wood fragments.

Cyan hauled herself back up and was on her feet in an instant, trembling and flexing the muscles in her arms and back in a vain bid to retract the spines, but they were biochemically linked to her emotions and wouldn't go back. For the thousandth time she found herself cursing Harlequin, wishing bitterly that she'd never met him, never submitted to his crazy experiments, never fallen in love with him.

No man was worth this.

As she stood seething, the sound of Magnus's laughter reached her ears.

"Ladies and gentleman, we give you Cyan X!"

Magnus rolled over and propped himself up on his elbows, slowly clapping, his eyes sparkling with mirth. Grabbing a piece of broken wood, he held it up to his mouth like a microphone. "Tell me, how does it feel to be the biggest freak in the whole of LA? I've heard that's really saying something."

"Damn you, Magnus." Cyan was shaking with rage and incipient shame. She spread her arms and bared her inch-long incisors, deliberately flaring out her spines. Blood dripped from the points where the emerging spikes had nicked her flesh on the way out of their implanted bone sheathes, and another of her thousand dollar dresses had been ripped to tatters. She knew she looked every bit the monster Magnus pronounced her to be, but she didn't give a hot damn.

"You think I asked for this?" she spat. "Bullshit. He was the one who made me—"

"Spare me the history lesson," Magnus drawled. "I've heard it all before. He made you do it, you agreed because you loved him... until you found out that he was just using you as a test subject for her—"

Cyan's foot whipped out and she kicked Magnus's elbows out from under him, knocking him flat on his back. He started laughing again, his laughter only increasing in volume as Cyan stepped up to him and rammed her stiletto heel hard into his chest.

Blood spurted and Magnus bucked slightly beneath her, staring up at her with a lascivious grin.

Cyan twisted her heel. "Remind me again why I let you live?"

"Because I'm the only one who'll still take you in."

Magnus watched with a smirk as the brilliant spark of righteousness drained from Cyan's eyes, leaving them hard and cold and dead.

He knew then that he had her.

She didn't move when he pulled her heel from his chest and sat up, nor when he reached up to take her hand and tug her down on top of him. Tangling his calloused fingers in her hair, he pulled her sharp, elfin face down to meet his, breathing in the scent of her perfume. He pressed his mouth to hers and kissed her greedily, delighting in the knowledge that she was his and his alone. He tasted the familiar tang of blood in her mouth as his hand crept triumphantly down her incredible body, toward the hem of her torn dress.

He paused as he heard the muted tap of heels on concrete. Somebody was trying to be quiet. Magnus inhaled then paused, glancing up in irritation.

"Seen all you want?" he asked the cowering Dana.

The beautiful she-wolf hesitated in the doorway, her wide-eyed gaze riveted on Cyan. Dana was stunning in her long white satin dress, but her face was ashen in the moonlight as she backed away from the scene before her. The two glasses of champagne she had been holding hit the ground with a crash, and she turned and fled through the door.

Magnus chuckled, heartily amused.

He jerked back as he felt the cold press of a blade digging into his ribs. His eyes flicked up, seeking

Cyan's, finding them alert and alive with a delicious malice.

"Correction," she purred into his ear. "I let you live because it amuses me, and because I enjoy teasing poor, dumb animals."

She twisted her body around and grasped the front of his shirt, giving him a quick peck on the cheek.

"Call me, baby," she grinned.

With that, she threw him off the rooftop.

IT WAS SIX stories to the ground, more than enough time for Cyan to retract her spines and smooth down her rumpled dress before vaulting back to her feet.

Cat-stepping to the edge of the club's roof, she watched with infinite satisfaction as Magnus dropped down the side of the building, screaming bloody murder all the way. She knew that the fall wouldn't kill him, but it would do definite damage to his pride. Revenge was always sweet, especially when it involved throwing your ex off a rooftop, but she for one didn't want to be there when he picked himself up and came looking for payback.

Speaking of payback, she had one more piece of business to take care of tonight.

She reached down to adjust the strap of one of her stiletto heels, then put her foot back down with a clunk and stepped across the deck toward her sword, whistling lightly under her breath. Retrieving it, she gave the blade a quick polish on the hem of her dress and then gave it a quick spin. The moonlight glinted off its fire-hardened edge as it whickered through the air.

She turned to go, pausing only to brush a single tear from her cheek before vanishing into the night.

CHAPTER TWENTY

Down in the hot, noisy clubroom of Wolfbayne, Skeet took a swig of beer and then thumped the bottle down on the tabletop with a hearty burp. "Screw Magnus. Ten large says I'll nail this Hunter guy's broad first."

"A wager? Interesting." Harlem's eyes gleamed as he mulled this over. "So be it. First one to bring back the body gets the cash, and let's up the ante." He glanced around the group, watching in private amusement as the werewolves around him leaned closer, hanging on his every word. "Winner takes all, and I do mean... all."

Skeet licked his lips, his drug-addled brain flaring with hope. "Cyan?"

Harlem inclined his head magnanimously. "We've been waitin' years to get a piece of that ass."

He glared daggers at the female werewolves nearby. They turned away from him with a titter and a toss of their glossy blonde heads. He curled his lip and reached for his drink. "Face it, boys, we're a laughing stock, a bunch of werewolves workin' for a stinkin' vampire. We are officially lower than scum. Hell, scum's so far above us I get a crick in my neck just lookin' up at it." He looked around at his men, from face to scarred face, and let his anger rise. "And for what?"

"For love," Skeet whispered, his voice husky.

Harlem snorted back a laugh. "Love ain't got nothin' to do with it, Fido. She's got us all under her pretty little spell, believin' that if we just does this for her, does that for her, then we'll have some kind of chance with her now that her an' Magnus are over."

He turned to Skeet. "Gimme your hand."

Skeet held out his hand, palm up. Harlem slashed it open with a flick of his claws, ignoring the younger werewolf's wince of pain. Harlem watched blood drip down onto the table, and then drew a heart in it with a long-nailed finger.

He looked up at the group with dark eyes.

"I say bullshit. We been workin' for Cyan for how long? Five years?" He leaned forward with a creak of leather, narrowing his eyes. "Face it, boys, we've been had. She's been screwin' us around for years and she ain't even..." He snorted, reaching for his drink, ignoring Jackdoor's giggle a moment later. "I dunno why we're even protecting her. Bitch is so hung up on that fuck-job vamp boss that none of us will ever get a look in."

"Hey, man, don't you mention him around me," growled Flame, his hand flying to touch the burned half of his face.

"Who? Harlequin?"

Flame slammed his drink down on the table and stood up abruptly, sending his chair flying over backward. He whipped out his fire-branded Colt and jammed it into Harlem's temple. "Dammit, man, I told you! Don't ever say that name!"

"Why?" Harlem took a sip of his beer, unconcerned. "He scare ya?"

"Fuck that," snapped Flame. "You scare me, you madman. That Harlequin guy? A thousand of you don't even come close."

"Thanks, man," said Harlem dryly, finishing up his beer. "Now how 'bout you get that peashooter outta my face before I stick it up yer ass and make you sing the YMCA? And it ain't even Tuesday yet."

"Fuck you, Jack," snapped Flame, baring his teeth. But he sat down anyway with a flounce, throwing his Colt down onto the table with a clatter.

The atmosphere in the room relaxed a little.

"Didn't he once butcher an entire city, just because he didn't like the food?" piped up Skeet.

"I heard that he made some European king eat his own foot to prove a point," added Mitzi, thoughtfully spinning his sword.

"You ain't heard nothin', you morons," snapped Harlem. "It's all publicity, their guys tryin' to scare our guys with a bunch of made up bullshit that's about as close to reality as Skeet is to ever gettin' laid. Forget him. Harlequin's outta the picture, so there's only one guy left standin' between us and Cyan."

The five werewolves looked at each other.

Unsheathing his claws, Harlem viciously scored them through the blood-heart on the table, driving his nails deep into the wood. Then he flexed his fist, popping them back.

"Right. So here's the new deal. Whichever one of you motherfuckers gets the hit first gets Cyan. We've been her lapdogs for too damn long, and I for one am sick of it."

He paused for effect. "Anyone agree?"

The other four werewolves leapt to their feet, waving their weapons and whooping as they toasted each other, ignoring the odd looks the rest of the swarming partygoers gave them.

Harlem alone remained seated, sipping his beer in smug satisfaction.

Idiots. They all thought they stood a chance. Cyan was his, of course, and it was just a matter of time before she realized it. However, this little wager was just a means to an end, and it wasn't the end he'd told the others it would be.

Sliding his hand deep into his pocket, he fingered the little silver coupon that sat there, while inside his mind, shadowy cogwheels spun. If he played his cards right, he'd get Cyan and a whole lot more besides. The shit was going to hit the fan; it was just a matter of picking which side of the fan he wanted to stand on.

Love makes fools of us all, he thought, but at least this fool had a backup plan.

CHAPTER TWENTY-ONE

THE FUNNY THING about life, Detective Jake Collins thought as he stared down at the body, was that just as you thought you'd gotten the hang of it, it jumped up and kicked you in the teeth, and then ran away giggling like some South Side wacko on speed. He rubbed a hand tiredly across his eyes and gazed gloomily around the city morgue. He gingerly lifted one corner of the bloodstained sheet that covered the body. He lowered the sheet again and patted it back into place, glancing almost guiltily around him. He turned toward the main door, his face setting into an expression of steely resignation.

"Please tell me we got him," he said.

Ned looked up from his report book and shook his head. "Our little birdie flew the coop. We're still trying to work out how."

Jake swore, lighting his fifth cigarette of the hour. "Did we get surveillance footage? We need to get a positive ID on this guy ASAP."

"Tapes on that street weren't rolling, some kind of power glitch." Ned shrugged, reaching up to scratch at the still-healing "H" tattoo on his arm. "We got a homeless guy in the office says he saw some big guy in a suit throw the body in the dumpster. Said the dude had weird eyes, like a demon or something."

"Demons. Great." Jake glanced down at his watch. "And it's not even six o'clock yet."

He blew a puff of blue smoke up at the ceiling and watched it drift slowly heavenward. As if it wasn't enough to have some deranged serial killer running around the city ripping people's throats out, now he had to deal with some guy cutting open beautiful women's veins, bleeding them dry, and then dumping their bodies in the trash. The whole force was spooked, and so was he. Just the thought of what was under that sheet made him feel queasy.

"Sir?"

"Hmmm?" Jake looked up. Ned stood in front of him, looking uncomfortable. Jake rolled his eyes, praying to a God he wasn't sure he believed in anymore for strength. "Yes? Out with it, man."

"I... well, I had a quick peek." Ned swallowed, a sick look on his young, thoughtful face. "What's up with her, sir?"

"I don't know, Ned, but I wish I did."

Ned remained silent a moment, turning his cap over and over in his hands. "So, this is like the third sign of the apocalypse, right? Scaly lizard-women turning up dead in dumpsters?" He gave a nervous smile. "What can we expect next, flaming toads falling from the sky?"

Jake shook his head firmly. "Ned, I'm a man of science. There are only three ways this world's

going to come to an end: fire, ice, or paperwork."
He sighed, staring down at the covered body.
"Where this case is concerned, option three's look-
ing more and more likely."

He hesitated, and then reached into his desk
drawer and handed Ned a police-issue pistol.
"Better take this out with you tonight."

"You sure?" Ned fingered the gun, an odd look
on his face.

"Sure, and don't look so nervous. Just remember.,
guns don't kill people, people kill people." Jake
sighed. "Unless you're on my watch, and then monsters kill people. Then I have to clean up afterward
and figure out what to tell the press."

"Sir, look, about the monsters…"

Jake got to his feet, scraping everything on the
morgue desk into a big cardboard file. "Don't even
go there. You won't believe me. My own department doesn't believe me. Some days even *I* don't
believe me, but the bodies keep showing up, and
someone, for some reason, keeps giving me money
to look into it. In this department, when that happens, you don't ask questions. I just bought a two
bedroom condo in Burbank, Ned. Don't mess that
up for me."

"But—"

"Enough." Jake set his mouth in a determined
line. "I want unmarked cars sent out to patrol the
area, one on each street for a six block radius
around where they found the body. Maybe someone saw something, heard something, whatever."

Ned saluted sharply.

Jake nodded, setting his mouth into a hard line. It
was all about the attitude, wasn't it? No matter
how freaked you were, no matter how foxed you

were, give people orders in a firm, authoritative voice, and they'd jump to do whatever you said, even if what you just said was a steaming crock of old horseshit. Better to give them something to do and let them put all their energy into doing that than waste it worrying about the actual matter at hand.

Hell, that was his job.

"So what do we tell the press?"

Assorted unworthy answers spilled out of Jake's brain and threatened to pour out of his mouth. He closed it with a snap and shook his head instead. "We don't tell them dick. This is the third female cadaver we've retrieved from that area this month. If word gets around that there's some sicko on the loose hacking women up and sticking their bodies in the locals' trash, it could be bad."

"It's already bad."

Jake looked up with a start as Sheriff Garcia strode into the room, two med lab boys scurrying at his side. The lab boys looked nervous, and Jake groaned inwardly. Those guys saw pretty much everything that went through the morgue, stuff that would turn the stomach of even the toughest of beat cops.

For them to be looking nervous did not bode well.

Sheriff Garcia stopped in front of Jake, a strange look on his strong, deeply tanned face. "Detective? I have someone next door I think you should see."

"Another wino?" Jake clasped his hands together, miming delight. "You shouldn't have, sir. You know I'm trying to collect the set."

"Don't get smart, Collins. It's something better: a woman."

"Already got one, thanks, although not for much longer if I keep up these late nights." Jake went to light another cigarette, and then noticed the still-smoldering one in his hand.

Sheriff Garcia waved away the smoke and scanned the morgue with deep suspicion. "Do we have a name for the casualty?"

"Loki Everton," said Jake, "thirty-one. She was a hot-shot model a couple years back, made the cover of *Vogue*, everything. Her people dropped her when she turned thirty. Next thing we know she turns up dead in a dumpster. The press is going to love this one."

He reached into his pocket for a pack of aspirin, popped two, and washed them down with a swig of cold coffee. He made a face.

"Yeah, well, we got one very pissed beauty therapist upstairs. Claims she knows the guy who did it."

Jake sucked in a breath so quickly he managed to inhale part of his half-swallowed aspirin. He bent double, coughing, waving Ned away as he tried to slap him on the back. "You're kidding."

"I'm serious. She says our Loki woman had been going to this guy for some kind of special beauty treatment. Said she had some kind of reaction to the stuff and tried to sue the guy." Garcia snapped his report book shut. "Coincidence?"

Jake swallowed the rest of his aspirin and straightened up, his eyes streaming. "Ned, I want that woman brought to the station right away for questioning. If she has any questions, tell her I'll deal with them after debriefing. In the meantime…"

He coughed loudly to clear his throat, then waved Sheriff Garcia over to the covered gurney, waiting until Ned had left the room before reaching down to take hold of the bloody sheet.

The Sheriff raised his eyebrows in a silent question as Jake started to pull it back. "Is that really necessary?"

Jake shrugged. "You tell me."

A moment later, Sheriff Garcia stirred. "Well," he said, "that's one I've never seen before."

UPSTAIRS, NED WALKED into the waiting room, a windowless office containing a ramshackle collection of wooden chairs, and closed the door behind him. He held out his hand to the beauty therapist. His heart sped up a little at the sight of the lithe, ravishing beauty sitting perched on the corner of the desk, her silky-smooth legs crossed demurely before her. He realized with a surge of shame that he was eyeing up the friend of a murder victim, and glanced down quickly at the collection of official release forms on his morgue clipboard.

"Sorry to keep you waiting, ma'am."

Dana smiled indulgently, surreptitiously rearranging her legs so that her short skirt rode up a little higher. "No trouble at all, officer," she purred.

CHAPTER TWENTY-TWO

THE NEXT DAY dawned, bright and treacherously sunny.

Kayla shivered as she gazed numbly down at the order she was unpacking in the back room of the store. More perfume. Great.

Twenty-three boxes of Addiction stared up at her, their cases gleaming in the yellow glare of the storeroom's strip lights. She reached for her craft knife to cut the tape on the next box and then glanced down at her watch, yawning.

She'd been at work almost an hour now, and already it felt like forever. The man she loved was dead. All she wanted to do was go home, curl up on the sofa, and just sleep the rest of her life away, only there was a fat chance of that happening until she'd paid her rent for this month. Mr. Holt had told her to take the rest of the week off, but even a cursory glance through the giant stack of bills that had arrived on her doorstep this morning had quashed that idea.

So here she was, bruised, broken, and numb, with seven-point-two-five hours left on the clock before she could get the hell out of this pathetic excuse for a job and go home to get some rest. Joy. Even on a good day the eight-hour stint on the perfume counter drove her crazy, but today she could actually hear the tiny sounds of her sanity tearing.

Muttering to herself, Kayla stabbed the knife into the top of the box and quickly slit the main tape seal. She dropped the knife and ripped the rest of it open by hand to vent some of her frustration. Pieces of cardboard fluff showered the floor.

"Poor box, what did it ever do to you?"

Kayla turned to Wylie, giving him a sardonic look. Her young goth friend sat sprawled on the supervisor's chair opposite her, boots up on the desk, absentmindedly picking his teeth with her Social Security card.

"Don't you have somewhere you need to be?" she asked him tiredly.

"Nope. I'm not needed at the bar till seven-thirty. Until then, I'm all yours, baby." Wylie watched with consternation as Kayla violently ripped the cardboard flaps off the side of the box, muttering under her breath. "Honestly, Kayla, enough. I think you've killed it."

Kayla emptied out the box, and then flattened it on the floor with a satisfying stomp of her heel. "It deserved to die. It had fulfilled its purpose."

"Fine, it can go to box heaven, then."

"Boxes don't go to heaven," said Kayla, "and we're not having this conversation."

"Sure they do, along with all the lost pens and scissors and broken staple-guns. You know it makes sense."

"So there's a box hell?" asked Kayla, drawn into the argument despite her better judgment. Since Wylie had lost his day job two months ago, these little conversations had come to make up a good portion of her day, much to the annoyance of her supervisor. Wylie seemed to relish the new-found opportunity to come and bug her at work, although Kayla knew that the fact she worked two counters over from the lingerie department probably had something to do with it too.

"Of course," said Wylie, examining a staple remover with interest before pocketing it. "It's where all the boxes go that get thrown out before they've fulfilled their purpose—flat-pack boxes that get bought and then never made up, gift packaging that never gets used, mailing boxes that languish in the attic for years before someone finds them and burns them, not knowing that by doing so they're condemning them to eternal damnation."

"You worry me sometimes."

"I worry myself."

"So," Kayla said lowering her knife for a second, "going by your little hypothesis, anything that doesn't fulfill its purpose goes straight to hell?" She frowned. "That doesn't sound right. What about puppies?"

"What about puppies?"

"The whole point of a puppy is for it to grow up to be a dog. So if a puppy dies before it becomes a dog, it goes to hell?"

"Of course not. It's been a baby dog, if only for a short while. It's fulfilled its purpose. Plus its parents have loved it, which means it'll go to heaven, and oh my God, I can't believe you've got me talking about dead puppies. Can we talk about something else?"

"So being loved gets you into heaven?" Kayla thought for a moment before spotting the flaw in the argument. "What about Hitler? I'm sure Eva Braun loved him. You mean to say that God was all like, 'Ooh, Hitler was loved! Clean slate, come bounce around on clouds with me?' I'm sure it doesn't work like that."

"Yeah, that's the thing I keep coming back to," said Wylie, settling back down in his chair. "Religion doesn't have all the answers, but I do know that whatever we believe, each and every one of our lives has a purpose, even if we don't find it out until the end, and only by fulfilling that purpose can we truly find peace."

Kayla put down her blade and gave her friend a long, hard look. There was no way he could know anything about Karrel, but still... she had to be sure.

"Wylie..." she started. "You ever see... anything weird, after someone you loved died?"

"Sure," said Wylie matter-of-factly. "My buddy Niko died five years back. Threw himself out the window of a derelict tenement building up in Santa Ana. Splattered himself across half the neighborhood. Not very clever. Cops arrived at ten-thirty in the morning and some rabid dog was eating him. Made the news and everything."

"You never told me that."

"Didn't see the point."

Wylie paused, gazing at Kayla thoughtfully. "Funny thing was, after that, I kept getting these... not exactly visions, more like little hallucinations. I'd dream about him real vividly, almost as if he was here in the room. Kept thinking I saw him out of the corner of my eye, sitting at his table at the diner, eyeing up all the hot waitresses. As soon as I looked properly then there was nothing there, but still... makes you think."

Kayla nodded uneasily.

"I mean," Wylie went on, scratching his head, "I don't believe in ghosts and stuff, but I do believe that something happens to you when you die. It's got to, right? Else why bother? Why have a life in the first place?"

Kayla reached down and lifted up another box, sawing distractedly at the tape binding with her Stanley knife. She took a deep breath, her thoughts racing in her head. "Can I tell you something weird?"

"Always."

Kayla hesitated, and then shifted her gaze down to the floor. "Yesterday... I kind of saw Karrel."

"What, you mean they let you see the body?"

"No. I mean *I saw Karrel*," said Kayla, agitated. She put down her knife. "I actually saw him, right in front of me. Clear as day, like you said. He talked to me. Told me stuff."

"Uh, Kayla..."

"I know! I know how it sounds. Crazy, huh? But this was real. He was right there, talking to me, like we're talking now."

"Like a ghost, you mean?"

"A ghost, a spirit, a specter, whatever." Kayla pushed her hair out of her face distractedly. "He told me he was murdered, and that nine people were responsible. He told me their names and every-thing!"

"Nine people? What, like one for every level of hell or something?"

Kayla blanched. "Don't even say things like that!"

"No, I'm fine." Kayla got to her feet, shaking her finger. "We've got a first aid box in the storeroom."

"Want me get it for you?"

"It's fine, really." Kayla forced a smile.

Wylie nodded, his hand lingering on her arm, his expression wistful as he gazed at her. Kayla pretended not to notice him floundering. She gently pulled her arm away to reach up and playfully ruffle his hair.

"Hold the fort. I'll be back in a sec'."

Turning, she strode toward the door at the end of the long, cluttered room. Pulling the key out, she unlocked the door and stepped inside the storeroom, clicking on the light as she did so.

Ninette and Phil were sitting calmly on the stack of boxes in the middle of the storeroom. They were dressed in full battle armor, which was spattered with what looked suspiciously like dried blood. Ninette had a stripped-down M16 machine gun laid across her lap like a toy, and Phil had a blood-soaked bandana tied around his muscled forearm. Behind them, air hissed from the ripped-out ventilation grill in the wall. The pair of them looked as if they had just been run over by a truck.

Phil gave her a little wave.

"'Scuse me, miss," he said with a grin, "could we have our car back, please?"

CHAPTER TWENTY-THREE

KAYLA PULLED THE door of the storeroom shut behind her and twisted the lock, then turned to face her two unexpected visitors.

"What the hell are you doing here?" she hissed.

"I told you," said Phil. "We need our wheels back. Plus, we're out of that stuff you put on your hair to make it not do this."

He pointed at his windswept locks and made a face.

"Hair gel?" hazarded Kayla.

"That's the stuff," Phil said, beaming.

Kayla rolled her eyes in disbelief. "Aren't you two supposed to be out hunting werewolves?"

"That's what we're doing right now," said Ninette, fiddling with the bolt on her machine gun. A radio crackled at her side and she quickly switched it off, looking guilty.

"You get a lot of werewolves in storerooms?"

"You'd be surprised."

"Look," said Kayla, with as much patience as she could muster. "I appreciate your concern, really I do, but I want my life back. Karrel's dead, and I need to move on. I can't do that if every time I open a cupboard, I find it full of vampire slayers."

"Werewolf hunters."

"Whatever." Kayla looked the Hunters up and down, shaking her head. "I mean, look at you two! This is the real world, and you guys look like something out of a movie. How did you even get in here dressed like that?"

Phil shrugged. "Because we look like something out of a movie. We just walked in here handing out paper fliers. People took pictures and asked what we were promoting. One guy even asked if we'd found a distributor yet. This is Hollywood, after all."

Kayla shook her head. "This isn't happening to me," she said. "This can't be real."

"You want to know about reality? Go live someplace else." Ninette stood up and handed Kayla her miniature radio. "Take this. After that little stunt you pulled there's no way we can take you back to base, but we're not just gonna abandon you." She flicked a wary glance at the door. "This visit is strictly off the record. We'll keep an eye on you as much as we can, but we can't watch you all the time. You see anything weird or just get that spooked-out feeling like something's watching you, hit the red button and we'll come get you."

Kayla folded her arms suspiciously, staring at the radio. "What's that little flashing light thing on the top?"

"Tracking device."

"Uh-uh. No way. I don't want anyone keeping tabs on me."

"Too late," said Ninette. "The wolves have already got a bead on you, and to be honest you're lucky to have survived the night. Wolves aren't exactly big on the whole 'patience' deal, but we have a plan."

"Oh, God."

"No, listen to me. Wolves are nocturnal, same as vampires, so here's what we'd like you to do. Go out tonight, to a public place like a bar or café. We'll watch you and see if we can lure any worms out of the woodwork. Don't glare at me like that. The wolves won't try to make a kill in public, but they will track you, which means at some point they'll show themselves and we can nab them. Case closed. We get our guys, and you get to go home and bake cookies. The end."

"So you basically want to use me as bait until you catch these guys?"

"More or less, yes."

"Well, that sucks." Kayla felt her anger rise, and struggled to keep her voice down. "I already told you, I don't want any part in this... in any of this! You think you can come in here and talk me into helping you catch a bunch of psycho killer werewolves, using me as the lure? Mmm, sounds good to me. Why don't you just paint a friggin' bull's-eye on my head and be done with it?"

"Look, I know you're upset, but—"

There was a loud knock on the door.

"Kayla?" came a muffled voice. "You all right?"

"Shit, it's Wylie." Kayla glared at Ninette. "I'll be out in a minute!" she called, as cheerfully as she could.

There was no reply. The door handle turned as Wylie rattled the door, trying to open it.

"Go on! Get out of here!"

"Take the radio first, and promise me you'll go through with the plan tonight."

Kayla stared down at the radio, then picked it up and shoved it into her pocket. "Fine! You win, but don't expect me to do any more than that. As soon as you get these guys I'm outta here. You understand? You can go back to your world and take your were-wolves and vampires with you, because I'm through. Deal?"

"Deal." Ninette sighed, glancing at Phil. "But I will say one thing."

She stood up straight, quietly tightening the blood-soaked bandage on his arm. "If you want to change the world, you've got to make sacrifices." She gestured down at her uniform. "This is ours. We didn't mean to drag you into this, but I'd be lying if I said we didn't need you to help us out on this one, maybe even join the team. I promise you you'll make a difference."

She dropped her gun into its oilskin shoulder holster and clipped the top as Kayla eyed her warily. "Or... you could just stay here, working that counter, earning a few bucks to pay the rent on that cockroach-ridden hovel you call a studio apartment. Maybe if you work real hard in a few years you'll be head counter girl... maybe even make supervisor, get your own office..."

She glanced around at the shabby storeroom. "Sounds real exciting, doesn't it?"

Kayla gestured toward the air-vent. "You can go now," she said levelly.

* * *

SEVEN HOURS LATER, Kayla sat miserably on a
sticky vinyl barstool in one of Tinseltown's most
notorious bars, the Snake Pit, watching the door.
People shouted and music boomed. She adjusted
her white dress for the thousandth time and
gazed down at her drink. It was green with a little pink paper parasol in it. She'd bought it a
good half hour ago to take the edge off her
nerves, and she still hadn't a clue what it was. All
she knew was that it had cost her exactly three-
point-four hours' worth of her daily mall wage,
and she was not happy about it.

She pulled the cherry off the end of the paper
parasol and fiddled with it, trying to stop her
mind from wandering, as it had been doing with
increasing frequency over the course of the last
hour, in a vain effort to escape the unspeakable
horror of what she was doing. Kayla resolutely
tightened her grip on her glass. She was here for
a reason, and she was going to see it through,
even though the thought of it made her want to
run screaming from the room.

She had made her choice, but that didn't mean
she had to like it.

Kayla popped the cherry into her mouth and
took a small sip of her drink, surreptitiously eyeing up the rest of the clientele, mostly men,
grunged-out and seedy-looking, wearing the
usual Friday-night-on-Melrose mix of leather
and black cotton. Their piercings glinted and
their over-pumped muscles flexed as they swag-
gered through the bar, downing shots and
clustering around the front window to play
"Gay, Straight or Actor" on the street outside.
They glanced at her appreciatively as she sat

alone at the bar, but so far nobody had as much as approached her, let alone tried to attack her.

Come on...

She downed another burning half-inch of her drink, hoping that she was doing the right thing. She knew she was putting herself in yet more danger by cooperating with the Hunters, but right now it was the only option she could think of. She'd thought briefly about calling the police, but what was she going to tell them? That a bunch of supernatural creatures were stalking her, could they please keep an eye on her and let her know if they saw any suspicious-looking werewolves loitering nearby?

Kayla took a deep breath, feeling the weight of the world on her shoulders. She snuck a furtive glance around the room, looking for Phil or Ninette, but there was no sign of them. Of course, they'd be undercover or in disguise, but still she couldn't see anyone who even looked like them. Either their disguises were pretty top-notch, or they'd forgotten about her. She hoped they would show up soon, because she was nervous as hell.

She leaned out of the way as a shrieking teen lurched past her, groping at the bar for her drink as her boyfriend laughed and shushed her. Kayla felt her head swim, caught between two realities. Already last night was starting to seem like a bad dream. She wished desperately that it was, that she could just go home and get on with her life. Trying to come to terms with Karrel's death was bad enough without all this crap dumped on top of it. Still, it was a new day, things might start looking up from this point on.

After all, she'd been attacked by supposedly unstoppable creatures before and had lived to tell the tale.

Just how bad could these werewolves really be?

OVER BY THE main door, there was a small commotion. A man had walked through the main entrance, completely ignoring the bouncer's request to show his ID. The bouncer radioed for backup while clutching at his bruised hand and fighting a weird urge to run shrieking from the building. A few people turned to stare, then quickly looked away in a show of studious unconcern.

The man was slender and cold. He was dressed in dusty black jeans and a black silk jacket that rippled with a raven's sheen. His jet-black hair was pulled back in a tight ponytail. He stopped just inside the door and scanned the room with practiced ease, his arrogant gaze as cold and expressionless as the eye of the CCTV camera above him.

The one he wanted wasn't there.

He walked through the room, knocking aside drunken people who blundered into his path. An eddy of outrage began to build behind him as he moved swiftly onto the dance floor, systematically looking from face to face, searching for the one he wanted.

He knew she was in here. It was only a matter of time before he found her.

He didn't even bother to react as the regulars turned away from him one by one as they felt his gaze on them. That was just how things worked around here. You didn't deal with trouble, you simply ignored it and hoped it went away, or happened to somebody else. The man knew that he was quite plainly trouble. As far as the clubbers were concerned, if they didn't look at him, he didn't see them.

That suited Mitzi nicely.

KAYLA WATCHED A waiter weave his way through the crush, a heavily-laden drink tray balanced on one hand and a double platter of burger, fries, and salad on the other. Patrons bumped and jostled him as he made his way over to an table of impatient diners sitting at the side of the bar. Kayla's heart went out to him. If Murphy's Law was working correctly tonight, she guessed, the fries would end up scattered on the floor, the beer would get dumped in some girl's lap, and the grossly-inflated cleaning bill for her chain store dress would come out of the poor guy's wages the next day. She had worked as a waitress herself when she'd first come to town, and had been relieved when she'd got the perfume counter job, just so she'd never be treated like that again.

Right now, she'd give anything to change places with that guy.

Something caught Kayla's attention and she twisted around on her barstool to look up at the nearby TV, currently tuned to the local news channel. She was surprised to see Julissa's beaming face on the screen.

Go, girl, she thought, faintly amused to see that the station was using an old tape of her. Julissa was twenty-six. In the video, she couldn't have been a day older than nineteen. That was bound to piss her off, which immediately made Kayla's day a little brighter.

The nipped-and-tucked newscaster shuffled her papers as she went on, beaming glassily into the camera. "Julissa Cortez was today named as the new face of corporate giant Genetica, beating off competition from over three hundred other young hopefuls to star in a new advertising campaign. Cortez will be appearing at the company's launch party later tonight to answer questions about the firm's revolutionary new genetic makeovers, which, despite meeting strong opposition from protesters, are billed to be the next big thing in beauty therapy. One controversial treatment even claims to be able to stop the aging process altogether, although the drug has yet to be granted approval by the FDA. Located in the heart of youth-obsessed Hollywood, Genetica was founded by—"

A warm hand descended onto her shoulder and Kayla turned with a sigh of relief, expecting to see one of the Hunters.

Mutt slid into the empty seat beside her.

Kayla's welcoming expression faltered and died on her face. She scowled, her flustered nerves jangling at the sight of him. Great, more drama. He was a different kind of trouble to the sort she was hoping to attract, and right now, she had no time for him. Not to mention the fact that he was putting himself in a crazy amount of danger from the Hunters by even being here.

She forced herself to remain calm, to keep her expression neutral, even as heat swept through her at his sudden nearness. "What do you want?" she asked, glancing quickly around her to see if anyone was watching them.

"A large Bloody Mary on the rocks, if you're buying."

"I meant..." Kayla stopped, glowering.

"You're glowering," said Mutt. "I'll take that as a 'no.'"

Kayla tossed her head, going through several different equally-scathing replies in her mind before giving up in disgust. "You know what?" she said, sipping on her drink. "I don't have to talk to you."

"You're right, you don't," Mutt said tonelessly, watching the screen above them, "but I think you should."

"Any special reason that doesn't have to do with your enormous ego?"

"My enormous what?" Mutt grinned. "Oh, my ego. I thought you said... never mind." He cleared his throat and started again. "Okay, just for starters, there's a werewolf sitting three seats down from you." He reached into his pocket for a pack of smokes and flipped the top open, his eyes glinting with amusement. "That a good enough reason?"

Kayla sucked in her breath sharply. Mutt's hand flew to her upper arm and gripped it, stopping her from turning.

"Don't look," he said in a monotone, idly stroking her wrist with a fingertip. "He's probably not here to kill you. I'm sure he's just here looking to get laid, same as the rest of us."

He paused for a moment, looking deeply into her eyes. "Probably."

Kayla struggled to remain calm while fighting the urge to bat Mutt's hand off her arm as if it was a hot iron. Memories of last night flitted treacherously through her mind, and it was all she could do to retain some semblance of politeness with the guy. She felt the heat of his hand flooding through the thin cotton of her sweater. A chill raced though her body as it responded, unbidden, to his touch.

She took a few careful breaths, reining in her anger at her own weakness. "You're telling me this because...?"

"Just wanted you to be aware of your own monumental stupidity in coming out into the open like this." Mutt glanced around, carelessly trailing his finger up her arm, across her collarbone. "I told you to be careful. They could be anywhere. They could be..."

"...anyone, yeah, you said." Kayla knocked Mutt's hand away in irritation and looked him up and down, letting a little of her disgust show in her eyes. "I'll take my chances, thanks all the same."

She glanced pointedly down at his other hand, which still gripped her bicep. When he didn't move it she shook her head in exasperation and slid down off her barstool, trying to make the move look casual. She had to get rid of this guy before the Hunters saw them together. Instead of releasing her, Mutt quickly shoved his chair back and stood, trapping her between his body and the bar.

"You think this is a game? Some kind of joke?" He clapped his hands together in front of her face, making her jump. "Come on! Get with it, girl! They're after you, get it? And they will not stop—absolutely will not stop—until you're dead. Period."

"I've told you once already," Kayla said levelly, "move."

Mutt's eyes fell to Kayla's semi-exposed cleavage. The heat between the two of them was all too obvious. It was all he could do to keep his hands from creeping lower, as her subtle scent—tropical spices, with a hint of coconut shampoo and that warm caramel perfume she wore—crawled through his nostrils and did treacherous things to his brain.

He blinked quickly and looked away, yanking back his libido on a choke chain. He'd promised Karrel he'd keep an eye on his girl and, pain-in-the-ass as she was, that was what he was going to do.

That was the reason he'd come here tonight, honest.

The heat of her glare burned through him. "Look," he started, "I didn't come here to cause trouble. I just need you to be safe. You shouldn't be out in the open. If I was one of them, you'd be dead by now." He stroked her hair back off her shoulders, casually exposing her throat, perfunctorily adjusting the twisted strap on her dress. "Think about it. Then go home."

"My home or your home?" Kayla asked acidly.

Mutt deliberately placed his hand on Kayla's forearm, squeezing gently. This time the arousal that flickered between them was inescapable. He stroked his thumb over the soft skin on the inside of her elbow, clearing his throat with an effort.

"Your call."

Kayla flushed. Mutt could see that he had her. He couldn't resist a grin as she opened and closed her mouth a couple times, the werewolf temporarily forgotten. As she floundered he leaned in and brushed his nose over the vein in the side of her neck, sending an unmistakable tremor through her.

"You know," he started, in a low, husky voice, "I fixed the bed."

"Jesus!" Kayla burst out. She shoved Mutt away, although to his secret delight she didn't push him too far. "What the hell is wrong with you? What about Bea? This time yesterday you were all cut up about her getting killed. Now you're back to hitting on your dead buddy's girlfriend. Did either of them mean a thing to you, or are you just full of it tonight?"

"I already told you, Bea meant something."

"Yeah, right," Kayla snorted. She twisted her body around to face Mutt, gripping his shoulder with one hand and swiftly running the other down his stomach. She pressed the heel of her palm hard over his groin, making him groan softly. "Sure feels like she meant a lot to you."

Mutt laughed, surprised and amused. He grabbed her hand and pressed it harder against him. "You don't get it, do you?" he asked, grinning as Kayla pulled away from him in exasperation. "I'm a were-wolf, honey. Want me to spell it out for you? Being what I am… it's a whole lifestyle thing. It means no remorse, no regrets, no mornings snuggling under the blankets watching Sunday morning cartoons with the girl I just laid the night before, talking 'bout picking out curtains and growing herbs in the window box. That's not what I'm about." He moved closer to Kayla, studying her intently. "I do what I want, with whomever I want, and I've never heard any complaints. It's part of the whole 'were-wolf' deal."

"So where does Bea come into your 'deal?'"

"You want the truth?" Mutt scratched his jaw. "We were close, sure. We hooked up every once in a while. She got my back, I got hers, but I never loved her. I never loved anyone."

"Now, there's a surprise."

"It's for a reason," said Mutt firmly, "and that's the way it's gonna stay." He studied Kayla's doubtful expression, and his grin widened. "I mean, come on! Look at me. I'm a Westside boy, born and bred. Can you honestly see me hookin' up with someone for keeps? The way I act..." He shrugged indifferently, straightening his belt buckle. "It's in my nature, always has been, always will be. Who am I to try and change it?"

"You look like a man to me," said Kayla, "and you sure as hell talk like one. So you're a werewolf too?" She shrugged. "Big deal. That doesn't give you an excuse to act like an asshole."

"It gives me the perfect excuse: I can't help the way I am."

"Bullshit. Don't go all Anne Rice on me, giving me that 'it's in my nature' crap. If being a jerk is in your nature then I don't wanna know you, man or wolf."

"Fine. Your loss." Mutt flicked a guarded glance toward the door, riled despite himself. "But you know what? I did care about Bea. She was one heck of a woman, and whoever killed her's gonna pay for it. I owe her at least that much."

"For what? Putting up with you?"

Mutt narrowed his eyes at Kayla. "You know what?" he said, then suddenly laughed. "Fuck it, and fuck you. You wanna see me kill everyone in this place in some crazy misguided revenge attack? Fine, I'll do it, but it won't bring Bea back. I could sit around on her grave for a year, cryin' and writing bad poetry on expensive handmade paper with bits of flowers stuck in it, but that wouldn't bring her back either."

He let his breath out hard and cupped his hands on either side of her hips. "But now something good's come out of all this, and you're acting like it's something bad. I'm attracted to you. I don't deny it. I can't help it, much as I can't help it that the only woman I ever gave a damn about is now pushin' up daisies in a ditch somewhere south of downtown. The world sucks, but we're in it, so we might as well make the best of it. That's my motto." He paused for a second. "What's yours?"

Kayla gazed up at him, uncertain, and then opened her mouth to reply. She closed it again and moved back hurriedly as a tall, black-clad boy with spiky hair emerged from the crowd and elbowed his way in between them, carrying an overloaded black plastic drink tray with flashing lights around the side.

"Okay," said Wylie, "I got one pair of beers, one double margarita with a twist, two lime sodas, one gut-wrenchingly expensive melon martini with some kind of unidentified fruit in it..." He looked up from his carefully balanced tray and raised an eyebrow. "Speaking of unidentified fruit, who's your friend?"

"He ain't my friend," said Kayla, a little too quickly.

"Oh really?" said Wylie, glancing pointedly at Mutt's hand, which still lingered on her arm.

Kayla shifted uncomfortably, sneaking a peak around her. She'd forgotten that Wylie still worked here. Yet another complication. She was close to bailing on the whole deal, but she had a feeling that this might just be the clincher.

"Really," Mutt said firmly, and this time it was Kayla's turn to raise an eyebrow, "and I was just leaving."

He released his grip on Kayla's arm, his eyes never once leaving hers. "Just be careful," he said in a low voice.

"Like you give a shit," Kayla hissed.

"You'd be surprised," replied Mutt, then left with what Kayla thought was a somewhat put-out glance at Wylie, casually trailing one hand across the back of her hips as he did so. Kayla swallowed, feeling things low in her body tighten at his touch.

Bastard.

Wylie set his drink tray down on the bar top, and then swept his spiky hair out of his eyes, peering behind him in bemusement. "Looks like Rent-A-Jerk just turned in for the night. Anyone I should know about?"

"He's nobody," said Kayla firmly. It was richly rewarding to see Mutt stiffen slightly as he walked away, shoving his way through the customers at the bustling bar.

Wylie leaned against the bar beside her, raising his eyebrows in a "tell-me-all" expression. Kayla gazed down at the tray of drinks helplessly. She couldn't deal with Wylie right now. She had to get rid of him.

"Look... I'm sorry. Not sure I'm much up for company tonight," she said, unable to resist glancing after Mutt.

"His company or my company?" Wylie asked quietly.

"Excuse me?" Kayla glanced over at Wylie, and something inside her lurched at the stony expression on his face. She got the unnerving feeling that he'd been watching her for longer than he made out.

"Forget it." Wylie shook his head with a strange little laugh, and then picked up his drinks tray with a flourish. "Have a fun evening, the pair of you. Maybe if you drink enough, you'll remember who your friends really are."

"Wylie..."

But it was too late. Wylie was gone, disappearing back into the crowd without so much as a backward glance.

Kayla watched him go with regret, but she didn't try to stop him. Relief welled inside her even as a cold hand of anxiety closed inside her chest. She'd make it up to him in the morning, but for now, he was one less problem she'd have to deal with.

The mission was back on.

Blinking, she snapped into an alert awareness. Her brain shifted and she glanced down the bar, three seats down, where Mutt had told her that there was a werewolf sitting.

The seat was empty.

Kayla felt a chill steal over her. A thought occurred to her and she flicked her eyes up the bar in the other direction. A curly-haired guy in trucker overalls was sitting in the third chair along from her. An untouched beer glass sat in front of him, and he was apparently absorbed in a dog-eared bass guitar magazine. Feeling her eyes on him, he frowned and started to roll his gaze in her direction.

Kayla snapped her eyes back to the front, sudden panic gripping her. The noise of the crowd around her seemed to amplify, and she became hyperaware of the door behind her. That guy had to be the werewolf, she decided. It was coming up to nine o'clock and his overalls were spotless. Besides which, no trucker she knew of would let a full glass of beer sit in front of him for that long without drinking it.

Mutt had said he probably wasn't there to kill her.

She glanced once again around the bar, but there was still no sign of Phil or Ninette.

Ah, crap.

Kayla was so busy freaking out about the trucker guy that she didn't see the scruffy, flint-eyed man sitting across the room from her, watching her intently in the mirror that hung over the bar. And even if she had, she would've been too nervous to notice the telltale bulge of the sawn-off rifle concealed beneath his bulky biker jacket.

HARLEM SWALLOWED A yawn as he popped the cap off his bottle of Corona with a polished thumbnail. He took a sip as he sat back in his chair and waited for the target to make a move. The beer tasted good, crisp and clean. He drained a good half of it before setting the bottle back down again, idly cracking his tattooed knuckles and whistling faintly under his breath. In his mind he heard his mother exclaim in annoyance at the sound, and felt her whip him across the back of his hands with her steel-edged ruler, the one she'd always carried with her in case one of her children misbehaved. She'd tried to pull it on him that time he'd led her out of the house, away from the watchful eyes of Daddy.

Harlem smiled faintly as he remembered the sound that ruler had made as it had sliced through Mother's skull—in one temple, out the other. People couldn't hurt you when they were dead, he'd found out, and the discovery had made the rest of his childhood a thoroughly entertaining experience.

Entertainment. That was the name of the game out here in Hollywood, wasn't it? Harlem grinned to himself as he switched his gaze back to the mirror, checking on Kayla. This girl looked as if she would be extremely entertaining, but he suspected there'd be precious little time for that. A vision of his dead buddy Rocco rose in his mind and Harlem's nostrils flared dangerously. Rocco had been a good friend, a good fighter. He'd fought by his side for nearly twelve years before that bastard Hunter Karrel had shot him, blowing his brains out and earning him nothing but death for his troubles.

This girl was his girlfriend?

Hell, that made her dead already.

Harlem adjusted his jacket and narrowed his eyes at the girl, visualizing a red crosshair on the back of her stupid brunette head. Skeet had been careless, barging into the Hunters' place after her like an unguided missile. The guy had no finesse, no style. He, on the other hand, would wait for the perfect moment before taking the girl out. The hit would be clean and quiet, a surgical strike, with no witnesses or clues left behind for the Hunters or the damned LAPD to get their grubby little donut-grabbers on.

Yeah, clean and quiet. Unless you counted all the screaming.

Harlem snorted in mirth, then lifted his empty beer bottle in a toast, his vengeful gaze fixed on the girl.

"Rocco, buddy," he said in a dry whisper, "this one's for you."

CHAPTER TWENTY-FOUR

OVER AT THE side-bar at the back of the room, Mutt paid for a fresh drink somewhat unwillingly, his mind still on Kayla. What was the deal with the girl? He'd warned her about the danger she was in, and she'd completely ignored him, as though dealing with the fact that she had a bunch of killer werewolves on her tail was something that could be put off until tomorrow.

Mutt sniffed, swirling a double Jack and Coke around in its glass as he moodily scanned the room. The girl was living in a fairytale, thinking she could ignore this one and it'd just go away. He studied the dark figure at the bar. The fug of smoke and the overlapping, eye-watering stench of alcohol and aftershave almost blew out his sense of smell. He closed his eyes, searching for a familiar scent pattern.

He opened his eyes. It was no good. He couldn't smell shit in here. His mouth briefly twitched at the inadvertent pun, and then he forced himself to sober up. If there was another werewolf in here, it was hiding very well. He knew that he should really scope out the place, go person to person, do some spot checks, but he was nearing the end of his very limited patience. He'd kept his end of the bargain, after all. He'd done all he'd promised Karrel and more, protecting Kayla above and beyond the call of duty.

Now, the girl was on her own.

Good luck to her.

Mutt turned back toward where Kayla sat alone at the bar, gazing down into her drink. He watched as she tugged down her absurdly short white dress, scooting herself back up on her barstool, glancing around anxiously and hunching her shoulders as though trying to disappear while still simultaneously staying in plain sight.

Crazy chick.

Mutt stared at her for a while. Then he rubbed his eyes tiredly and put his drink down on the bar. God help him, he was going to have to go back and save her life again, wasn't he? He was involved now. He hadn't meant to be, he didn't want to be, but now that it had happened, there was absolutely nothing he could do about it. Some long-dead part of him felt warm at the sight of her, and dammit, he wasn't going to let her die until he found out why.

He was really just doing his dead buddy a favor, Mutt told himself as he got up from the bar and made his way back across the crowded room. A promise was a promise, after all. It didn't mean that he actually liked her. Once upon a time he would've been swayed by the girl's looks, but now he considered himself all grown up and immune to such immature and ephemeral things as perfect hair and silky skin and incredible breasts and legs like a race-horse and....

In the name of all that was holy, who on earth was that?

Mutt's eyes almost bugged out of his head as the tall, leggy woman strode into the bar as if she owned it, which, judging by her arrogant stare and "fuck you" gait, she probably did. She was wearing some kind of shiny black vinyl creation that left precious little to the imagination. What it did leave, it made very sure—by means of a variety of straps and lace and tantalizingly placed zippers—that imagination would be lying on its back fanning itself frantically and begging for a cold shower before it had even taken in the rest of details, like her buckled white lambskin corset. Her almost unbearably low-slung black velvet jeans revealed just a peep of her golden belly and diamond-jeweled g-string.

Mutt stared, dumbstruck.

Pausing by the bar, the stunning woman reached into her purse and pulled out a pack of French cigarettes, sliding one slowly between her luscious lips in an unbearably suggestive way. Replacing the pack in her purse, she cast around for a lighter, which Mutt was only too glad to offer her, appearing at her side as if by magic, before she had even gotten her bag fully closed. The woman's eyes slid up to his with cool amusement, before she leaned forward to touch her cigarette to the flickering flame.

Judging by the expression on her jaw-droppingly beautiful face, it was the most pleasurable thing she had ever done.

Mutt mentally slapped himself several times as the woman straightened up and looked him over thoughtfully, her gaze running over his body like a warm caress. A bone-deep shiver ran through him. The world around him seemed to fade away until all that remained were her gorgeous eyes, drawing him in, pulling him down, holding him under until he willingly stopped fighting and just stared at her with a goofy smile on his face, hoping to God that he wasn't drooling.

He'd never seen anyone with violet eyes before.

The woman's lips moved and he gazed at them lovingly, watching the way her cherry lip-gloss picked up the subtle colors of the fairy lights strung above the bar. Then she laughed and Mutt blinked, clearing his throat.

"What?" he asked, dazed.

"I said, quit drooling. It's not attractive." Reaching out, the woman pretended to wipe Mutt's chin. Mutt noticed a Spanish fighting bull bracelet around one slender wrist, and his hands moved of their own accord to take her arm. He kissed her hand in a daze, a word coming to him through the fog of his otherwise useless high school education.

"*Encantado*," he sighed.

The woman laughed again. Mutt hoped desperately that he'd just said "charmed to meet you" in Spanish, rather than "I'll take the squid" or "your grandmother is a fish," which was how his luck usually ran. To his immense relief she bowed her head and smiled up at him through her long, mascara-blackened lashes.

"Good to meet you too." She paused a moment, sweeping him with a smoldering gaze. Mutt felt his internal organs starting to melt, and whimpered very slightly.

Leaning forward, the woman placed her cheek alongside his, her subtle perfume and the sudden nearness of her making his head swim. "You wouldn't happen to know where the restrooms are?" she whispered. "I don't come here very often."

"Would you like to?" Mutt asked huskily.

"Excuse me?"

Mutt silently pointed to the green restroom signs, not trusting himself to move or speak or do anything that required any kind of higher-level brain activity.

The woman giggled, twining her fingers with his. "I get lost real easily. Can you take me there?"

The way she had said it had left even less to the imagination than her outfit did. His mouth opened and closed a couple of times like a fish's, then curved back into that goofy grin. The woman tightened her grip on his hand and smiled down at him, the sight of her corseted cleavage deftly silencing his last remaining functioning brain cell.

There is a God, thought Mutt fervently. He stepped around the woman and led her in a daze through the heaving crowd toward the women's restrooms. Perhaps he was going to get lucky tonight after all.

KAYLA FINISHED UP her second drink of the evening and glanced up, a little fuzzily, to check that the werewolf trucker guy was still sitting at the bar.

He had gone.

Kayla's head swam as she pushed herself to her feet a little more abruptly than she had meant to. She peered around, trying to be inconspicuous in the not-very-inconspicuous way of the somewhat inebriated.

"Ah, great," she muttered, trying to remain calm and failing miserably. It was official: the Hunters' plan sucked. There was still no sign of Phil or

Ninette, Mutt had vanished, and she was all alone and drunk off her ass with a werewolf in the room and nobody here to save her.

Forget the plan. It was time to split.

Grabbing her bag off the back of the chair, she turned and groped her way along the bar until she reached the door. She slipped outside and strode as quickly as she could to the nearest brightly-lit building, which turned out to be a strip joint. Practically throwing the ten dollar admission fee at the woman behind the grill, she pushed her way past the massive bouncer before diving into the welcoming warmth and darkness on the other side.

It was hot. A sparse crowd of locals sipped slowly from their beers as a pair of tired women cavorted onstage. An off-duty sheriff sat in an end booth, doing his very best to look like he was just there for the food. The place was run-down and seedy, and nobody looked up when she entered. In these kinds of places it was wise not to stare, apart from one guy who Kayla guessed was a tourist, a ratty-looking guy who gaped at her as if she was some kind of off-duty stripper.

She felt his beady little eyes on her as she merged with relief into the crowd by the bar, offering herself some measure of cover. She waited until her heart had stopped pounding before moving swiftly to the far wall, her eyes scanning frantically until they lit upon the reassuring silver shape of a payphone. There was nothing else for it. She was going to have to call the police and hope that they could do something—anything—to protect her.

Fumbling in her pocket, she pulled out a quarter and jammed it into the slot, ready to call 911. She remembered that dialing the emergency services was free, and unthinkingly hit the coin release lever to get her quarter back.

The lever jammed.

Kayla hit the receiver button to start again, but when she put the phone to her ear she was met with a dead electronic tone. Impatiently she jiggled the receiver up and down, but all this seemed to do was to make the tone increase in volume. In frustration she struck the coin slot with the flat of her hand, trying to dislodge the coin, then struck the money return lever with her fist.

The lever snapped off in her hand.

Kayla stared at it for a moment, glanced guiltily behind her, and jammed it back into place. Hanging up, she spun around and scanned the room, hoping to see a second pay phone, but it seemed she had wrecked the only phone in the place.

Beginning to panic, Kayla walked up behind a guy in a leather jacket sitting with his back to her in a nearby booth and tapped him on the shoulder.

"Hey... can I borrow your cellph..." Kayla's voice tailed off as she saw the trucker guy turn to face her, now wearing a jacket over his overalls.

He had followed her.

Kayla felt the blood drain from her face.

Abruptly, she turned and barged her way back through the crowd, desperate to get out of the place and away from the guy who she was sure was stalking her. She walked into something that refused to yield, like walking into a wall.

At first she thought it was a statue, some kind of fancy bar decoration bought from a Hollywood prop shop. Her gaze traveled up the guy's body until it reached his face, and her blood turned to ice. In the red-blue light of the bar, the man's face looked as if it was carved out of white marble, his thin-lipped mouth set in a hard, straight line. His clothing was so black it seemed to swallow the light. His eyes were two spooky black orbs, the pupils and the whites completely hidden behind some kind of space-age black contacts, making him look like some kind of alien mannequin.

The guy's eyes flickered down at her, and Kayla realized that he was real. As she stepped convulsively back from him she felt the world slowing down, until the only thing moving was her heart as it clenched in her chest.

He was the one.

She knew it with a blind certainty that had nothing to do with logic and everything to do with her gut. He was a werewolf, and he was here to kill her.

There was nothing she could do but run.

Before her brain had even caught up with the situation her feet were moving, backpedaling away from the guy, unable to tear her eyes away from him. His head turned in creepy slow motion to follow her.

People milled around her, dancing, laughing, oblivious to the danger they were in. Kayla watched, transfixed by terror, as the black-eyed man reached behind him and drew a long *Jian* from a hidden scabbard in his backpack. A burst of strobe light from the stage illuminated it in nightmare snapshots as the man brought it down in front of him, silver flashing against black. Kayla realized with a jolt that the crazy guy was actually going to try and kill her. She should've stayed with Mutt, she realized, or taken her chances with the Hunters. Too late for regrets now.

Mitzi felt a cold chill of satisfaction as he gazed down at the terror-stricken girl.

The hit was acquired.

An explosion of sound tore through the packed strip joint. Kayla screamed reflexively as something whistled over her shoulder in a dull implosion of air. The black-eyed man jerked and dropped his sword with a clatter. He stared stupidly down at it, then his head snapped up and he glared at something behind Kayla, his smooth white face twisting into an ugly expression of outrage.

Before Kayla could register what was happening a second explosion rang out, spinning the man half around. A bloody crater opened up in his shoulder and the man clutched at it, baring needle-like teeth in an expression of pain and fury. Someone was shooting at the guy who had been about to kill her.

It was great, but now wasn't the time to start handing out thank you notes.

Whirling, Kayla ran for her life.

SITTING IN ONE of the covered plastic booths, Harlem lowered his smoking sawn-off shotgun, nodding in grim satisfaction as all around him the club exploded into chaos.

He liked chaos. It was what he did best.

The crowd miraculously parted like the Red Sea as terrified people scattered in all directions to reveal Mitzi, standing alone in the center of a streaming V of people. Glowering, the older were-wolf assassin turned until his blind eyes were facing Harlem.

Baring his teeth, he raised a bloodstained middle finger.

Chuckling, Harlem blew him a kiss before getting to his feet to scope out the crowd. That took care of the competition, for now. He knew that the others were probably close, but for the moment, out of sight was out of mind. He was always one to give his rivals a sporting chance, whatever that meant.

His glinting eyes locked onto the bouncing hair of the Hunter's girl as she made a beeline for the exit. A wave of pleasure spread through him at the thought of the upcoming kill. He didn't know the bitch's name, but he was going to make pretty damn sure she learned his by the time she died, which would be—he theatrically checked his watch—in about two minutes and counting.

Damn, he loved this job.

Tucking his shotgun back into the shoulder sling hidden beneath his biker jacket, Harlem nonchalantly made his way down to the lower level. He slipped unseen into the rapidly vanishing crowd as he followed Kayla toward the back door.

CHAPTER TWENTY-FIVE

THE PROBLEM WITH running for your life, Kayla soon realized, was that people didn't know you were running for your life. They thought that you were running because your parking meter was about to run out, or that you'd left the oven on, or that you were on drugs and being chased by invisible shrimp.

Of course, everyone got in your freakin' way.

She was three blocks away from the strip club, cutting through an overflowing Irish pub in a vain bid to throw her pursuers off. People glared at her as she shoved her way frantically through the overheated throng. The women snapped catty insults, the men grabbed her arms and pressed themselves against her as she squeezed past them.

"Hey, Rosita, where you running to?" laughed one guy, a short Mexican with a missing front tooth. He grabbed her in a bear hug and swung her around in a parody of a dance as she passed him, shoving his bristly, foul-smelling face into hers. Kayla pushed him away and continued running, not hearing the stream of lewd insults he hurled after her.

She thumped through a dividing door and burst out onto a roof terrace, her heart pounding in her ribs. She'd covered half the distance to the iron gate on the other side when a hand seized her arm.

"Julissa?"

"I know. It's hard to believe, isn't it?" Julissa gushed. She was dressed in a green satin dress that contrasted perfectly with her rich chocolate eyes. Her hair was flowing long and loose over her shoulders, swept back by the evening breeze. A pack of her equally gorgeous girlfriends surrounded her, watching Kayla with the kind of rapt attention that indicated they knew instant entertainment when they saw it.

Kayla, however, was in no mood to defend herself. She turned to Julissa, trying to pull herself free from her grip. Julissa hung on determinedly.

"What do you think?" Her face scrunched into a grin and she did a little twirl, still holding onto Kayla's arm. "Don't I look fabulous?"

"Sure. Whatever." Kayla tried to tug free, her gaze still riveted on the door. "Now go look fabulous somewhere else. I gotta go. *NOW!*"

"What's the rush? You got some kind of painting emergency you gotta get back to?"

"Huh?"

"Your face." Julissa pointed. "Ever heard of Wet-Wipes?"

Kayla reached up to wipe at her face.

Her hand came away smeared with red.

"Uh," she said, "yeah." She cleared her throat.

She groped at the last remaining thread of patience that prevented her from ripping her arm from Julissa's hand, shoving her into the mini-swimming pool and making a run for the gate. She pulled again on Julissa's arm, but Julissa refused to let go.

"Present for you." She thrust a small silver post-card into Kayla's hand.

"And this is…?" asked Kayla, through gritted teeth.

"Only an invite to the party to end all parties. It's at midnight tonight."

Kayla glanced down at the postcard. Julissa's face was emblazoned across the front, with the slogan "GENETICA—Your Passport to a Better You" stamped down the side.

"It's a new company I'm modeling for. I'm going to be the star!" Julissa grabbed Kayla's hand and ran it over her own arm. "Feel how smooth my skin is! All from just one little injection!"

"I'm delirious with excitement," growled Kayla. "Really. In fact, I think I'd better leave before I explode with joy all over the patio. Because human blood? Kinda hard to get out of silk without dry cleaning."

Julissa pouted. "Hey, I've only been waiting all my life for an opportunity like this! Everyone who's anyone's going to be there. They'll be giving out free treatments and everything." She eyeballed Kayla. "You'd better make it. It would do you some good to take a little pride in your appearance, boost your sales figure a little. You're looking a little ragged around the edges after, you know…"

Kayla stopped, her hand on the gate. "You know… what?" she said, her voice dangerously calm.

"After what happened to your boyfriend," Julissa went on blithely, pulling out a compact mirror to check her reflection. She took out a lipstick and reapplied it to her lips, smacking them loudly. "You know you can always call me if you need someone to talk to about that. Him being dead and all... that's gotta suck."

"I don't have your number," replied Kayla, in the same tone of voice generally reserved for saying things like, "I'd rather drink the boiling oils of Hell from a skunk's ass, thanks all the same."

"You don't?" Julissa looked up from her compact. "Here, let me give it to you."

Suddenly, being chased by a psychotic sword-wielding werewolf assassin paled in comparison to putting up with Julissa for one more second.

"Just forget it!" she snapped. "I can't make it tonight, anyway."

"Somebody's jealous," said Julissa smugly.

"I'm not jealous!" Kayla burst out. "I just have a life that contains more important things than lip gloss and manicures, and the vast quantities of scorn you heap on people whose shoes don't match their belts!"

"Yours don't, by the way."

"Look at me," Kayla groaned. "I. Don't. Care. Why should it matter how I dress or what makeup I wear or don't wear to work? Hell, you worked beside me for twelve months before you even bothered to learn my name, and even then you only did it in order to have something to yell across the store when you needed someone to cover for you while you picked up your mail-order Prada pumps."

"Your point being...?"

"That sometimes, just sometimes, people do things that don't directly benefit themselves, things that nobody else will ever know about." Despite the danger she knew she was in, Kayla stalked toward Julissa, scowling, unable to let the argument go. "You don't give a crap that my boyfriend just died. All you care about is looking good in front of your friends, pretending that you care when in actual fact if I did ever get around to calling you to talk about Karrel, you'd probably pretend to be a Spanish restaurant. You'd probably even take my order just to get rid of me!"

Julissa blinked. "Who's Karrel?" she asked.

That did it. Kayla walked up to Julissa and pushed her as hard as she could into the swimming pool.

As Julissa resurfaced, spluttering, Kayla felt the back of her neck prickle. Turning, she saw Julissa's six clones step forward, blocking her exit, wearing identical expressions of vengeful glee. At the same time the door to the bar swung open, loudly rebounding off its stoppers.

Trucker Guy stepped through.

KAYLA FROZE, PANIC knifing her brain. Turning, she faced the girls opposite her.

"Move," she growled.

The tallest girl stepped forward, a Gwen Stefani look alike clad in the latest Eighties revival fashions from the Hollywood catwalks. "I think she needs to cool off a little, don't you?" she said.

Her eyes flicked to the swimming pool and back, and she grinned nastily.

There was a murmur of catty assent from the other girls. Moving as one, they spread out to block Kayla's path to the gate.

"Oh, for crap's sake." Kayla feinted to the left and made a determined break for the gate, only to find herself seized by six pairs of immaculately manicured hands and dragged back toward the water.

Kicking and struggling, she flung a panicked glance at the door. Her eyes widened in horror as she saw Trucker Guy stop in the doorway with a jerk. His eyes lit up at the sight of her, and his hand moved down toward his bulging pocket.

With a sudden burst of strength, Kayla broke free of the girls, flinging them aside so violently that five of them went down like ten-pins, sprawling on the wet concrete. The sixth hung on determinedly, making a grab for her hair. Kayla planted one foot against an ornamental mini palm tree and heaved with all her might, sending the girl flying across the patio. The girl crashed into a drink table and vanished over the other side, taking down the suited waiter in the process.

Kayla ran to the gate and heaved on the handle. It was locked.

She spun around, her hair flying.

Trucker Guy shoved the startled girls aside in his efforts to get to her.

Kayla grabbed the handle of the iron gate in both hands and pulled with all her might. There was a twisting, groaning sound of tortured metal. The gate bulged outwards around the handle, as though it were made out of rubber rather than steel. One more heave and the entire locking mechanism popped out of the gate, spraying metal rivets all over the concrete.

Finally, the gate swung open.

Scarcely aware of the sudden silence from behind

her as the astonished girls gaped, Kayla fled through the gate and pelted around the corner... straight into the arms of a uniformed sheriff.

Gasping in relief, Kayla clung to him, swinging him around and pointing back the way she had come. "You gotta help me! There's some crazy guy chasing me! He's got a gun!"

The sheriff looked down at her, his tough, scarred face breaking into an expression of concern. "What's your name?"

"Kayla."

"Well, Kayla, don't you worry, you're safe now. My cruiser's just around the corner. Come with me and we'll call backup."

Taking her hand, the sheriff jogged off down the street. Kayla followed him in a buzzing rush of adrenaline, almost tripping several times as she spun around every few seconds to check for the trucker. As they turned onto the next street she slowed, peering around the corner. The street stayed reassuringly empty.

"Wait!" she hissed, tugging the sheriff to a halt. "I don't see him!"

"Oh, you don't need to worry about him," said the sheriff. He turned back to Kayla and pulled out a service issue .22 revolver. He leveled it at Kayla's head.

"You need to worry about me," he said with a grin.

CHAPTER TWENTY-SIX

KAYLA STARED INTO the barrel of the gun, her heart pounding on overdrive. She watched in absolute confusion as the sheriff aimed the red dot of the laser sight between her eyes.

CRASH!

The service door behind them flew open, rebounding off the brick wall. Kayla spun around to see the trucker step out. He drew a black army rifle from the recesses of his jacket, his steely-eyed gaze fixed grimly on her.

In her amped-up state, Kayla realized that these two crazy men were going to try to kill her. She wished desperately that she'd brought Karrel's handgun with her. At least then she'd have stood a chance.

However, to her surprise, the trucker aimed his rifle at the sheriff. He winked at Kayla.

"Duck!" he shouted.

Kayla liked that idea so much that she obeyed immediately, throwing herself to the ground.

Gunfire blazed over her head for the second time that evening. She heard the sheriff cry out and glanced around in time to see him reeling backward while the trucker advanced on him, emptying his shotgun and blowing him backward down the alleyway through sheer firepower. The sounds of the gunshots ran together into one long burst of ear-splitting noise, bouncing back off the damp brickwork around them in a harsh echo.

The final empty cartridge tinkled to the ground, rolling down the sidewalk.

A deadly silence descended.

Kayla pushed herself up, ears ringing. She gaped at the body of the dead sheriff. He lay just ten feet from her in a slowly spreading puddle of blood.

A shadow fell across her. The trucker loomed over her, reloading with a swift, military efficiency.

But he wasn't looking at her. He was watching the body of the sheriff.

The sheriff suddenly sat up, his face contorting in a rictus of hate.

Kayla felt the world spin around her.

The trucker snapped shut the breach of his rifle, then extended a hand down to her in greeting. "Lieutenant Dan Ferro, Unit D, Hunter code two-eight-two-nine, shirt size twenty-seven and a half. I vote that we get our asses outta here and back to base before Dogboy over there gets up."

"Who?"

"The werewolf."

He pointed to the sheriff as the man began scrambling to his feet. Lifting his rifle, Ferro snapped off a quick shot that blew the man's right knee out. Kayla screamed and clapped her hands over her ears at the noise. The sheriff collapsed with a howl, clutching at his leg and rolling over onto his front. He turned to Dan, snarling in rage and pain. As Kayla watched in increasing disbelief the sheriff's fingers morphed into giant taloned claws. His bullet-riddled jacket split open to reveal two black, diseased-looking wings, five feet of ragged skin stretched between clawed bone structures.

The sheriff/werewolf tried to get to his feet, using his wings to give himself an extra push off the ground. He collapsed, and then tried again.

"They make werewolves with wings now, do they?" said Kayla, in a worryingly calm tone of voice. She got to her feet, keeping her distance from both men.

Dan nodded an affirmative, chewing his gum thoughtfully. Under the yellow glow of the streetlight he seemed younger than she'd thought he was. Wisps of his curly brown hair blew into his eyes as he glanced briefly in her direction, flashing her a look of sympathy. "Bunch of 'em got experimented on by vampires, back in the eighties. A nasty business, but we got the big head honcho guy who did it, or so they tell us."

"You mean there are more of these things around?"

"Nah." Dan popped his gum. "Most of the test subjects were killed, but some escaped, know what I'm sayin'?" Dan watched the winged werewolf carefully, his finger still on the trigger. "That sack of shit's called Jackdoor. We've been after him for a while, practically all the time I've been training."

"Jackdoor." Kayla frowned. "Where do I know that name from?"

Dan shrugged. "Dunno. Anyway, they sent me to keep an eye on you, but then Flap Happy over there showed up and I got to kill two birds with one stone, so to speak." He beamed. "Pretty neat for my first solo mission, eh? You want some gum?"

"I'll pass, thanks."

"Suit yourself." Dan shrugged and popped a fresh stick of sugar-free Juicy Fruit into his mouth, then crumpled the gum paper and raised his rifle again, peering through the laser sights. He squeezed the trigger, sending a round blasting into Jackdoor's head. The unfortunate man plummeted to the ground.

Despite herself, Kayla winced.

Shouldering his rifle, Dan strode nonchalantly up to the prone Jackdoor, motioning for Kayla to follow him. He nudged its cratered head to one side. "You know, I got shot once," he said in a conversational tone of voice.

"Er, Dan…" Kayla said, backing away.

"Up on Melrose. Some kind of gang initiation thing. Humans, not werewolves. How fucking ironic is that?"

"I think it's still…" Kayla pointed, too grossed-out to speak.

"And guess where they shot me? Right in the… *whoa!*" Dan jumped back as Jackdoor's razor-sharp teeth snapped an inch from his ankle. The werewolf raised its head and hissed up at him, one side of its face coated in blood and gore from its temple. It was still in human form, but its eyes were wild, its movements jerky and unpredictable like a wild animal's. Kayla could see fur starting to sprout around the edges of the man's face as it began to change forms, grimacing with the effort.

"Hardy li'l creep, aintcha?" said Dan as he raised his rifle, aiming it at Jackdoor's forehead at point-blank range.

He pitched face-down on the ground as a crowbar connected solidly with the back of his skull.

Kayla spun around to see a figure step out of the shadows.

He was dressed in a biker's getup with an abundance of chains hanging about his person, the rust-colored stains on several of the thicker ones suggesting that not all of them were for show. He swung his crowbar back up with a flourish and laid it over his shoulder like a lady's parasol.

"You've gotta be pretty thick-skulled to work in this profession," said Harlem, cracking his knuckles. "Don't you agree, Kayla?"

HARLEM ENJOYED THE horrified look on the Hunter girl's face at the sight of him. He strode cockily past her and peered down at the weakly twitching Jackdoor. The guy had a hole in his head the size of Texas. Cool.

"Oh, that's gotta sting," he said. "Anyone got a Band-Aid?"

CRACK! He slammed his crowbar across Jackdoor's forehead as the man reached pitifully up to him. The werewolf dropped back onto the street, unconscious.

"Sorry, bud."

Harlem kicked the rifle from Dan's outstretched hand, grabbing the young Hunter by the collar and dragging his unconscious form over next to Jackdoor. He dropped him on top of the bleeding werewolf as if Dan was a carcass at a slaughterhouse.

He gazed down at the pair of them, the lights of a passing LAPD helicopter reflected in his fiery eyes. "It's like dumb and dumber, ain't it? But wait, the credits ain't rolling yet."

He hurled his crowbar at Kayla's feet as she tried to make a break for it, the thick metal bar smashing into the cracked concrete just inches from her. Kayla froze, staring down at the crowbar. She turned to face Harlem, a rage burning deep within her.

"You're one of them," she said, her voice unnaturally calm, "a werewolf."

Harlem inclined his head modestly. "The name's Harlem. Remember it. There'll be a test later."

"Harlem." Kayla's eyes flashed fire. "I know you! And Jackdoor too! You guys killed Karrel! I knew I recognized that name!"

Harlem cocked a scarred eyebrow. "Nice detective work there, princess. Who tipped you off, Captain America down there?"

"No, Karrel told me," snapped Kayla. Her fear evaporated like water off a hotplate. She felt her muscles tense as a dark fury swamped her. One of Karrel's killers was standing right in front of her, bold as brass. Why the hell hadn't she brought a weapon out with her this evening?

She hung back, glaring at him.

"I hate to break it to ya kid," Harlem said, "but yer boyfriend's dead. Worm food, if that. There wasn't much left of him when we was done, and I think Skeet ate what was left." Harlem's face lit up with an unholy glee. "Gave him terrible gas, as I recall."

"He's not dead," snapped Kayla, clenching her fists. "He's here. He told me to kill all of you scumbags to avenge his death."

"He told you to do what?" Harlem was grinning like a skull. Pulling out Dan's rifle, he tossed it into the air and caught it by its barrel in his leather-gloved hands. He offered the other end to Kayla with extravagant politeness. "Go on, then, shoot me. Be my guest."

Kayla snatched the rifle from him, her eyes flashing suspiciously. She aimed it at Harlem. It had to be a trick, but she sure as hell wasn't going to hand it back again now that she was armed.

"Pull the trigger. That's the little curvy part underneath," Harlem prompted. He opened his jacket invitingly, exposing his broad, tattooed chest.

Kayla slid her finger into the trigger guard, her pulse pounding, her mouth going dry. This guy was either very stupid or on a hell of a lot of drugs to hand her a piece like this and invite her to shoot him.

Her heart thumping, Kayla aimed the gun right in the guy's face and started to tighten her finger on the trigger. Something inside her rebelled. She'd never shot anyone before. It was harder than she'd thought it would be, with the guy just staring at her like that. She'd seen it done a million times before in the movies, but in real life it felt so... wrong. Just a tiny movement of her finger and a human—or not-so-human—life would be ended. Just like that.

She swallowed, steeling herself.

"Sorry! Time's up!"

Harlem's hand blurred and the rifle leapt out of Kayla's hand as though it were possessed. Kayla jumped back and sucked on her stinging fingers, then glanced down at the rifle as it hit the ground. A heavy iron throwing knife was embedded in the stock, inches from where her fingers had been.

She yelled as Harlem crashed into her, grabbing her by the throat and swinging her around before hauling her in close to him. He smelled so strongly of blood and alcohol that it made Kayla want to throw up. He tightened his grip on her throat, preparing to snap her neck. "Say hi to Karrel for me."

"Go to hell!" gasped Kayla.

Harlem shrugged. "'Better to reign in hell than to serve in heaven.' That's my philosophy."

"I thought your philosophy was 'kill everything that's moving and date whatever's left?'" said a smooth female voice.

Harlem looked up.

"No rest for the wicked, eh, Harlem?" Ninette stepped out of a shadow, clad in a black body suit. Its smooth lines were broken only by a commando belt containing a dizzying assortment of weapons. She held a strange contraption in her gloved hands, a bulbous, blackened steel cylinder attached to a flared barrel. Behind her, lights blazed on and a jet-black SBV trundled forward, aiming a dozen chromed lights at the scene. The driver's door burst open and Phil jumped out, training his favorite AK on Harlem's head.

Harlem's bloodshot eyes lit up with glee.

"On the contrary, I'll be resting very **well** tonight, thanks to our little Kayla."

"Huh?" said Kayla.

She felt the blood drain from her face as a multitude of dark shapes appeared through the milky white fog that was rolling slowly up the alleyway toward them. Phil and Ninette stood their ground, weapons leveled warily, as two dozen werewolves stepped out of the fog and padded up the alleyway to join Harlem. They growled softly, their yellow eyes fixed unwaveringly on the humans.

CHAPTER TWENTY-SEVEN

POLICE SIRENS SOUNDED in the distance. The two young Hunters clicked the safety catches off their weapons, apparently unbothered by the odds. The werewolf pack spread out in a flood behind Harlem, forming a bristling semi-circle behind him and blocking the alleyway. Several were in human form, wielding street pistols. Skeet headed the pack, armed with a pair of ugly curved knives. He fell in beside Harlem, a gleeful look on his face.

"Great plan, Batman," he sniggered. "We did just what you said."

"Good boy," said Harlem, eyeing Ninette smugly. "Set a kit to catch a cat... and bingo! I reckon these two'll fetch a handsome price from you-know-who, along with that little wolf boy we bagged back at the club."

A wave of guilt hit her. *Mutt.* She'd just left him there, without a thought that he might be in danger too, if anyone had seen him talking to her. "What have you done with him?"

"Relax, darlin', he's perfectly safe—" Harlem threw back his head and laughed at Kayla's expression. "—*ish*."

"You son of a bitch!"

Kayla started struggling madly, her gaze flying to the two Hunters. She saw them glance briefly at each other. Phil made a quick hand signal and raised his eyebrows. Ninette nodded grimly then turned back, aiming the barrel of her weird weapon at Harlem. Her finger hovered over a red button on the side.

"Release the girl and I'll let you live," she said.

"*You'll* let *me* live?" Harlem laughed out loud, glancing at the werewolf pack behind him. "D'you hear that boys? She'll let me live." He flicked his arrogant gaze over Ninette, drinking in every inch of her stunning, Amazonian figure. "Well, I'm sure glad you put my mind at rest on that one, sugarplum. I was getting worried there for a moment, all of you two against the twenty million of us. Jeeze."

There was a click. Phil had disengaged his safety catch. He glared at Harlem. The moonlight reflected off his polished battle armor, the picture of military efficiency.

"Drop it," Harlem growled.

Phil didn't move. Harlem stared blankly at him, then took hold of Kayla's head and started to twist. Kayla felt vital things inside her neck crunch and grate. She yelled out frantically, digging her nails into Harlem's wrist as hard as she could. The werewolf didn't so much as flinch.

"I ain't askin', kids. Drop the slingshots or the girl comes back in two bits."

Harlem twisted Kayla's head further, making her cry out in pain. She started to choke. There was a tense couple of seconds and then, unwillingly, the two Hunters placed their weapons on the ground. Skeet sauntered over and gleefully picked them up, juggling them like toys. Kayla saw Ninette go very still as Skeet examined her weapon, his blunt face scrunching into a slow, stupid frown as he tried to figure out what it was. He turned it over in his hands a couple of times, and then paused as a low whining sound came from the stock.

Beep...beep...beeeeeeeeeeee...

KA-CHINK!

Skeet jumped as twin barbed darts shot backward out of the weapon, each followed by a comet-like tail of red elastic silk. The darts embedded themselves in Skeet's neck while their tails wrapped themselves around his body and tightened, reeling back into the gun. Skeet shrieked in pain and surprise and dropped the weapon, scrabbling at the barbs buried in his neck. The gun hit the ground with a hiss of compressed air and exploded, sending a dozen more darts shooting into Skeet's body, swathing him in a mummy-like cocoon of silk.

The werewolf stumbled and fell to the ground, swearing and struggling, hopelessly entangled.

"Ah, for fuck's sake," snapped Harlem. He pulled what looked like a modified mini-chainsaw out from under his jacket, his gaze fixed on Ninette. "You want a job done properly..."

"Wait! Cyan said not to kill them!" Skeet cried, from ground level.

"Thank you, Skeet," replied Harlem pleasantly, swinging his chainsaw. "Remind me again precisely why I picked you to help me out on this little mission?"

"Cause you said the others was too scared of Harlequin to—"

"Skeet, someday before I kill you I'll explain to you the meaning of a rhetorical question," Harlem snapped.

"Harlequin?" Phil stared at Harlem, and then slowly smiled. "And Cyan? I thought we killed her back in—"

"Well, you thought wrong," Harlem snapped.

Phil shook his head, his eyes lighting up with mirth. "So, remind me which part of 'I'd rather burn in the merry fires of Hell than work with lousy stinkin' vampires' you decided to go back on?"

"You shut your mouth," Harlem growled, tightening his grip on Kayla's throat. Kayla coughed and spluttered, pulling frantically at Harlem's arm.

Phil grinned and gave a little shake of his head. "Not content with rescuing a two-timing backstabbing traitor like Cyan from a well-deserved death, you run around behind her back making deals with her genocidal lunatic and all-round scary son of a bitch ex-partner, a guy so messed up that he orders the complete extinction of his own race in order to justify his own pathological sense of aloneness?" Phil shook his head in wonder. "I have to say, I'm impressed."

"I'm bored already." Harlem turned to the gun-toting werewolf behind him. "Drop them."

"But boss, Skeet's right. Cyan said—"

"I don't care what Cyan said, you miserable little—"

A low, menacing growl started up from the werewolf pack behind him. There was something about the pitch of the growl that made Harlem pause, glancing behind him. Every eye was on him. As he turned to face the pack their growling increased sharply in volume, like a breeze gathering before a storm.

"What the...?" Harlem started.

He frowned as a medium-sized wolf with a tawny, silver-splotched coat stepped out of the pack and took a couple of steps toward him. It was bleeding from a bad double-puncture wound on its neck, and did not look happy. Harlem eyeballed the creature as it stopped a few feet from him and glared, the fur on its back bristling.

Kayla's jaw dropped in recognition.

"Mutt?" she whispered.

Several things happened at once. The silver were-wolf attacked, flying toward Harlem in a blur of scrabbling claws. The rest of the pack took off after it, fangs flashing. As the pack closed in on them, Kayla saw Phil grab his big machine gun off the ground and point it at Harlem. There was a dull *CRUMP*. Harlem's body jerked beneath her as a round of hot lead drilled into his shoulder. Harlem looked up at Phil, outraged. Phil took the opportunity to shoot him again.

Taking advantage of the distraction, Kayla slammed her elbow into Harlem's stomach and sank her teeth into his arm, twisting his wrist up and away from her throat as hard as she could. Harlem tightened his grip on her and swung her around so that her flailing legs sideswiped the nearest attacking werewolf. Then he flung her aside with a grunt and hit the power switch on his chainsaw, his eyes blazing with fury as the first werewolf launched itself at him and locked its jaws on his chainsaw arm.

Kayla hit the ground, rolled in a storm of gravel, and then pushed herself back up to her feet with a speed born of frenzy. Phil lifted his AK and took careful aim at the were-pack as they flooded toward them, trying to settle on a target.

"NO!" she cried.

Phil flung her a bemused look and paused, his finger on the trigger.

"Don't shoot. You'll hit Mutt!"

"Who?"

"The werewolf!"

"Girl, you're nuts!" Phil took aim again.

Kayla ran over to him and grabbed his arm, ignoring his warning look. "Please! Just wait!"

Phil started to reply, then broke off in bemusement as he saw the werewolf pack swamp Harlem like water flowing over a rock, snapping at his exposed torso with their razor-sharp teeth. Harlem retaliated, his face a mask of outrage. He swung his roaring chainsaw at the wolves nearest to him. Blood flew against the nearby wall and snarls turned to squeals. Kayla saw the chainsaw connect with the belly of one smaller gray wolf, its intestines flopping to the ground a second before its lifeless body followed suit.

She turned away, sickened.

"What the hell?" Ninette stared at the unfolding action, and then swung to face Kayla. "Start talking. Who's Mutt?" she asked urgently.

"A friend," Kayla gasped.

"Bullshit, girlfriend," snapped Ninette. "Those are *werewolves*, not friends."

Kayla pointed at one dark shape as it dodged and ducked through the mass of creatures attacking Harlem. "That one is... he said he was friends with Karrel?"

Ninette's hazel eyes widened in realization. "That's the little shit from lab eight!" she burst out. "I thought it looked familiar! And you let it out..."

Kayla was no longer listening. She stared at the silver wolf as it dodged and ducked through the melee, trying to get to Harlem. She gave a shout as she saw three of the human-form werewolves converge on the wolf. They pumped several shots into it to knock it down before grabbing it and hauling it toward a parked black minivan.

Without even thinking Kayla started forward, desperate to save Mutt, then yipped and jumped back as something struck the ground beside her. Skeet had managed to pull one arm free from his red silk bonds. He awkwardly aimed a small Ruger pistol at her, his finger tight on the trigger.

"Kayla! *RUN!*" yelled Phil.

He jerked and crashed to the ground as Skeet fired three rounds into his chest.

Kayla froze in shock, staring at Phil's unmoving body. Then Skeet shifted his aim and emptied his pistol into Ninette's back, sending the young Hunter spinning to the ground just a few paces from Phil. Silence descended, broken only by the roar of Harlem's chainsaw as he fought off the were-pack, half a block away.

Then that, too, fell silent.

Kayla slowly turned to face Harlem, staring at him in horror as he casually sheathed his chainsaw and stepped out of a large pile of bleeding wolf bodies. Not one of them was moving. Feeling her gaze on him he turned and winked at her, then started moving unhurriedly in her direction.

Kayla's heart slammed against her ribcage.

Whirling, she fled like a ghost down the alley.

CHAPTER TWENTY-EIGHT

KAYLA TORE THROUGH row after row of long, darkened back lots, putting as much distance between herself and the bloodbath behind her as she could. Police sirens whirred on the main road, converging on the sound of gunfire, but they were too far away to be of any use to her.

She ran four, five, six, seven blocks without tiring. She finally slowed and stopped with a jolt, panting, scanning the street behind her.

It was empty.

For a moment she thought she was home free, and then...

A voice. Drifting out of the fog.

"Kayla," it cried, singsong. "Kaaaaylaaaa."

Kayla backed up against the wall of the alley, taking refuge in the shadow of an overflowing dumpster as she peered frantically back down the street. Harlem calmly strode out of the wall of roiling fog that filled the street like an image from hell.

His biker jacket was shredded by gunfire, his face and hands streaked with blood.

Worst of all, he was still grinning that awful grin.

Something gave way inside Kayla's head at the sight of him. She was amazed to find herself stepping out of the shadows and into the open, balking at running any further. She stared at the invitingly empty street ahead of her and swallowed hard. It was pointless, wasn't it? She knew she could run and run forever, but a feeling in the pit of her stomach told her that somehow, this guy would still find her and kill her.

Enough running.

It was time to fight back.

Kayla's fists clenched at her sides as she turned to face the insane, blood-slicked werewolf. Her long, tangled hair hung across her face as she guardedly watched him approach.

Harlem stopped a short distance from Kayla and regarded her with interest. He reached up to slide his thumbs under the tattered remains of his jacket, dropping it softly to the ground as if divesting himself of a shroud.

"'Yet from these flames no light,'" he murmured, "'But rather darkness visible...'"

Kayla blinked, trying to place the quote.

"Milton, huh?" she said.

Harlem shrugged, his eyes never leaving hers. Kayla quickly backed off a few steps. She found that she was unable to look away, fascinated and appalled at Harlem's exposed torso. The guy was built like a prize fighter. Muscles like sacks of snakes were trapped behind taut, bulging sinews. His broad chest was marred by two dozen sucking bullet holes. His blood-spattered mini-chainsaw hung from a strap rigging down his back, where its modified diamond shape fitted snugly in the groove between his slab-like muscles. A barbed wire tattoo ran down his corded arm between two black-and-red pornographic demons, criss-crossing his stomach before disappearing into the top of his filthy jeans. What was left of his hair fell forward into the spiky mess of his thick mohawk, ungelled now and flopping into his face, making him looked like some punk-ass lead singer who had just butchered the rest of his metal band.

Kayla had a feeling that tonight, he wasn't going to be the one singing.

She stood her ground. Harlem walked right up to her and stopped, cocking his head to one side as though he expected her to run screaming. When she didn't, his smile grew wider. His kohl-rimmed eyes burned with a deep, dark, and somehow knowing malice, as if the thoughts scurrying around in her head like frightened mice were written on her forehead for him to read and dissect.

Harlem laughed as though guessing her thoughts, then reached up to wipe the blood from his face. "Done running?"

"Depends," Kayla said, willing her voice not to shake. "You done quoting dead English poets?"

His smile died as he stepped closer to the girl and looked her over, his eyes glittering fiercely. She was a pretty piece of ass, no mistaking. Standing there in that little dress, lungs heaving as though in the throes of passion, the avenging angel look on her sweet little face promising him a whole world of fun and games. It was almost a shame to waste her so quickly. Still, orders were orders, and a bet was a bet.

A picture of Cyan rose in his mind and he banished all thoughts of letting the girl live. She was a means to an end; that was all. He felt his mouth go dry in anticipation of the fun to come as he sauntered toward her, not even bothering to reach for the knives he kept in his belt. The girl's neck was so skinny he could probably snap it one-handed. No need to dirty his chainsaw any further.

Kayla stood her ground, one hand clenched tightly around her lucky coin necklace. She lifted a piece of thick metal piping from a nearby gutter and hefted it apprehensively as Harlem approached her, centering herself, letting all those martial arts moves she'd seen on TV and in the movies fill her mind. She could do this. Karrel had told her that he'd given her his strength. So far, that seemed to be true. With her new powers, all she had to do was get in a couple of good strikes and this guy would be down for the count.

Simple.

Harlem reached out for her with one great dirty hand. Kayla swung the pipe madly and batted his hand away. Concentrating fiercely, she spun the length of metal around in a diagonal arc, the pipe whistling through the air.

THUNK!

More by luck than aim she cracked Harlem in the ribs. The werewolf grunted in pain and surprise, and Kayla quickly grabbed the other end of the pipe and slammed it broadside into his chest, shoving him backward with every ounce of strength she had left in her body. She expected him to go flying through the air, as Mutt had done.

Instead of falling, Harlem merely stumbled back a couple of paces, surprised. Then he grinned and raised an eyebrow, rubbing his chest.

"Nice technique. For a girl."

The werewolf's arm blurred and suddenly he was holding the pipe. Kayla gasped and quickly backed off as Harlem dismissively bent the two-inch thick pipe up into a U shape and tossed it aside with a hollow clang. His eyes glittered as he moved closer to her, running his gaze down Kayla's trembling body.

"Ordinarily, I like my women how I like my coffee—ground up and in the freezer— but for you..." Harlem licked his lips, his eyes bright with violence. "For you, I'd be willing to make an exception."

He slammed into her, sending her sprawling to the ground. Kayla gave a yell of alarm, and desperately twisted her body to the side as Harlem's steel-heeled boot came stomping down, missing her face by inches. She rolled over and kicked upwards at the werewolf's kneecap as hard as she could. Harlem sidestepped her wildly flailing leg and clamped his hand around her ankle, lifting her bodily off the ground and flinging her across the alleyway. She crashed into a pile of stacked wooden crates.

Kayla tumbled across the ground in a storm of flying woodchips and broken panels. Rolling over groggily, she pressed the back of her hand to her mouth, watching dumbly as blood—her blood— flowed from a deep cut in her lip.

"Ah, fuck," she muttered.

Her old feelings of helplessness rolled through her as Harlem began striding toward her, cracking his knuckles. She almost choked on the acid taste of fear and bile that rose up into her mouth. This wasn't a game! This was real! This guy had killed Karrel and her two new Hunter friends and Mutt's entire wolf-pack, and now he was about to kill her too, or worse. Kayla's limbs turned to jelly, as though she had water instead of blood running through her veins, and she came to a hard realization.

She was no match for this guy.

She had to get out of there.

Kayla lurched to her feet and took off into the night, Harlem's insane cackle of triumph floating down the street behind her.

FEAR ADDED WINGS to Kayla's feet as she darted down a little side alley, pelted along parallel with a buzzing electricity grid station, and then burst out onto the main street.

Finally. Lights. Life. Civilization. People.

Immediately, Kayla realized that this might not have been such a great idea. It was a Saturday night, and the place was awash with activity. People thronged the sidewalks, flowing down from the cheap parking lots of the malls in the general direction of Hollywood Boulevard, with its bars and clubs and late night shopping. Kids ran screaming around the legs of their parents, while tourists struggled with cameras and backpacks, blocking the sidewalks with their enormous maps, endlessly photographing one another against the familiar landmarks of the area—the Walk of Fame, the Hollywood sign, Ripley's Believe-It-Or-Not, Grumman's Chinese Theatre. It was close to ten o'clock but the area was lit up as bright as day, teeming with life, music, and humanity.

It wasn't the kind of place you'd really want to lead a homicidal werewolf to.

Kayla snapped a frantic glance behind her, hoping against hope that he wouldn't follow her. For a moment she thought she'd lost him. Then her heart jumped into her mouth as she saw Harlem emerging from the side alley. His vengeful gaze scanned the faces in the crowd, grimly searching for her. Kayla saw passing tourists stop and stare at him as he stepped casually out into the crowd, the festive streetlights overhead reflecting off his blood-covered torso. Nobody seemed particularly alarmed. It took Kayla a second to figure out why.

This was Hollywood, wasn't it? The land of movies and illusion. No one was going to bat an eyelid at the sight of a semi-naked guy covered in bullet holes walking down the street, because it obviously wasn't real. The guy was an actor, promoting some new movie, and that was just fake blood and some wicked prosthetics. Just a block away, there was a guy dressed in a Spiderman outfit balanced on a fire hydrant, handing out lollipops and fliers to the crowd. Over the crosswalk, three of the Mystery Men were emerging from Mel's Diner, clutching take-out bags and bickering about the price of valet parking.

Kayla watched as a young family stepped right in front of Harlem, blocking his path. The father snapped a flash photo of the werewolf. His ten year-old son peered up at Harlem, wide-eyed, breaking into a huge grin.

"Hey! Cool chainsaw!" he said.

Harlem ignored him, pushing his way rudely past the family as he searched for Kayla. The crowd briefly parted and his vengeful gaze locked with hers. He shoved his way toward her, his pace slowed by the sheer mass of humanity in his path.

Elbowing her way across the sidewalk, Kayla jumped down into the road and started sprinting down the side of the bus lane, praying that she wouldn't get hit by a taxi or stopped by the cops. Getting a ticket for jaywalking was the least of her concerns, but the last thing she wanted was some cop giving her shit and demanding to see photo ID when she was about to get her head hacked off by a psychopathic, chainsaw-wielding werewolf.

She increased her pace, leaping back onto the sidewalk as a packed Metro night-bus roared past, spewing out a gust of foul-smelling wind and whipping up a storm of trash behind it like dirty plastic snow. A young man clutching a sheaf of postcards grabbed her arm as she passed by, pressing a card into her hand.

"Do you have an agent?" he babbled, "'cause with a look like yours, you could make big bucks if you'll just sign up for—"

"I don't want to be an actress," snapped Kayla, shoving past him.

"Yeah, right." The man smirked. "That's what they all say. So, if you take us on as your representati—hey!"

Kayla sent the man sprawling into the gutter with a wild shove and plowed on.

A gap in the traffic beckoned and Kayla tore across the road, hoping to throw Harlem off. A screech of brakes from behind her told her that this wasn't a smart move. She threw a glance over her shoulder just in time to see Harlem vault over a moving cab. He snarled at an oncoming stretch limo so that its driver had to turn the wheel hard to avoid him, missing a brand-new white Mercedes by inches. Horns blared and cars jolted to a surprised halt as Harlem leapt over them, crossing the four lanes of traffic in a series of seven-foot jumps. As he reached the other side the tourists on the sidewalk applauded, obviously thinking that this was some publicity stunt, while a pair of cops reached for their radios, leafing through their nightly filming permit schedules with confusion.

Kayla whirled and ran on.

The glowing lights of a packed restaurant drew her. Surely Harlem wouldn't follow her in there?

Inside, it was hot and bright. Kayla blinked painfully as she barged her way past the line of people waiting to be seated and strode into the clattering, noisy depths of the restaurant. She ignored the handsome young waiter who tried to hand her a menu. Breathing hard, she smoothed down her torn, dirty clothes and walked with as much restraint as she could to the back of the room, as though she was going to the restroom. Her last few shreds of sanity kept her from breaking into a full run. She needed to hide, to breathe, to come up with a plan. She couldn't think straight to save her life, and right now, that was precisely what she needed to do.

She reached the other end of the room and paused by the kitchen. With a furtive glance behind her she put her hand on a door labeled "Employees Only," her pulse hammering in her throat. Some sixth sense made her turn as she pushed the door open, throwing a last, quick glance across the restaurant.

A waiter was standing at the door, talking to someone outside and looking a little freaked. As she watched in horror, he looked right at her and pointed a helpful finger in her direction.

Adrenaline jumpstarted Kayla's heart. Shoving her way through the door in a blaze of fear, she ran through the small, dark room on the other side, a storage area cluttered with half-unpacked boxes and crates and discarded refuse bags, a rat's nest of disuse. For one heart-stopping moment she thought she might have reached a dead end, but then her frantically groping fingers found a handle buried under a swathe of hanging uniforms and she heaved with all her might.

It was locked.

A crack of light fell across her as the door behind her started to swing open.

In a frenzy Kayla leaned back and put her entire weight onto the handle, turning it as hard as she could. To her infinite relief, the locks popped off with a crack and the door swung open. This whole "super-strength" thing was helpful, but still, she knew she was no match against someone who was armed.

Kayla barreled through, almost plummeting head-first down the industrial metal stairs that lay on the other side. Catching herself on the doorframe and swinging around, she jumped down the steps three at a time and raced down the short passageway at the bottom, twisting and turning in the maze-like lower levels of the restaurant. The smell of dust and damp filled her nostrils, but she kept running, searching for a way out. She heard someone come down the stairs heavily behind her and increased her pace, stumbling into walls, tripping over boxes in the semi-darkness until finally her groping fingers found an unlocked door set into the wall at the end of the passageway.

She was free!

Jerking the door open, Kayla hazarded a quick glance behind her. There was no sign of pursuit. She tensed her body to lunge through the door and continue her mad dash, but something made her glance again over her shoulder.

Lockers lined the wall behind her. Man-sized lockers.

Before she knew what she was doing she flung the door wide as though she had just run through it, letting it crash loudly against the wall. Then she ran for the lockers, pulling open the nearest empty one and diving inside. She waited there in the darkness, heart hammering, pushing herself as far back as she could from the wire ventilation grill on the front of the locker. Claustrophobia set in almost immediately. It was hot and cramped, and smelled sickeningly of rotting food, but she knew instinctively that it was the right thing to do. If she kept on running, Harlem would just keep on chasing her. Could werewolves see in the dark? God, she hoped not.

The light around her faded as the door swung closed.

Footsteps came down the stairs heavily, scraping and ringing on the metal steps. They sounded in no particular hurry. Kayla shrank back from the grill, trying to hold her breath as the footsteps clumped slowly toward her locker. Her heaving lungs betrayed her and she put both hands over her mouth. Her body screamed for air, her heart thumping so loudly in her chest that she was sure Harlem could hear it.

Time seemed to pause as the footsteps passed by her locker and headed toward the door. Then they stopped. Kayla screwed her eyes shut, everything in her silently begging Harlem to take the bait, to go on through the door after her so that she could slip back quietly up the stairs, find the waiter, and stay in the restaurant while he called the police. They would come and take her to safety before—

The door of her locker was torn open.

Kayla screamed, throwing up her hands as she prepared to make a last, futile fight for her life.

Nothing happened.

Kayla fearfully opened first one eye, then the other.

"That's a really great scream you got there," said Phil, cautiously removing his hands from his ears. "You ever thought of auditioning for the Home Makeover show?"

Kayla dived out of the locker, nearly knocking it over in her haste to get out. "Phil! Oh my God! I thought you were dead!"

"So did I. I need to call the guy who invented flak jackets and buy him a beer." Phil tapped his chest.

"Harlem!" Kayla's gaze flew to the stairs. "Is he here?"

"Who, Big Bubba?" Phil shrugged. "Nah. He ran off with half the LAPD after him. Cops caught him chainsawing a Scientology recruitment guy in half. They waited until he was done before they went after him, though." Phil rubbed his jaw thoughtfully. "Can't think why."

"Thank Christ for that." Kayla started moving toward the open back door, then stopped, frowning, as her brain nagged at her.

"Phil? Where's Ninette?" she asked.

"See, that's the thing."

Kayla turned to Phil. His usually cheerful face was somber.

"They took her, Kayla," said Phil, picking at the bloodied strap of his AK. "They took my girl."

CHAPTER TWENTY-NINE

KAYLA HAD TO jog to keep up as she followed Phil out the back of the restaurant and headed toward his parked SBV. Half his armor was missing and his face was cut and bloodied, but he didn't seem to notice.

"I got two cars coming to rendezvous with us on Venice Boulevard, and I've rung in a city-wide alert that should hopefully give us a few leads on where those scumbags are headed." Phil pulled out his remote to unlock the car with a quiet beep.

"So what now?"

"We drive. Maybe we'll find them, maybe not. Either way, we ain't going home tonight."

"Shouldn't we wait and see if they make some kind of ransom demand?" asked Kayla.

Phil swung sharply around to face her. Kayla took a step back when she saw the look on his face. "They've got Ninette," he said simply.

Kayla nodded. She understood.

"They took Mutt, too," she added, a little defensively.

"The werewolf?" Phil looked at her weirdly. "Did I mention that you're crazy?"

"Twice."

"Then I've covered my bases, but don't worry, we'll get them back. Because guess what?" Phil gave her a chilling grin. "We've got something of theirs, too."

Phil hit a tab on the back of the car to open up the trunk. The hatch swung open. Skeet peered up at them, his enormous body bent almost double and covered in blood. He was still swathed in sticky red fabric. He did not look like he was having a good time.

"Hello, Skeet," said Phil pleasantly. "How many body parts would you like to keep?"

"Is that a rhetorical question?" he asked.

EIGHT MINUTES LATER, they knew all they needed to know. Kayla watched Phil as he bundled Skeet back into the trunk, not sure whether to be impressed or scared.

She rubbed her arms, shivering in the cold. "So... those red syringe thingies... remind me what's in them again?"

"That chemical with the reeeeally long name." Phil shoved Skeet's head back down, holding him in place as though trying to stuff an over-full suitcase. "Remember, we told you. The red one stops werewolves from changing. When they're in human form they're tough little motherfuckers, but as a wolf they're stronger. Plus there's the added bonus for them that wolves can't talk and tell us where the hell their boss has taken my girl."

Phil glowered down at Skeet, who was stuck mid-change, his grimy, unshaven face covered with ratty brown fur, his hands semi-morphed into claws.

"If he so much as lays a finger on her..."

"I know, you said. 'You'll rip off my head an' feed it to me.'" Skeet stopped, frowning in sulky confusion. "That don't make no sense. How can I eat my own head?"

"I'm the one asking the questions here!" snapped Phil. He slammed the trunk on Skeet and jumped into the car. "You sure you know where this Genetica place is?"

"Positive," said Kayla as she buckled up, her mind still on Skeet. She wanted to kill him so badly that she'd barely been able to see straight, but Phil said they needed to keep him alive, in case they needed bargaining material. She'd eventually agreed, with reluctance.

She shook herself, trying to stay focused.

"So what is this place?" Phil asked her.

"Genetica? Some big new gene therapy clinic. They've been all over the TV for weeks. It's their big opening night bash tonight. Lots of famous people are going, so the place will be crawling with security. We'll have to be careful, but if that's where they've taken Ninette and Mutt, we'll have to risk it."

"You sure you know how to get there?"

Kayla shrugged. "I have this." She reached into her pocket and pulled out the postcard Julissa had given her, feeling like a super sleuth, trying not to look too smug.

Phil took the card from her and examined it. He turned it over. "Gee, I dunno. You got anything better than that?"

"Better?" Kayla burst out. "It's got the address and phone number of the place on the bottom..." She stopped. "That's sarcasm again, right?" she said.

"You're learning," said Phil, as he started the engine.

DETECTIVE JAKE COLLINS lowered his infra-red scope and turned to Ned, who was perching precariously on a low wall near the edge of the roof. He was clutching a night vision camcorder in one hand, staring fixedly down at it. Behind him, five black-clad LAPD SWAT troopers fiddled with their sniper rifles, shuffling their feet and avoiding each other's eyes.

Jake fumbled with his lighter, still gazing down the road. "How's the new battery on that thing holding out?" he asked carefully, without looking around.

"Good, boss," muttered Ned.

"So, you got all of that, then?"

"In seven-point-one surround sound," said Ned mechanically, "and the digital zoom worked just great."

His stomach heaved and he quickly pressed his palm over his mouth, his worried eyes flitting back to the street below. "A little too great, perhaps."

"Excellent," Jake said brightly, attempting to light his already-smoldering cigarette. "So do we call *Weird News*, or just get ourselves committed right now?"

"Well... let me think about that, boss." Ned pulled the strap of his camcorder off his hand and carefully set it down on the ledge of the roof. Then he pulled a .22 pistol out of his waistband and shot Jake twice, neatly in the stomach.

Jake crumpled to the ground, staring wide-eyed up at his partner. Ned pulled out a lens cleaning cloth and carefully polished his fingerprints off the handgrip of his pistol. Then he laid the gun on the rooftop next to his boss's writhing body.

"Sorry, sir," he said, retrieving Jake's cigarette pack from the ground where it had fallen. "I guess people really do kill people, but you gotta admit, the gun helps."

Straightening up, he pulled out a cigarette and lit it, then turned to face the SWAT troops, blowing a plume of smoke up into the night air.

"Now, for your next exercise. Anyone fancy bagging themselves a werewolf?"

CHAPTER THIRTY

PHIL HONKED HIS horn as he and Kayla sat in the interminable traffic on the road to Downtown. He'd retracted the guns and fins on the SBV before they hit the main roads. As they inched their way up the 10 freeway, they blended in perfectly with the Saturday night crowds heading out to party on Sunset Boulevard.

"Come on, come on," Phil muttered. "Tell you something, this 'being a superhero' business sucks. If Batman lived in LA, I swear he'd be dead from traffic fumes by the age of thirty, and Robin would be running a gay bar up on Melrose, complaining about the rising cost of spandex and how they just don't make spangly pants the way they used to."

"And they'd never find parking for the Batmobile," added Kayla. "Can you imagine trying to valet that thing?"

Phil looked at her thoughtfully, drumming his fingers on the dash. "That's the problem with superheroes, they just don't fit into the real world."

"Maybe that's the world's fault."

"Or maybe if they fit in, they wouldn't be super."

"You Hunters seem to do pretty well."

"Yeah, right," said Phil. "We live underground in a big steel bunker, which, by the way, gets really crappy cell phone reception. We're not allowed to tell our friends or family what we do for a living in case it gets them killed, or us killed, or everybody killed, and we don't get to go to IHOP nearly enough." He took an exit off the freeway in a fit of frustration, decelerating down the steeply curved off-ramp onto the surface road below. "Trust me, it sucks being a hero."

"But you get to save people's lives."

"Yeah, whatever." Phil fiddled with the stereo. "Give me giant triple-stacked chocolate-chip pancakes with whipped cream anyday, or even a kick-ass movie."

Kayla gave a little laugh.

"What?"

"Nothing. I guess the grass is always greener."

"Meaning?"

"Forget it." Kayla pulled a cloth out of the gun rack beside her seat and started scrubbing some of the dried blood off her skin. "I guess people always think stuff's more glamorous than it really is. Everyone thinks their life would be better if only they were famous, or a superhero, or whatever. Truth is, it often makes things worse."

"I wouldn't mind being famous," said Phil distractedly, clearing a batch of AK clips off the dashboard as he hunted for his road map.

"You say that because you guys used to be in a band, right?"

Phil glanced up at her in surprise. "Why do you say that?"

"Well, let's see." Kayla looked Phil over. "One, you're not a goth but you're wearing black nail polish; two, you say 'kick-ass' a lot; three, you have band stickers on your machine gun; and four, you keep spare guitar strings in your weapons case." She folded her arms and sat back smugly in her seat. "Coincidence?"

"I don't say 'kick-ass' that much," Phil mumbled.

"Yes, you do. Besides, this is Los Angeles, also known as 'Slash City.' Nobody ever just does one thing. Everyone here is a waiter-slash-actor, or a bargirl-slash-screenwriter, or a receptionist-slash-porn star. People come to LA to be in the movies or in music, then wind up working in a mall to earn a living while they wait for their dreams to come true. Then their boyfriend gets killed by werewolves and they find out that not only do vampires exist, but that an alarming number of them want to kill them for no particular reason. It all goes downhill after that."

Kayla broke off, a wistful look on her face.

"So if I was in a band," Phil went on, after a respectful pause, "which I might not be, you wouldn't tell anyone, would you? Hunters aren't supposed to have outside commitments. It makes us vulnerable, whatever the hell that means, but it's why we came to LA in the first place, and it's what we wanna do when I'm through with all this."

"I'll take it to the grave," said Kayla.

Phil turned onto a long, tree-lined street that led to the parking lots of Genetica. Spotlights wheeled in the sky around the brightly lit main building. The area was packed, people and paparazzi swarming around while the valet parking guys tried to deal with everyone at once.

"So what about you?" asked Phil, trying to change the subject. "What do you want from LA?"

Kayla considered this, trying to shift her suddenly fatalistic mood. "Me? Well, two days ago, all I wanted was for my supervisor to get off my case and Karrel to ask me to marry him so I could get out of that crappy dead-end apartment block before I hit thirty and actually *do* something with my life. Now, Karrel's dead, I'm on the run from a werewolf hit squad, I got two new friends kidnapped by monsters, and all I can think about is what I'd give for a hot shower, something to eat, and a change of clothes."

"That's why we wear black all the time," said Phil smugly. "Doesn't show the blood, onstage or off." He reached into the back and tossed a bag at her.

"What's this?"

"Spare Hunter's uniform. Should fit you."

"Do I get a gun and a badge too?"

"You're funny."

"But what if you need backup?"

"Sorry, kid. You're sitting this one out. We're getting Ninette and your buddy back, and then we're dropping you home. This shit is far too dangerous."

"No way! It's my fault they took your girl and Mutt. I want to help you get them back, and I'll do whatever it takes. Even if that means joining the Hunters after tonight, but I need to come in with you and help fight. If anything's happened to either of them, I'll never forgive myself."

"Let me just check... nah, that won't fit on your tombstone. Can you say it again, in fewer words?"

"I won't need a tombstone. I just need a chance to prove myself." Kayla paused. "It's something that I need to do, for Karrel, and for me."

"Girl, you're crazy. You wanna save lives? Go give blood. You join the Hunters, you're just gonna wind up getting yourself killed, or worse."

"What's worse than getting killed?"

There was the slightest hesitation before Phil replied. "Seeing someone you love get killed."

He sighed and pulled a small, filed-down gun from his belt pack. He passed it over to her, along with a handful of spare clips. "Silver frag rounds, filled with garlic. One shot'll take down a vamp or a wolf. Use them wisely, 'cause they cost an arm and a leg to make, sometimes quite literally."

Kayla examined the clip. "All you Hunters use these?"

"Nah. We give them to newbies to get up their confidence."

"Great." Kayla pocketed the pistol as Phil turned the SBV into an empty parking spot. "So when do I get a real gun?"

"Never, but don't worry, you won't need one."

"Why not?"

"Why? Girl, you're with the professionals now, you won't ever need to... whoa!"

Phil hurriedly slammed on the brakes as the car rebounded off the curb and stalled. "Sorry! Little curb-check there." He glanced into the side mirror to see an alarmed valet running toward them. He pointed in delight. "Look, I made the little guy run! That's ten points to me!"

"We're all going to die, aren't we?" sighed Kayla.

"Hey." Phil slipped a flak jacket over her head. "Now you're starting to sound like a real Hunter."

CHAPTER THIRTY-ONE

"ANOTHER GLASS OF champagne, madam?"

Julissa gave a sigh of contentment as she lifted a shining crystal glass off the waiter's silver tray. She took a sip, swilling the sharp, sweet amber liquid through her teeth as she gazed happily around her. The plush ballroom was awash with important people—celebrities, TV stars, musicians, models, actors, the works. They all sipped their drinks and talked loudly and animatedly about themselves as they waited for the climax of the evening—the grand unveiling of the new treatment that claimed to actually reverse the signs of aging.

The enormous room was laid out with lavish tables of food and drink. Original art hung on every wall, specially commissioned for the event, the general theme being "beauty." As with every Hollywood affair the décor was larger than life. The centerpiece of the room was a magnificent mahogany table featuring three top Belgian supermodels sprawled semi-naked amid platters of imported exotic fruit, handing out snacks and drinks. On an opposing table, a beautifully muscled male model stood on a wooden plinth, his equally semi-naked body carefully airbrushed to give his flesh the appearance of white marble. At the start of the evening he'd been handing out brochures to giggling young ladies, now he was smoking a cigarette and talking on his cell phone to his agent as the speeches went on and on.

Julissa turned her attention back to the main stage, where just minutes ago a prominent up-and-coming rock band had been playing during an interlude. It was nearly time for her to go on. She took another sip of champagne to drown the butterflies in her stomach. Now Jagos's guy was back up on stage, waxing lyrical about the many wonders of his company's treatments and calling up smiling ex-patients to demonstrate. He'd told her that she would be the final star up on stage—living proof of the effectiveness of Genetica's new wonder-drug, with before-and-after videos and blood tests to prove it.

Julissa looked down at her hands, turning them over and over, marveling for the hundredth time that day at how perfect they looked. Each and every one of the tiny marks, sun splotches, scars and minute wrinkles that were as familiar to her as—well, as the back of her hand—had just... gone. The last time her skin had looked this perfect she'd been fifteen years old. With each successive treatment her skin had just got better and better, glowing with an inner radiance that already made her friends green with envy.

But their compliments just washed over her. She'd always known how good she looked, even before this treatment thing, but now there was only one person's opinion and approval she craved. And he wasn't here.

Julissa adjusted her voluptuous cleavage and snuck a hopeful look around the room, taking another quick sip of her champagne. She'd asked her agent to mail Tyler's agent an invite to this bash, explaining in her handwritten cover letter how good the TV exposure would be for his career, while subtly hinting that if he showed up to this gig, it wouldn't just be the free treatment pack he would be taking home at the end of the night. It had taken her the best part of the afternoon to compose the four sentence note, writing and rewriting it until it was perfect, which in itself was deeply pathetic. Right now, Julissa didn't care. She just wanted Tyler to be here. The fact that he wasn't was deeply disturbing to her, as was her realization that she still gave a damn.

That was the trouble with love: it wasn't over, even when it was over.

She transferred her troubled attention back to the stage as Jagos finished up his speech and turned to face her, smiling.

"And now, ladies and gents, the moment you've all been waiting for. The new face of Genetica and the first ever recipient of our age-defying wonder drug Rev-X, Julissa Cortez!"

The crowd applauded. Julissa put down her glass and stood up straight, smiling for the cameras as they panned around in her direction.

Finally, her big moment had arrived.

She was on.

She lifted her jeweled satin dress and started to walk down the isle toward the front of the stage. Then she stopped, glancing down at her nails.

That was odd. She could've sworn they hadn't been that long a minute ago. She frowned down at them, bemused. They were almost an inch long and pointed at the ends, more like the claws of an animal than the nails of a human.

Still, no time to worry about that now. Julissa quickly fumbled in her purse for her satin gloves, and slipped them on, still smiling.

There, all better.

She took two more steps toward the front, and then stopped again as a quiet ripping sound reached her ears. She looked down. The ends of her gloves had split open and the white French-polished tips of her nails were poking through.

The TV cameras swung to track her as Julissa determinedly clenched her fists, hiding her nails. She continued walking up the steps toward the stage.

UP IN THE control room of Genetica, Magnus rested his bandaged knuckles on the mixing deck. He peered contentedly down at the TV monitors, watching the festivities in the ballroom down below. He had a makeshift splint on one leg, and one side of his face was blackened, swollen, and covered in white surgical tape.

He looked up and grunted in greeting as Skyler Banks came in.

"The delegates just arrived. Everything is in place," said Skyler.

Magnus nodded, and then turned his attention back to the TV monitors. "Look at them down there, lapping it up." The big werewolf stared at the screen, his broad, arrogant face lighting up in wonder. "If tonight goes well, we'll be laughing. You know how much Hollywood's finest would pay for a drug that totally stops aging? And that's without our little deal with the suppliers in Europe."

"They beat Japan, eh?"

"By thirty mil... guess they should have brought more pocket change over on the boat with them." Magnus rubbed his hands together, cackling gleefully. "Get used to the good life, little man, 'cause that's what we'll be living after tonight."

"You know," Skyler said uncomfortably and handed Magnus a shot glass of whisky. "I just keep thinking about that last seven percent."

"What of it?"

Skyler swallowed. "I just... I don't want there to be any comeback. If those scary-ass motherfuckers from England get wind of the fact that that this stuff ain't ready to roll yet, it would be the end, for us and for you. We'd both lose everything."

"And what do you know about loss?"

"Enough." Skyler folded his arms and leaned back on the doorframe. "There was this one time in Italy when we were fighting this big coven of witch-demons, and—"

"Shut up," said Magnus, without rancor. The blue light of the TV monitors played across his unshaven face. It took Skyler a couple of seconds to recognize the look on the werewolf boss's face.

Magnus was afraid.

Skyler stared.

"Let me tell you about loss, Mr. Banks," Magnus said quietly. "When was the last time you were so fucking terrified, so scared shitless, that you couldn't even breathe?"

Skyler was silent.

With a sigh, Magnus turned his back on him and crossed to the large oval viewing window. He reached to pour himself another shot of whisky.

"Before this," Magnus waved down at his powerful werewolf body, "I had nothing, less than nothing. The Southside tenement building I lived in... I remember once catching rats, skinning them with Dad's penknife, and trying to cook them. We were always so fucking hungry. Crime ain't crime when you're starving. You go without food a couple days, the rules of the jungle start to kick in. Everything starts to look like food—purses, autos, houses... then finally, people. It's like baby steps on the path to hell."

Magnus gazed out at the ballroom, sipping his drink. He gave the shadow of a smile as a memory sparked.

"We're all animals in the end, as much as we like to pretend otherwise, but do we lock up a dog for stealing a cookie? Fry a lion in the chair for killing a deer? No, but that ain't the way the LAPD sees it. Every man has a choice, or so they say. To kill or not to kill, that is the question. The cops think they're the answer, but they ain't always the right one, and they sure as hell weren't the right answer for me. Got bit by some loco bitch while I was in the county lockup, and that was the end of it. She took my life, and gave me another one, one I never asked for."

Magnus stared down at the ballroom below him, at the happy, tanned people as they milled about, drinking his wine and eating his food. "Some days, I wish she'd just killed me and been done with it."

"But you've achieved so much!" said Skyler, passing his boss another whisky shot. "Look around you. You're top dog now. You own all of this. You've got every werewolf in the state kowtowing to you and every major player across the globe waiting in the wings, offering you millions for the chance to pick clean your kill. You can go anywhere you want, and do anything you want. You don't have to answer to anyone."

Magnus shook his head slowly. "You're wrong, Mr. Banks. There is one person I must one day answer to: the one person nobody can escape, except for vampires."

Sklyer got his meaning.

"But with the formula... if it succeeds, I mean, you won't ever have to worry about dying, about it all someday coming to an end. You could live forever!"

Magnus raised his glass to Skyler's, and then knocked back his whisky. "The trouble with 'someday' is that it always comes sooner than you think, Mr. Banks, and you can't really lose what was never yours in the first place."

His expression suddenly became fixed as he gazed down at the crowds below them. He pointed a black-nailed finger. "Speaking of trouble, what's *she* doing down there?"

"Cyan? I invited her."

Skyler jumped as Magnus thumped his fist down on the drink cart, pulverizing it and sending bottles spinning across the floor.

"So uninvite her," Magnus snarled, all vulnerability suddenly gone from his face. "Then tell all your little Hunter buddies that it's open season on her and her pack of neanderthals. Cyan is off my books, permanently."

"You know," a new voice said, "neanderthals were actually quite bright, or so I've heard."

Magnus jumped and spun around as the big punk werewolf stepped past Skyler into the control room. Dana tailed him, leaning smugly back against a bank of security monitors and wrapping her white furs around herself. Harlem glanced down at the smashed drink cart. He selected an unbroken bottle of Russian vodka from the heap, holding it up to the light to read the label. "Or so I've read," he added.

"Security!" cried Magnus, jumping up.

The door creaked open and a uniformed man leaned through. Magnus opened his mouth to bark an order, and then closed it again with a tired sigh. The guard's eyes had been carved out, blood daubed in two circles on his cheeks like pantomime rouge. Flame stepped through the door behind him, wearing a waiter's tuxedo and a silver half-mask that covered the burned portion of his face.

He dangled the dead guard from a clawed hand, watching blood drip onto the plush carpet.

"Evening, all," he wheezed. "Anyone order the vegetarian?"

Magnus glared at Skyler as the three werewolves moved to flank him. In the ballroom downstairs the ceremony continued, a round of applause rising up from the crowd as Julissa took the stage.

Magnus folded his arms, his face tight with anger. "I take it this means you're declining my offer, my very... *generous*... offer."

Skyler spread his hands expansively, relaxing for the first time all day. "What can I say? Money talks, old man, but you have to choose who you listen to, and I've been listening very hard lately."

"Cyan," rumbled Magnus, his eyes flashing with anger.

Skyler saw Harlem's high-cheekboned face swivel in his direction, and he shifted uncomfortably. "The vampire can be somewhat persuasive," he admitted, feeling his cheeks start to burn, "but this isn't about her. It's about me."

Skyler leaned forward, the light from the ballroom bathing his clean-shaven face with a wash of pink light. "See, you don't make plans with your sworn enemies without having a guarantee that they're simply not going to have you as a snack when they're done with you. A no-kill-fee clause, if you will."

"I gave you my word," growled Magnus.

Dana sniggered nastily, folding her arms.

"Dead men tell no tales, or so they say," said Skyler, rising to his feet, "nor do they make promises they don't intend to keep." He took a sip of his drink, feigning nonchalance. "Tell me, Magnus, without that cure, how long did they give you to live? A week, maybe? A month?"

Magnus flicked a disgusted glance at Harlem, who spread his hands in a "who, me?" gesture.

"Let me tell you about loss, Magnus," said Skyler blithely. "You're right, in a way. You can never lose what you never had in the first place. This life isn't yours, and your wonder drug, your so-called immortality cure, that isn't yours either. It never has been. We have some new players in town, and it looks like you've just been out bid." He grinned. "You ever heard the phrase 'hostile takeover' before?"

He glanced over at Harlem, who reached under his torn jacket and handed him a bloodied minichainsaw. Skyler hefted it, glancing around him appreciatively.

"Nice booth, this. Soundproof, or so I'm told."

Magnus's face didn't flicker. He had ruled over the werewolves for decades. He was more than used to being threatened, and this puny man didn't even come close to raising his hackles. He got to his feet slowly, looming over Skyler and ignoring a warning growl from Flame. His teeth seemed to lengthen as he spoke, glittering in the light of the console.

"Mr. Banks, I believe there has been a miscommunication. There are two cardinal rules in the world of business, which I'm sure you'll one day learn. One, don't fuck who you work with; and two, don't run around making secret pacts with people who have a sworn duty to kill you. Both of which you are currently in violation of."

"So?"

"So—" A coughing fit wracked Magnus and he took a swig from his whisky bottle to stifle it. "If you kill me, which by the way I can't wait to see you try, you'll just be stepping one rung sideways on the ladder to hell. They'll get you in the end. They always do."

"Kill you?" Skyler laughed out loud. "Why would I kill you when it's far more profitable—and entertaining—to keep you alive?"

He nodded to Flame, who pulled the door open wider. A half-dozen uniformed SWAT team members flooded into the control room. They surrounded Magnus, their automatic weapons primed and ready. Ned strode in behind them looking decidedly apprehensive, a pair of reinforced steel handcuffs dangling from one hand.

"Is this him?" he asked Skyler timorously.

Skyler nodded and then turned back to Magnus, a look of triumph on his face. "Pop quiz: do you know how much trouble you can get in for marketing an untested treatment to the general public? And of disposing of the evidence in dumpsters when your test patients have minor side effects, such as death?"

Magnus glowered at Skyler. He'd been ready for this. The vamps might own the county sheriffs and the paperwork guys, but the regular beat cops knew nothing about vampires or werewolves. They were mere pawns, used purely to bring in suspected werewolves under false charges and deliver them to their vampire enemies.

He knew all their tricks, and so long as he stayed within the law, or pretended to, he was safe.

"I have no idea what you're talking about. My business is totally legitimate." Magnus jerked his chin toward the ballroom window. "Every person down there signed a waiver just for the pleasure of being here tonight. If they choose to sample our beta products then it's on their own heads, and I've got the signatures to prove it." He folded his arms smugly. "The law can't touch me, and you know it."

"Yeah, I know it's legal for a human to do something like that," said Skyler, "but remind me again, what rights do werewolves have?"

"Werewolves?" Magnus laughed nastily, then winked at the cops and made a little 'crazy person' gesture toward Skyler. "No such thing." He took another swallow of whisky, then turned and winked at the pale-faced Ned, who was staring at him as if hypnotized. "Looks like I'm not the only one who's been drinking tonight."

A sudden, panicked look came over his face. His whisky bottle dropped to the ground as his fingers violently clawed, locking up. A spasm of pain ran through him and his knees buckled, sending him crashing to the floor.

He turned to Skyler, wide-eyed, as fur started sprouting from his face.

"What have you done to me?" he shouted.

"Me? Nothing." Skyler leaned in closer, a hint of smugness in his voice. "But a word to the wise: tip the bar staff a bit better next time and they won't spit in your drink."

"What?" Magnus stared at the whisky bottle, lying on the floor beside him. It was nearly empty, but he could clearly see a faint green layer on top of the amber liquid. "No!"

"Sorry, boss," said Skyler. The SWAT team moved to surround Magnus. They threw steel ropes around him and shoved his limbs into block restraints as he writhed and thrashed on the floor, helpless as the transformation gripped him. Skyler watched the show with infinite satisfaction. Then he beckoned to Dana, who trotted forward and smugly pressed a glass vial full of red liquid into his hand. Skyler squatted down next to the stricken werewolf and jammed the syringe into his thigh.

"You go this far, and no further."

Magnus gasped, his transformation halted by the serum, painfully stuck halfway between a man and a wolf. His half-formed muscles bulged as he strained against the reinforced metal restraints. He rolled over and glared up at Skyler, his red-eyed gaze unfocused. "If they lock me up I'll be dead in ten days," he hissed. "Why not just kill me now? Let me keep my pride?"

"You ever seen that Monty Python sketch? You know, the one where the guy pays a fortune for a dead parrot?" Skyler whispered back.

"Sure, why?"

Skyler smiled. "They don't know you're a dead parrot."

He straightened up as Ned crossed the room toward him. The young detective's eyes never left the half-transformed figure of Magnus as he pulled out his check book. Finally, the fabled leader of the werewolves! And he'd caught him! The vampires were going to owe him big time for this one. Maybe they'd even give him his own office.

Skyler smiled as he patted the nervous young man on the shoulder, handing him a half-dozen more syringes of red liquid. "Would you like his collar and leash, or shall I mail them to you?" he asked Ned brightly.

CHAPTER THIRTY-TWO

KAYLA AND PHIL slipped soundlessly through the deserted back rooms of Genetica, heading for the stairwell. Getting in hadn't been a problem, thanks to Bobo the security guard's weakness for short skirts, and the fact that Kayla was still wearing one. Right now the guy was sleeping off a major concussion in a minor flower bed, and Phil had himself a new Taser. He spun it nonchalantly around his finger as they cautiously made their way through the staff areas of the building, looking for some clue as to where Ninette and Mutt had been taken.

"So, you never told me how to kill a werewolf," said Kayla.

"You really want to know?"

"Sure."

"Well, before you kill it, you first need to do three things," said Phil, as they cautiously headed up the stairs to the first level. "First, you need to make sure it really is a werewolf. You've got about three seconds to decide what you're dealing with before it eats you, shoots you, or both. Vampires are easy to spot—the teeth are a straight-up giveaway."

"Like that security guard back there?"

"Uh-huh. Werewolves are harder to spot if they're in human form. They have a different bone structure, bigger teeth, more hair, but that stuff's easy to hide. You have to be one-hundred-percent sure it's a werewolf before you kill it, 'cause the last thing you wanna do is to smoke a human, even one working for them."

"So how do I tell the difference?"

"Simple," said Phil. He pulled out a pocket flashlight and tossed it to her. "Check their eyes. Animals like cats and dogs have a reflective bit at the back of their retinas. You've seen cats' eyes at night, right? It's why they can see in the dark and we can't. Vamps can see in the dark too, but they have a bigger brain to process the available light with, so they don't need that extra shiny layer. Werewolves are more primitive, less evolved."

"So I have to shine a light in their eyes before killing them?" Kayla looked worried. "That's practical."

"The flashlight's a 'newbie' thing too," said Phil. "You soon learn what to look for. Take this guy, for instance."

Kayla spun around as a tall security guard came lumbering around the corner. He stopped dead at the sight of them and reached for his gun.

"Vampire, werewolf, or human?" asked Phil calmly.

"Erm..." Kayla gulped, then remembered herself and whipped up her flashlight. "I can't tell! He's wearing shades!"

"Wearing shades indoors at night—that says 'vampire!' to me."

Phil casually shot the guard with his Taser, sending him plummeting to the ground, and then kicked the gun away from his convulsing, smoking body. "Or possibly 'actor.'"

Kayla stared down at the man. "How do you tell?"

"Actors don't get up again if you give them a chance to lie down," said Phil, as the enraged security guard lunged to his feet, his hair smoldering. His eyes lit on Kayla and he ran at her headfirst, snarling.

"Second thing you gotta do is to pick your weapon," said Phil, leaning back on the wall and folding his arms like a lecturer in class. "Keep it as low-tech as possible: Tasers for humans, bullets for werewolves, and... what do we use to kill vampires with?"

"Er..." Kayla shot a panicked glance at the furious guard as he blundered toward her.

"Pointy thing?" Phil prompted, making a little stabbing motion.

"Right!" Kayla's hands made a mad tour of her new weapons belt and pulled out a steel stiletto. She gripped it uncertainly. "Can't I just shoot him?"

"Gunshots attract attention," said Phil calmly as the man rushed him, teeth bared. Without moving from his comfy position on the wall he stopped the vamp's charge with a swift chop of his gloved hand to the guard's throat. Then he gave him a shove, sending him reeling back in Kayla's direction. Kayla raised her stiletto determinedly as the guard closed in on her. Then she suddenly leapt aside, balking at the thought of actually stabbing someone, monster or not.

"Help me! I can't do this!" she cried.

There was no reply. Phil had gone.

The vampire spun and faced her, snarling.

Kayla smiled ingratiatingly as the creature advanced on her, whipping the stiletto behind her back. "Er... would you believe I'm looking for the restrooms?" she asked.

BOOM!

Kayla struck the sheet-metal door at the end of the room, making it vibrate like a gong, then plunged to the ground upside-down, cracking her head on the wooden floor. Rolling over dizzily, she blew her hair out of her eyes and propped herself up on an elbow. "I'll take that as a 'no.'"

With a growl, the vampire guard went for her again, kicking the stiletto out of her hand and grabbing her by the ankle. He yanked Kayla flat on her back and then reeled her in toward him, snarling. Kayla made a mad grab for the guard's dropped gun and managed to snatch it up. She remembered Phil's words, and flung it at the guard's head as hard as she could. It bounced off his forehead with a satisfying crack, and he relaxed his grip on her ankle just long enough for her to pull free. Snatching her stiletto off the ground, she steeled herself and grabbed the guard in a flying tackle, thumping the steel spike as hard as she could into his heart.

Or she would've done, if he hadn't gone for her throat at the last minute.

Kayla stared, horrified, as the guard lunged backward with a bloodcurdling shriek, six inches of cold steel projecting from his eye socket. Galvanized by an electric current of fear and revulsion, Kayla threw herself aside as the half-blinded guard came at her full speed, crashing through the cheap steel railings that bordered the top of the stairwell and plunging down headfirst with a howl. He smashed into the railings below, finishing up impaled through the chest on one of the sharp metal rails. Blood gushed from his weakly struggling body, pouring down the stairs in a red tide.

Kayla stared down at him, trembling. She almost jumped out of her skin as Phil clapped a hand on her shoulder. He stepped up beside her, peering with bemusement down the stairwell.

"Well," he said, "I can see you have a few anger management issues we're going to have to work through, but in the meantime, I should probably give you this."

He handed Kayla a small steel cylinder.

"What is it?"

"Silencer," explained Phil with a grin. "Goes on your gun so you can use it without waking up the neighborhood. And don't glare at me like that."

"Why not?" snapped Kayla, angrily screwing the silencer onto the end of her pistol.

"Because when you're glaring at someone, you're not watching your back," said Phil. He gave a little nod over her shoulder.

Kayla spun around to see three enormous security guards burst through a door at the end of the corridor. From the thunderous look on their faces, she doubted they'd fall for the "restroom" line.

"Hunters!" snarled the lead guard, cracking his knuckles.

"They're all yours, baby," said Phil, with infuriating calmness. "Try again. Human, vampire, or werewolf?"

Kayla focused desperately on the lead guard: not a big guy, but broad, and his suit didn't seem to fit him quite right. Weird hairline.

"Werewolf?" she hazarded.

"Attagirl!"

"And I kill it... how?"

"Chop its head off or destroy the heart." Phil glanced down at his watch. "In your own time."

"Oh, great." Kayla raised her pistol with unsteady fingers and fired three shots at the lead guy's chest. He immediately went over backward and hit the ground with a satisfying thump.

Strike one.

Immensely heartened by this, Kayla shifted her pistol sights to the second guy, fighting to keep her aim steady. This was just like all the shoot-em-up arcade games she'd played as a kid, she told herself desperately as she squeezed off another shot, spinning the guard around and bouncing him off the side wall, Except, said a nasty little voice in the back of her head, the blood in those games was digital. You couldn't hear the dull, sick thud of metal striking human flesh, or see the shockingly red craters the impacts opened up in the guards' bodies with each pull of her trigger.

The second guard snarled at Kayla as his buddy went down, revealing ugly, jagged teeth. Kayla quickly fired two more shots into the guard's chest, knocking him down before she whipped her sights around to the next guard.

Strike two!

She screamed as something smashed into her chest with incredible force, just an inch above her heart, knocking her clean off her feet.

She hit the floor with a bruising thump and gasped, curling into a fetal ball as great hot stabs of pain shot through her. Holy crap! She'd always wondered what it felt like to get shot, but she hadn't thought it would hurt this much. She felt like she'd been kicked by a steroid-crazed mule.

"I'm hit!" she cried, unable to believe it.

Phil reached down and grabbed her by the front of her jacket, hauling her back upright.

"Good job you're wearing a bulletproof jacket, then," he said with a wink.

He released her. Kayla staggered on her feet, shocked and freaked. She glanced down fearfully at herself, expecting to see torn flesh and glinting white bone. All that was visible was a tiny hole in the black cotton of her combat top, through which a flash of metal glinted.

"Jesus!" she cried, relieved.

The final guard reached them. Kayla yelled as the man grabbed her and yanked her back against his broad chest, going for her throat. She felt his hot breath on her neck and swung her gun up over her shoulder. She jammed it into the man's chest where she judged his heart would be and pulled the trigger. There was a sharp, muffled bang and the guard went down, pulling her over backward with him, still clutching her by the throat. Kayla fought free of his heavy body, then wildly lunged to her feet, breathing heavily, staring down at the twitching body of the guard.

Phil glanced up at her, still leaning on the wall, his cell phone open in one hand. "Congratulations," he said mildly, "nice shot"

"What are you doing? Are you texting?" Kayla cried in disbelief.

"No," Phil lied, closing his phone with a snap.

"Yes you were!" cried Kayla. "I just nearly *died*, in case you didn't notice, and you're standing there checking the football scores!"

"I was calling backup, actually," said Phil, sounding hurt.

Kayla shook her head, too glad to be alive to be angry. "So what's the third thing you have to do to kill a werewolf?" she asked, morbidly curious.

"Shhh!" Phil held up a hand, listening.

"What?"

Phil turned his head to listen as the muffled sound of applause came from a partially open door down the hallway. He moved silently down the hallway to open the door a crack.

They both gazed out at the massive, brightly-lit ballroom just visible on the other side of the balcony. There was a stage at one end topped by a JumboTron video screen and flanked by long tables bearing food, drinks and some kind of merchandise. The rest of the hall was packed with around two hundred elegantly dressed people, all watching the stage while tuxedoed waiters moved amongst them.

And up on the stage...

"Julissa?" Kayla said in surprise.

Sure enough, her co-worker's face loomed large on the video screen, smiling and waving as she was presented with some kind of award. Despite herself, Kayla was impressed. She knew how much Julissa liked to brag, but for some reason she never thought the girl might really be doing what she claimed to be doing.

Kayla turned to Phil, pulling on his sleeve excitedly. "That girl on the stage—I work with her! She's the one who gave me the invite card. She said she was some kind of model for these people."

"Vampires," said Phil, staring down at the hall.

"What?"

"The place is full of vampires. There are dozens of them." Phil reached for his cell phone as though in a trance. "This is huge. I've never seen so many of them in one place before, and under the same roof as werewolves? It's unheard of." He watched the room intently for a moment, then shook his head in wonder. "This is too weird even for me. I'm calling the team in."

"I thought you already did."

"I was going to, after I checked the football scores," said Phil, looking faintly sheepish. He started punching numbers, frowning in concentration. "What's the party for again? I see a lot of famous faces down there."

Kayla reached for her invite. "Product release bash. Some kind of breakthrough anti-aging drug thingy. Very controversial. It's been all over the news. "

"Anti-aging?" Phil glanced up at her. "Sounds suspicious. I'd get your friend out of there if I were you."

He turned his back on her, pressing the phone to his ear. "Mikey, I need an extraction team, stat. I'm sending you the satellite coordinates. Could you give me your ETA, or at least an ATA... what?" His eyes flicked guiltily at Kayla, and he lowered his voice. "MapQuest it, then, for God's sake, and do it quick."

Snapping the phone shut, he turned and marched off up the corridor.

"Where are you going?" asked Kayla, racing after him.

"To find Ninette, and maybe get some answers."

CHAPTER THIRTY-THREE

THE FIRST THING Ninette noticed upon waking was that she was cold. Not your everyday, just-woken-up cold, but a real bone-deep, I-passed-out-drunk-in-the-freezer cold. Her fingers were almost completely numb, and it felt as if her eyelids were stuck together with crazy glue. On the plus side, no one was sitting on her legs and going through her pockets. Still, there was a definite feeling of menace surrounding her, as though Fate itself was watching, waiting for her to wake up so that it could inflict itself on her in some new, horribly cruel way.

Gasping, she jerked into full wakefulness.

Her head swam as she took in the unfamiliar surroundings. If her blurred eyes weren't deceiving her, she was lying in some kind of lab filled with odd-looking machinery and high-tech animal cages. The ceiling above her was criss-crossed with snaking cables, and little chrome lamps hung on bare black wires. There was a low, irritating hum in the room that seemed to be keeping her brain from focusing.

She rolled her head to one side and stared around her in utter incomprehension. How had she gotten here? Had she been drinking Jaeger and Red Bull with the lab tech boys again? Or had something far worse happened?

She shuddered. Come to think of it, there was nothing worse than Jaeger and Red Bull, except possibly the lab tech boys themselves.

A door swung open behind her with a double click of heavy duty locks. Ninette tried to roll over, but alarmingly, she found that she couldn't move. That did not make her happy. Her body was a well-oiled machine, honed through many years of fighting demons, vampires, and assorted nasties. She was at the pinnacle of fitness, with nearly every kind of martial art in existence under her jeweled belt, plus several new styles of her own. Ordinarily she could kick a full-grown hell-demon's ass and still have energy left over to teach her mid-afternoon kickboxing class. When you'd had the kind of life that she'd had, it paid to be able to defend yourself, and not just from the monsters.

Right now, she felt as weak as a kitten.

She was going to make someone pay for it soon.

The next thing she knew, cold hands were touching her face, rolling it from side to side as a bright light shone into her pupils. Ninette winced, reaching up to slap the hand away, but her arm wouldn't respond. Some kind of drug, she thought, although that wasn't much comfort to her. She settled instead for scowling, her fifth favorite expression.

"Who are you? What's going on?" she demanded. Her voice sounded as if it was coming from a long way away. She concentrated as hard as she could, trying to fight off the effects of the drug. "If I have to add 'where am I?' to that, there's going to be trouble, blood, deaths, and quite possibly evisceration."

"Relax, doll," said a scratchy little voice. "My name is Cerik. You're with friends."

"Whose friends?"

"Not yours, that's for certain."

Ninette's vision cleared a little and she looked up at the man standing over her. He was poorly dressed and painfully thin. He seemed to loom rather than stand, although he wasn't very tall. He wore leather gloves and an ill-fitting white lab coat.

Vampire, she decided.

Ninette nodded at the syringe he was holding. "Touch me with that and you'll have about two seconds left to regret it."

Cerik laughed, reaching up to pull at the silver collar around his neck. "Relax, doll, this isn't what you think."

Ninette focused all her mental energy on her arm as the vampire reached out for her wrist, flicking the syringe to remove an air bubble. As he went to slide the needle into her arm she managed to lift it, batting the syringe out of his grasp.

Cerik raised an eyebrow. "Not bad. I've heard many tales of the Hunters, of their bravery and strength. That was why I sent for you."

Ninette paused, looking up at the vampire in confusion.

"For me?"

Cerik nodded gravely. "I need you to help me. In a minute I'm going to set you free, but first there are some things you need to know."

KAYLA SHOVED HER way through the well-dressed crowd that packed the ballroom, grumbling to herself. It wasn't bad enough that she was stuck rescuing Julissa, but now she had to do it dressed like a waitress. Porn-star-slash-waitress, she corrected herself, judging by the length of her skirt. Before leaving her to search for Ninette, Phil had warned her that Hunter garb would be too easily recognizable to any vampires in the room. Two minutes and a quick bit of hands-on training with the Taser later, she had herself a new identity.

Kayla pointlessly pulled up her little black pleated top in a vain attempt to cover her cleavage, pulled the skirt down to cover her ass, then hefted her drink tray and plunged into the fray. She prayed that no one would actually try and order a drink from her before she reached Julissa.

The room was hot and noisy, and she had to push past a lot of beautiful people in expensive clothing to get anywhere near the stage. With a lot of shoving and elbowing she managed to reach the aisle by the stage. It was currently being kept clear by several menacing security guards, who gave her the kind of grinning, lecherous looks that under any other circumstance would've earned them a slap.

Kayla was within ten feet of the stage when a bony hand clamped down on her shoulder. She spun around with a shout, her hand instinctively flying to the gun tucked inside the waistband of her skirt.

"Miss Steele?"

Kayla closed her eyes and gave a silent groan. Here she was, on her very first mission with the Hunters, braving werewolves and vampires and God knew what else, only to run up against something infinitely more terrifying.

"Mr Holt," she stammered. "You're here. You look very…"

She swiftly ran through her inner list of polite adjectives and drew a blank. Her fifty-two-year-old supervisor had squeezed his five-foot-two frame into a fitted blue nylon suit clearly intended for someone at least thirty years his junior. He wore an unfortunate toupee that looked like a crazed ginger cat attacking his head.

"…blue," Kayla said. She licked her lips and glanced up at the stage quickly, checking on Julissa. "What are you doing here?"

"Same thing as everyone else," said Mr Holt. He eyed her with undisguised lust. "Signing up."

"For what?"

"Freebies. If you get on their books today you get a free sample of the stuff they used on Miss Cortez." Mr Holt's beady little eyes shone, and he rubbed his sweaty hands together in glee. "They say it's still under testing, but it'll be over a thousand bucks a shot when it's released next month, and they're just giving it away for free by the door!"

Kayla turned to see a pair of semi-naked male models standing by the door, handing out tubes of green liquid to a long line of party guests.

Mr Holt winked at Kayla, lowering his voice. "Quite frankly I think it's a load of bull, but when you get to my age you'll try anything once." He straightened up, his watery blue eyes drinking in

Kayla's indecent waitressing outfit with obvious enjoyment. "What might you be doing here? You know the store's policy on moonlighting. If I find the Dior line stocked on the Chanel shelf again..."

"I'm not moonlighting." Kayla shook herself. Lives were in danger. She didn't have time for this. She turned to go, only to be restrained by Mr Holt's surprisingly strong grip on her upper arm. Kayla tensed, fighting an almost uncontrollable urge to break free and push the old lecher into the punch bowl.

"Pay attention when I'm talking to you, little missy," drawled Mr Holt, reeling her back in. Kayla opened her mouth to reply, and then paused.

"Are you wearing fake nails?" she asked.

"Fake what?"

"Your hand." Kayla pried it free from her arm and held it up.

Mr Holt stared at his inch-long nails in surprise. "Those aren't mine," he said, somewhat foolishly. His eyebrows shot up. "And my hand... it's not mine either."

"Then whose hand is it?" asked Kayla, wondering if someone had pushed Mr Holt into the fruit punch bowl before her.

They both jumped as a shrill scream pierced the ballroom. All talking stopped, and a hush descended in its wake. The image on the JumboTron beside them blurred as the bored cameraman impulsively swung his rig around at the audience to zoom in on the commotion. Kayla peered upwards as the image of a young woman at the back of the crowd came up on the screen. She was jumping around in a frenzy, clutching her face with both hands.

"Help me! Somebody help me!" she shrieked.

A stir of consternation rippled through the crowd. Kayla watched the screen as the girl's date tried to calm her, taking her hands and gently trying to remove them from her face. He gave a cry and leapt back from her as if stung. The cameraman automatically zoomed in for a close-up. A whiplash of reaction crossed the room, followed by a collective intake of breath as the woman's face filled the screen, full-frame.

"Jesus!" cried Kayla.

JULISSA STOOD HELPLESSLY clutching her speech notes as Jagos left her side and strode across the stage, past the band, to the cameraman. He wrenched the feed cable out of the wall, and then turned back to the crowd with an ingratiating smile.

"Sorry, folks," he called over the PA. "There's been a little technical hiccup. Please bear with us while we—"

Another scream pierced the ballroom, then another. Panicked, the crowd turned toward the source of the noise. A loud hubbub of conversation rose.

Julissa hurried over to Jagos and grabbed his arm. "What's going on? That lady… what was wrong with her?"

"Nothing. Everything is…" Jagos's eyes suddenly widened and he took a slow step back from her. "Tell me, Julissa," he said in a deliberately calm voice, "exactly which products did you try today?"

Julissa shrugged. "Just the one they were giving away by the door when we came in. It was like a little green squirty thing you took with some water. I think most people tried it. Why?"

"Oh, no reason," said Jagos. He backed away from her, his face set in an expression of polite horror.

"Then why are you looking at me like that?" Julissa looked around for a mirror. There was a bank of reflective steel panels set at the back of the stage. She pulled away from Jagos and hurried over to them, peering worriedly down at her own reflection.

Julissa screamed.

KAYLA STARED AROUND in panic as the crowd started to fragment, buzzing around in confusion. Tanked up on free wine and cocktails, the mood was rapidly degenerating into an angry unrest that threatened to turn into downright disorder. She stood on tiptoe, trying to see over the hundreds of jostling heads in front of her. "What's going on?" she asked.

"Search me. the girl must've had an allergic reaction." Mr. Holt scratched at his own face in nervous sympathy. "Kids these days, allergic to everything. Now, if they'd had a proper upbringing, like I had…"

Kayla shook her head. "I don't like this. I'm going to talk to Julissa." Kayla turned back to her supervisor. "Maybe she…" Her voice tailed off.

"Maybe she what?"

"Er…" Kayla swallowed, staring at her supervisor. Maybe she was tired and her eyes were doing weird things, but the man's face looked odd, odder than usual. His cheekbones were protruding and his jaw seemed somehow more pointed than she remembered it being.

"Speak up, girl! Cat got your… Ow!" Mr. Holt's hand flew to his mouth, and he looked down stupidly at the blood on his fingertips. His fingers went back to her mouth, and his face froze. "My teeth have gone nuts. I just bit my tongue. What's happening?"

Kayla spun around, urgently scanning the crowd. A tide of stunned disbelief slowly spread through the room as people mindlessly backed away from each other, pointing and yelling. Tuxedoed men watched in disbelief as their beautiful dates grew horns and scales. Supermodels stared down at their hands as their nails grew long and lustrous... and then kept on growing, morphing into terrifyingly huge claws.

Kayla turned to Mr Holt, whose teeth were now almost an inch long and still growing. "I'll tell you later!" she called.

NINETTE STOOD TENSELY beside Cerik at the lab door, buttoning up her Hunter's uniform. She rubbed her arm briskly and flexed her shoulders, working the last of the stiffness out of her joints. The anti-sedative injection Cerik had given her had done its job nicely. The pair of them gazed at the clicking, humming metal containment gates on either side of the lab door. The little blue lights flashed in synch with the lights on Cerik's UV collar. The vampire tugged on it, sweating.

"Are you sure you want to go through with this?" she asked, putting a hand on his arm.

Cerik nodded, just once. "It's the only way. If they suspect in the slightest that there's been a leak, they'll simply move their operation. You'll never catch them in time. All your precious humans will be lost forever."

"Just one question: why?"

Cerik shrugged. "Same reason any guy'll give you right before he does something unbelievably stupid: for her. What other reason is there?"

Ninette nodded. After what she'd seen in her short, packed career, it wasn't really possible for her to feel sympathy for any vampire. In Cerik's case, she managed to feel a small amount of grudging admiration.

"And you really think they'll buy it?"

Cerik glanced over his shoulder at the trashed lab behind them. They'd done a good job of it, over-turning chairs and smashing equipment so that it looked like a struggle had taken place. As far as it was possible for a vampire to go any paler, Cerik managed to. "They're werewolves," he said, as though this was the only explanation needed.

Ninette stepped back from Cerik, looking from him to the flashing gate and back again. She knew vampires didn't have souls, but that didn't mean they couldn't feel emotion, like fear or love, or make sacrifices, like Cerik was about to.

She glanced over at Cerik. "If she doesn't make the right choice," she asked quietly, "what then?"

"Then I'll see you—and her—on the other side. Now, quickly, go."

Ninette nodded once. Then she turned and walked through the door, heading quickly down the corridor.

A few moments later, there was a loud beep and a brief *WHOOMPH* of fire from behind her, followed by the dull thud of a body hitting the ground.

Ninette walked on, without looking behind her.

CHAPTER THIRTY-FOUR

PHIL PROWLED THROUGH the empty, darkened offices on the twelfth floor of Genetica, a pair of night vision goggles strapped over his face. The world around him was revealed in green crackling lights, the thermal overlay on the picture showing heating pipes as white hotspots in the walls around him. A pile of unconscious human guards lay just inside the door behind him, stashed out of the way to avoid drawing unnecessary attention.

A movement on his right caught Phil's attention and he quietly skirted his way around a pair of office cubicles, drawing his snub-nosed silenced Glock pistol as he did so. He made his way toward the door, which was firmly closed. Sidling along the wall, he gingerly reached out for the doorknob to open it. Bracing himself, he gripped the knob and turned it, letting the door creak open.

A wash of bright light flooded out and Phil winced, pushing up his goggles. He froze as a young female voice called out, "Hello?"

Quickly stashing his pistol inside his jacket, Phil straightened himself up as much as he could. He removed his goggles and stepped confidently around the door.

Inside, he found himself in a warm, brightly lit office. A jaw-droppingly beautiful receptionist sat at a computer behind a polished mahogany desk, reading a magazine to combat the boredom of her night shift. He hesitated in the doorway, feeling somewhat foolish in his black combat gear and body shields. He hoped that she'd think he was a cop.

"Can I help you?" she asked.

"Sure," said Phil. He smiled winningly and walked over to the desk, reaching into his pocket. "Where do you keep your hostages?" he asked pleasantly.

"Our what?" asked the receptionist, popping her gum.

She gave a yelp as three barbed Taser darts buried themselves in her shoulder. Her body jerked, then she slumped backward and slid off her chair, blue sparkles of electricity arcing over her slim figure.

Phil quickly jumped over her desk, minimizing the solitaire game she was playing on her computer and accessing the networked server, searching for any kind of company records.

He'd cracked three passwords and was busy hacking into Genetica's employee list when he felt something warm and wet dripping on his shoulder. He brushed it off, excitement buzzing through him as he scrolled through a long list of names and faces, some of whom were quite high-ranking pillars of the community. It seemed that Genetica had its greasy little fingers in a lot of pies. One glance at the company bankroll was enough to confirm that the amount of money going both ways was quite incredible. It all looked legitimate, and yet he had a gut feeling that this company was being used as a front for developing something extremely nasty. End-of-the-world nasty.

But what, exactly?

Phil paused, his cursor over name eighty-six on the employee list.

"No way!" he breathed.

Behind him, a floorboard flexed.

Phil was already moving when a steel chair whistled through the air where his head had been, smashing the computer off the desk and embedding itself in the monitor, exploding it in a spray of fizzing blue sparks. Phil snapped his body into a tight roll and was on his feet again a second later, whipping up his Glock as he stared up at the thing that was looming over him.

It had mandibles, he noticed with the detached, out-of-body curiosity that came from extreme terror, and slime. Lots and lots of slime. The fact that it was wearing the shredded remains of the receptionist's jacket wasn't entirely lost on him as he immediately put six rounds through its face at close range. The wounds spurted yellow blood before almost immediately healing again. Phil raised an eyebrow, impressed. You saw something new on this job every day, whether you wanted to or not. This creature was fresh out of the catalog labeled "RUN!"

The secretary-beast reared up over him, hissing in fury. "Hey, uh—" He glanced at the lurid pink name tag still dangling from the creature's upper carapace. "Cindy? Would you be a doll and tell me where a guy might find a really big can of bug spray around here?"

Cindy hissed at him again, cocking her reptilian face as her shining silver eyes honed in on his gun.

"Never mind." Phil dived behind the desk and Cindy brought her serrated tail down on top of it, reducing it to splinters. As shards of wood rained down around, him he rolled away and took shelter behind an iron filing cabinet. Reloading his Glock, he lunged out from behind the cabinet and fired two shots at...

Nothing.

Phil's face froze. His eyes ticked sideways, and then up.

"Ah—" he started.

WHAM!

Phil plowed through the wooden wall at the end of the room, smashing it to firewood and sliding halfway into the room next door before friction halted his violent slide. "...crap," he finished. His right knee stabbed at him and he winced, checking the hydraulic mountings on the mechanized brace he wore. A broken tube hissed air. He swore and tried to plug the leak with a finger. His head snapped up as a sound like a hyena laughing rang out, raising weird echoes from the metallic office walls.

Adrenaline hotwired Phil's system. He lunged to the side and snatched up his pistol, which lay amid the ruins of a potted fern. He swung it toward the door in one smooth motion and then paused, his head slowly turning to take in the new room he found himself in.

The secretary's office opened out onto an open-plan office that took up almost the entire floor of the building. The windows that lined the room on all four sides had been boarded up and painted with tar. The walls and ceiling were almost completely covered in a flickering mass of equipment, heart monitors, and EKG machines.

Phil swore under his breath and slowly rose to his feet, scarcely daring to breathe as several hundred glowing eyes locked in on him in the fragmented semi-darkness. A giant clawed hand uncurled from a shelf above him and flexed, insect-slow. A loud trill came from a covered cage somewhere in the vicinity of the ceiling.

It did not sound friendly.

Phil hurriedly tucked his pistol away and pulled out a shortened version of his AK with a sawn-off barrel and a stripped-down stock. He had to fight to keep his hands steady as he slammed a new clip in and chambered a round. He swung the barrel of the gun around, at a loss as to where to aim first.

So *this* was what Genetica was really developing, and there were so many of them...

The *click... click... click* of claws on tiles echoed through the room. Phil spun around to see the giant, hunched, insectoid shape of Cindy appear silhouetted in the hole in the wall, backlit by the office light. Her flattened face turned in his direction and she lowered her head, making a barking noise of query.

"Sorry, girl," said Phil, as he sighted his AK on her throat, "I'm taken, but maybe we can do coffee sometime."

He stared at the demolished wall he'd just crashed through. It was packed full of giant bundles of explosives and olive-colored claymore mines, wrapped in red tape. A spaghetti of wires and fuses connected them together, leading back into the guts of the building. There had to be a hundred pounds of plastic explosives in that wall, and that was just what he could see from here.

Phil's heart gave a quick double-thump.

The entire place was wired to blow!

There was an angry screech from the doorway. Phil whipped around and reflexively sent a double-tap of lead slamming into Cindy's thorax. The secretary-beast screamed, setting off a wall of jabbering noise from the creatures in the lab behind her. She shook her head in irritation and came at him, unsheathing foot-long stabbing bone spurs, which burst from her elbows and the palms of her hands.

Phil held down the trigger as the creature flew at him, yelling, spraying her with bullets and sending a vapor cloud of yellow blood mist up into the air. The Cindy-beast was nearly upon him when there was a flash of white light and a sound like a mini-thunderclap, deafeningly loud in the confined space. Cindy exploded, her liquid flesh flying off her bones while her spurred skeleton thunked into the wall on either side of Phil, trapping him inside her steaming ribcage.

Disgusted, Phil used the butt of his rifle to smash his way out of the smoldering insectoid skeleton. He turned to see Ninette standing in the light of the doorway, covered in blood, her blooper gun smoking.

She gazed around at the wrecked room and shook her head. "Just tell me one thing," she said as Phil ran over to embrace her. "You got her lawyer's number, right?"

* * *

BACK IN THE ballroom, Kayla shoved her way through the jostling, shouting crowd, heading for the stage as quickly as she could. The situation was rapidly turning nasty as panic spread through the hall like wildfire. Up on the stage the tanned, well-dressed figure of Jagos had gotten hold of the microphone again and was appealing for calm. Nobody paid him the slightest bit of notice. A scuffle broke out over by the door as the uniformed security guards firmly pulled the doors shut and stood in front of them, folding their arms, watching the stage as though awaiting instruction.

Nobody, it seemed, was leaving.

Kayla caught a glimpse of Julissa cowering at the back. Kayla started forward resolutely, and then jumped back as a model with a sheet of black hair and a panicked expression loomed out of the crowd and grabbed her by the shoulders, begging her to help. Kayla stared at her in shock. The woman's eyes had no pupils. They glowed a dim blue color that was slowly spreading out to suffuse her face. Even as Kayla watched her skull flattened, as though invisible hands were pulling at it, and then a horn burst out of her nose, splitting her face open in a horrific gush of blood. Kayla pulled free and spun away, only to crash into a stern-looking businessman in a tuxedo. He was perfectly normal apart from his fang-like teeth, which were ten inches long and still growing. He grabbed her arm and loomed over her nightmarishly, foaming at the mouth.

"Whash happening to me?" he gasped.

Kayla shook herself free and ran on, dodging and ducking through the deformed crowd as people reached out to her in terror. It was time to make a rescue, and then get the hell out of there.

"Julissa!" she shouted.

Somebody grabbed her shoulder. She spun to look into the deep black eyes of one of the bouncers, then gasped and reached into her belt for her gun.

The bouncer was a werewolf!

Before her brain had a chance to kick in she had aimed her silver-bullet pistol at the bouncer's heart and pulled the trigger. The muted crack of the gunshot rang through the room, and a sudden wave of silence spread out around her as people turned one by one to stare at her, their animal eyes locking in on her gun as though transfixed.

Kayla stood frozen as the werewolf security guard clutched at his heart, his lips pulling back from his lengthening incisors in a grimace of pain. He slowly toppled forward and fell with a crash across the remnants of the drinks table.

Kayla threw herself at the steps as the crowd surged forward and a sea of clawed hands reached out for her. She grabbed hold of the hand rail and hauled herself up, taking the steps two at a time, running out onto the stage. The crowd followed her, their fear and panic swiftly turning to rage, now that they had a focus for their plight. Kayla scrambled across the speakers at the front of the stage, shoving her way past the bemused four-piece rock band. Julissa was huddled in a corner between two amp stacks.

"Come on! We've got to get out of here!"

Julissa turned frightened eyes up to her and Kayla jumped back, clapping a hand over her mouth. Julissa's beautiful, doe-eyed face was covered in a quilt of spines, forming a peaked, needle-like crest that swept in an S-shape from her hairline to her cheekbones and down her jaw. Her Cleopatra eyes were jet black from edge to edge, and two tiny fangs projected from her lower jaw making her look like a bulldog puppy.

Kayla backed away, staring at her coworker in shock.

"Just tell me," Julissa said, her voice almost unnaturally calm. "Do you think we sell any products that'll cover this?"

Kayla shook her head, finding her voice on her third attempt. "I think we have more important things to worry about."

The two girls turned to face the room as the stage flooded with freakishly deformed partygoers, their expressions murderous. Kayla looked from one intent, animalistic face to the next as she fingered the Glock pistol she held behind her back. She had one clip left, but she couldn't shoot these people. They weren't monsters. They just looked like monsters. She hoped.

"What the hell are you doing here, anyway? I thought you said you couldn't make it tonight," Julissa hissed. She seemed quite unaffected by her transformation, as though her sheer force of personality was keeping her human—for now. "More importantly, what on earth are you wearing?"

Kayla sighed. Even here, even now, Julissa was still Julissa.

"Tell you what," she said brightly, as they backed away from the snarling horde. "You hold the fort while I just pop next door and change into something that's appropriate for fighting off two hundred people who've just turned into things you don't usually see outside of a Tarantino movie. Then you can pick me out a nice belt to match the bloodstains on my shoes while I die trying to save your worthless ass. Deal?"

"Are you making fun of me?"

"No, I'm making fun of me. I've had far more practice. Let's go."

The two girls ran across the stage toward the stage exit. They stopped as it flew open and a man and a woman stepped out.

The man Kayla recognized instantly as Jagos, the well-dressed European guy who had been giving the speeches up on the stage. The woman had to be another model, Kayla guessed—until she saw her eyes. They were the color of a chemical explosion at dawn, set in a face that would be more at home breaking hearts in a silent movie than leading a security team in downtown Los Angeles. Her features were sharp and cruel and beautiful, with knife-edge cheekbones and plush, glossed lips. She was dressed in a white spun-silk dress and wore a necklace strung with tiny freshwater pearls.

The woman fixed the two girls with a piercing look, while behind her two guards wearing thick designer sunglasses and clutching police batons stepped through the door, looking menacing.

Kayla felt the woman's eyes boring into her brain.

"It's you," said the woman, sounding surprised.

"Sorry doll," breezed Julissa, tossing her head. "I'm a little busy right now, but if you'd like an autograph, you can email my publicist."

"Not you, her."

"Me?" asked Kayla, confused.

There were two quiet, efficient-sounding clicks, and the next thing she knew she was staring into the barrels of two enormous gilded Magnum pistols. Through a haze of disbelief she saw the two guards glance at the woman as though asking for permission to shoot her. Kayla quickly pulled out her own pistol and leveled it at the woman, feeling Julissa's shocked gaze on her. She backed up a couple of steps, trying to look as businesslike as she could.

"Julissa?" she asked quietly, staring at the woman's teeth. "Just one question: is your dress real silk?"

"Of course. Why?"

"Then I'll apologise in advance."

Kayla aimed her pistol at the woman's heart and pulled the trigger.

Blood sprayed, and Julissa screamed.

When she stopped screaming, Kayla stared at the smoking hole in the vampire woman's chest. A flash of metal glinted through the torn, bloody flesh. Kayla's pulse started pounding. What the hell? She'd just blown a fist-sized hole in the woman's chest, and she hadn't so much as flinched. Neither the silver nor the garlic seemed to have affected her either. What kind of vampire was she dealing with here?

Oh, this was going to be bad.

Both girls backed up warily as the woman stepped forward, staying her two guards with a hand. Torn veins and muscle fibers oozed and flexed inside the hole in her body where her heart should've been. Julissa gave a little yip of fright, clasping her hand over her mouth. The woman laughed, wiping blood off her chin, and then touched the wound in her chest with a long-nailed finger.

"Good shot, Kayla. Karrel would be proud."

"Karrel?" Kayla jerked the gun up to aim at the woman's head. A loud growl came from behind her. Julissa tugged on her arm urgently, but Kayla shook her off, sweating. Her entire world narrowed to the two little black sights lined up neatly on the woman's forehead, asking the question that she knew she didn't want answered. "How do you know Karrel?"

"Easy," said the woman, with a grin. "We killed him."

CHAPTER THIRTY-FIVE

KAYLA DIDN'T STOP pulling the trigger until she ran out of ammo. Julissa cowered behind a metal-plated Randall amp while Kayla fired round after round into the vampiress, who laughed merrily, holding out her arms and spinning in the hail of bullets like a young girl dancing in the rain. Time slowed down and the world closed in around Kayla, until all she was aware of was the smooth feel of the gun in her hand, her finger on the trigger, and the two crosshairs lining up on the vampire woman's heart. She was vaguely aware of someone screaming, but she ignored the sound, compartmentalizing everything but the driving urge to kill the monster standing before her.

This woman, this thing, had killed the man she loved. The only way this was going to end was with one of them dead.

Then her gun clicked on empty.

Kayla gave a shout of frustration. The woman was still standing!

Worse, she was grinning.

Kayla swore and backed off hurriedly, fumbling in her pocket for her last clip. It wasn't there. She clenched her fists as the woman caught her eye, smiling a terrible bloody smile, and then opened her hand to reveal her clip. She dangled it between two lacquered fingernails.

"Looking for this?"

An instant later the air moved and her pistol was snatched from her grip by Jagos. Kayla struck out at him in sheer blind rage, but he caught her wrist, held it, and then slammed the butt of his gun into her stomach, winding her.

Gasping, Kayla folded up and dropped to her knees, unable to breathe.

"Kayla, look out!" cried Julissa.

Through a haze of pain Kayla looked up and saw the hired rock band marching across the stage toward them, clutching their instruments as though they were weapons. There were four of them, all panther-like young men in their late twenties, dressed in the latest "what-the-fuck" punk fashion that seemed to involve a lot of leather and piercings and dangling chains. Half-inch fangs burst through their gums and their fingernails lengthened into black claws as they walked, blood dripping down onto the stage. The mutated audience spilled up onto the stage behind them, snarling mindlessly. The band drove them off, fangs flashing, before turning their attention back to the two girls, their eyes shining a soulless black.

Kayla backed up two steps, her eyes flashing between the two vampires behind them, the vampire rock band in front of them and the monster audience penning them in around the sides.

They were trapped.

A merry peal of laughter rang out. Kayla tensed as the vampire woman loomed over her, wiping the blood from her face, slicking it over her eyelids and along her cheekbones like a small child playing with paint. Then she took Jago's velvet-gloved hand and pressed it to her lips, her gaze still on Kayla.

"Jagos, be a good boy and go check on our party guests, would you?"

"Sure thing, Cyan."

Jagos pushed past Kayla, ignoring Julissa's furious stare. Striding across the stage, he pulled out a walkie-talkie and started marshalling the security guards. They formed a cordon around the edge of the stage to hold the mutated audience back.

"Cyan." Kayla's face registered sudden awareness as she put two and two together, then hardened as more important considerations came to mind. "I should have known. Where's Mutt?" she demanded.

"Who? You mean your little werewolf boy?" Cyan gave a nasty little smile. "After what happened between him and Karrel, I'd have thought you'd be keeping well clear of him."

"Excuse me?"

Cyan flashed her teeth in a smug little grin that made Kayla want to hit her. "You mean he never told you? Dear, dear. I'd have thought Karrel would've at least mentioned something about me, what with our little... history... together."

Kayla felt a cold hand wrap around her heart and squeeze. "History?" she spat.

The woman's eyes crinkled in mirth and she made a dismissive gesture. "That's in the past now, which is where you're about to be."

"Wait!" Kayla took a step toward Cyan, and then yelled as she felt an arm go around her throat. She twisted her head around frantically to see a pair of deep crimson eyes drilling into her own. The vampire lead singer hauled her backward, away from Cyan. She heard Julissa shout something very un-model-like as the bassist grabbed her in a headlock, dragging her off across the stage. The pair of them kicked and yelled as Cyan raised her bloodied hands in the air, waving them as though conducting an orchestra.

"Kill them!" she cried.

"Why does everyone keep saying that to me today?" yelled Kayla.

The two guards raised their guns again, aiming them at their foreheads.

Kayla tensed, preparing to die.

Then the guards' bodies jerked and they cried out. Their guns crashed and Kayla felt their bullets whiz past her, missing her and Julissa by inches. There was a flash of silver and bloodied swords burst from both of the guards' chests, blue flames flickering around the edges of the wounds. The flames raced upwards in tandem, and for a sudden, shocking instant both guards were lit up from within by a searing internal light, revealing every blood vessel, and every bone. Then the light went out and their flesh turned to black ash, dropping off their flaming bones, which collapsed in a steaming heap.

"Hunters!" cried Cyan.

Phil and Ninette stepped forward into the space freshly vacated by the exploding vampire guards, their swords raised. Ash billowed around them and a ripple of surprise went through the crowd of monsters behind Kayla. In the sudden silence, the sound of the guards' scorched bones cooling and cracking was audible.

Ninette lowered her sword, winking at Kayla.

"Did we miss the canapés?" she asked.

CYAN DREW HER sword and turned to square off against the two Hunters, blood running down her face. "Don't you people ever stay dead?" she growled.

"I was gonna say the same thing about you," said Ninette, switching her grip on her own *Jian*, "but I'm cool to kick your ass again, no big deal."

She glanced across at Kayla. "You okay?"

"Just peachy," gasped Kayla, tugging at the muscular arm around her throat. "Nice entrance, by the way."

"This is Hollywood. It's expected." Ninette dropped smoothly back into an en garde position. The air hissed as she swung her sword up to block a wild swing from the outraged Cyan, her eyes still on Kayla. "By the way, what the hell are you wearing?"

"That's what I said!" cried Julissa.

"Who's she?"

"That's Julissa. I'll explain later," said Kayla. "We're co-workers. This is all her fault."

"Okay, she'll explain now."

"Idiots!" Cyan spun around at the end of her swing and then stamped toward them, her sword held high. "You're all going to die!"

"No, we're all going to die, you crazy bitch," snapped Ninette. "There's a bomb in the building."

"Bullshit," Cyan snapped, but the look in her eyes betrayed her sudden anxiety. Her hand crept to her belt and she hit a button on her high-tech walkie-talkie. The glassy silence around her only amplified the hiss of static that poured out of the speaker. Judging by the look on the vampiress's face, this was not good.

"What did you do?" Cyan hissed, switching frantically between equally silent channels.

"We didn't do nothin', girlfriend," said Ninette. She tossed Cyan a charred metal UV collar. "Recognize this?"

Cyan's eyes scanned the writing on the side. "Cerik... what have you done with him?"

"He's dead. Thanks to you."

"Who's Cerik? What the hell is going on?" cried Kayla.

Ninette's eyes didn't leave Cyan's. "I'll explain later. We've gotta get these people out of here, right now. This building is wired to blow. It could go off at any minute."

"The people stay!" Cyan snarled, motioning to the werewolf bouncers as they moved to flank the stage, shoving stray audience members back into the pit. At the back of the room, vampire guards blocked the exits, slamming heavy wooden bars across the two main doors.

"But these people are monsters!" Kayla protested. "The immortality drug backfired!"

Cyan eyed her with pity. "What are you talking about? The drug trial was a total success."

"*Trial*?" Julissa swung around and stared daggers at Jagos, who stood smugly at the end of the stage. Her hand flew to the tiny scales covering her skin, and she touched her tiny pointed teeth with the tip of her tongue. "You're telling me this shit wasn't properly tested?"

"Oh yeah, it was tested all right," said Ninette, still glaring at Cyan. "On you, and on all the people here tonight, and it worked just fine."

"You mean...?"

"That's right," said Ninette grimly. "There is no 'immortality' drug. These people have been set up."

Ninette jerked her head at the ballroom, now swarming with a whole army of mutated monsters. "This was what the vampires wanted all along, to test their genetic-engineering crap out on us humans, using the werewolves' anti-aging research facility as cover to do it. Think about it. What better way to ensure a steady stream of willing human volunteers than by promising them what everyone in Hollywood dreams of—eternal youth?"

Ninette turned to face Cyan, raising her sword as she started to circle slowly around the vampire, blocking her exit.

"Thought you had them fooled, didn't you? Thought no one would suspect a thing?"

Cyan shrugged indifferently, her eyes glittering in the ballroom light. "What is there to suspect, sweetie?"

"Oh, come on!" Ninette burst out. "Big Daddy vamp Harlequin vanishes under mysterious circumstances, and overnight a whole shitload of vampires just lay down their arms and let themselves be captured and put to work for their mortal enemies? *Please!*"

"This was Magnus's gig, not mine. He just hired me to do his... how do you say? Wetwork?"

"So I hear." Ninette stared at the vampiress with cold loathing. "Magnus may have been a dog, but he wasn't a fool. From what I heard, he wired every test result he got to his handy hideout in Mexico, then rigged this building with enough TNT to blow a hole in the side of a mountain, just in case."

Cyan paled.

Ninette shook her head, advancing on Cyan. "Magnus has been onto you from the start. If he doesn't get his aging cure, you don't get your test subjects."

"But there is no aging cure!" Cyan burst out.

"Exactly," said Ninette coldly, "and I think the old man upstairs just figured that one out... right about when the cops came to take him away."

"Cops? Here? Tonight?" Cyan backed up a couple of steps, staring at Ninette in surprise. "Why? We control the cops—you Hunters know that, but we didn't order any troops tonight."

"Someone must've found you out." Ninette paused for a pointed moment. "Somehow."

Cyan stared at Ninette for a long moment, and then grew very still. "Harlem," she breathed.

Ninette nodded. "Poetic justice, ain't it? The vamps do a bunch of fucked-up experiments on werewolves, make a wolf who can read minds, and then hire him to do their hit-work, and you thought he wouldn't be a threat to you guys why, exactly?"

"He will die for this," hissed Cyan, tightening her grip on her sword.

"Doubtful. I'll bet he's a long way away by now, while you're standing here in a wired building, yakking to me." Ninette inspected her nails calmly. "I guess you should've thrown the dog a bone from time to time instead of leaving him out in the cold all night, for it seems that he just screwed you, in a manner of speaking." She grinned, eyeing Cyan, unable to resist turning the knife. "Let's face it, sister, what self-respecting vampire would sleep with a werewolf?"

The sound of Cyan's back teeth clenching together was audible. When she spoke, her voice was icy.

"And the bomb?"

"Is ready to blow, yes," said Ninette, eyeing the captured Kayla and placing her hand on the hilt of her sword. "Magnus has gone, but the bomb hasn't yet been activated. We're guessing he placed the trigger in the charge of a second party, as a failsafe. We looked for the fuse everywhere upstairs but couldn't find it, which is why we're now downstairs, reasoning with you in a slapdash last minute attempt to try and convince you to call off your guards and let these poor people out of the building before whoever has the detonator device decides to use it."

"And if I don't?"

"Then we're more than happy to kill every vampire in the place, including you, but that's gonna take a bit longer than you saying one word and freeing them. Our backup team and what Phil just described to me as a 'whole shitload' of cops are currently about eight minutes away, so if you go now and let us free these people, you might just avoid a good ass-kicking."

"Forget it, Hunter," snapped Cyan, raising her sword. "I don't make deals with humans."

"Yeah, Cerik said you might say that," said Ninette sadly. "He confided in me, before he... lost his head."

"So you *did* kill him." Cyan relaxed slightly.

"No, he killed himself, after he told me all kinds of interesting things."

Cyan's smile dripped off her face.

Ninette raised her sword, circling around the vampiress, her lithe body tense with disgust. "To be honest with you, I oughta just kill you right here where you stand, but I'm not going to. You have one last chance to live."

"Which is?" asked Cyan, with ill grace.

Ninette licked her lips, glancing over at Phil. "Cerik died for you, Cyan, not for your cause, or for your race, or for anything else you've had him busting his balls working on for the past eight years. He died willingly because he loved you, plain and simple, in order to give you something precious—a chance to put all of this right."

"Ninette!" Kayla yelled, eyeing the vampire security guards who were shoving their way through the audience, heading toward the stage.

Ninette ignored her.

"We all want something, Cyan," she continued. "Some people want fame and fortune, others just want love. Some people want it so much they're willing to die for it." She stopped circling, her eyes simmering with contempt. "But if you really want to get a handle on a person, really and truly, then ask him what he's most afraid of. Then you'll really start getting somewhere."

"Guards!" yelled Cyan, raising her sword, all pretense at calm now gone.

"I don't think they can hear you, sweetie," said Ninette, kicking at the pile of ash at their feet, "but I'll bet that someone upstairs can, or so Cerik told me."

That did it.

Cyan bolted for the door, then skidded to a whirling halt as Phil moved suddenly to block her path, watching her warily. Every ounce of humor was gone from his face as he moved with her, every muscle tense, his eyes as cold and intent as a jungle cat sizing up wounded prey. Cyan's gaze flicked between the two Hunters and she hissed, her canines flashing as her last nerve snapped.

With a snarl, she attacked.

CHAPTER THIRTY-SIX

PHIL AND NINETTE rushed forward as the enraged vampiress hurtled toward them, swinging their swords up to meet hers in a defensive cross. Blue sparks sprayed as metal met with a clang, and within seconds the three of them were engaged in a full-on sword fight, the two Hunters ducking, stepping, and blocking the vampiress's lightning-fast strikes. There was a yell from beside her and Kayla dropped into a half crouch, only to see Julissa grab the arm of the bassist who was holding her and twist it around before performing an impressive karate throw on the man, hurling him to the floor.

She danced away from the man and backed up toward Kayla, watching him cautiously.

"What?" she said, seeing Kayla's incredulous expression. "Don't tell me you didn't sign up for those self-defense classes at work?"

"I took the needlework class," replied Kayla, bewildered.

"Good call. So you can use your handy new skills to darn my black belt once I've finished saving your ass—"

Julissa broke off as the lead singer lunged at them, his fangs bared. The guy feinted toward Kayla and then pulled up short with a grin, his red eyes flicking from one girl to the other. He made a sudden lunge at Julissa, taking her to be the weaker target. Kayla moved to intercept him, body-slamming him to the ground, blindly trusting in her new-found strength to block the man's charge. The impact knocked the breath from her, but she recovered quickly and grabbed the guy by the collar. Like she'd done this thousand times before, she plucked a silver stiletto from her belt, reached under his guard, and smoothly drove it up into his...

"Ow!"

Kayla dropped her stiletto with a clatter and clutched at her wrist, then stared up at the vampire, who eyed her maliciously before opening his jacket to reveal a Kevlar vest strapped tight across his ebony chest.

"You think we'd play an LA gig without wearing one of these?" he sniggered. "Girl, you crazy!"

Kayla backed away warily, and then ducked to grab her knife off the ground. As she straightened up, an arm seized hers from behind. She snapped her body around to find herself face to face with the vampire guitarist, an older guy with metal spikes piercing his forehead, nose, and chin, and a British flag emblazoned across his black T-shirt. Without hesitation Kayla brought her other hand up, cracking the guy across the nose with her pistol and then shoving him into the lead singer. The pair reeled backwards, then quickly recovered their balance and came at her again, spreading out to flank her. The singer snapped his arms down hard to the side, ejecting six-inch claws from his fingertips, while the vampire guitarist ripped the guitar from around his shoulders and hefted it by its neck like a club.

The pair of them advanced on Kayla, snarling.

Kayla stood her ground, not wanting to turn and flee in front of Julissa. This was her big chance to prove herself to the girl, and she wasn't going to blow it.

The guitarist reached her first, swinging his guitar savagely at her face. Kayla felt the heavy wooden body whistle over her head as she frantically threw herself to the side.

CRACK!

Kayla staggered backward clutching at her nose as a flash of white filled her vision. The guitarist had elbowed her in the face at the end of his swing. Kayla gasped in pain, thrown off-balance. She dizzily raised an arm to ward the vampire off as he came at her again, whirling the body of the guitar around and lifting it triumphantly over his head, ready to split her skull open.

The man's muscles tensed and Kayla yelled in fear, but nothing happened. A look of bemusement crossed the guy's pierced face, and then he glanced behind him to see Phil holding onto the guitar tightly.

"Man, what are you doing?" yelled Phil.

The vampire bared his teeth in fury. "Let go!"

"No way!" cried Phil. "This is a classic Fifties Les Paul! Are you insane? You get blood on this, you'll ruin the finish!"

The vampire guitarist paused, a wary look on his face.

"You know guitars?" he asked.

"Well, *duh!*" Phil yanked the guitar from the vampire's grip and cradled it protectively. The nickel-plated pickups gleamed in the light. Phil stroked a hand reverently over the pick guard. "It's practically mint!" he breathed. "I've never seen one in this good a shape outside a collection before. Where did you get this?"

The vampire grinned, his chest swelling with pride.

"Looks the biz, dunnit? But it's a '58 reissue from the custom shop. I'd love a real '58 but they're goin' for two-fifty large."

Saving the world could apparently wait for a moment. "Love the fat neck," he murmured, swinging the guitar around and fingering an experimental chord. Kayla slipped away to safety. "But I gotta say, I prefer P-90s over the Humbuckers."

"I once saw a '57 gold top with P-90s on eBay for five grand, but it had a wraparound bridge and the intonation sucks on those things," said the vampire, refusing to be out-cooled by a mere human.

"Five grand?" Phil whistled. "It must have a repaired headstock or the finish was really fucked... whoa!"

He lifted the guitar out of the way as Julissa dodged past him around the back of the amp stack, the vampire drummer right on her tail. "Watch it!" He shook his head in good-natured bemusement, and then turned back to the guitarist, leaning back on the wall. "As I was saying..."

Behind the amp, Julissa dodged left, then right, glaring at the drummer over the top. This day wasn't going at all how she'd planned it. Instead of being up on stage, basking in the adoration of hundreds of people, she now had scales and fangs and was being chased by a guy that looked like something straight out of *Lost Boys*.

Well, there was only one thing left to do about that.

With a kamikaze cry she burst out from behind the amplifier, running right to the edge of the stage. The drummer chased her, fangs bared, charging her at full tilt. Julissa waited until the very last moment before stepping aside, as though she were fielding a bull. Unable to stop in time, the drummer rushed right over the edge of the stage, disappearing with a wail into the vengeful hands of the mutant audience.

Julissa straightened up, peering down into the pit. She pulled a face as gristly crunching sounds filled the air.

"Drummers," she scoffed, and then turned and ran for her life.

Back onstage, Phil plugged the guitar in and strummed a few notes, oblivious of the chaos going on around him. "Man, that Marshall sounds amazing. Did you have it modified?"

"No way, dude." The vampire puffed up his chest. "It's a '76 hundred watt. I just got lucky."

Phil shrugged, trying not to look impressed. "Well, *I've* got a triple rectifier, and when I use channel two on the vintage setting with a Boss compression pedal and a ten band EQ pedal boosting 700 and 3k in the F/X loop, I kind of get that sound."

The vampire shook his head, folding his arms. "First up, no way you get that sound and second up, you need to lose all that shit and get one great-sounding head, 'cause life's too short, man, know what I'm sayin'? Hey, you got a pen? I'll give you the number of that custom shop."

"Phil!" yelled Kayla from ground level, her arms locked above her to hold off the slavering lead singer. His fangs snapped just inches from her face.

Phil glanced over at her, frantically patting his pockets. "One minute!"

"I don't have a minute!"

Phil rolled his eyes, then gave up his hunt for a pen and reached into his belt-holster for his gun.

It wasn't there.

He pulled a pained face. He sighed and turned to the vampire guitarist, a look of deep regret on his face.

"I'm sorry, bro. This is gonna hurt me far more than it hurts you."

He gazed down sadly at the guitar in his hands, steeling himself. Then in one quick move he swung the guitar's headstock up hard against the amp, smashing it off at the neck. He whipped around and drove the broken neck upwards, staking the vampire through the heart. As the creature screamed and exploded in a cloud of flaming white ash, Phil strode over to Kayla and grabbed the vamp singer by the scruff of the neck, hauling him off her. He removed the creature's protective vest, and then punched the neck of the guitar through his back, into his heart.

Dust and flaming embers rained down around him.

Phil reached through the cloud and took Kayla's hand, helping her to her feet. Kayla dusted herself down, coughing hard and wiping vampire drool off her cheek.

"Thanks," she said wryly.

"I'd say 'don't mention it' but I wouldn't mean it," sighed Phil. "Mention it. Lots. Preferably in front of important people with money who can buy me another one of these." He lifted the smashed and bloodied Gibson.

They both jumped as a loud crash boomed through the room. Kayla looked up to see the stage barrier give way. Audience members started climbing up onto the stage, heading straight for them. A woman who was plainly recognizable as a famous LA beauty pageant winner grabbed one of the vampire bouncers in a headlock and sank her fangs into his throat. Blood spurted and the man screamed. A moment later she tossed his limp body aside and headed for Kayla and the Hunters, the only three people left in the room who looked even remotely human.

"Um, Kayla?" said Phil, as the ravening beauty queen approached them, blood running freely from her mouth. "Remember that whole 'run' concept we talked about?"

"Vividly," replied Kayla.

"Great, 'cause now's a good time to try it out. No pressure or nothin'."

Kayla was already halfway across the stage and accelerating. She heard Phil fall in behind her, and the pair of them put some serious muscle into running. A vampire roadie sprang into their path as they reached the overturned drum kit. He snarled, and Phil staked him with a swift jab of his broken guitar neck. Phil tore over to where Ninette was still locked in deadly combat with Cyan, over by the stage door.

"Honey, time to go!" called Phil, reaching into his ammo bag for a fresh gun.

"Just a moment!" replied Ninette breathlessly.

Kayla stopped beside Phil and watched helplessly, afraid to interfere. The pair seemed pretty evenly matched, one dressed in black cotton, one in white silk, their swords clanging and singing in an intricate dance of interlocking razor-sharp metal. One of Ninette's strikes hit home, opening a bloody slash across the vampiress's belly, dousing her already ruined ballgown in fresh blood. With a cry of vengeance, Cyan retaliated with a blindingly fast swing at Ninette's side, slicing open a mirroring wound across her ribs.

The young Hunter jerk in pain, pulling to the side, her sword hesitating for a second. In that second, Cyan whirled around in a lightning-fast strike and aimed her sword at Ninette's stomach.

Without even thinking, Kayla grabbed the broken guitar from Phil and swung it up protectively toward Ninette's body. A fraction of a second later Cyan's sword tip punched through the solid wooden body of the guitar at gut level, the bruising force of her strike knocking Ninette backward and tearing the guitar from Kayla's grip.

The guitar dropped to the ground, Cyan's sword embedded two inches deep in the pickguard.

Ninette's hand flew to her belly. It came away bloody where the sword had punched through, scratching her skin. She flung Kayla an incredulous look.

"Damn, girl! You learn fast!"

She whipped her sword up as Cyan tried to flee, raking a hand through her tangled hair. "And you—hold your vampire ass right there."

"It's too late," panted Cyan. She flung back her head and laughed. The sound choked off into a cry of pain as twin foot-long bone spurs violently punched through her elbows and from beneath her wrists, the two interlocking blades driving downwards toward the floor with the sickening sound of tearing flesh.

Cyan spat blood onto the floor in contempt as she straightened her arms and rotated her wrists, locking the bio-blades together with a double clunk. Then she slowly turned to face the Hunters, her forearms transformed into a pair of gleaming organic swords.

"Now that's something you don't see every day," murmured Kayla.

"Cool, aren't they? If you enjoy having a carving knife shoved through your wrists on a daily basis." Cyan clenched her fists and held her bio-weapons up before her, half as threat, half as defense.

Phil protectively moved between Cyan and the two women.

"Last chance. Let these people go."

"Too late." The vampiress laughed, blood running down her arms and dripping onto the floor. "They're already here. Can't you hear them?"

Phil paused, his finger tensing on the trigger. He could hear something. A drawn-out rumbling sound filled the air, like a dumpster truck driving full tilt toward the hall, and getting closer by the second.

Cyan grinned. "Just so you know, Cerik was full of shit. You think we tell our staff the truth? That was our bomb, not theirs." She threw Ninette a desultory look. "Magnus wasn't all that bright, sweetie, and neither, it seems, are you."

Ninette stared. "So where's the trigger?"

The windows on all four sides of the ballroom burst into a hailstorm of flying safety glass. Dozens of black-clad troopers came through the broken frames, rappelling into the room on toughened steel drop lines. White light stabbed into the room as a helicopter screamed past, its searchlight flooding through the broken windows.

For an instant, the Hunters were distracted.

In that split second Cyan ducked and ran for the stage door, wrenching it open and throwing herself through it as she made a break for freedom. Phil's bullets crashed harmlessly into her back as she fled.

"Shit!"

Phil instinctively started to give chase, and then lurched to a halt, swearing. He clenched his fists, unwillingly turning back to the roomful of people. He had a duty. There was a bomb ticking upstairs, and he couldn't just leave people here to die when there might be a chance he could save them.

Turning abruptly away from the door, he hurled the broken Les Paul to the floor to vent some of his frustration. Then he clicked over effortlessly into combat mode, scanning the room, sizing up the situation.

There were at least thirty fully armored troops, heavily armed with automatic rifles, police batons, and stun guns. Their slender torsos were protected with gunmetal gray adjustable body amour. As they deployed they dropped clinking silver gas canisters that spewed out sweeping clouds of orange sedative gas into the crowd. A wave of coughing and hacking rose up and people dropped to the ground, clutching their throats. The troopers rushed up to them as they fell, rolling their weakly struggling bodies over and slapping metal restraint cuffs on them.

Ninette stepped up beside Phil and lightly touched his arm as he walked to the edge of the stage, shielding his mouth from the gas, scanning the crowd like a bloodhound. He had less than a minute before the gas would reach them.

"Whatcha think?" she asked tensely.

Phil stared intently at the troopers as they swarmed down the walls, trying to ID them. "Not SWAT," he said, "wrong body amour."

"Cops?"

Phil shook his head. "Outdated gear."

"Then what?"

Phil's eyes narrowed as he stared at the nearest trooper. He clutched at Ninette's arm in sudden horror.

"What?"

"We gotta go. Now!"

"Why?"

Ninette jumped back as Phil drew his Glock and emptied his clip into the nearest trooper's face. Black blood spurted and the wounded man gave a screech of outrage. Ninette gasped as the man spun around to get a lock on the source of the gunfire. Half his lower jaw was missing and his right eye was a bloodied crater, but he didn't even seem to notice.

Phil ejected his clip in a hurry and slammed in a fresh one. He backed away, dragging Ninette with him.

"Remember that army we thought the vampires might be building?" he asked grimly.

"Uh-huh?"

"I think they built it."

CHAPTER THIRTY-SEVEN

NINETTE STARED IN horror at the seething roomful of hissing, snarling monsters, even now being sedated and checked over by the vampire troopers. The main door crashed open and more vampire guards flooded in, nodding to the troopers as they started hauling their semi-conscious victims toward the door.

Phil tightened his grip on Ninette's hand as they took cover behind a stack of three enormous amps. "Looks like the vamps pulled the old Trojan horse trick, in reverse."

Ninette shook her head in admiration. "Guess that's what happens when the boss gets lazy and doesn't check up on what his staff is doing all day. If it's not surfing internet porn, it's building mutant vampire armies in the basement. Go figure."

"But how are they gonna get away with this? There's gotta be two hundred people in here! The cops'll be all over this shit when, tomorrow morning, hundreds of families file missing persons' reports."

Phil stared hard at Ninette. "The bomb?"

"Shit! The vamps are gonna blow this place sky high the second they've got their new 'army' out! An explosion this big, the cops won't even bother looking for the bodies!"

As one, the Hunters turned and raced across the stage toward the exits.

"Kayla!" yelled Ninette. "Get out of here! The building's gonna blow!"

"I can't!" came the reply.

"Why?"

"Door's locked!"

Phil ran over to Kayla, joining her by the stage door. He tugged on it fruitlessly, and then aimed his Glock at the deadbolt.

"Stand back, guys," he ordered.

Kayla covered her ears as the lock exploded in a blaze of twisted metal. Phil yanked it open, hurrying Kayla and Ninette through, grabbing Julissa by the hand and setting off.

They ran in a blur through the darkened, carpeted corridors of backstage Genetica, crashing through room after room without meeting any resistance. Any door that was locked, Phil simply blasted open. In less than five minutes they burst out into the main lobby of Genetica, but as Phil and Ninette sprinted for the exits, Kayla slowed and stopped, staring behind her.

"Guys, wait!" she called. "We're missing someone!"

"Who?"

"Mutt! We need to find him!"

"No, we need to get the hell outta here before that bomb goes off and turns us all into crispy critters. Unless you're wearing factor ten-thousand sunblock, in which case, you go right ahead and rescue that little snapping, snarling bundle of joy."

Kayla gave Phil a hurt look and resolutely headed back the way they'd come. A second later she felt Ninette's hand close on her shoulder, spinning her back around.

"New kid!" she barked. "I say move, you move. You hear me?"

Kayla pulled herself free. "I have to find Mutt!"

"Sorry, girl. If the vampires have got this guy then he's already dead. You go looking for him, it's your funeral."

"Either way, I can't just leave him to die."

Tightening her jaw, Kayla grabbed the Colt pistol from Ninette's hip holster and froze as a vampire lobby clerk stepped out from behind the main desk. He moved directly into their path, drawing his pistol.

"Nobody leaves!" he yelled, with impressive bravado.

K-CHAK! The clerk found himself looking into the wrong end of three Glocks, a Colt, and a Ruger.

"We insist," said Phil.

As the clerk opened his mouth to reply, the lobby light blew out and the ceiling exploded. Tiles and pipes rained down around them.

"Oh, for crap's sake," cried Ninette, glaring at Kayla and covering her head as rubble crashed down all around her. "Are they doing a two-for-one offer on fuck-ups today?"

A hissing, deformed thing wearing a shredded bell-hop's uniform smashed through the remains of an air vent and dropped down in front of them. Uncurling itself in a snap, it lunging straight for Ninette's throat in a blur of alien motion. Its head rocked back as Phil smoothly unloaded three rounds into its armored reptilian skull, then two more into each of its kneecaps. It screamed, swinging around to face him.

"Whoa!" yelled Phil, jumping back.

There was a loud cracking sound like a half-cut apple being pulled apart. The creature's tooth-filled, vertically-set mouth opened and kept on opening, a red fissure running swiftly down its jaw and throat and chest and belly as though it were being sliced open by an invisible scalpel. The entire front of its body split apart to reveal a gory, glistening body cavity lined with teeth and dripping with acidic digestive juices.

As the Hunters backed away in utter horror, the giant mouth swung open like a Venus Flytrap on hinged rib joints. With a quick striking motion, the creature flew at the screaming lobby clerk and snapped its body shut around him. The guard's screams abruptly cut off as the creature bit down with a crunch, severing the man's dangling limbs as though they were spaghetti.

The two Hunters emptied their pistols into the creature, to no visible effect. Their guns clicked on empty and they backed up, drawing their swords and assuming defensive positions. The creature turned to face them, hissing, its malevolent blue eyes zeroing in on them with icy intelligence.

Kayla watched the creature's legs tense as it snarled at the two Hunters and prepared to pounce, opening its mouth a second time.

Then it paused, blinking.

"Julissa?" it said, in a muffled voice.

Kayla, Phil and Ninette slowly revolved to face Julissa, who stared up at the nightmarish apparition in a kind of stunned fascination. Her expression turned to one of shock as she recognized its voice.

"*Tyler?*" she gasped.

The Hunters hurriedly scrambled aside as the Venus Flytrap vampire took a hesitant step toward Julissa, its multi-jointed claws scraping gauges in the marble floor. It closed its enormous mouth in an intricate shuffle of bones and cleared its throat, looking faintly sheepish, as though it were a dog that had just been caught in the act of stealing a bone.

Julissa walked forward as if in a dream, peering up at the nightmarish beast. As its head came down into the light she could see Tyler's familiar features rearrange themselves around the edges of the gaping vertical mouth. She cleared her throat, feeling unreality dance inside her.

"So, this is why you couldn't make it tonight?" she heard herself say.

The Tyler-creature hung its head. "I left you a voice-mail," it started, and then jerked to one side as Phil fired a round through its left shoulder. It retaliated with a vicious sweep of its spiny tail, knocking him off his feet and sending him crashing into a nearby wall. He rolled and continued firing from ground-level, then gave a yell as the creature swatted the pistol out of his hands.

"No you didn't!" snapped Julissa, her brain firing on pure instinct. Fighting down the urge to laugh hysterically, she pulled out her cell phone and checked it. "Oh," she said, "I think I had it on silent. Shit. Hang on."

"Er, Julissa," said Kayla, flicking a frantic glance toward the exit.

Julissa shushed her sternly as she pressed the phone to her ear, watching the Tyler-monster all the while. She listened for a moment, her face changing from suspicion to outright disgust. "You said you were working tonight!"

"I am working." The creature protested weakly. It lifted a forelimb, waving the tattered remains of the bellhop uniform at Julissa.

"Guys," said Ninette, trying to talk without moving her mouth as she helped Phil up and pulled out her own blooper gun. "I don't think this is the best time to—"

"Oh, I think it's the perfect time." Julissa's fear vanished and she was suddenly extremely angry. Lying to her was one thing, lying to her in the face was another. She stormed up to Tyler, put her hands on her hips, and directed two thousand watts of pure outrage at him. "You asshole!" she shouted. "All this time I thought you were..." She floundered, casting for words.

"What?"

"Famous!" burst out Julissa. She looked Tyler up and down in disgust, flinching as Ninette's silenced blooper blew three large, steaming holes in Tyler's chest. When the noise abated she uncovered her ears and glowered up at him. "And here you are, working as a common guard!"

"A vampire guard... freaky mutated thing," modified Phil, nodding to Ninette as she dropped her empty gun and pulled a length of glinting glass wire out of a spool on Phil's belt. They pulled it taut between them and advanced on the Tyler-beast. He glanced at them in irritation and deftly extruded a hooked claw from his midsection, snipping the wire in two.

"Well, that just takes the cake, doesn't it? You dump me, blow off my invite to the party of the century, and then show up looking like a dog's dinner without so much as a phone call to warn me that there's a small chance you might not actually be here. Do you have any idea how long it took me to get my hair like this?"

She reached out to finger the remains of Tyler's uniform, the disdain on her face speaking volumes. "And that's not even real Armani! They sell those fakes up at Beverly Center Mall, I've seen them! Honestly, the nerve!"

She shook her head in disgust, tears threatening. It was the perfect end to the perfect night. "Just tell me straight," she whispered, "are you even union?"

"That was what I wanted to tell you," sighed Tyler, rubbing his eyes with a mandible. "Baby, you and I need to talk."

Tyler's voice choked off and an expression of shock crossed his face. Then he burst into flames and exploded in a swirling cloud of incandescent ash. Julissa shrieked and jumped back as chunks of bloody flesh rained down across the room, along with the gristly, half-digested remains of the lobby clerk.

Phil and Ninette cocked their pistols through the smoke and aimed them at the dark, menacing figure of...

"Mutt?"

Kayla stared at the young werewolf in utter relief as he lowered his bloody silver stake, grimly wiping bits of exploded vampire bellhop off his face.

"What the hell are you doing here?" she cried.

"Nice to see you too, Kayla," said Mutt tonelessly. "Caught your little performance in the ballroom. Thought you might need some backup."

"Well, you thought wrong." Kayla blew vampire dust out of her eyes and swept a hand through her hair, attempting to tidy it. She licked her lips, painfully aware that she had a rapt audience. "We're doing just fine, thanks all the same."

"So I see." Mutt brushed a bloody chunk of ash off his sleeve as the dust settled, ignoring Kayla's glare. "For fuck's sake, yuck. Filthy creatures, vampires."

"And I suppose werewolves are better?" asked Ninette, aiming her pistol at Mutt's heart. Phil moved smoothly into position behind her, pinning Mutt in his sights.

"Werewolves?" Julissa's brain finally caught up with the conversation. "And vampires? Would somebody like to explain what the hell is going on? My boyfriend just exploded, in case any of you missed that! And everyone in the hall back there turned into monsters, and those two guards turned to big poofy piles of ash when you stabbed them, and that psycho lady got her heart blown out and didn't die, and I'm going to need some crazy heavy foundation if I'm going to go back to work on Monday, and now he's a werewolf. So what are you two?"

"Hunters," said Mutt quietly, wiping his stake on his sleeve before dropping it back into his pocket. He was in pretty good shape apart from the pair of fresh bruises marring his forehead and left cheek. Kayla's eyes trailed down his torso, and she shook herself. The guy had been in the room for thirty seconds and already she was eyeing him up. She needed to get a grip on her hormones and concentrate on more important things, like not dying.

"Werewolf hunters, to be precise," she corrected, shooting Mutt a look. A second ago she had been ready and willing to lay down her life for the guy. Now she felt the echoes of her anger at him starting to creep back. What was the deal with that?

"Great," said Julissa. "So they've got their guy. Is this the part where we all go home and eat cookies?"

"I'm not the werewolf they're after," snapped Mutt. "I've got nothing to do with any of this."

"Yeah, right," snorted Kayla.

"Really, I'm on your side, but there's no time for this. Call off your dogs, Kayla. There's something I need to tell you."

"What did he just call us?" asked Ninette. Phil thumbed off the safety catches on his Glocks and aimed them at Mutt's heart, his fingers hovering over the triggers.

Mutt glanced at Phil, darkness flooding his face. "You don't want to do that."

"And why not?"

Mutt swallowed as he slowly opened his jacket. "Because it could be messy."

"Kayla," said Phil quietly. "Get out of here, and try not to look back."

Kayla's heart dropped into the pit of her stomach and she backed away, staring wide-eyed at the dozens of explosive rounds taped to Mutt's sculpted torso. A detonator device was clipped to his belt, the orange and red LED lights flashing. A silver UV trigger collar glinted around his neck.

"No!" she cried.

"Kayla, I'm not asking you," said Phil. He grabbed Ninette's hand and started to back toward the exit, keeping his Glocks trained on Mutt. "Take your friend and run. The pair of you."

"Might be wise to do as he says, guys," added Mutt.

"You're going to just leave him here to die?" cried Kayla in disbelief.

"He's a werewolf, Kayla," said Ninette harshly. "He should die."

Kayla rushed to Mutt's side and stared helplessly at the wires, her composure vanishing as the reality of the situation hit her. "We've gotta get this thing off you!"

"Sorry, babe," said Mutt, holding up his hands and stepping quickly away from her. "It's rigged to blow if tampered with. You know the drill. Got twenty pounds of grade A plastique under here. This little lot goes off, it'll set off the fuse for the bomb in the ceiling above, and then the one above that, and the one above that."

"So get out of the building!"

"I can't!" Mutt fingered his UV collar, sweating. "I go through any door and this thing'll trigger a charge, blow my head off, and then detonate the plastique. I'm screwed either way."

"So why are you even here? Get away from us!" cried Julissa.

"Because I had to warn you," said Mutt.

"Warn us? About what?"

"Aw, are you guys leaving already?" asked Harlem, stepping around the corner. Kayla's eyes flew to the detonator device in the werewolf's clawed hand and her heart gave a nasty thump. Cyan followed Harlem at a short distance, her smug, vengeful gaze darting between Phil and Ninette as they aimed their pistols at her head. She waved her spurred bio-swords at them in a taunting reply. Flame, Mitzi, Jackdoor, and Dana brought up the rear of the group, dragging a giant covered crate with them, its metal edges scraping loudly on the marble floor.

Mutt bared his teeth at Harlem. "Where is he?"

"Who?"

"Freakin' Ronald McDonald, who d'you think?"

"I dunno what you're talking about, buddy," said Harlem. He raised an ironic eyebrow as the door behind the reception suddenly burst open and...

Skyler ran in.

"Guys," he called breathlessly. "We've gotta get this lot loaded into the trucks stat. The Feds could be here any minute, and—"

Skyler's voice tailed off as his eyes caught up with his brain. Phil and Ninette crossed their arms and glared at him. He blinked, taking in the nightmare scenario before him—the ceiling caved in; vampire guts strewn everywhere; Karrel's damned girlfriend still alive and standing guard over the rapidly-mutating former cover girl of Genetica; and in the corner, two of his highest-ranking commandos aimed guns at the bloodied and grinning form of the woman he loved.

The vampire woman he loved. The color drained from Skyler's face.

Phil readied his gun. "The whole gang is here! Glad you could join us. *Sir.*"

CHAPTER THIRTY-EIGHT

NINETTE DREW HER sword, her disbelieving gaze riveted on Skyler. Kayla grabbed a spare Glock pistol from Phil's belt and trained it on Skyler's head.

"Lemme guess," said Phil, his aim unwavering. "This isn't what it looks like, you were framed, and this was all a set up?"

"I can explain." Skyler held up his hands.

Phil edged around his commander, lining his sights on the man's throat. "You can explain this shit? And this?" He indicated the werewolves behind him and the exploded remains of Tyler with an angry jerk of his head.

"Phil, please."

"What the *fuck*, Skyler? I trusted you, man! We both did."

Kayla nervously glanced from Phil to Skyler and back again. She had never seen Phil angry before. Somehow, that freaked her out more than anything else.

"Stay away from him, guys," said Mutt in a low voice. "He's been working with them all along, helping fund this Genetica freakshow, staffing it with the very vampires you Hunters have been busting your asses catching, and you don't even want to know what's in that crate."

"Skyler? Is that true?" demanded Ninette.

"Oh come on!" Skyler burst out. He straightened his suit and rose to his full height. "I'm your commander! He's a werewolf! You'd take his word over mine?"

Phil stared at Skyler. "You tell me," he snapped.

"Don't believe a word he tells you," said Mutt, his eyes not leaving Skyler. "Good thing about being a hostage, you learn all kinds of nasty secrets. This guy's a lying, backstabbing son of a bitch. He's worse than her." He jerked his head at Cyan.

"That's a compliment, coming from you." Cyan eyed Mutt with a wicked grin. "And speaking of nasty secrets..."

"Don't you dare."

Cyan made a big show of biting her tongue. Something in Kayla's chest lurched as she saw the look that went between them like a pulse of electricity.

"Mutt," she said quietly, "what's in that crate?"

"Nothing," Mutt snapped.

Cyan gave a little mock gasp. "You mean you didn't tell her?"

"Tell me what?" asked Kayla.

"Much as I hate to interrupt this little fucked-up family reunion," said Harlem, "we're outta here." Harlem gazed at Kayla for a moment, his eyes sparking with amusement and recognition. He reached inside his jacket, pulled out a Coda net gun, and fired it at the two Hunters. They dropped to the ground, hopelessly entangled in the rapidly constricting steel net. Kayla managed to snap off a shot at Harlem before she too was caught. Julissa was the next to fall, followed by Skyler.

"Sorry, bud," said Harlem, seeing Skyler's outraged expression. "You stay too. I don't do the whole 'sharing' thing, money or women."

He handed Cyan the detonator, delicately wiping a fleck of blood off her lips before stepping in close and planting a lingering kiss on her open mouth. He ran his gloved fingers down the bio-blades projecting from her wrists and elbows. He cupped her jaw, breathing in deeply as he touched his forehead to hers. "Set the timer for me, baby. Daddy's got some important business to take care of."

He shot Skyler a triumphant look and headed off toward the main door. Sounds of a helicopter descending filled the lobby. Skyler pulled on the net impotently as Flame helped Jackdoor push the giant crate. The two werewolves disappeared through the main door, slamming it behind them.

CYAN PEERED DOWN at her captives as they struggled and swore. She tapped her long nails on the remote detonator. She swung around to face Mutt, who stood opposite her, clenching his fists in fury.

"How long should we give them? A minute? Three minutes?" Cyan licked her lips, running her eyes over Mutt's lean body with regret. "Lots of things you can do in three minutes."

"Don't you ever shut up?" Mutt felt Kayla's accusing glare burn into him as he turned to face Cyan, squaring off against her. His eyes flicked down to the detonator. If he could just get it away from her he could end all this and save himself; save everyone.

He poised to rush Cyan. The vampiress pulled out a silver pistol and aimed it at Kayla's head.

"Don't even think about it, cutie."

Mutt glared at her.

"Back up now. Go on. Good boy."

Unwillingly Mutt took a step back, then another, until he hit the wall. He felt his face burn with humiliation and fury as he stared at the vampiress with cold loathing.

"There now," Cyan cooed, "that wasn't so hard now, was it?"

"The second I get out of this…" Mutt growled.

"Mutt? Is that your name?" interrupted Skyler from floor level. "Let me out. I can help you."

"Shut it, creep."

"I'm not the enemy!" Skyler cried. "I'm working undercover with the werewolves, not working for them! I'm trying to save the Hunter operation, don't you get it?"

"And the award for Bullshit Artist of the Year goes to—"

"Ninette, tell him! I'd never hurt you guys. You've got to believe me!"

Ninette wriggled a serrated knife out of her boot and started trying to saw through the net. "You really are full of shit, aren't you?"

"No! You have to listen to me. Cyan! Don't go. You're in danger."

"From who?" Cyan scoffed, halfway to the door.

"From Harlem!" Skyler tried to roll into a sitting position. "I heard him and Skeet talking last night at the club. They don't give a rat's ass about this racket. They're just going to sell off the contract for some quick cash. The whole reason they blew this operation and shipped Magnus off to the cops was to get to you. That was Harlem's plan all along!"

"To me?" Cyan stared. "Why?"

"Come *on*, kitten, use your head! Without Magnus's protection, do you have any idea what those wolves are gonna do to you?" Skyler slid his fingers through the netting. "It'll start with a candlelit dinner for five, and go downhill from there."

"Harlem?" Cyan shook her head with a titter. "That cat don't scare me. I've worked with him for ten years, and he's never once touched me. He knows Magnus would kick his ass."

"And you know me, Cyan. You know I wouldn't bullshit you."

"He's lying!" snapped Mutt. He walked rapidly back and forth, staring at the gun in Cyan's hand. "He doesn't give a damn about the Hunters, or you. He wants control of Magnus's empire, and he's using you to do it."

"What makes you think that?"

"Because Karrel told me." Mutt paused a moment. "The night before you had him killed."

"That order never came from me!" Skyler shouted.

"But you knew about it!"

"And I opposed it, right up until the end."

"I'm not listening to this bull."

"It's the truth, like it or not," snapped Skyler, "Karrel's death was for the greater good, for the survival of the Hunters."

"How do you figure that one, buddy?" asked Phil in a low voice. Mutt glanced quickly over at him. There was something about the way the guy had said "buddy" that made the hairs stand up on the back of his neck. He watched the downed Hunter warily.

"I can't explain now," Skyler said glancing quickly at Cyan, "but there are great things going on, things that none of you can even conceive of, things that could tip the balance of good and evil in this world forever, and Karrel nearly jeopardized them."

"Oh my God, is that guy still talking?" asked Mutt in exasperation.

"So the Hunters really did kill Karrel," said Kayla coldly. "Who gave that order?"

"It's not important," said Skyler brashly, "and quite frankly, if your two friends had told anyone besides me their suspicions about the vampire's master plan, they might've wound up having a little 'accident,' too."

Skyler turned back to Cyan. "Cyan, baby, I'm making you a deal here. You know the score, what I've got planned. Right now, I have legal, legitimate control of everything—the Hunters, the werewolves, everything. After tonight I'll have ties with the vampires, too. You walk out that door now, and Harlem will have control. He'll have access to Magnus's assets, his manpower, everything. Your life won't be worth shit, but if you let me out, I'll get rid of him for you. We'll rule LA together. Everything will be perfect."

"What a crock of shit!" said Mutt.

"You—shut your mouth," snapped Skyler. "Cyan, you know what I'm saying makes sense. This is your one shot to make the choice you should've made... before all this began."

Cyan gazed at him for what felt like forever, then gave an almost imperceptible nod. The vampiress swiftly lowered the detonator and backed around Mutt, keeping her gun trained on Kayla's head. Skyler beamed at her as she sliced through the steel net with her bio-swords. He flashed the two downed Hunters an apologetic look, and they headed for the doors.

"Sorry, guys. If you want me to save the Hunters, I have to do this. Your sacrifices—like Karrel's—will be for the greater good."

"Fuck the greater good!" shouted Phil.

"I'll put that on a T-shirt," said Skyler, "and wear it to your funeral." He turned to face Cyan, reaching carefully around her razor-sharp bone spurs to take her dainty hand in his. "You finally made the right choice," he said. He gave a sigh of happiness and brought her hand to his mouth. Then he tightened his grip and rammed her arm down and back, stabbing her in the gut with her own bio-blade.

"Sorry, baby," he whispered. Cyan's knees buckled and she clutched at him, her mouth open in a little "O" of surprise. "I've got an empire to run. I have no time for women."

He took the remote trigger from her, gave her a shove, and watched as she fell to the floor, blood gushing from the depths of her gaping belly

"Three minutes good enough for you, kitten?" Skyler punched the activation button on the detonator. A muted bleeping filled the room, horrifically loud in the suddenly claustrophobic atmosphere. There was a collective intake of breath as he smugly held up the timer, revealing a row of red numbers counting down to zero. He turned and pitched it as hard as he could over the railings of the high-ceilinged lobby. With a little wave, Skyler turned and fled out the door.

CHAPTER THIRTY-NINE

THE ROOM ERUPTED into chaos.

"You! Get the detonator!" Ninette yelled, frantically struggling to free herself.

Mutt had no idea where the stairs were. Even if he got up to the correct floor in time, there was no guarantee that there was an off button on the timer. He was all out of choices, and the bomb was counting down.

"There's no time!" he yelled.

With a growl Mutt stepped over the pinioned body of Cyan to reach the Hunters. The vampiress rolled over weakly as he passed her, blood pouring in a red river down her arm and back where a good five inches of the bio-blade projected through her spine. She tried to pull the blade from her belly, but the foot-long spur on her elbow was locked deep between her armor-plated ribs.

"Help me," she gasped, her beautiful eyes filled with pain.

Mutt ignored her. He grabbed the netting that bound Kayla and tore it apart with his bare hands, grunting with the effort. Metal links spattered and plinked across the floor as the steel netting squealed, heated, and then broke. Kayla quickly shoved her way out of the netting and scrambled to her feet, helping Julissa up behind her. Mutt freed Phil and Ninette in a similar fashion.

"Now get outta of here! Scram!" cried Mutt.

In an adrenaline-rush of emotion Kayla saw the two Hunters hesitate, glancing at each other. Did they have a plan to save him?

She cried out in disbelief as they simply nodded to Mutt, their expressions somber. Phil reached out to clap Mutt on the shoulder in awkward thanks before turning and starting toward the door. Julissa quickly outdistanced them, reaching the exit in record time and hurling herself through it, shrieking in fear.

"Move it, Kayla!" cried Ninette, glancing at her watch. "Two minutes!"

Kayla balked. "I'm not leaving him!"

"Why not?" asked Cyan weakly, from ground level. "He'd leave you to die, if he had the chance. Just like he left Karrel."

"What?"

"Kayla, get your ass outta here!" yelled Phil, holding the main door open.

"One minute fifty, guys!"

"Just wait!" Kayla stared down at Cyan, her heart in her mouth. "What did you just say?"

"Why don't you tell her?" panted Cyan. "It's not like you have anything to lose at this point."

"Shut your face, Cyan!"

"Tell me what?" demanded Kayla.

"That Karrel died because of him," said Cyan smugly.

Kayla stared down at the vampiress, shocked. She swung around to face Mutt. "Is this true?" she demanded.

"It's true," he mumbled

"One minute thirty!" yelled Ninette. "Kayla! Move your ass!"

Kayla barely heard her. All her attention was desperately riveted on Mutt. "What did you do?" she whispered. She gazed into his gorgeous amber-green eyes, lit up from below by the blips of blue light from his UV collar.

"Kayla, I'm sorry," said Mutt, reaching out to touch her hand. "I didn't mean to get involved, but things just happened. The Hunters paid me to..."

Kayla slapped him. Hot tears of betrayal stung her eyes as she backed away from him, shaking her head in disgust. She joined the other two Hunters as they yelled at her to hurry up. The four of them vanished through the exit.

The hall door swung shut, leaving Mutt alone with Cyan. A terrible silence descended, broken by the sound of Cyan laughing weakly.

"Well. That was heroic," she coughed, between giggles, "but completely pointless. You think she'll swallow that half-baked crock of horseshit? Wait until she finds out the *real* truth. Then you'll wish you'd let her die here with you."

"Zip it, bitch," snapped Mutt. He was a were-wolf. Being altruistic did not come easily to him. He didn't need any more provocation.

"Or what?" grinned Cyan.

Mutt kicked her in the face, bouncing her head off the tiled floor. She slumped to the ground, unconscious.

"Sorry, babe," said Mutt. "No time to hunt for the mute button."

Moving away from her, Mutt's hands flew to the detonator pack strapped to his belt. He tried to shove it down over his pelvis, but it caught on his hipbones. He tried pulling it the other way, holding his breath, but his shoulders were too broad to pull it off over his head, and if the wire broke in the process…

He didn't want to think about that right now. There was only one course of action left to him, and he really, really didn't like it.

He reached into the inner lining of his jacket and pulled out a syringe filled with green liquid. He tried not to think about what he was about to do, while inside his head, an internal chronometer continued silently counting down.

Mutt quickly shed his jacket, taking care not to disturb any of the tubes of plastic explosives taped to his body underneath. He flexed his hand a couple times to pump a vein in his forearm, then placed the syringe in the crook of his elbow.

Yeah, this was gonna hurt.

He shoved the sharp needle into his vein and depressed the plunger, gritting his teeth against the pain that he knew was coming. For a second or two nothing happened. Then he shuddered as he felt the acidic liquid sear through his veins, burning everything it touched. He blinked rapidly, sweating, feeling the liquid work its way up his arm and into his throat, then downward into his heart.

Mutt swore violently and inventively as a stream of molten agony coursed through his bloodstream, burning every organ, every shred of his inner being that it touched. Everything in him screamed out at the wrongness of what he was doing. He felt a wave of biological static pass through his mind as his brain made one last-ditch attempt to protect him from the pain. Every cell in him started to mutate, transforming at a frightening rate.

His head thumped back in agony. The empty syringe went flying as his whole body cramped. His muscles convulsed as his bones began to elongate, changing density and mass. A sense of pressure filled his head as his face flattened, then his mind whited out as his skull pressed in on his brain to form its new shape. Blood started to flow from his mouth as Mutt bit through his tongue to try and halt the agony. His fingers blazed with pain as claws stabbed through his nail beds. His back cracked and bowed as his spinal column rearranged itself to accommodate a tail, the bones and cartilage that made it leached from his rapidly-flattening rib cage.

Then the pain went away. He collapsed onto the floor, panting shallowly.

As the red fog in his head dissipated, Mutt peered muzzily around him, gripped by a mad sense of urgency that he couldn't quite put his finger on—if he had a finger. His huge furry paws scrabbled on the tiles and pushed his body upright into a world devoid of color. He howled at the dizzying, overlapping cacophony of scents. He shed his crumpled clothes and headed for the smells of the outdoors.

He paused as something jangled behind him. Something was caught around his hips, something that flashed and bleeped and smelled bad. Mutt lifted his muzzle and delicately sniffed it, his eyebrows drawn together in canine worry.

Aw, shit!

Awareness suddenly filled him, along with a tidal wave of adrenaline. Mutt quickly reversed a couple of steps, then scraped the dangling belt gently against a strut projecting from the reception desk.

Careful now.

One step at a time, Mutt eased the main bomb pack off his body, the steel band easily slipping over his narrowed hips and dropping with a *clink* onto the strut.

And then he was free, bounding across the lobby toward the door in a skitter of claws. He was almost through the door when he paused. Smelling her blood, he turned and glanced back across the lobby to where the still, silent form of Cyan lay.

Dammit!

He growled to himself in disgust and darted back to her. He seized her wrist between his jaws, sinking his razor-sharp teeth through her soft, buttery flesh until they met with a click and locked through the bone of her forearm. The smell of vampire was so strong that he had to fight not to retch as he raced for the door... and stopped.

Mutt swallowed, feeling the UV collar around his throat bob up and down with the movement. He closed his eyes and whined in sudden misery. The second he went through the door, the collar would activate and trigger the bomb.

There was only one thing left to do: run.

Mutt reared up and lunged through the open door, hearing his collar send out a quiet electronic signal even as his frantically scrabbling paws hit the steps outside.

A giant hand of heat picked up Mutt and flung him through the air, flailing and howling. A sound like crashing water filled the air as a shockwave of fire shot from the bomb pack and blossomed through the lobby. It shot upwards through the building as ten floors of TNT sequentially activated. Mutt was barely aware of his fur burning as he hung suspended in the air. Time slowed to a crawl, his consciousness violently crashing to white as the edge of the explosion overtook him, enveloping him in a blast of searing heat.

Then the ground rushed up to meet him, and everything went black.

CHAPTER FORTY

THE NEWLY APPOINTED Detective Ned Crawley slammed on the brakes of his patrol car as the explosion rocked the grounds of Genetica. He stared through the side window and watched, dumbfounded, as the building he had left thirty minutes ago blew up in a stunning display of pyrotechnics. He pulled up the emergency brake as a rush of hot air and flying debris swept over his squad car, cracking the windows. He jolted forward violently as the car behind rear-ended him.

Then all was still.

Ned killed the engine and, dazed, got out of the car. He joined the rest of his squad as they stared up at the giant mushroom cloud of roiling fire billowing out of the Genetica building. White smoke rolled toward them like fog, carpeting the grounds of the building with a thin layer of ash.

The SWAT trooper next to Ned cleared his throat. Ned swung into brisk action, raising his walkie-talkie to his lips and barking orders into it as he stared at the blazing building. The chromed windows were blown out into angry black teeth on the first, fifth and ninth levels, and he could plainly see flames flickering behind the windows on the remaining floors. It wouldn't be long before the whole thing caved in on itself.

Ned's heart skipped a beat, his eyes flying back to the dark shape of the LAPD chopper. It was still sitting on the ground in the parking lot. Ned let out his breath in a quick pant of relief. Thank God it hadn't taken off before the building had blown up, or months of tracking and research would be down the tube. As he watched, its doors slammed and boomed up into the air, swinging lightly as the secondary wind from the explosion coursed over it, carrying its precious cargo with it. He still couldn't believe he had actually caught Magnus. Hell, it almost made having to put up with eight long months of that jackass Collins worthwhile.

Almost.

A movement on the grassy lawn in front of the building caught Ned's eye. He frowned at the dark shape lying in the grass, hoping that it wasn't one of his SWAT guys. He glanced around, then sighed and reached back inside his car to grab his radio. He'd better check, if only for the sake of appearances. Those guys were expensive to replace.

Ned walked across the springy grass, ready for anything. He scrunched up his face as he approached it. It was definitely a body. Ned drew his gun and walked cautiously up to it, then froze as the body rolled over to face him, coughed loudly, and groaned in pain.

The creature lying sprawled on the grass stared up at him with green, pain-filled eyes that locked on his briefly before rolling away in despair. It had a blunt, snub-like muzzle and powerfully clawed hind legs. There was a charred silver collar around its throat. Its broken limbs were folded awkwardly under it, multiple wounds bleeding out onto the grass through the melted remains of its fur.

Ned grinned, unable to believe his luck. Another werewolf—two in one day! The other guys in his department were lucky if they could bring in two a month. He was going to be getting a big Christmas bonus from the vampires this year.

The werewolf snapped at him weakly as he approached, baring its teeth in a token gesture of defiance.

"Well," said Ned, his eyes gleaming as he pulled out his block cuffs, "what have we here?"

IT WAS OVER. They had lost... or had they?

Kayla put a hand on the cool glass of the window as the Hunter vehicle rumbled its way through Genetica's back lot. A painful mix of feelings welled through her: fear at how close she had just come to dying, fury and confusion at what she had just found out about Karrel, and a desperately twisted anguish at the death of Mutt.

Julissa sat beside her, her head down and eyes closed from the sedative injection Ninette had given her. Her fangs seemed to have receded a little, but the scales that coated her face and neck had definitely gotten worse.

Kayla shivered. It didn't look very "over" to her.

Phil put the monster car into third gear and hit the gas, booking down the white gravel driveway. The vamps had been loading the last of the mutated humans into a series of sleek black trucks when they had fled down the steps of the building. They had slammed their tailgates and taken off before the Hunters had gotten anywhere near the parking lot. Ninette had radioed their backup and they had agreed to meet at a rendezvous point to track the vampires down before they got away with several hundred ex-human abductees.

There was so much work to do. Kayla had a nasty feeling that this was just the beginning.

Right now, all she wanted to do was go home.

Ninette tilted the rearview mirror in her direction and she turned her head away numbly, watching the plush greenery speed past.

"You know he deserved to die," said Ninette, after a moment.

Kayla didn't reply. Her eyes stung with sudden, annoying tears. She clenched her jaw tightly and stared furiously at a tiny crack in the window, focusing all her attention on it to keep from thinking.

So Mutt was dead. So what? She'd barely known the guy. In that short time he had done nothing but lech on her, annoy her, and poke her with a succession of increasingly sharp mental sticks. He had pretended to be Karrel's secret best friend before revealing that hang on, sorry, back it up there, it was actually him who was somehow responsible for his death.

Sure, he deserved to die, so why couldn't she stop thinking about him?

Kayla sighed. It was no good. There were too many pieces of the jigsaw missing for her to make sense of this or even know how to feel. She had to do something about it before it was too late. They had to go back. Maybe they could scope out the site and find out if Mutt really was dead. If any vampires had managed to escape maybe they could catch and interrogate them to find out more.

Yeah, right, said a snide little voice in the back of her head. You're just hoping that by some miracle he made it out alive.

She told the voice to shut it.

BLAM!

Something struck the side of the SBV with such force that it slid sideways across the road, peeling around in a tight, smoking circle before winding up facing back the way it had come, buried nose-first in the crumpled remains of a white Mercedes.

Yeah. So much for "over."

Steam hissed from a broken radiator as Kayla shook herself and pushed herself back up in and her seat. Beside her, Julissa lifted her head and hissed like a spooked cat.

Kayla screamed as the window next to her exploded inwards, sending shining pebbles of glass spraying across the inside of the leather-lined cab. A bone-white sword flashed downwards, cleaving its way through the solid metal of the car door. Bloodied hands gripped the edge of the door and ripped it open.

The next thing Kayla knew, she was sailing through the air as strong claws sank into her shoulder and pitched her out of the car. She rolled on the asphalt and popped up to her feet again with a speed born of terror. The horrifically burned figure of Cyan X stalked toward her, her bio-blades at the ready.

Kayla almost threw up at the sight of the vampiress. All the skin had been burned from the right side of her body. Her gorgeous black hair hung in ragged strands around the singed mess of her face. White bone and hints of bluish internal organs glinted through the ravaged skin of her belly where Skyler had stabbed her, revealing her pelvic bones and parts of her ribcage. Cyan was barefoot and her dress was in shreds, but still she maintained a stately grace, her violet eyes shining with malign intent.

"Running again?" she hissed.

"It's my new favorite thing to do," Kayla said. She circled warily around Cyan, her eyes ticking sideways to the crashed SBV. Inside, she saw Phil trying to force the smashed driver's door open, bleeding from a cut to the forehead. Beside him, Ninette wrestled with the control stick, trying to shut off the auto-locking mechanism that had jammed their seat harnesses, trapping them in the car.

She was on her own.

Kayla backed up a couple paces, beyond exhausted, trying simply to keep her feet under her. She heard sirens wail in the street outside, getting closer, but knew they couldn't save her in time. Cyan was unstoppable and, from what she'd seen, pretty much unkillable. If she was going to live for longer than the next ten seconds, she was going to have to think fast.

As the vampiress raised her bloodied bio-blades and snaked toward her, a flash of inspiration struck.

"So where's Harlequin?" Kayla asked, all innocence.

Cyan drew up short as though she'd just walked into a wall.

"Only," Kayla carried on, flagrantly bullshitting, "I'd have thought he'd be here, by your side, over-seeing the building of this great vampire army of yours. That's what you're trying to do, yes?"

Cyan sneered, amused. "You're good, but not good enough." She wiped the blood off her face and moved closer, swinging her hips seductively. "Chica, you don't know the half of it. Our army is just the beginning, the sideshow. Wait until you see the real deal. When we're done, you humans will be finished, for good."

Kayla backed off quickly.

"But you love him, don't you? Harlequin?" she continued, sneaking another peek at the car. The vampire flinched every time she mentioned that name, and a flare of hope echoed inside her. She had to keep her talking.

"What makes you think that?" purred Cyan.

"No woman with any self-respect would go through the crap you went through," Kayla indicated Cyan's organic weaponry, "without there being a man at the end of it, somehow."

"You think I did this for him?" Cyan's nasty laugh turned into a gasp of pain as her flash-fried skin began to crack. "Get real, honey. No one gets ahead these days with what nature gave them. This is Los Angeles, the City of Angels. If your wings ain't as white as the next girl's, reach for the bleach or get the hell out of town. Know what I'm saying?"

"But you're a vampire. If the next girl gets in your way, just kill her."

"Newsflash, newbie: there are worse things out there than vampires or werewolves. Things that steal your man, think they're better than you, and won't ever—ever—just fucking die." Cyan raised her blades as if to fend off the memory, scowling. "Who can blame me for wanting to get the one-up on her?"

"On who?" Ninette had managed to get the SBV's side-door partway open, but the metal was too buckled and twisted to go any further. The door was stuck.

Cyan smiled cruelly, her mouth snapping shut. "That would be telling." She lunged forward, her blades hissing around in a sweeping ar.

"*KAYLA!* Heads up!"

Something whirred toward Kayla and her arm automatically snapped up to catch it. She looked down at the silver-plated sword in her hand, and then flung a furious glance sideways at the car.

"You just threw a sword at me!" she yelled.

"You're welcome," Ninette called cheerily through the three-inch gap in the door.

Kayla's senses twanged. She spun around and swung her sword up just in time to deflect Cyan's murderous blow to her head. The impact drove her backward and almost knocked her off her feet, wrenching every joint in her arms, from her wrists to her shoulders. She cried out in pain as she recovered her balance, gasping at the power behind the vampiress's strike. She backed away as Cyan began circling her, cat-stepping on the glass-strewn concrete, a nightmarish apparition in bloodstained white satin.

"Love makes us do some crazy shit," the vampiress murmured, moving softly closer. She flared her blades out, eyeing Kayla soulfully. "But who are you to judge me? That wolf-boy just risked his life to save you. And just so you know..." She paused, her eyes bright with malice, "Your little boyfriend died for him, not because of him."

"What?" Kayla stared, feeling her heart contract painfully.

"You heard me. Karrel was protecting the werewolf. He wound up getting himself killed rather than spilling the beans and clearing his name. All very heroic. What I want to know from you, my dear little Hunter girl, is why."

A loud banging started up inside the SBV, coming from the trunk.

Cyan ignored it.

"I don't... I'm not a..." Kayla shook her head helplessly. She bumped up against the back of the SBV, her mind whirling.

After all that, Mutt had been innocent, and she'd left him behind to die.

"Oh, just drop the act," snapped Cyan. The banging from inside the trunk got louder. "Why would a hot shot high-ranking Hunter like Karrel Dante risk his life for a mere werewolf? What did he know that we didn't?"

"I don't know!" shouted Kayla. "I don't know anything! All you people keep asking me these questions I don't know the answers to and I've had enough! If you'd told me werewolves even existed two days ago, I would've laughed in your face. I didn't even know Karrel was a hunter until last night!"

Cyan narrowed her eyes at Kayla. She lowered her blades and backed off slightly, nodding her head. "You're telling the truth."

"Thank you!" snapped Kayla.

"I have no further use for you."

Too late, Kayla realized her mistake. She swore and tried to roll away as Cyan's blade whickered through the air in an inhumanly fast strike. She cried out as

Cyan's sword punched through the muscle beneath her arm an instant later, the blade burying itself elbow-deep in the trunk of the SBV, impaling her like a butterfly on a pin.

Kayla gasped, a wave of molten agony pouring through her arm. Cyan smirked and raised her second blade in front of Kayla's face, taunting her with it.

"Time for lights out, kitty cat."

"Fuck you!" Kayla spat.

"Very poetic." Cyan twisted her blade, locking it as she prepared to deliver the death blow. "But they say the greatest thing you can do is to die for love. Don't sweat it. When you and your little wolf-boy are reunited in Heaven, you can discuss it."

Inside the trunk behind her, something thumped again.

"See?" grinned Cyan. "Even the car agrees with me, but there's one thing I really should tell you before you die."

Cyan leaned closer and Kayla recoiled at the stench of blood and charred flesh. The vampiress's charred lips stretched back into a grim smile as she whispered in her ear.

"Karrel was never yours. It was me he loved, not you. Your relationship—everything he ever told you—that was just a cover."

"Bullshit!"

Kayla stared up into the vampiress's smug face, her free hand dropping painfully downwards as she groped at her belt. With a shout of vengeance she pulled her Taser out and jammed it into the gaping wound in Cyan stomach. Blue bolts of electricity snapped through the air as the Taser grounded itself through Cyan's bio-mechanically enhanced body.

The vampiress shrieked and tore her bio-sword from Kayla's shoulder, then used it to viciously bat the weapon out of her hand.

She yelled something at Kayla, but Kayla was no longer listening. She was buoyed up on a current of pure animal rage. Her eyes locked in on the vampiress's unprotected neck and she spun around with a furious growl, swinging her own sword around in a vicious arc, aiming to sever Cyan's head.

A clawed hand punched through the trunk of the SBV. A moment later, the entire back end of the car flew open with a screech of tearing metal. Skeet spilled out, the tattered remains of his bindings hanging from his hairy, semi-transformed body. With a snarl, he threw himself in front of Cyan in a vain effort to protect her.

Kayla's sword passed cleanly through his neck.

Skeet stared at Kayla, his eyes disbelieving before his head tumbled from his shoulders. He collapsed in a cold, dead heap on the asphalt. Blood flowed out of his severed neck, pooling on the ash-strewn concrete.

Kayla stared down at her sword in surprise.

"Damn, that's sharp," she said, then stumbled, clutching at the trunk as the world swam around her. Darkness speckled at the edges of her vision.

"It should be," said a voice, "it was Karrel's."

Kayla looked up with blurring eyes to see Ninette step up behind her. She moved in front of Kayla protectively and then rounded on Cyan, her own sword at the ready.

"You'd better run," she growled.

Cyan gave a ghost of a smile as she pointed to the side of the building, at the grass below the steps.

"By the way, I think the pound just swiped your new puppy. Better be quick if you want him back."

Kayla swung around and stared shakily. A group of cops was gathering around a dark, vaguely canine shape on the grass. They hauled it onto a strapped gurney and started loading it into an LAPD helicopter.

"Mutt?" she whispered.

When she turned back Cyan was gone. She had sprinted for the cover of a nearby group of out-buildings. Ninette caught Kayla as she lunged after her.

"We have to get Mutt back!" she cried.

"And she's off on that one again. Listen, Kayla... the cops have got him. He might not even be alive. You go running over there in your condition, they'll get you too, not to mention blowing our cover." She waved a hand at the remains of the Genetica building. "You fancy explaining that to the local Sheriff's department?"

Kayla nodded numbly. All the fight went out of her and she slumped back against the car, her wounded shoulder pouring blood. She stared down at Skeet's dead body. It was a victory of sorts—her first werewolf kill.

One down, eight to go.

"So what now?" she asked, after a moment.

Ninette raised her gaze to the horizon, her face troubled. A wind kicked up, whipping her hair across her face. "We'll take you in until this mess is sorted out. We may as well start training you. We'll start you with some Aikido and basic weapons training, and progress to teaching you the Dark Arts if you pass the test. Then we'll go from there."

"The Dark whats?"

Ninette smiled faintly. "You'll see," she said. "We have no idea what the vampires are planning next, but I do know that there's a storm coming. We want you to be ready when it hits."

Kayla leaned against the side of the wrecked car, gazing down at the sword in her hand. She wiped the blood off it onto her black skirt and then buffed it lightly on her sleeve, swinging it experimentally.

"Just one question," she asked. "Do I get to keep the sword?"

A GHOSTLY SHAPE moved swiftly through the rolling gray cloud of ash slowly settling around the building. Rays of glaring red light from the setting sun refracted through the swirling particles as they spun around and around, gently resolving themselves into a figure.

Karrel Dante opened his eyes and stepped out into the fading light, brushing a fine layer of ash off his Hunter's uniform. He straightened up and watched keenly as a pair of beat-up old Land Rovers screeched to a halt in the parking lot. Karrel gave a grunt of recognition as the familiar shapes of Tony and Dan jumped out, running toward the wreck of their team leader's vehicle. Backup had at last arrived. Dan had a bloodstained bandage taped to his forehead, but he otherwise seemed to have recovered from his little encounter with Harlem.

Sizing up the situation in an instant—one dead werewolf, one wounded civilian—the two Hunters ran to join Kayla and Ninette, urging them to help Julissa into the back of the first vehicle. Phil slammed the door behind her and jumped into the driver's seat. Tony rolled Skeet's heavy, lifeless body into a thick plastic body bag and heaved it into the trunk of the second vehicle. Doors slammed, and the two Land Rovers took off across the ornamental lawn in a spray of fake grass.

Karrel sighed, wistfully gazing after them. He knew that Kayla wasn't in for an easy fight, but for now, she would be safe, he hoped.

Closing his eyes he breathed in deeply, hoping to catch a hint of her perfume on the night breeze. All he could smell was blood and ash.

Karrel turned back to watch the tail lights of the two Hunter vehicles vanish into the coming night. The first of the cops was arriving from the opposite direction, screaming down the winding road in a blare of sirens. Arriving in front of the building, they spilled out of their sparkling white squad cars and spread out to cordon off the building. Behind them, the full moon started to rise in the cloudy dusk.

As the first rays of moonlight filtered down through the cloud layer, the world... changed. The scene before him suddenly flickered to gray and back again in a quick pulse of light, revealing a black, horrific snapshot of the underworld beneath. For a split second, the falling dusk became a howling void. The scurrying police squad turned into a bunch of moving skeletons, lit from within by tiny colored lights.

Then, just as suddenly, the world snapped back to normal like a rubber band. It made Karrel's brain hurt.

He backed up two steps until he was touching the parking lot wall. He flattened himself against it, his heart hammering. The world around him turned to a howling gray void once again. The sky blackened and an icy wind swept over him, bringing with it the stench of decay and rotting flesh.

Karrel cried out and sagged, turning to clutch at the wall beside him as a bright, agonizing flash of light shot through his mind. Something caught in his throat and he coughed hard, his eyes streaming. He looked down in confusion to see blood spatter across his hand.

What was happening to him?

A second flash of light split his vision and he collapsed against the wall. The air around him erupted in an ear-splitting cacophony of noise. A sudden wash of heat seared its way across his face. Karrel's eyes flew open and he gasped.

The parking lot was on fire.

Spectral flames spurted from the manholes and drains. They raced across the concrete sidewalk toward him, the ghostly white fire licking hungrily at the oxygen-rich air. The fire roared at him, pouring over the few remaining parked cars and up the scrubby, vandalized palm trees in a silver river, turning the place into a cocoon of fire.

Every street light in the lot exploded at once in the intense spectral heat. Karrel ducked and covered instinctively as a deadly rain of shining glass fragments poured down.

He looked back and saw the figure.

It was standing hunched in a pile of rubble from Genetica, almost obscured by the flames. It was crouching over and shrouded in shadow, but the sight of it made Karrel's stomach clench nastily.

It was vaguely humanoid, in that it had a head and limbs and a torso. Beyond that, all resemblance ended. It had way too many legs. Its long, skeletal limbs folded and tangled together at obscene angles, joining its body in a mesh of red, torn flesh and snapped bone. Its head was triangular and eyeless with a black, tooth-filled void where its mouth should have been. It looked like a giant preying mantis covered in flayed human skin. The stench of it was indescribable.

Karrel covered his mouth and nose with his hand as his eyes started to stream. What kind of sick shit was this?

The thing's head revolved around until it was facing him, and its blind eyes locked in on his with unnerving accuracy. Karrel's hand went instinctively to his belt, going for his hunting knife.

It wasn't there. Or rather, it was there, but he couldn't touch it.

How was that even possible?

Karrel froze, every muscle in him tensing as the thing began to make an odd, scratchy sound. After a second, Karrel realized it was laughing. It unfolded itself in a flowing, graceful movement that might have been beautiful had it not been so goddamned freaky. It rose to its full, nine-foot height and turned to face him.

"What the hell are you?" Karrel whispered.

The thing tilted its head, shadows spilling across its alien face. It opened its mouth and a breath hissed from it in a single, drawn-out word.

"Deaaaaatttthhhhhhhh."

Goosebumps raced across Karrel's flesh. He forced himself to move away from the wall, to stand up straight, to challenge the thing. Every instinct in him coiled like a spring as his training kicked in, jolting his semi-paralyzed mind back into action.

"You're Death?" Karrel shook his head, trying to master his fear. "I thought you'd be taller."

"Not *the* Death. *A* Death. We are many."

Karrel edged around the thing, his courage growing. "Yeah? The death of what? Insects? Creepy crawlies? I could've sworn I trod on something that looked like you in the men's room yesterday."

The thing made no response to the jibe, staring down at him as flames crackled around it.

"So what next? Huh?" Karrel felt the world start to spin around him. He still couldn't believe this was happening. "I'm dead, I get that much. But I'm a ghost now, right? I made a deal with Heaven. Is this the bit where you waft me out of here, give me my little golden harp and tell me to report to God every Tuesday night for band practice until I've avenged my death here on Earth? That how it goes?"

The thing continued to stare. Karrel could've sworn that its expressionless face took on a sudden look of pity. The flames around it burned still brighter.

"What?" he asked.

The thing cleared its throat with a rattle. "There's been an error. You've been classified a suicide. You belong to Hell now."

Karrel gasped. A terrible sense of realization seeped through him like a sluice of cold, icy water.

"No," he said.

He backed up a few short faltering steps, breathing fast in horror. "I didn't... Oh, Christ! You're Death! You saw what happened! I made a bargain!"

"Not with us, you didn't. You must come with me now."

"Says who? Fuck that!"

With a sudden lunge, Karrel made a bolt for freedom.

He hadn't taken two steps before a hideous, paralyzing pain shot through him. He cried out, but kept on running, forcing his legs to keep going even as the phantom flames enveloped him. The pain became too much. He stumbled and crashed to the ground, writhing soundlessly as the flames poured over him. The sickening sensation of his flesh melting away from his bones almost undid him, even though his logical mind told him that his skin was still intact, that the flames weren't real.

Gritting his teeth, he rolled over and clawed toward the road on his hands and knees. Then his body rocked as something slammed down through his back. Karrel jerked and cried out. Hot, metallic blood surged up his throat and filled his mouth as what felt like a giant serrated sword shoved its way deeper into his ribcage. Karrel almost blacked out as he felt himself being hoisted up into the air and dangled in front of the thing's blind face, pinned on one of its giant scythe-like front limbs.

He stared up at the creature, numb with shock. Despite the darkness he could see every detail, from the tiny veins that flecked the raw skin of its throat to the twitch of its exposed facial muscles. He coughed weakly, marshalling the last few dregs of his remaining energy to speak.

"I didn't kill myself! You can't do this!"

The thing shook its head. "Nonetheless, you committed suicide."

"I was murdered, damn you!"

"You had a chance to save yourself. You chose not to take it."

"That's not suicide!"

"Your partner was nearby. He could have saved you."

"Yeah, and gotten himself killed in the process. I was trying to save his life!" Karrel glared at the creature, panting around the pain of his battered insides. "I can't believe this! This is such bullshit! What about the soldier who throws himself across a grenade to save his buddies? The mother who hides her kid and runs out of the house to draw off knife-wielding crazies? Do they go to hell too?"

The thing just stared at him.

"Answer me!" shouted Karrel.

"Well, officially, they're borderline," the thing started, looking uncomfortable. "The good deed should balance out the sin. It's a judgment call—your final fate depends on who's on duty at the Gate to judge you. You could have gotten away with it, had you not drawn our attention by returning to Earth."

"But my deal—"

"The deal's off." The thing clattered closer to him, rubbing its forelimbs together greedily. "Now that you're back in the world again, new rules apply. You had a chance to go to heaven, but you rejected it. That in itself technically makes you a candidate for Hell."

"You're sending me to Hell on a technicality?" Karrel hooted. "That's so twisted! You guys are worse than my insurance company!"

"Apologies. I have a quota to fulfill."

"A quota?" Karrel started struggling. "Fuck you! Get me my lawyer!"

The thing shook its head sadly. "Plenty of those where we're going."

With a whooshing sound the spectral flames around them leapt higher, closing in on them, liquefying the very ground around them until it boiled apart into its component molecules. Karrel yelled as he was dragged downwards with the thing into the ground, passing through the concrete as though it were nothing more than quicksand. He had a brief, confused impression of metal, stone, and dirt as he plunged deeper into the earth, kicking and struggling all the while. They sank faster and faster, speeding through the cold, dead earth at breakneck speed, until Karrel practically blacked out from the insane velocity.

He finally hit the ground. Hard.

Karrel felt as though every atom in his body had been forcibly ripped out of place and jammed back together again. His head pounded with a sickening sense of displacement. His blood felt as though it were boiling in his veins. As his consciousness returned, even though he was on his way to Hell, a bolt of fear shot instinctively through him. He grabbed at his stomach frantically, expecting to find a jagged, spurting wound where the thing from the parking lot had stabbed him. To his surprise, his skin was unbroken.

Then a savage sense of terror hit him as the sound of crackling flames reached his ears. Karrel took a deep breath.

This was it, the afterlife.

Then he opened his eyes.

"Dear God," he gasped, "is this really Hell?

CHAPTER FORTY-ONE

KAYLA STOOD ON the pier, her back to the wind. She gazed out over the dark, calm waters of the bay. It was just coming up to sunrise. The blackness of the night sky above her already held the faintest tinges of purple, shading to a light yellow-blue around the horizon. The blue mountains of Malibu loomed on her right, shrouded in a tumbling, early morning sea fog.

Kayla breathed in a deep lungful of the cool, damp air, trying to calm her nerves. She was casually, but efficiently dressed in a camo-green cotton tank top and jeans, with her hair up in a businesslike pony-tail. The white bandage on her shoulder seemed to glow in the pre-dawn light. She nervously adjusted her wraparound thermal shades, and then reached down to stroke the unfamiliar tops of the half-dozen silver stakes in the band around her thigh.

Far from being an ending, Karrel's death had just been the beginning. The personal tragedy of his murder had linked her to something far bigger than herself. In doing so, it had given her a direction, a purpose to her life that she had been lacking before.

In the seven days since Genetica, she had made a lot of long-overdue changes to her life. She started by quitting her crappy job at the mall in order to dedicate herself to training with the Hunters. If she only had thirty days to avenge Karrel's death, she wanted to make sure that she didn't waste a single second. She hadn't seen Karrel again since they'd met in the restroom, but she'd dutifully passed the information he'd given her on to the Hunters. With Skyler gone, she'd felt confident enough to fully brief a select couple of units on his case. They already had a handful of leads—one of which they were pursuing tonight. With Ninette and Phil's help, she'd been able to mobilize enough manpower to ensure that if Karrel's killers showed their faces anywhere around town, they'd be quickly caught and picked up.

It was a start, but it still wasn't enough.

Kayla only hoped that they wouldn't be too late.

She studied the deep waters below her for a couple more seconds, then let out her breath in a soft sigh. She impatiently glanced over her shoulder at Ninette, who stood beside her wearing lace-up army combats, a black tank top, and a look of cool concentration as she scanned the waters beneath them.

"Any luck?" she asked.

Ninette shushed her and held up a finger.

"What?"

Ninette pointed.

Kayla peered over the railings into the water below. Two humanoid shapes were visible on the thermal overlay in her shades, glowing yellow-red amid the graduated blackness of the ocean. She lifted her shades and squinted down at the water. With a bit of effort, she could just make out the dull white gleam of two surfboards bobbing up and down on the waves next to the pier.

Her heart fell. "It's just a couple of surfers."

"Surfers? At this hour of the morning?" Ninette said, looking at her sideways. "Don't you think that's a little odd?"

Kayla stared at her for a moment before her eyes lit up. "Gotcha," she said.

As she reached for her radio, a bloodcurdling scream pierced the stillness of the night. It came from the parking lot behind them. Kayla jumped, throwing a panicked glance over her shoulder. Ninette remained motionless, staring down at the sea, whistling under her breath.

After a moment, Kayla turned back to face the water, trying to calm her jangled nerves. "Perhaps you shouldn't have given the keys to that monster car of yours to the valet," she said. "Do you think he needs a hand?"

"Nah, he'll be okay." Ninette's face was expressionless, but Kayla knew her team leader well enough by now to discern the faintest gleam of mischief in her hazel eyes. "They wanna charge fifteen bucks to park your car for you at six in the morning, they can earn it. The car can look after itself."

"So I hear."

Kayla glanced eagerly back down at the water.

The two surfers had gone.

She turned to face Ninette in dismay, but her new team leader was already moving, jogging across the rough wooden boards of the pier toward the steps leading down to the beach. Kayla followed her, feeling a distinct and unsettling sense of déjà vu. She tried hard not to look at the charred, blackened swing set that sat a short distance back from the pier, the empty swings rocking back and forth quietly in the night breeze. It was ironic that her first mission was here of all places, but it gave her a strange sense of completeness, of things coming full circle.

She only hoped that things wouldn't end here.

She followed Ninette down the steps and across the sand. Phil was already waiting for them at the water's edge beneath the pier, decked out in black camouflage gear. Julissa stood a couple of paces behind him, clutching a slim silver sword and looking deeply unhappy about it. The remains of a splintered surfboard lay at their feet, half immersed in the water.

"I still don't see why I had to be part of the beach scouting party," Julissa grumbled as Kayla joined her. She flashed Kayla a withering look, then hurriedly stepped back as the black water washed perilously close to her four-hundred-dollar Lucky jeans. "In fact, as a pastime, beach scouting is highly overrated. Why couldn't I be the one up there on the pier, having fun and ice cream while tracking down the vampires and werewolves and—hey!"

Ninette shone her flashlight in Julissa's face in reply. A wave of pearly-black scales rippled over the surface of Julissa's skin and her eyes started to change color on contact with the light, her pupils slitting and her irises flashing a reflective silver-yellow. Tiny teeth began to erupt from her jaw.

"All right, fine!" Julissa waved a hand in annoyance, shielding her eyes from the light. Ninette pointed the beam away from her face and it swiftly returned to normal, her smooth skin just visible in the early light. She rubbed her face irritably. "Point taken, I'm a freak. But you know what? When did that ever stop anyone from being famous?"

"Hardly ever," said Kayla, shooting Ninette a look. "I hear going out in the light is overrated, too. I'm sure you'll cope."

"That's what I said!" said Julissa, impervious to Kayla's sarcasm. "Anyway—look! I found a clue!"

Ninette dutifully redirected the beam of the flashlight down to the surfboard at their feet. The board was so battered that it was hardly recognizable. At one end, beside a set of deep tooth marks, she could make out the name "Gridz" sprayed in artistically blocky lettering. The ankle leash had been chewed off.

A frown flickered over Ninette's brow as she studied the board. "Looks like something ate our surfer boys."

"Or maybe that's what they want us to think," said Kayla.

Ninette raised her eyebrows and shared a glance with Phil. Kayla rubbed her chilly arms and turned to gaze out at the booming surf.

"So what's our next move?" she asked.

"Now, we wait." Ninette stepped up beside Kayla and switched her flashlight off. "And keep your voice down. Not very big on patience, werewolves, so if they're here, they'll show themselves soon enough. In the meantime, just keep quiet and watch. Keep your mind open, and your senses tuned to the breeze. You'll need to use every instinct you have in a situation like this, so listen to your gut. Reach out with your mind to pinpoint exactly where the wolves might be, like I taught you."

"Or you could just radio base and ask them where the werewolves are," said Phil, stepping up beside them. "We've got thermo-satellite tracking in this zip code—ow!"

He rubbed his ribs where Ninette had elbowed him, and turned to grin at her. A low, rumbling growl came from the road behind them.

Instantly he and Ninette were moving, slipping into the shadows beneath the support struts of the pier and motioning for Julissa and Kayla to follow them. The four of them watched as a lone beach patrol truck rumbled down a dirt road and rolled to a halt at the edge of the sand. A lifeguard with a handheld floodlight and a pair of night vision binoculars jumped out and strode warily down the beach.

"Hello?" he called, playing the floodlight beam over the waves. "C'mon guys, I already told you once this week. You know you're not supposed to surf after dark."

The lifeguard's voice trailed off as the water under the pier foamed, then burst outwards in an explosion of white spray. Two enormous blond werewolves crashed out of the surf and pounded up the beach, tongues lolling, salt-water flying from their thick sun-bleached manes. In the beam of the floodlight Kayla saw that both wolves had broken surfboard leashes attached to their hind legs. She felt a small surge of satisfaction.

She was learning.

With a yell, she snapped her thermal-vision shades up and burst out of cover with the two Hunters, moving to intercept the werewolves. As she drew her sword—Karrel's sword—she wondered briefly if Karrel was watching her. She wondered if he would be proud of her. Death merely ended a life, not a relationship. She fully intended to make the most of hers from now on.

Karrel may be dead, but her love for him lived on. She had a feeling that the fun was only just beginning.

CHAPTER FORTY-TWO

IN THE DARKNESS of the desecrated club, something moved.

A match flared and touched the wick of a tall candle. A pale, sickly orange light filled the room, mercifully not strong enough to reveal the details of the hundred-odd werewolf and vampire bodies strewn about on the heaped furniture, lying in separate pools of violent death. Flames flicked down the hallway, threatening to encroach upon the blood-soaked red plush carpets.

Jagos felt a drop of sweat form on his forehead despite the chill in the air. It started to slide in a tickling path down the side of his face. He wiped it away and cleared his throat.

"I like what you've done with the place."

Harlem smiled, though his expression had very little to do with humor. Turning his back on the sweating human, he wandered over to the smashed bar, humming a cheerful little ditty under his breath.

He selected an unbroken bottle of rum from the shattered shelves and poured himself a generous shot. "Keep the change," he informed the blinded and gutted barman who hung over the bar, his spilled entrails obscuring the Club Wolfbayne sign beneath.

"C'mon, man, we're waiting," said a voice. "Don't keep us in the dark like this."

Harlem half-turned, growling softly under his breath. Jumping flames reflected in his eyes as he stared at the three wolves who sat sprawled on a leather sofa, the one remaining unbroken piece of furniture in the place. His eyes crinkled briefly at the sight of Dana perched daintily on the arm of the sofa, her soft white hair cascading over her shoulders, a look of polite horror on her face.

She was the only one who had avoided the bloodbath, watching from a safe distance as he and his boys had completed the final bloody stage of his plan. After slamming the doors on the place, they had systematically slaughtered every one of Magnus's disciples, save the handful of panicked-looking vampires standing in a tight, hushed huddle at the end of the bar. The three surviving delegates from Europe, Japan, and Asia were sweating, but their faces bore the pale, sly look of those who knew that their money, if not their loyalties, would keep them alive.

They stared as though hypnotized at the large covered crate that stood in the middle of the room. The faint sounds that came from inside it were unnaturally loud—clinking noises and an occasional, drawn-out scraping sound, like nails on a chalkboard.

Now that he had everyone's attention, Harlem turned around and moved back toward the crate, raising his drink in a toast as he did so.

"Welcome, gentlemen, to the dawn of a new age, an age where werewolves and vampires work together hand in hand and go skipping up the bloody garden path to wherever the crap it may lead them, crushin' the puny humans underfoot and ensuring centuries of fun and frolics, and rivers of blood. Yeah, that's the speech Magnus would've made at this point, but he's gone now, so get the fuck over it. It's my turn."

Harlem took a sip of his drink, swilling the amber liquid around reflectively in the bottom of the glass, before clearing his throat. He turned to address the room, or what remained of it.

"Ding dong, the witch is dead, but Hell ain't Hell without someone to laugh and point at your flaming ass while you're in there. I don't respect any man who don't grab a fast buck when it's waved in front of him, even if it's hanging from a hooker's panties, so today I'm auctioning off a fun little friend to whoever can throw the most cash at the wall and make it stick. Non-sequential bills, please, but I do also take MasterCard. These are modern times, after all."

Harlem cocked his head, winking at Dana. He pitched his shot glass into the roaring fireplace and turned to face the crate.

"Jagos, the curtain, please." Harlem blew the man a kiss, and then meaningfully flashed his teeth at him.

Jagos stepped over the bodies on the floor until he reached the crate, trying to avoid the worst of the blood. His Gucci shoes were ruined, but now probably wasn't the time to bring it up. His career with Magnus hadn't gone at all as he had planned. If he could just get in with this new pack, then one day he might be doing a little ruling of his own. This Harlem guy didn't seem as bad as everyone said, and if he got the big bucks he was anticipating for the secret weapon in the crate, his life just might start looking up.

He took hold of the curtain, and then wearily turned to face their audience like a patient magician's assistant.

"Ladies and gentlemen, I give you—"

Harlem broke off as a banshee shriek rang out. He swung around quickly. The red velvet curtain billowed inwards. There was no sign of Jagos.

Raising a curious eyebrow, Harlem took a step forward, hyper-conscious of the delegates' panicked gazes on him. His heart sped up as he edged forward, peering gingerly through the flapping curtain. The thought that he might have fucked up occurred to him briefly, before being crushed behind the monumental wall of his ego. It would be fine, just a little miscalculation of tensile strength in the main restraints. All he had to do was...

The crate exploded.

Harlem threw himself frantically to the ground as wooden shards and twisted metal punched holes through the ceiling of the devastated club. Light streamed in and the vampires screamed in pain as they dived for cover, their flesh smoking from the unexpected UV exposure.

A dark figure rose up from the shattered remains of the crate. Its powerful muscles flexed as it snapped the last remaining chain that tethered it to the wall, and it turned to face the room. Hot blood poured from its gaping maw as it rose to its full height and bayed insanely at them, splattering blood up the nearby walls. A second later, Jagos's skinned remains landed on the leather couch, scattering the remaining werewolves. They fled the room with cries of panic, the sound of slamming doors echoing through the club.

Harlem alone stood his ground as the skeletal, sinuous form of the monster whipped around to face him, its murderous black pinwheel eyes searing into his brain as foot-long razor-edged talons reached out for him.

With a triumphant grin, Harlem clicked the red button on his remote. There was a click and a hum as the creature's UV collar activated, pouring blinding blue light into the room.

The monster screamed in pain as its skin started to char and the stench of burning flesh filled the air. Its naked, corpse-white hide flashed chrome silver before rapidly plating itself in a rippling wave of armored black scales, protecting itself from the light.

Harlem let the light burn for a moment or two longer, making his point. Then he shut the UV collar off, watching as the shocked creature reached up with taloned fingers to touch its own hide in wonder as its scales retracted.

Its neck pulsed as it cleared its throat with a menacing rumble. "What have you done to me?" it croaked.

"Just a little genetic surgery, bud. It's nothing to be ashamed of."

"Genetic what?"

Harlem stepped back, beaming. "Welcome to LA, Harlequin," he grinned. "I think you're gonna like it here."